Praise for

WILBUR SMITH

'A thundering good read is virtually the only way of describing Wilbur Smith's books'

IRISH TIMES

'Wilbur Smith . . . writes as forcefully as his tough characters act'

EVENING STANDARD

'Wilbur Smith has arguably the best sense of place of any adventure writer since John Buchan'

THE GUARDIAN

'Wilbur Smith is one of those benchmarks against whom others are compared'

THE TIMES

'Best Historical Novelist – I say Wilbur Smith, with his swashbuckling novels of Africa. The bodices rip and the blood flows. You can get lost in Wilbur Smith and misplace all of August'

STEPHEN KING

'Action is the name of Wilbur Smith's game and he is the master'

WASHINGTON POST

'A master storyteller'

SUNDAY TIMES

'Smith will take you on an exciting, taut and thrilling journey you will never forget'

THE SUN

'No one does adventure quite like Smith'

DAILY MIRROR

'With Wilbur Smith the action is never further than the turn of a page'

THE INDEPENDENT

'When it comes to writing the adventure novel, Wilbur Smith is the master; a 21st century H. Rider Haggard'

VANITY FAIR

Wilbur Smith was born in Central Africa in 1933. He became a full-time writer in 1964, following the success of *When the Lion Feeds*, his first published novel. An international phenomenon, his readership built up over fifty-five years of writing, his works include the Courtney Series, the Ballantyne Series, the Egyptian Series, the Hector Cross Series and many successful standalone novels, all meticulously researched on his numerous expeditions worldwide.

The establishment of the Wilbur & Niso Smith Foundation, in 2015, was driven by Wilbur's passion for empowering writers, promoting literacy and advancing adventure writing as a genre. The foundation's flagship programme is the Wilbur Smith Adventure Writing Prize.

Wilbur Smith passed away peacefully at home in 2021 with his wife, Niso, by his side, leaving behind a treasure-trove of novels and stories that will delight readers for years to come.

For all the latest information on Wilbur Smith's writing visit www.wilbursmithbooks.com or facebook.com/WilburSmith.

David Churchill is the author of THE LEOPARDS OF NORMANDY, the critically acclaimed trilogy of novels about the life and times of William the Conqueror.

Also by Wilbur Smith

Non-Fiction

On Leopard Rock: A Life of Adventures

The Courtney Series

When the Lion Feeds
The Sound of Thunder
A Sparrow Falls
The Burning Shore
Power of the Sword
Rage
A Time to Die
Golden Fox
Birds of Prey
Monsoon
Blue Horizon
The Triumph of the Sun
Assegai
Golden Lion
War Cry
The Tiger's Prey
Courtney's War
King of Kings
Ghost Fire
Legacy of War
Storm Tide
Nemesis
Warrior King
Fire on the Horizon

The Ballantyne Series

A Falcon Flies
Men of Men
The Angels Weep
The Leopard Hunts in Darkness
The Triumph of the Sun
King of Kings
Call of the Raven
Fire on the Horizon

The Egyptian Series

River God
The Seventh Scroll
Warlock
The Quest
Desert God
Pharaoh
The New Kingdom
Titans of War
Testament

Hector Cross

Those in Peril
Vicious Circle
Predator

Standalones

The Dark of the Sun
Shout at the Devil
Gold Mine
The Diamond Hunters
The Sunbird
Eagle in the Sky
The Eye of the Tiger
Cry Wolf
Hungry as the Sea
Wild Justice
Elephant Song

WILBUR SMITH

WITH DAVID CHURCHILL

CROSSFIRE

ZAFFRE

First published in the UK in 2025 by
ZAFFRE
An imprint of Bonnier Books UK
5th Floor, HYLO, 105 Bunhill Row, London, EC1Y 8LZ

A CIP catalogue record for this book is
available from the British Library.

HB ISBN: 978–1–83877–911–5
TPB ISBN: 978–1–80418–888–0

Also available as an ebook and an audiobook

3 5 7 9 10 8 6 4 2

Typeset by IDSUK (Data Connection) Ltd
Printed and bound in Great Britain by Clays Ltd, Elcograf S.p.A.

MIX
Paper | Supporting
responsible forestry
FSC® C018072
FSC
www.fsc.org

The authorised representative in the EEA is
Bonnier Books UK (Ireland) Limited.
Registered office address: Floor 3, Block 3, Miesian Plaza,
Dublin 2, D02 Y754, Ireland
compliance@bonnierbooks.ie
www.bonnierbooks.co.uk

This book is for my wife

MOKHINISO

who is the best thing
that has ever happened to me

This novel, like all of those published after his passing, originated from an unfinished work by Wilbur Smith. Wilbur worked closely with each of his co-authors on storylines that met his rigorous standards. Wilbur's wife, Niso Smith, his long-standing literary agent, Kevin Conroy Scott, and the Wilbur Smith Estate's in-house editor, James Woodhouse, continue to work tirelessly to ensure that the body of work that Wilbur left behind reflects his vision in his absence.

THE COURTNEY FAMILY IN CROSSFIRE

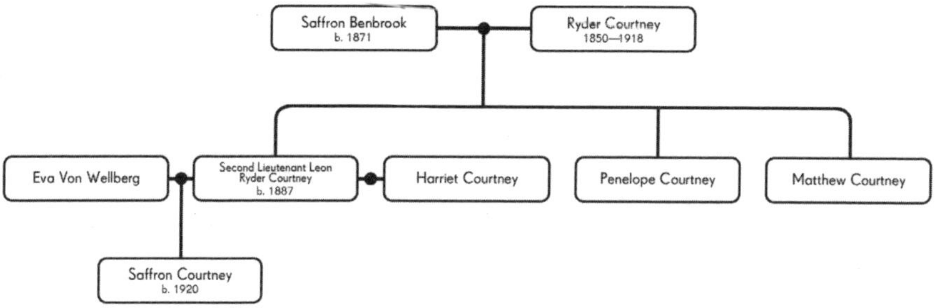

Find out more about the Courtneys and see the Courtney family tree in full at www.wilbursmithbooks.com/courtney-family-tree

WASHINGTON DC, LATE APRIL 1943

The sun was shining on the nation's capital, the temperature rising into the low seventies, but a gentle breeze kept the air nice and fresh. It was the kind of weather that makes a man find a good excuse to be out of the office for a while.

Joe Lewandowski spotted his contact, the individual he knew only as Foxglove, walking towards him. Lewandowski's code name was Shadow. He dropped the smouldering stub of a cheap cigar at his feet, ground it into the earth of East Potomac Park and strolled over.

He nodded back towards the sign he'd been leaning against. 'You want to play miniature golf?' He grinned, hoping to get Foxglove to relax, loosen up a little, make this look like a normal conversation. Just in case anyone was watching.

'No, thank you,' said Foxglove, tight as a drum.

'Not in the mood, huh?'

Foxglove shrugged.

'Okay, suit yourself.'

Lewandowski had been checking for tails since he'd got into his Chevrolet pickup truck, more than an hour earlier. It was automatic, like looking both ways before crossing the street. He'd not spotted anything suspicious, but now they were in the park he checked again for anyone who looked out of place. He nodded to himself, then looked at Foxglove. 'Let's head on down to Hains Point. You ever been there?'

2

'No.'

Lewandowski grunted. 'Well, it's where the Anacostia and Potomac rivers meet—'

'What's that got to do with it?' Foxglove protested.

'You said it was even more important than usual that we're not overheard,' Lewandowski said curtly. 'Well, Hains Point is practically surrounded by water. Makes it real hard for anyone listening in. Now, let's walk.'

Lewandowski led Foxglove onto the path that ran around the park, and was about to turn right, towards the point, when he stopped and pointed. 'The White House is right over there. Couple miles away, maybe less.' He grinned. 'So near and yet so far, right?'

'No, not so far,' Foxglove said. 'Not for what I have in mind.'

Since his arrival in Washington in the fall of 1937, Lewandowski's cover occupation had been running a small construction company, AOK Contractors. He had the name painted on the doors of his truck, with a phone number and the words WORKING HARDER FOR YOU. To his friends and neighbours, he was just like them – a regular blue-collar guy, striving to join the ranks of the middle class. Most of the time, he was jovial and easy-going, but he was known to be short-tempered if someone screwed up on the job. The other regulars at his local bar usually called him 'Joey L', but sometimes, when he got a little overheated, it was 'Crazy Joe'.

Lewandowski was his real name, so in a way he was hiding in plain sight. When he was posted to Washington, his superiors had assured him that the Americans had no knowledge of his identity, for the simple reason that while the FBI was responsible for catching foreign spies on American soil, the United States possessed virtually no counter-intelligence capacity beyond its own shores.

So he stuck to his own name, and wasn't bothered that his accent, though broadly working-class American, still had an Eastern European edge to it. After all, America was a nation of immigrants. Occasionally, someone might ask, 'So, Lewandowski, huh? What kind of name is that?' And Lewandowski would say, 'Polish, where my parents were born.' And that was also true: his family came from the port city of Gdansk – or Danzig, as it was called in German, which was the language that the majority of its citizens spoke, being of Prussian descent. But there was no need to tell anyone that.

The important thing was that Lewandowski looked like a man at home on a building site. He was of average height, a little overweight maybe, but it was more muscle than flab. He had a thick neck, and today his tie was loose and his shirt was open enough to show a sprinkling of curly black chest hairs.

All the way along the path, Lewandowski acted the part of the jovial builder, Joey L. Only when they reached Hains Point, and it was safe to talk, could he be his true self: the experienced intelligence officer, Jozef Lewandowski, whose rank was equivalent to a British or American major.

Lewandowski looked at Foxglove, who was leaning on a railing and gazing out over the water. There were clear views across the two rivers to Maryland, or south to the new Washington National Airport on the Virginia shore. There was no one else in sight. 'So, what do you have to tell me?'

Foxglove turned to him with a slight smile. It conveyed the superiority felt by someone who knows something important that the other person doesn't. 'Churchill is coming to Washington in the next two to three weeks. The exact dates haven't been confirmed. They won't do that until the last minute . . .' A fractional pause, another smile, and then, 'For security reasons.'

Lewandowski nodded, trying to look as if Foxglove hadn't just dropped a bombshell. 'Why?'

'To plan the invasion of Europe. He's bringing his most senior military commanders. They'll be meeting their American equivalents every day at the Federal Reserve Building. By the time they head back to Britain, they'll have decided when and precisely where they're going to attack in France and southern Europe.'

'And you can get us that information?'

'I believe so, yes.' Foxglove looked at Lewandowski and added, insistently, 'They're confident of victory. They think it's just a matter of deciding on the means to achieve it.'

'Good for them,' said Lewandowski, brushing aside Foxglove's account of Allied triumphalism. 'Still, I guess now I understand why you were antsy about this meeting.'

Foxglove straightened, took a step away from the railing, and turned to face Lewandowski. 'No, you don't.'

'I'm sorry?' Lewandowski was startled by the superior – almost dismissive – tone that had entered his asset's voice.

'You're missing the bigger picture. The real opportunity.'

'Yeah? So enlighten me.'

'Churchill will be taking meetings with Roosevelt at the White House. Those will be public knowledge. But there will be at least one private meeting, too, away from the security that the presidential mansion provides.'

Lewandowski's eyes narrowed. *Surely Foxglove couldn't really be suggesting* . . . 'And your point is?'

'Isn't it obvious? Roosevelt and Churchill, two pathetic old men. A sickly cripple and a drunkard. And yet their people worship them. They are the living symbols of the Allied cause.' Foxglove paused for a second and looked Lewandowski in the eye. 'Imagine if they were both killed.'

'Dear God . . .' Lewandowski quickly glanced around again. If anyone had heard what Foxglove had just said . . . But the only other person in sight was a mother pushing a pram about thirty yards away.

'Are you serious?' Lewandowski hissed. It wasn't a rhetorical question. Part of him still hoped this was Foxglove's twisted idea of a joke.

'Absolutely. I know exactly when, where and how it can be done. But maybe you don't have the guts for it . . .'

Lewandowski could see that Foxglove was completely serious, but what explained the undercurrent of mockery – even contempt? Lewandowski and his bosses had never seen Foxglove as anything more than a source of low-grade information.

But looking back, Lewandowski could remember moments when Foxglove had betrayed a barely suppressed sense of superiority.

Or maybe it was something else. What if Foxglove had been working for the other side all along, and this was a trap designed to lure him out of the shadows and into the hands of the British secret service or the FBI? What if Foxglove were handling him, rather than the other way around? Lewandowski was tempted to just walk away. But could he afford to throw away such an opportunity? If he could make it work – the greatest assassination plot of all time – he would have all the medals, promotions and beautiful women that any man could ever ask for.

All right then, Lewandowski told himself. *Keep talking*.

'You are certain about this? And you will be able to provide details of the time and location?

'Of course. I wouldn't have told you otherwise!'

'This will need careful consideration,' Lewandowski said. 'At the highest levels. I hardly need to tell you that such an operation cannot be allowed to fail.'

Foxglove laughed. 'I should imagine not.'

'You don't seem troubled by that possibility.'

'Why should I be? I don't expect it to fail,' Foxglove said, with a smile.

There was that supercilious attitude again. Lewandowski felt a powerful desire to wipe the smirk off Foxglove's face. 'Listen to me. If a British or American army suffers a humiliating defeat, what happens to the generals who are responsible for the disaster? They are . . . What is the phrase? "Relieved of their commands." But in our world, they are relieved of their lives, and the officers under them, too.'

Lewandowski's meaning was clear: *the same thing will happen to you if this goes wrong*. But Foxglove simply said, 'Then we'd better make it work,' cool as ice, indifferent to the threat.

Lewandowski sighed. He needed to reassert his control over Foxglove, and he knew how to do it. But that would have to wait for another time and place. For now, he would stick to business. 'As I said, I will report our meeting to my superiors.'

'Tell them they don't have much time to make up their minds.'

'I am aware of that.' It was Lewandowski's turn to smile. 'Of course, there is another possibility . . .'

'What is that?' For the first time, Lewandowski detected a note of unease in Foxglove's voice.

'Churchill and his generals have to get from one side of the Atlantic to the other.'

'And?'

'Who's to say that they will survive the voyage?'

• • •

It might have been spring in softer, southern climes, but winter had still not loosened its grip on the Scottish Highlands. The distant mountains were topped with snow, the wind was bitter, and the sky over Loch Morar was an unbroken sheet of slate-grey cloud, with not the faintest glimmer of sunlight.

The brightest colours for miles around were the deep sky blue of Saffron Courtney's eyes and the rosy glow of her skin. She had been on her feet since dawn, hiking alone across rough terrain, and she shivered as she looked out across the deepest freshwater lake in the British Isles. More than a thousand feet to the bottom, and who knew what monsters lurked in those black depths?

Saffron checked her watch: a little after 11.30. She had to be back at the Special Operations Executive training centre at Arisaig House by 13.00, and there were more than seven miles to go. She was wearing army boots and had a thirty-pound pack on her back. If she forced marched for five miles and ran the final two, she would make it in time, but she'd need to get a move on.

As she turned to leave, Saffron glanced back across the loch. The view was bleak, but so spectacular that she wanted to commit it to memory. Yet, as she looked at the water, its gloom seemed to trigger something. She could almost feel the cogs of her brain moving, like the tumblers of a lock falling into place, until a door, deep in her subconscious, opened.

Suddenly, the blackness reaching into Saffron's soul was not that of fathomless water, but of deathly, endless night. Though her body was still standing by a Scottish loch, her mind had moved to a smaller, shallower body of water: a ceremonial lake called the Hofvijver in the Dutch city of The Hague.

It was as if a time machine had dragged her back, into her past. It was getting dark, and Saffron could see the silver flashes on the black collar of SS-*Hauptsturmführer* Karsten Schröder's uniform and the silver skull and crossbones on his cap. She could hear his voice as he tried to force himself on the woman he believed was a loyal Nazi sympathiser called Marlize Marais. She smelled his sweat, felt the rough bark of a tree bruising her back as he pushed her hard against it, and the thrust of one hand beneath her skirt and between her legs while the other grabbed hold of her hair.

Panic rose inside her, as if it were all happening again. And then, the sudden time-shift of a dream moved to later that evening, when she was no longer standing up, no longer the helpless victim. She was sitting astride Schröder's semi-conscious body, feeling the faint flutter of his breath against the palm of her hand as she stifled his feeble attempts to cry for help. She re-lived the tug of the hatpin as her other hand pulled it from her hair, and the resistance she'd felt as she pressed it down with murderous precision and . . .

Saffron screamed. It was a primitive, wild yell of fury and frustration, the cry of a woman possessed by a demon she could not conquer. Then she ran, desperate to escape the ghoul's grasp, forgetting any thought of walking even some part of the way back to her base, as she dashed up to the village of Morar, past the hotel, past the station and on to the road to Arisaig.

Saffron had not covered a quarter of the distance when the pain of running began to slow the overworked muscles of her long, slender legs. It clawed at her hammering heart, and squeezed the air from her chest. No matter how hard she sucked in the next breath, her lungs were never satisfied.

Saffron didn't care. She welcomed the pain because it was an antidote to the all-consuming visions. The more her mind focused on her physical agony, the more the nightmare receded.

Her route took her along a beautiful coastline with views across the water to the islands of Eigg, Rhum and Skye, but Saffron saw nothing but tarmac in front of her. She arrived at Arisaig, her vision blurred by sweat, her heart pounding. Running downhill along the drive that led from the Fort William road to the forecourt of the house, she hurled herself through the front door, staggered across the lobby to the great hall and collapsed on the floor.

A minute later, an army sergeant – one of the training centre's instructors – passed through the hall. He spotted Saffron, ran across and squatted beside her.

'Better get the doc to take a look at you, miss,' the sergeant said. He lifted Saffron to a sitting position, slipped the pack off her back and then pulled her to her feet. Draping one of her arms across his shoulder, he half-dragged her to the surgery.

The sergeant was a short, squat, powerfully built man. Saffron was a couple of inches taller than him, but forty pounds lighter. Together, they resembled a bulldog leading a hobbled, over-raced greyhound.

'What have we here?' asked Dr Hamish Maguire, as Saffron was placed, semi-conscious, in a chair opposite his desk.

'Miss Courtney, doc,' the instructor said.

'Aye, so it is,' Maguire said, walking round to the other side of his desk, then leaning against it as he looked down at her exhausted figure. 'And what reduced her to this sorry state?'

'Looks like she overdid it on a cross-country exercise.'

'Well, it's not the first time she's overdone it, eh?'

'Not by a long chalk,' the instructor agreed.

'How long was it she held out last year? Forty-eight hours?'

'More like seventy-two,' the sergeant said, unable to hide his admiration for an act of endurance that had passed into Arisaig legend. All the trainees were put through an interrogation session that was as close as possible to the actual experience of capture and torture by the Gestapo. Holding out for a single day was regarded as an achievement. Three days was unheard of, but the effort had left Saffron confined to bed for the best part of a week.

Saffron opened her eyes and let out a soft groan.

'Very well, Sergeant, I'll take it from here,' Maguire said.

As the instructor left the room, the doctor picked up one of Saffron's arms, which was hanging limply over the side of the chair, and took her pulse. It was fast – one hundred and twenty beats a minute – but this was the strong, solid heartbeat of a twenty-three-year-old woman in prime physical condition. Maguire could feel it slowing, even as he was taking his reading.

Saffron lifted her head and opened her eyes. 'I promise you, doctor, I'm perfectly all right.' Her diction was that of an upper-class Englishwoman, but tinged with the tighter cadence of

British colonial Africa. She pulled herself a little more upright. 'Really, there's no need for me to take up your valuable time.'

'Och, I'm in no hurry,' Maguire replied. 'As a matter of fact, you're my first customer today.'

Saffron nodded, too exhausted to find a reason to argue.

'You know, you're very highly thought of around here,' Maguire said. 'Old Fairbairn used to say that you were one of the half-dozen most naturally gifted fighters he'd ever trained. He's no longer with us, of course. His methods are greatly in demand elsewhere.'

'Oh,' Saffron said, then fell silent.

Maguire continued. 'I remember observing how remarkable it was that someone as charming as you, who shows no signs of aggression or bad temper in normal circumstances, should have such a capacity for violence when required to display it. Fairbairn pointed out that all the best fighters are like that. They have cool heads, are not easily provoked and never knowingly seek trouble. But when trouble finds them, they don't hold back.'

Saffron shrugged, and for a moment she looked more like a bored schoolgirl than an SOE operative.

'But even the toughest fighter is still a human being,' Maguire said, looking at her carefully, as if searching for some clue hidden deep inside of her.

'The sergeant mentioned your bravery when they gave you the Gestapo treatment. But what I remember are the nightmares you had afterwards. Your screaming frightened poor wee Nurse McLintock. I can't help but wonder whether you've been having another run-in with our German friends . . . at least in your mind.'

Now Saffron sat upright, suddenly alert. 'What makes you say that?' There was a sharpness in her voice now.

Maguire smiled. 'Well, now . . . This is a very secretive establishment, of course. But still, when senior officers come up from London to see how we are getting on, and we pour them a dram or two, it's only natural that they should talk about our former pupils and how they are getting on in the real world. And you being one of our most remarkable trainees . . . Let's just say that, while I do not know any specific details of your recent mission, I am aware that you had to be pulled out in a hurry and were, I quote, "Being hunted by half the bloody Gestapo in the Low Countries."'

Saffron shrugged, with a little grimace. 'Something like that.'

Maguire's voice hardened, became less avuncular, as he said, 'Miss Courtney, you were sent here by your superiors to rest, relax and do a moderate degree of physical and technical training. The aim was to send you back south in tip-top condition. It was not to have you running across the Highlands as though Hitler's minions were still chasing you. That is what I believe you were doing, and since there are no reports of Nazis in the neighbourhood, I must conclude that the enemies that you were running from are in your mind. Is that a fair assessment?'

Saffron turned her eyes away from his and buried her head in her hands. 'I'm all right,' she said, her voice muffled. 'Really . . . I'm all right.'

'Don't worry, lassie,' Maguire said more gently. 'It's nothing to be ashamed of. I suspect you've had experiences that would have troubled the toughest, most battle-hardened veteran. But we must deal with them, because untreated distress is no better than an untreated disease. It gets worse over time, and it can prove fatal. Now, look at me . . .'

Maguire waited while Saffron took a deep breath, then pulled her hands from her face and turned to him. 'Am I on the right track?' he asked.

Saffron nodded.

'And would you like me to get you some help?'

She didn't answer. It was not in her nature to admit her weaknesses. And Maguire did not try to force her. He just kept looking at her, waiting for signs of a decision. Finally, she nodded.

'Good girl,' Maguire said. 'There's a chap in Harley Street who can help you – an excellent man, a real leader in his field.'

Saffron winced. 'Will you tell Brigadier Gubbins? I don't want him to think I'm not fit for duty.'

'On the contrary, this will make you much fitter for duty, as he well knows. Believe me, you're not the first of his people to need this kind of treatment. Now . . . You have three more days up here. My orders to you, as your doctor, are to get plenty of rest, eat as well as our rations will allow, and take occasional gentle exercise. And I do mean gentle, Miss Courtney – no more hurtling around the Highlands.'

Saffron smiled. 'Yes, doctor.'

'That's the spirit.' Maguire walked towards the door to show Saffron out. He opened it for her, but before she stepped through, he added, 'And the very best of luck to you, for the rest of this blasted war.'

• • •

Dr Clement Thackeray did not resemble Saffron's idea of an eminent Harley Street practitioner. He was a tall, thin man, with a shock of grey hair and round tortoiseshell spectacles, and was dressed in grey flannel trousers, a heathery tweed jacket with leather patches at the elbows, and a pale blue cotton shirt, worn without a tie. If anything, Thackeray reminded Saffron of the eccentric, unworldly professors she had encountered during her brief pre-war studies at Oxford, and the state of his consulting room only added to that impression. There were shelves on every wall, crammed with piles of books in any old order. Yet more volumes were heaped on a table and on the desk, behind which Thackeray himself sat.

'Please, make yourself comfortable,' Thackeray said, getting to his feet and pointing to one of a pair of armchairs arranged in front of a marble fireplace. The weather was milder in London than Scotland, and the fire had not been lit.

Saffron did as she was told. There was a table beside her chair with a small jug of water, a glass and an ashtray.

'Do please feel free to smoke.' Thackeray's voice was warm, tinged with a gentle Yorkshire accent that made him seem reassuringly down-to-earth. He was smoking a pipe whose sweet tobacco scented the air.

'Thank you, but I don't,' Saffron replied.

Thackeray took the pipe from his mouth. 'Would you rather I extinguished this?'

'Not at all.'

'Very well, then . . . Before we start talking about your particular situation, let me tell you something about myself, and what I do, and how you and I might be able to work together.'

Saffron smiled and gave a nod of assent, so Thackeray continued. 'I am trained as a surgeon, and was working towards becoming a cardiovascular specialist. Then the war broke out – the last show, I mean. I signed up for the Medical Corps, was posted to Flanders and that's where I spent the next four years. Ended up getting attached to the Fifth Army under Gough.

Went through the Somme and Passchendaele, and witnessed that utter, senseless carnage. What troubled me the most, though, was seeing chaps I knew to be good soldiers, brave men, unjustly branded as cowards, when they were no longer able to fight for mental, rather than physical reasons. It was perfectly obvious to me that they were as badly wounded as any poor soul who'd lost a leg or been blinded. But the wounds were in their minds.'

Thackeray took a packet of tobacco from the side pocket of his jacket and refilled his pipe as he spoke. 'I swore that if I got through the war in one piece – which I did, not a scratch on me from beginning to end . . . Well, I was going to learn about the human mind under stress, and the toll that extreme experiences of all kinds – be they physical or emotional – take on us all.'

'May I ask you a question?' Saffron said.

'By all means,' Thackeray said, applying a match to the fresh tobacco.

'Have you experienced this kind of trauma yourself?'

Thackeray finished lighting his pipe and smiled. 'Well done, lass, good question. And the answer is, yes, I have. Had to be invalided home in March of '18. I could no longer bring myself to apply a scalpel to human flesh. So . . . how does that answer make you feel?'

'Better,' Saffron replied. 'It means you won't judge me the way someone else might.'

'I wouldn't ever judge you,' Thackeray said. 'Certainly not in any moral sense, and nor should anyone else with the slightest shred of professional competence, let alone human decency. Now, I want you to tell me once – and only once – about the event that you believe might have traumatised you.'

'Why only once?'

'Because I don't want to ingrain it any deeper in your mind. I want us to move beyond it . . . but it helps to know what we're moving beyond.'

'Of course.'

Saffron described how she had killed Karsten Schröder. The furious blur of images that had overwhelmed her mind by the shores of Loch Morar was transformed into a coherent account of events, from meeting the SS officer at a weekend conference for the Dutch and Belgian Nazi parties, through to the night-time walk across a park that had led to his attempt to force himself on her, and her immediate, deadly response to that assault.

When she had finished, Thackeray said, 'Thank you. It can't have been easy telling me all that. Now, what we must do is isolate the specific traumatic element. Was it the man's attack on you, or your retaliation against him . . . or both?'

'The retaliation . . . I know you say you won't judge me, but I can't help thinking that I must be some kind of monster to be able to do such a thing.'

'I assure you that you aren't. After all, you fought back against a vile attack by an enemy combatant in wartime. No court would consider that a crime. Moreover, if you were truly evil, or possessed by some kind of psychopathic disorder, you would have felt elated, rather than traumatised by the events you described.'

'Thank you. That's a great relief.'

'Good. Freeing yourself of any feelings of guilt will certainly help. For now, though, tell me, was this occasion in Scotland the only time that you've had this kind of waking nightmare, or have there been others?'

'That was the only time where I could actually see and feel what happened, although I have had a couple of nightmares about it.'

'What about sudden emotional outbursts, like losing your temper or breaking down in tears?'

Saffron thought for a moment. 'Yes, one.'

'Tell me about it.'

'I was walking through Hyde Park on Sunday afternoon a couple of weeks ago with my friend Margaret, Brigadier Gubbins' secretary. A boy was coming the other way, trailing a kite. He was running as fast as he could to try and make it fly. He was looking back at the kite and not at where he was going, and he bumped into me.'

'How old was this boy, would you say?'

'I don't know . . . Seven or eight, maybe.'

'Big enough to give you quite a bump, then?'

'I suppose so. But I reacted as if I'd been attacked. I started screaming at him, and then at his mother . . . Honestly, I was hardly aware of what I was saying or doing, and I can't remember any of the details now. All I know is that the boy ended up in floods of tears and his mother was furious with me, and Margaret had to try and make the peace, bless her. Several people stopped to watch what was happening and I could see them looking daggers at me. I made a total fool of myself.'

'In their eyes, maybe. In mine, you simply expressed the pain that had been building up inside you.' Thackeray leaned forward. 'Imagine lava building up beneath a volcano. The pressure gradually increases until something makes it erupt. And in the case of the human mind, that eruption can either be internal, as it was at Loch Morar, or external, as it was in the park. So now we need to find out what it was that triggered you.'

'But I thought I'd already told you that – it was the boy and his kite.'

'There might have been other triggers you were unaware of. What about Loch Morar?'

Saffron shrugged. 'I don't know . . . I only remember the blackness. The scene looked like a black-and-white photograph . . . and the black made me think of Schröder's SS uniform.'

'Very well, then, can you remember seeing anything black that day in Hyde Park? Like, say, a priest or a nun in black clothes, or a woman in a black dress, someone in mourning . . .?'

'Not that I'm aware of, no.'

'Hmm . . .' Thackeray settled back in his chair and drew on his pipe. 'Whereabouts in Hyde Park were you, exactly, when the boy with the kite bumped into you?'

'We were strolling beside the Serpentine.'

Thackeray nodded. 'So, water, like the lake where the traumatising incident occurred. So it could be that the association that triggers your reactions is not related to blackness, but to water.'

'Of course, that makes sense!' Saffron exclaimed, with the enthusiasm of one who thinks a tricky problem has been solved.

Thackeray gave a wry smile. 'I said "could be", not "is". We may find, as we go on, that the trigger is some other, completely different thing that is not obvious at the moment. But the aim of our work will not be to drive all your bad memories out of your mind. What happened, happened, and there's no undoing that. But if we understand what causes your extreme reactions, we can, with any luck, enable you to take charge of those memories and deal with them. Do you follow me?'

'Absolutely.'

'Good – then we have our plan. But before we go any further, I have one additional question. Was that night in The Hague the only time that you have killed a man?'

Saffron's eyes suddenly lost their focus, as if she was staring at something at a great distance. She said nothing, turning her face away from Thackeray. She chewed her bottom lip as she considered, then she said, decisively, 'No, it was not.'

• • •

'How's the head-shrinker, Courtney?' asked Brigadier Colin Gubbins, the officer in charge of all SOE's operational activities. He focused on Saffron with his piercing, chilly blue eyes and added, 'Any use?'

Gubbins was a small man, a couple of inches shorter than Saffron. But his drive, energy and ferocious determination made up for any lack of stature. The SOE agents whom he commanded looked on him with awe, and not a little fear.

'I think so, sir,' Saffron replied. 'I saw him this morning. It was my third appointment. He seemed to think we were making progress.'

'Huh,' Gubbins grunted. He was about to say something, but stopped as he saw a waitress approach, bearing a teapot, milk jug, sugar and two cups. Gubbins had, for once, left his office and taken Saffron to the cafe beside the Serpentine in Hyde Park. She had not dared tell him that it might not be a good idea. So far, however, the sight of water had not disturbed her. Perhaps, she thought, just recognising the trigger was enough to disarm it.

Gubbins waited until the waitress had poured their teas. 'Got something for you – a job. Thought it might be a pleasant change after that business in the Low Countries.'

'That sounds intriguing,' Saffron said.

'Ever been to America?'

'No, sir.'

'Well, then, now's your chance. As you may know, Baker Street is not without enemies. And I'm not just talking about the Hun.'

'Baker Street' was the term by which the staff of the Special Operations Executive referred to themselves, since their existence was still highly classified.

'I know that we're not universally popular,' Saffron said. 'Some people in the military and intelligence hierarchy think we're . . . well—'

'A bunch of bloody amateurs,' Gubbins snapped. 'And fiascos like the one you discovered don't help.' He lowered his voice to ensure that he could not be overheard, and angrily muttered, 'Damn near every bloody agent we sent into Holland or Belgium being picked up by the Abwehr and Gestapo the moment they set foot on foreign soil.'

'Well, at least we know, sir. Now we can do something about it.'

'Indeed we can, Courtney. But only if we stay in business. I've been talking to Hambro.'

Saffron's ears pricked up. Sir Charles Hambro, the head of a merchant bank that bore his family's name, was director of SOE and thus Gubbins' boss. He was also a close friend of Winston Churchill.

'He and I see the situation the same way,' Gubbins said. 'The PM's a staunch supporter. Got Baker Street going in the first place, said its job was to set Europe ablaze. Anyway, Hambro told me he'd had a word with the PM about your recent adventure. Can't say I was entirely happy about that . . .'

'No, sir,' said Saffron, knowing how much Gubbins disapproved of casual discussion of his unit's missions, even in the heart of Downing Street.

'Apparently the PM lapped it up. Loves a good yarn. Dare say he would, being a journalist for so many years. But he's also a politician, and must keep people happy, particularly if they are very senior men whose support is essential if we are to win the war. So it's a damn serious problem if many of those men are dead set against us.'

'Did Sir Charles have any thoughts about how we might keep them on side?'

'Yes, he did. His suggestion was that we should open a second front, as it were, in the United States. We have friends in Washington, mostly chaps in the same line of business as us, but we need more, and we need them to say nice things about us, and our importance to the Allied cause. That way, the PM can say that our American allies regard Baker Street as a vital means of softening up Europe, preparing the ground for an eventual invasion, and so forth. And that should keep the wolves of Whitehall away from us.'

'So where do I come into it?' Saffron asked.

'You are going to be the front line of our propaganda offensive. You will travel to New York, and then Washington. You will be given introductions to various powerful and influential gentlemen and use your considerable charms . . .'

Saffron flinched. Brigadier Gubbins was not the kind of man who made complimentary remarks about his female agents. For him to even imply that she might be remotely attractive was unprecedented.

'. . . to persuade them of our merits.'

'Yes, sir,' Saffron said, praying that none of her astonishment was evident in her voice.

'Not, I might add, that I am asking for some sort of Mata Hari act.'

'Of course not, sir,' Saffron said.

'Just make it clear that we do work that may be unusual, but it is vital for the war effort and will bear fruit when the moment comes to invade Nazi Europe. And take your gong. It'll impress the Yanks.'

Many SOE staff, particularly the women, dressed for work in civilian clothing. But Saffron preferred the uniform of the Auxiliary Territorial Service, the female branch of the army, if only because it saved time not having to think about what to wear in the morning. She glanced down at the band of red silk, crossed by four vertical blue stripes, above the left breast pocket of her uniform blouson. This was the ribbon of the George Medal, awarded for conspicuous acts of gallantry by civilians. The bronze oak-leaf badge beside it indicated that she'd been mentioned in dispatches. This was an honour reserved for military servicemen. Hers had been a complicated war.

'Yes, sir,' Saffron said. 'But should I wear uniform or civilian dress when I get to America?'

'Use your discretion. I imagine uniform for formal daytime meetings and civilian for social events in the evening would be the general idea.'

'So how do you think I should set up these meetings and social events in America?'

'Ah, well, that's why I want you to go to New York first. There's a chap there by the name of William Stephenson. Runs an outfit called British Security Coordination from an office in the Rockefeller Center. The name on the door, however, is the

British Passport Control Office, and that is what you should always call it in public.'

'Yes, sir, I understand. What do I need to know about Stephenson, sir?'

'That he's a man to be taken seriously. Has the ear of everyone who matters in Downing Street.'

'Including the PM?'

'Particularly him. They listen to him in Washington, too. Stephenson came from nothing. Born in Canada, was adopted after his parents had to give him up. Too poor. He went to France in the last show with the Canadian Army, got himself transferred to the Royal Flying Corps, shot down almost twenty Hun planes, won the Military Cross, got shot down himself, taken prisoner, and then escaped from his POW camp.'

'Goodness, that's quite a record.'

'That's not the half of it. He was a Forces boxing champion – middleweight, if I recall. After the war he invented some kind of gadget that lets you send photographs by wire to anywhere in the world. Made him a fortune. Owns factories, a film studio.'

'So, he's rich.'

'As Croesus. And he's got a nose for politics, too. Back in '34 or so, he was telling anyone who'd listen that the Nazis were rearming and planning to take over Europe. Churchill believed him – that's what brought them together. The good thing is, Stephenson has a soft spot for our outfit, so he'll set you up with contacts in Washington. He'll even bankroll your trip. No room for it on our budget, but Stephenson pays for BSC himself, so he won't notice one more name on the payroll.'

'There's no need, sir. I'm . . . well . . . I'm not without means.'

Gubbins made a movement with his lips that might have passed for a smile. 'I'm aware of that, Courtney. But we are operating exchange controls, and you can't take any significant sum of money out of the country.'

'No, sir, but . . .' Saffron stopped. *My father would be furious if he thought a Courtney was sponging off someone.*

'But what?'

'Nothing, sir.'

Gubbins turned his blue eyes on hers. For a moment, unless Saffron was imagining it, they seemed a fraction less icy than usual. 'Well, I'll let you and Stephenson argue over the money.'

'Yes, sir.'

'In any event, you'll be going over to America on the *Queen Mary*. She sails from Gourock in three days' time.'

Saffron frowned. 'Gourock?'

'Port on the Clyde, outside Glasgow. It's the main entry and exit point for American personnel.'

'I'd better get moving, then. You know what the trains are like these days.'

'Indeed I do. Your friend Miss Jackson has booked you a berth on tonight's sleeper from Euston.'

'Oh, Lord,' Saffron gasped. 'I really will have to get going. Do you mind if I dash off, sir?'

'Why? Is there some sort of a problem? Damn train's not leaving for five hours. Can't possibly take that long to pack.'

'For a man, no, sir. But for a woman who has been ordered to take evening wear, that means sorting out shoes, and bags, and jewellery . . .'

Gubbins grunted. 'One more thing before you go. Stephenson is doing a favour for me, so he asked whether you could do one for him.'

'What kind of favour, sir?'

'Not sure, exactly. He said he needed someone capable of what he terms "sleuthing". I told him you had shown yourself eminently capable of uncovering information. Before you ask, no, he did not say what it was, other than it's a private, hush-hush project. In my view, Stephenson's got a bee in his bonnet about something, but he doesn't want to go public until he's sure of his facts.'

'That sounds interesting.'

'Yes, but let me tell you what I told him, very firmly. You, Miss Courtney, are on a mission that is of extreme importance to me personally, and to our unit as a whole. But it is not intended to be physically or psychologically taxing. Think of this as a working holiday.'

'Absolutely.'

How ironic it was to hear talk of holidays from Gubbins, Saffron thought. As everyone at Baker Street knew, their CO never left his office before ten at night, and had not been known to take a day off since the beginning of the war.

'Bearing all that in mind,' Gubbins continued, 'both for your sake and mine, I do not – repeat, not – want you getting mixed up in any rough stuff. The last thing we need is for the Americans to find you causing trouble in their own country. That would hardly make them warm to us.'

'Quite, sir.' Saffron could not help adding, 'What if Mr Stephenson needs me to do something important?'

'By which, I take it, you mean something that involves active service?'

'I suppose so, yes.'

Gubbins leaned forward in his chair. 'Listen to me, Courtney. Your fighting spirit does you great credit. But sometimes the politics of war are as important as any military campaign. Our outfit's continued existence hangs in the balance, and if we go under, the brave men and women resisting the German occupation of Europe will lose their best, most committed ally. I'm sure I don't need to tell you how much the Nazis would welcome that.'

'No, sir.'

'You did a damn fine job in the Low Countries. But you'll be doing an even better one if you can win over influential Americans and make them understand how vital it will be to the success of any invasion of Occupied Europe to have well-trained, well-equipped resistance forces harrying the Nazis behind their lines.'

'I understand, sir.'

'Good. Now go and get packing.'

• • •

Before the war, Saffron's father, Leon Courtney, had bought a flat in a Victorian mansion in Belgravia which had been converted into modern apartments. It was one of the smartest parts of London, halfway between Sloane Square and Knightsbridge. Leon had intended it to be a pied-à-terre for himself and his second wife, Harriet, Saffron's step-mother. But they were now at home in Kenya for the duration of the war, so Saffron had taken it over for herself.

She was standing in her bedroom, a woman of twenty-three years of age, packing for a trip of indeterminate length that would require her to look good in front of very powerful people and, quite possibly, their high society wives, in a country she had never visited before, whose climate she did not know.

Even her capacity for calm, cold-blooded reasoning was coming under strain. The bed itself had disappeared beneath a mass of strewn clothes, and her two large, monogrammed Louis Vuitton suitcases were still half-empty. Saffron looked at her watch. It was 18.55, and the train left Euston at 20.00.

From the hall, she heard the telephone ringing. Saffron ignored it as long as she could, but whoever wanted to talk to her wasn't taking no for an answer. 'Dammit!' she muttered, then tiptoed her way across a carpet strewn with shoes and bags, and picked it up.

'There's someone at the front door with a parcel for you, miss,' said the doorman. 'Says it's compliments of Brigadier Gubbins' office.'

'Thank you, Hollins. Please send him up.'

Saffron opened her front door, stepped on to the landing and watched as a young man wearing khaki fatigues and a motor-cycle helmet ran up the stairs, two at a time. 'Quicker than the lift,' he said with a grin, and handed over a foolscap envelope.

'Do you need me to sign for it?' Saffron asked.

'No need, miss,' the messenger replied. 'Righto then, better be on my way.'

Saffron walked back into the flat, examining the envelope. The address was in Margaret Jackson's handwriting. They had spoken on the phone just after Saffron arrived home. Margaret had promised to send a telex message direct from their office to Leon's, letting him know where Saffron was going and, since she could not get money out of England, politely inquiring whether he had means of providing her with the necessary resources.

'It's very nice of this Stephenson chap to offer to help,' Saffron had said. 'But I don't want to go cap in hand to a total stranger.'

'I wouldn't worry, darling,' Margaret had replied. 'The entire country's going cap in hand to Uncle Sam.'

'Maybe, but my father wouldn't like it, I can tell you.'

'Good point. Fathers usually don't take kindly to their daughters being given money by strangers.'

Saffron opened the envelope to find a typed note, to which two military travel passes were paper-clipped: by train to Glasgow, and by sea to New York.

> Darling Saffy,
>
> Here are your tickets. I have booked you a room at the Central Hotel in Glasgow. And I have a message from Sir Charles himself. He says, when you get to the ship, enter via Gangway A and say you are travelling with Colonel Warden's party. No, I don't have any idea what that means, either! But he was most insistent: say you're with Colonel Warden. Have a wonderful time. I am so jealous! Lots of love, M xx

There was one more line to Margaret's letter:

> PS. Telegram sent to Pater. Instant reply received! 'Send Saffron my regards and tell her the matter is in hand.' What a useful father!

It was now 19.05. Saffron had to be in a taxi on the way to Euston by 19.30. Now, at last, the ruthless side of her nature kicked in. She threw one of her cases to the far side of the room. In the one that remained, she packed two evening gowns, both black, so that she only had to add a single pair of black silk gloves and evening shoes. Two daytime outfits followed: one dress, one pair of trousers with two different blouses, two cardigans for cool days, and two pairs of shoes – pretty sandals and practical flats. Add to that her underwear, nighties, two spare uniform shirts, jewellery, evening bag, makeup and washbag . . . She had to sit on the case to close it, and buckle leather straps around it to prevent the contents bursting out, but the job was done.

Unfortunately, that still left Saffron's black evening coat, trimmed with mink at the collar and cuffs. There was nothing to do but wear it over her uniform – hardly regulation, and a strange match for the battered khaki canvas shoulder bag that had been her constant companion on all her wartime adventures, but by this point she was past caring about how she looked. She was in the taxi by 19.35, and on the train with two minutes to spare. Her mission was underway.

• • •

Saffron stood on the quayside at Gourock, in the damp grey chill, breathing in the cool air. There had been no porters at the local station, so she'd had to carry her heavy case herself. Around her, a sea of human chaos surged and eddied. Jeeps, trucks and ambulances were revving their engines and tooting their horns, trying to force a path through the thousands of men crowding the docks. And though they were on the west coast of Scotland, it felt more like New York.

The vehicles had white stars stencilled on their bonnets and side panels, and most of the men around her were wearing various forms of US Army Air Forces uniform – from formal, collar-and-tie service dress, to motley get-ups topped with fur-lined leather flight jackets and caps. And the accents of the men, who were barking orders or exchanging foul-mouthed curses, would have been more readily found in the Irish bars of Boston or the stockyards of Chicago than on the banks of the Clyde.

Everyone had come for the same reason as Saffron: to get aboard the vessel that loomed over them. Saffron gazed up at RMS *Queen Mary*. She had never seen – let alone stepped aboard – a vessel that could possibly compare with her.

She heard her father's voice calling across the drawing room of their Kenyan home from his big armchair. He'd wanted to show her a cutaway drawing of the newly commissioned *Queen Mary* in the *Illustrated London News*. 'Look at that, Saffy!' he'd exclaimed. 'She'll weigh eighty thousand tons when she's finished!'

Saffron smiled at the memory. She must have been nine or ten. 'Golly,' she'd said, wanting to share Leon's excitement, but unable to see what was so thrilling about all those numbers.

'Maybe you and I can sail on her one day, eh? Cross the Atlantic from England to America. They say there'll be a telephone in every room, a splendid restaurant, and even a cinema. Then we'll cruise into New York past the Statue of Liberty. Wouldn't that be grand?'

'Yes, Daddy,' Saffron had said, a little more enthusiastically, because she knew what America was. But she didn't love it the way she loved her pony, so the next words she spoke were: 'Can I go riding now?'

Leon had sighed, exasperated, as if he was thinking, 'A son would have understood what I was talking about.' But she knew now, looking back, that it also meant, 'And a mother would have known what to say to her daughter.'

Saffron had reached up on tiptoe, wrapped her arms around her father, and rested her head against his chest, knowing that he would bend his head and kiss her hair. 'Run along, then,' he'd said, and then, 'But we'll sail on the *Queen Mary* one day – that's a promise.'

'Well, here I am, Daddy,' she said to herself. 'And you were right. She's as big as you said she would be. But look what they've done to her.'

The black hull, white upper decks and red and black funnels of the Cunard-White Star Line's livery had vanished. Instead, the great ship almost merged into the cloudy sky beyond her, vanishing into the rain and sea spray being whipped into Saffron's face by the wind coming off the water. The *Queen Mary* had been converted for use as a troopship, and every inch of her hull and superstructure had been covered in the dull, dove-coloured paint that had inspired the nickname she had recently acquired: the 'Grey Ghost'.

Saffron cast a professional eye – the eye of an SOE agent – over the superstructure of the great liner. She spotted a four-inch naval gun and half-a-dozen Oerlikon cannons, which fired 20mm explosive shells at a rate not much slower than the Vickers machine guns that were mounted in batteries of four, so that they could be fired by a single gunner, along the topmost deck.

Well, I hope they have better luck than I did, she thought, casting her mind back to that perfect spring afternoon, almost two years before to the day, when the blissful calm of the Aegean had been torn asunder by the screaming bombers dropping from a cloudless sky. *The only plane I even hit was . . .* 'No,' she muttered. 'Don't.'

Saffron looked at her leather suitcase, then back at the ship. There were less than a couple of hundred more yards to go, but it might as well have been a mile, given the time it would take to fight her way to the gangway. She was about to pick up the case when she heard the toot of a horn. She turned, ready to give the insolent brute behind the wheel a piece of her mind, but stopped, entirely disarmed by the sight that confronted her.

The noise had come from an open Jeep. A red cross on a white background was painted on its bonnet. There were two men in the vehicle. The one behind the wheel looked unremarkable – no sooner seen than forgotten. His passenger, however, was another matter altogether.

He was leaning back in his seat with one foot up on the dashboard, wearing a khaki greatcoat, unbuttoned, bearing a lieutenant's insignia, a peaked US Army Air Forces cap, pushed back on his head, and a pair of tinted Aviator glasses for which there was no conceivable need on this grey northern day. A lazy smile spread across his chiselled, absurdly handsome face. He pulled down his glasses and looked over the top of them, with velvety brown eyes. 'Well, howdy, ma'am,' he called over to Saffron, in an exaggerated cowboy drawl. 'Looks to me like you could use a ride.'

The only thing worse than a man who thought he was God's gift to women, was a man who was right to think it. Saffron immediately found the lieutenant wildly attractive and absolutely infuriating in equal measure. She wondered how to take him down a peg or two. 'I could use a porter,' she replied. 'Are you available?'

'Any time, for a passenger like you.' The lieutenant sprang out of the car and walked over. He was, Saffron noted, at least six feet tall. He paused a couple of steps away from her and took a second to admire her. The normal ATS uniform was not designed to flatter the female form, but Saffron's fitted her like a piece of elegant haute couture daywear – which, indeed, it was. Her immediate superior at SOE was Major Hardy Amies, head of the Low Countries section. He was also one of London's leading couturiers, and before the war he had made several evening gowns for Saffron. As a special favour to her, since she was a loyal customer and a valued subordinate, Amies and his seamstresses had created two identical uniforms which were correct in every regulation detail, but made of the finest worsted fabric and cut to emphasise her figure. As Amies had told her: 'Any self-respecting Guards officer would have his dress uniform tailor-made. Why shouldn't you do the same thing?'

Saffron waited patiently while the lieutenant completed his inspection.

'Don't mind me asking, ma'am, but are those for real?' he asked, nodding towards her medal ribbon and badge.

'Quite genuine,' Saffron replied. She could see now that he was at least six feet two. She had to tilt her head to look him in the eye. She felt the need to impress him. 'I was mentioned in dispatches for fighting off some Italians in the Western Desert when I was driving a general around. And this . . .' she pointed at the George Medal, 'was for gallantry in the face of the enemy . . . but that's a long story.'

The lieutenant gave a long, low whistle. 'Not bad,' he said, grinning. 'But apart from that, what have you done for the war effort?'

Saffron knew he was joking, but she gave him a straight answer. 'A lot . . . and in places you wouldn't believe. But I'm afraid I'm not allowed to discuss that. Now, if you could get me to the ship before we all die of old age, I'd be eternally grateful.'

'Let's go, then.' The lieutenant picked up the heavy case as if it was a shopping bag and swung it on to the back seat of the

Jeep beside his own kitbag and a black briefcase. He looked at the driver and said, 'Hey, Jimmy, get in the back.'

'Sure thing, Doc.' Jimmy grinned, and took up a position perched on top of the kitbag.

The lieutenant waited until Saffron was settled in the passenger seat before getting behind the wheel and starting up the engine. 'Might take a while,' he said, easing the car into the sluggish stream of men and machinery, 'but we'll get you there before she sails.'

'Thank you,' Saffron replied. 'By the way, I need Gangway A.'

'Well, there's a coincidence – so do I.' The lieutenant grinned. 'Maybe we'll have the same bunk, too. I want to go on top.'

'So, you're a doctor?' Saffron asked, ignoring the innuendo.

'Yes, ma'am. Dr Clayton Malachi Stackpole the Third, if you want the whole dang thing. But most folks just call me Clay, or Doc.'

'I'm Saffron Courtney.' A thought occurred to her. 'I suppose I'm Saffron the Second, because my grandma's Saffron Courtney, too.' Stackpole was turning out to be less irritating than his first impression suggested, so she decided to reward him with a friendly smile. 'My close friends call me Saffy. But as you say "ma'am" so charmingly, do feel free to continue.'

Stackpole laughed. 'Yes, ma'am.'

'What kind of medicine do you practise?'

'Orthopaedic surgery.' Stackpole's voice became more serious. 'Broken bones, traumatic injury, that kinda thing. I studied at the University of Texas Medical Branch in Galveston, qualified as a doctor three years ago. Figured I'd spend my time dealing with busted-up oilmen, cowboys who fell off their horses . . . Ha! Turned out my first big job would be putting wounded fly-boys back together.'

'Will you be sailing with us to New York?'

'Yes, ma'am. I've got a few patients on board, mostly aircrew injured in raids over Europe, so I'll be looking after them on the voyage.'

'Poor boys,' Saffron sighed.

'Yeah, some of them are beat up pretty bad. But I guess you could say they're the lucky ones. At least they're going home. So many of our guys never will.'

'I know, it's the same with our Bomber Command. An awful lot of aircraft don't come back.'

'Hey, let's not get all gloomy here,' said Stackpole, making an effort to sound cheery. 'I got a few days' leave, so figure I'll spend 'em in New York. How about you?'

'Funnily enough, I've got a few days in New York, too. Then I'm off to Washington.'

The soldiers and civilians in front of them were pressed so tight that the Jeep had come to a dead halt. Stackpole switched off the engine and turned to Saffron with a quizzical look in his eye. 'That stuff you said about doing things you couldn't tell me about. You weren't kidding, were you?'

'No.'

'So, why are you going to the USA?'

'I can't tell you that, either. But you could say it's a diplomatic mission.'

'You sure don't look like a regular diplomat.'

'I think that's rather the point.'

'Yeah, I can dig that. You ask some old senator, "Won't you give poor little England another aircraft carrier?" And he'll say, "Sure thing, honey," and throw in the aircraft for free.'

Saffron laughed, thinking to herself that it might be an interesting voyage with Dr Stackpole on board. '"I can dig that . . ."?' she asked. 'I understood what you meant, but I've not heard that phrase before.'

'It's what the jazz cats say, the kind that make my old man go, "You listening to that damn racket again?"'

'If you're a Texan, shouldn't you be listening to . . . I don't know . . . cowboy music or something?'

'Huh . . . Guess I deserved that, giving you that old "aw, shucks" routine. But no, I don't listen to hillbilly music, or old-time dances, any of that hayseed stuff. See, I caught the jazz bug when I got to Galveston. It was just a couple hours' drive up to Houston, then catch the Sunset Limited overnight to New Orleans. Heard music there that changed my life. Never looked back since.'

'I love Dixieland jazz,' Saffron said. 'Such fun to dance to.'

'Yeah, it's pretty good . . . for beginners.' Stackpole gave a sly half-smile. 'But you should hear the new stuff. Charlie Parker blowing his sax, Art Tatum on piano, Dizzy Gillespie on trumpet. Man, those cats are cool.' He saw the blank look on her face. 'Don't feel bad you never heard of them. These guys have got a sound that's so new, it's never even been recorded yet. They call it bebop, and I promise you, it's like no other music mankind has ever played.'

'It sounds interesting.' Saffron was struck by the genuine enthusiasm in Stackpole's voice.

'Well, then, I tell you what, Miss Saffron Courtney the Second,' Stackpole said. 'I won't let you leave New York City till you've come to hear this music with me. We won't go to the regular jazz clubs on 52nd Street. I'll take you way uptown to Harlem, joints like Monroe's, where Bird and Dizzy play their hottest licks. Believe me, baby, it will change your life.'

Before Saffron could reply, Stackpole restarted the engine, said, 'Hold tight,' and thrust the nose of the Jeep through a narrow gap in the crowd and onto an open stretch of tarmac at the edge of the dock, in the shadow of the looming ocean liner. There was a gap of about twelve feet between the hull and the dock – enough room for the Jeep to fall into – but Stackpole didn't seem to care as he raced along until he came to a halt by the main gangway leading up to the ship.

Jimmy jumped down from his perch. He took the kitbag out of the back of the Jeep and gave it to Stackpole. He then handed over the doctor's black bag.

'You want me to carry the lady's bag?' Jimmy asked.

'No, we'll manage,' Stackpole said. He looked at Saffron. 'That all right by you?'

'Absolutely.'

'Then in that case, Jimmy, you can head down to the base. And, uh . . .' Stackpole reached into his greatcoat and pulled out a wallet. Saffron watched as he extracted a handful of ten-shilling and pound notes. 'Guess I won't be needing these any more. Here, you take them.'

'Gee, thanks, Doc,' Jimmy said. 'Appreciate it.'

'My pleasure.' Stackpole watched as Jimmy got in the Jeep and awkwardly begin to reverse the vehicle back along the dock, then he turned his attention to the men on the gangway.

'Well now,' he said. 'No son of Texas would ever allow a beautiful woman to stand in line with such a gang of scoundrels and ruffians. Can you carry my medicine bag?'

'Of course,' Saffron replied. 'I can take my case, too.'

'No need.' A moment later Stackpole had her suitcase in his left hand and the kitbag on his right shoulder. 'Follow me, ma'am,' he said.

'Wait a moment.' Saffron buttoned up her coat, so that her face was framed by the glossy black fur of the collar and her dark, lustrous hair. She reached into her canvas shoulder bag, pulled out a lipstick and applied two confident swipes.

'Oh, yeah,' Stackpole said, grinning. 'That'll do it.'

'Then let's go.'

Clay Stackpole got to the foot of the gangway and called out, 'Hey, fellas, make room for the lady.'

The gangway was solid with men and baggage. But somehow they stood aside to reveal a clear path all the way to the entrance to the ship. Saffron walked up it, smiling graciously at the men who were watching her with slack jaws and dumb grins as the wolf whistles rang out around her. Stackpole followed behind, weighed down by luggage like a devoted servant.

'That was fun,' she said as they entered the gaping hole in the *Queen Mary*'s steel flanks and went aboard.

A handful of US military police – all non-commissioned officers with pistols holstered on their webbing belts – were positioned by the entrance, telling the boarding men where to go. One of them took Stackpole's travel pass and identity papers and checked them. He reached into a box behind him, pulled out a red card and said, 'Follow the red signs, sir. They'll take you right to where you want to go.'

'Thank you, Sergeant.' Stackpole handed over Saffron's suitcase and gave her one of his cheeky grins. 'I'll see you later. Don't get seasick, now.'

'I won't, doctor,' she replied.

'Are you sure you're supposed to be here, ma'am?' the sergeant asked.

'Yes, quite sure. Here are my papers.'

The sergeant scanned them and handed them back. 'Well, these are okay. But I sure as hell don't know where to send you.'

'I was told to ask for Colonel Warden's party.'

'Well, I can't help you there, ma'am.'

A new voice entered the conversation: 'Don't worry, Sergeant. I can.'

A young man, not much older than Saffron, had materialised at the sergeant's side, apparently out of thin air. He had dark hair and a strong brow shading direct, piercing eyes. But these very masculine features were offset by full, almost feminine lips. He was wearing a beautifully cut charcoal-grey suit and held a clipboard in one hand.

'I'll take it from here,' he said, in an upper-class English accent. He looked at Saffron. 'And you are?'

'Saffron Courtney. My CO is Brigadier Gubbins, but it was Sir Charles Hambro who mentioned Colonel Warden.'

The Englishman nodded. 'Ah yes . . . we know Sir Charles very well. So, let me see . . .' He examined his clipboard. 'Courtney . . . Courtney . . . Ah, yes, there you are. My name's Colville. Christened John Rupert, but everyone calls me Jock. So, just follow me . . .'

'I'm so sorry,' Saffron asked, 'but could you possibly give me a hand with my bag?'

'Oh, don't worry, I'll send a man down for that.' Colville looked at the military policeman. 'Guard it with your life, Sergeant.'

Colville led Saffron towards a flight of stairs. Two Royal Marines, armed with pistols, like the American MPs, were standing guard at either side of the bottom flight. 'Miss Courtney is with me,' the man said.

'Yes, sir,' said one of the Marines.

The other grinned and added, 'Lucky you, sir.'

Colville nodded. As he and Saffron climbed the stairs, he said, 'Actually, we're both rather lucky. Almost all the original cabins have been stripped and converted into troops' accommodation. This ship was built to carry just over two thousand paying passengers. Can you believe they can cram fifteen thousand men in here for some voyages? Poor chaps are packed in tighter than sardines.'

'How many are there on this voyage?'

'About eight thousand, including us, the Americans and fifteen hundred Jerry prisoners, captured in Tunisia. I gather they're being taken to camps in the wilds of Texas and New Mexico.'

'Are we all crammed in together, too?' Saffron asked.

Colville laughed. 'Good Lord, no! The finest suites and staterooms on the main deck were left as they were, in case of need. You're going to be travelling in style.'

They emerged from the stairs into a large hallway in the heart of the ship. Though the mass of humanity was less dense here, the air of activity was equally palpable. Three young men hurried by, arguing about their bosses' cabin assignments. 'I'm sorry,' one insisted, 'but a permanent under-secretary is at least as senior and as deserving of priority as a presidential envoy.'

Two older men in uniform strolled past more slowly, deep in conversation. Both wore the red collar tabs that indicated they were senior staff officers. Saffron snapped to attention and saluted as they passed, but neither man seemed to notice her presence. More suits and uniforms scurried by in every direction.

Apparently oblivious to these goings-on, Colville looked around at his surroundings, then said, 'Right-ho, you should be just along here.'

'When will I meet Colonel Warden?' Saffron asked him as he led her to her cabin door. 'I feel I ought to say thank you.'

'Oh, I'm afraid that may not be possible – not for a few days, at any rate. The colonel will be very busy.' Colville unlocked the door and handed Saffron the key. 'But don't worry, I have a feeling he'll make a point of meeting with you before we get to New York.'

• • •

In a squat, reinforced concrete building outside Hilversum, in the Netherlands, a young woman in her early twenties took off her headset and put it down on the desktop beside her typewriter. She pressed a switch on the radio monitor fixed to the wall above the desktop and removed a single sheet of paper from the typewriter. Rising to her feet, she walked across the room that was about ten metres square, filled with other women glued to more radio sets, towards a man seated at a raised desk.

'Excuse me, please, Herr Kranz,' she said. 'This was just sent from the British Special Operations Executive in London.' She added, 'It is in clear.'

Her supervisor, *Hauptmann* Marius Kranz, reached out to take the piece of paper. 'Thank you, Lise, you may return to your post.'

Kranz did not speak English with any degree of fluency. But he understood enough to know that Lise was right. This was an unencrypted message, sent in plain English. Then again, Kranz smiled to himself, it would not have made any difference if it had been encrypted. The *Englandspiel* project, under *Oberstleutnant* Hermann Giskes of the Abwehr, the Reich's military intelligence agency, had long since broken all of SOE's codes. As a result, almost all the British agents who had been parachuted into the Low Countries – more than fifty in total – had been captured and then imprisoned or killed.

Until, that is, one agent – a woman – had managed to survive for months undercover and then escape back to England, leaving a trail of destruction behind her. And here was her name, COURTNEY, in the message in Kranz's hand. So what should he do with it?

This was not a serious question. 'My girls', as he liked to call his staff, were not cryptographers. Their job was to transcribe encrypted messages, not decipher them. But they had learned to recognise the particular 'hands' or Morse code tapping skills of individual operators, and could thus identify where messages were coming from, even when they could not decipher what they said. It was Kranz's job to prioritise those messages that needed the most urgent attention of the Abwehr's code-breakers. He was like a traffic cop at an exceptionally busy intersection, determining which intercepts could move and in what direction.

This particular message, which required no decryption, should obviously go straight to Giskes. But it seemed to Kranz that there were others who would want to read it, too. For what the Abwehr did not know was that while Marius Kranz had been a devoted Nazi Party member since 1935, a fierce patriot and a devoted admirer of the Führer, he was also a double agent.

Kranz sent a constant stream of confidential information to another intelligence agency that was both more hostile to, and more detested by, the Abwehr than Britain's Secret Intelligence Service or the Soviet People's Commissariat for State Security. Its name was the *Sicherheitsdienst*, or SD. It was part of the larger SS apparatus, and it served as the intelligence service of the Nazi Party.

In the Darwinian culture of Nazi Germany, in which both people and organisations were encouraged by the Führer to compete with one another as savagely as possible so that only the fittest survived, the Abwehr and SD were mortal enemies. The Abwehr regarded the SD as crude Nazi fanatics. The SD, in return, considered the Abwehr to be a nest of turncoats, whose loyalty was to the old, pre-Nazi Germany, not to the Third Reich.

Both agencies, Kranz reasoned, would be intrigued by this message between two very senior men in separate enemy intelligence agencies, apparently linked by a woman. So he discreetly copied it, word for word, on to a sheet from his own notepad. He sent the original direct to *Oberstleutnant* Giskes. Then he picked up the phone on his desk, called a number and said, 'Good afternoon. This is Herr Schmidt from the post office. I have a telegram for Frau Müller from her son.'

'Thank you, Herr Schmidt,' came the reply. 'I will ask her to come and collect it.'

• • •

There was a white Bakelite telephone in Saffron's cabin. At the front, where the dial would normally be, a round piece of card had been stuck to the set, on which the words YOU CAN TELEPHONE TO ANY PART OF THE WORLD WHILST AT SEA, were printed in neat capital letters. In pre-war days, this had been one of Cunard's proudest boasts, but now the line was dead. All the pleasures that the boat would have provided for a young woman – from the swimming pool, steam baths and beauty parlour to the restaurants, bars, night-club, ballroom, and the lounge that converted into a cinema – had been stripped away. Not that Saffron cared. She had a first-class suite with a blissfully comfortable double bed, and a bathroom in which to take hot, deep baths – extravagant indulgences after two years of rules stipulating no more than four inches of hot water in a bath, no more than once a week. There was even the choice of fresh or sea water.

Three times a day, an elderly steward called Clancy arrived with simple but edible meals, accompanied by sensationally good wines. 'Still got some of the pre-war stuff in the ship's cellar,' he told her. 'Save it for when we've got proper VIPs on board.'

That gave Saffron the opening to ask, 'So what's going on here? On this voyage, I mean.'

Clancy frowned. 'What do you mean, miss?'

'Well, I'm basically stuck in my room, except for a bit of exercise time up on the promenade deck, morning and after-noon. But when I do get out, I keep seeing young chaps rushing about the place, some in civvies, some in uniform, and then there are the bigwigs wandering around, too. I've seen at least one field marshal and a couple of admirals, and all sorts of important-looking chaps in suits.'

Clancy looked puzzled. 'You mean, you're not with them?'

'Not really. I've got one of their cabins, apparently, but I have no idea what's going on.'

'Oh . . . Well . . . Then I'm afraid I can't say. But I'll tell you one thing. I've looked after some fancy passengers in my time. But there's one on this voyage that takes the ruddy biscuit.' He winked and tapped the side of his nose. 'You keep your eyes peeled, miss. That's all I can say.'

By dinner on the second day, Saffron and Clancy were firm friends. 'Do you have any contact with the rest of the ship, where the Americans are?' she asked.

'Not personally,' the steward replied. 'But I've got mates working on that side of the ship. Why do you ask?'

'I was wondering if you could get a message to one of their officers. I don't know where he is exactly . . . but I don't think there'll be anyone else with the same name.'

'I should think not, miss!' Clancy exclaimed, casting an eye over the envelope that Saffron had handed him. 'US Army Air Forces Lieutenant Clayton Stackpole the Third, MD . . . Blimey! What is he, American royalty?'

'He does sound a bit like it, I agree.'

'Well, you leave it to me, miss. The Yanks have set up a hospital bay for their wounded lads. I expect they'll know your doctor there.'

Shortly after noon on the following day, Clancy reappeared, bringing lunch. 'Got something else for you,' he said, rummaging through his food trolley. He held out an envelope. 'Your Dr Stackpole replied,' he said. 'And I don't blame him, I'd have done the same.'

The envelope contained a short note and a Hershey's chocolate bar.

Hey, Saffron II, great to hear from you. But it would be even better to see you. *There's a big open space at the back of the sun deck, I think it's called the cabin class games area. Can you meet me there, starboard side, at 1600? I think I can get away for a few minutes then. I've got to warn you, it won't exactly be private. But I can bring more Hershey bars. How can you say no?*

Saffron smiled, then looked at Clancy. 'Please tell your friends to tell my friend that the answer's "Yes".'

• • •

In the Reich Main Security office on Prinz-Albrecht-Straße, in the heart of Berlin, a couple of hundred metres from Hitler's Reich Chancellery, two officers of the *Ausland-SD* – the overseas intelligence service of the SS, and therefore the direct competitor of the Abwehr – had met to discuss the intercept passed to them by Marius Kranz.

One of the officers, *Sturmbannführer* Hertz, represented the organisation's Section B, whose responsibility was espionage in Western Europe. His counterpart, *Sturmbannführer* Preminger, worked for Section D: espionage in the American Sphere. Both were involved, because the matter at hand involved a British agent travelling from the United Kingdom to the United States.

'The message seems to be very simple,' Hertz said. He had gone over it often enough to be able to recite it from memory. '"Miss Courtney is safely embarked. ETA at your end, five or six days. Hope she's of use. But don't work her too hard. Remember she is on holiday." It is addressed to Stephenson. He is, as you well know, the chief of British intelligence in America, based in New York. It is signed Gubbins, who is the chief of the sabotage and espionage agency, SOE.'

'The two men are known to be friends,' Preminger observed.

'Quite so. "Miss Courtney", though, is a less familiar name. But I have made some inquiries. Now, as you know, the Abwehr have turned a small number of SOE agents who were sent into the Low Countries. It struck me that these agents may have known of, or even worked with, Miss Courtney while they were all still in London. So I asked the Abwehr to speak to their people.'

'Were the Abwehr their usual helpful selves?' Preminger inquired.

Hertz laughed. 'It took a little persuasion, not least because the former SOE agents were initially reluctant to co-operate – until it was made clear that if they didn't, they'd get the same treatment as every other captured British agent. Which is to say, interrogated, tortured, sent to a camp and then killed.

'So, I can now tell you that her full name is Saffron Courtney. Age, twenty-three. Height, approximately one hundred and seventy-five centimetres. Athletic build, blue eyes, naturally dark hair, almost black.'

'She sounds like a very attractive woman.'

'That is one way of describing Saffron Courtney. Another might be that she is a dangerous enemy of the Reich. Because the description that I have just given you is remarkably close to that of the Hatpin Girl.'

'*Mein Gott!* . . . The hell-bitch who killed Schröder, in The Hague? Why has no one made the connection before?'

'As you can imagine, that same question occurred to the Abwehr. After Schröder's death, all SOE agents in captivity, whether they had been turned or not, were given a description of Marlize Marais and asked if she was one of their people. Not surprisingly, those agents who were not co-operating said nothing. But even the doubles said that they did not recognise the description. Yesterday, when they were asked why they had not identified Saffron Courtney, they swore that it had not even occurred to them that it could be her. This is not entirely implausible, because, for obvious security reasons, active agents do not have any idea about one another's missions, and they often do not fraternise with one another.

'Anyway, so far as the Abwehr's people know, Courtney has never engaged in espionage duties. Her job at SOE is to liaise with the Dutch and Belgian governments-in-exile in London. One of her former colleagues admitted that he did not know her, but said she had a reputation as, quote, "a spoiled little rich girl". Apparently she has her uniforms hand-made, and lives in a luxurious apartment bought by her father.'

'So why is she going to America?' Preminger asked. 'Clearly it is not for a holiday. The British can be frivolous people, but surely not even they would send anyone across the Atlantic for no other purpose than rest and recreation. It must be code for some other kind of activity. Would you agree?'

Hertz frowned. 'Yes. But if this is an operational matter, why was the message not encoded? And what are we to make of the phrase, "Hope she is of use"?'

Preminger shrugged. 'That is the mystery. What kind of mission would a British spy carry out in the homeland of her nation's greatest ally?'

'What we do know,' said Hertz, 'is that she is "safely embarked". It seems certain that the ship in question is the British ocean liner *Queen Mary*, which left Scotland on the fifth of May, the date the message was sent, bound for New York. I am reliably informed that Admiral Dönitz has ordered his U-boats to intercept it.'

Preminger nodded. 'Well, that would solve our problem at a stroke. But let us assume that Miss Courtney reaches New York on the tenth or eleventh of May. We have agents in New York. We can pick up Miss Courtney's trail as she disembarks. The *Queen Mary* may now be painted grey, but from your description, Hertz, Miss Courtney will be easy to spot. So we will keep her under observation until her true purpose in America becomes clear.'

'In the meantime, I will see if we can find more evidence linking the SOE agent Saffron Courtney to the killer Marlize Marais.'

'And then,' said Preminger, 'if they are truly one and the same woman, our superiors can decide what they want to do with her.'

• • •

Getting to the sun deck was not exactly straightforward. Saffron had to show her ID to the British military policemen guarding the VIP area and be checked off the list of passengers in Colonel Warden's party – and she couldn't help wondering why it was his party, when there were plainly so many officers aboard who were far above his rank. When that had been done, she was handed a pass that would allow her back in.

A few steps later, she had to be checked into the US Army Air Forces section of the ship and be handed a second pass to allow her back out. Saffron's cabin was on the main deck. The promenade deck was the next one up, with the sun deck above that. Saffron forced her way through teeming throngs of men who crowded each deck and all the ladders – as she had been told by Clancy to call the stairs – between them. All the men were friendly, most of them respectful, but some were a little too friendly, and even Saffron became worn down by the suggestive remarks, the whistles and the men's hands on her arms, her body and her backside as she went by.

'Follow me,' Stackpole said when he met her at the entrance to the games area. He wasn't wearing his cap, but his brown eyes were still hidden behind his Aviator glasses. It had been raining earlier and the deck was slick with water, but the clouds had now passed and the sun had emerged.

Stackpole tapped the shoulder of a man wearing a khaki uniform, who was standing by the rails, looking out to sea. 'Thanks, Mac. I'll take it from here.'

'No problem, Doc,' Mac said.

'I gave him five bucks to save me a prime spot,' Stackpole told Saffron.

She barely managed a smile. Stackpole looked at her, frowning. 'Something wrong?'

Saffron leaned against the balustrade, looking out to sea. She sighed and said, 'Oh, it's all right.'

'Uh-huh.' Stackpole nodded. 'Guess that's female for, "No, it's not all right at all." Right?'

Saffron put on a brighter smile. 'Yes, I suppose it is. But it's nice to see you, Clay. Better than sitting alone in my cabin all day.'

'Gee, thanks. Good to know I'm better than that.'

'Oh, don't worry, you are. The only company I've had since we left Gourock is the steward, Clancy. He's very sweet, but about a hundred and ten years old.'

'Whoa! Hold up! You have a steward?'

Saffron smiled, feeling a little better. 'I have, and he serves me three meals a day, plus elevenses and tea.'

'What? Three meals? We only get two. And we have to stand in line with our mess tins and pray that whatever gets slopped into them is edible.'

'At last!' Saffron exclaimed, delighted by the news of Stackpole's privations. 'For the first time in the war, there are Americans getting less food than the British. And,' she went on, deciding to rub it in further, 'I have a rather splendid suite with my own private bathroom.'

'Oh, I get it. The Limeys are all in the lap of luxury while Uncle Sam's boys are crammed tighter than steers in a railroad truck. Well, I gotta tell you, lady, I am calling my senator about this when I get home.'

'I'd happily let you share my cabin, but I don't think that would be allowed,' Saffron teased.

'Would you now?' Stackpole replied with a grin.

'Separate beds, of course.'

They both laughed and turned to look out to sea.

Stackpole fell silent. He grimaced.

'What's the matter?' Saffron asked.

'Just praying a U-boat doesn't get us,' Stackpole said. 'All the guys I'm looking after . . . Be kind of ironic if they survived bombing missions at twenty thousand feet over Europe, then got sent to the bottom of the ocean. I guess we've got a couple of little friends riding shotgun. Hope that's enough.'

A Royal Navy escort destroyer, HMS *Ottoman*, was sailing beside the *Queen Mary*, steaming slightly ahead of the liner and a few hundred yards off its beam. There was another, just like her, HMS *Ondine*, on the other side of the ship. They were both tiny by comparison to the vast ocean liner. 'I imagine the

Admiralty knows what it's doing,' she said, but her mind was elsewhere.

The promenade deck on the ship, where Saffron took her daily walks, was enclosed. Tall windows ran along its entire length; they could be opened to let in the sea air, but the weather had not been good, so they had remained closed. This was her first chance to look at the sea and test Dr Thackeray's theory that water might be a trigger for her panic attacks.

Saffron stared hard at the rolling grey swell of the ocean waves and the creamy bubbles of the ship's wake, but felt nothing. 'Maybe it has to be a lake,' she murmured to herself.

'What's that?' asked Stackpole.

'Oh, nothing . . . Just thinking about something a doctor said to me.'

'You want to tell another doctor about it?'

'He wasn't your kind of a doctor – more interested in my brain than my bones.'

'Well, I gotta admit, brains are not my specialty, but I can certainly—'

Before Stackpole could finish his sentence there was a piercing screech from the tannoy speakers located all over the ship, a crackling sound, and then a very English voice saying, 'Attention! Attention! This is a message for Miss Saffron Courtney . . .'

Saffron recognised Jock Colville's voice, as he repeated her name again. 'Would Miss Saffron Courtney please proceed at once to the promenade deck. I repeat . . .'

The massed American airmen on the sun deck burst out in mocking catcalls, whistles and impersonations of Colville's very British accent. 'I've got to go,' Saffron shouted over the noise. 'I don't know where I'm staying in New York, but you can get hold of me through Mr Stephenson at the British Passport Control Office, Rockefeller Center.'

'Stephenson . . . Passport . . . Rockefeller . . . Got it,' Stackpole shouted back, then added, 'Follow me! I'll run interference!'

Saffron frowned at the unfamiliar phrase, but its meaning became obvious as Stackpole barged his way through the crowd, clearing a path for her. He came with her all the way to the US checkpoint.

The MP grunted and held out his hand for Saffron's pass and ID. As the MP let her through, Stackpole shouted, 'Stephenson, at the Rockefeller Center. I won't forget!'

Saffron waved back, then turned to present her papers to the English guard, a corporal. Jock Colville was standing beyond him, tense with impatience and pent-up nervous energy. 'For God's sake, man, let her through!' he called as the corporal carried out the slowest, most painstaking of inspections. Finally he waved her through.

Colville grabbed Saffron's arm and practically dragged her after him. 'Where the hell have you been?' he snapped. 'We've been looking everywhere!' She shook herself free of his grip.

'Why? What's so important?'

'Not what – who,' Colville said. They had reached the door to the cabin class promenade. 'Well, here we go,' he said. 'You're about to meet Colonel Warden.'

Saffron was at the stern end of the promenade deck. The man she was meeting was right up by the bow. But even at a distance of more than a hundred yards, with his back turned, wearing a navy-blue greatcoat and matching peaked cap, the silhouette was unmistakable. It was something to do with the sturdiness of his posture, the legs a little apart to support the short, stocky body. But the puffs of cigar smoke being swept away in the wind were the clincher.

'Excuse me a moment,' Colville said. He upped his pace and went ahead. He bent his head to speak to the cigar-smoker, who turned around to observe Saffron as she approached.

'This is Miss Saffron Courtney, sir,' Colville said. 'Miss Courtney, may I introduce you to the prime minister, Winston Churchill.'

Saffron found herself shaking hands with her country's leader, the embodiment of British defiance. The set jaw, the glowering eyes . . . the features of the man she was facing were so familiar to her from a myriad of photographs and newsreels that there was something strangely unreal about seeing them in the flesh. And yet, here he was, so close that she could smell the cigar smoke.

Churchill had been in conversation with two other men: a silver-haired naval officer, who appeared to be in his late sixties, much like the prime minister, and another younger, much taller man in a smartly cut double-breasted suit.

'Ah, Miss Courtney,' Churchill said. 'I have heard a great deal about you.'

'Sir . . .' Saffron began. 'Prime Minister . . . I hope that what you've heard has not been too off-putting.'

'On the contrary, it made me eager to meet you for myself. Now, may I introduce you to Sir Dudley Pound, the Admiral of the Fleet? He is the man who, by winning the Battle of the Atlantic, has made it safe for you and me to cross the ocean on this magnificent vessel. And this is Mr Averell Harriman, the president's special envoy to Europe.'

Harriman gave a practised smile. It was broad, but flat, Saffron noticed. The corners of his mouth barely rose above the horizontal. 'Pleased to meet you, Miss Courtney,' he said.

Before the conversation could go any further, a naval officer with a lieutenant commander's stripes on his uniform jacket appeared and hovered, somewhat anxiously, behind Admiral Pound. He coughed politely and then said, 'You're wanted on the bridge, sir. The news we were waiting for has arrived.'

'Ah . . .' said Pound. 'Excuse me, Prime Minister, Mr Harriman, Miss Courtney.'

'Off you go, Pound.' Churchill watched the Royal Navy men hurry off, then turned back to Saffron. 'I believe they've found a U-boat. They told me earlier today that there might be one in the vicinity. I replied by ordering a machine gun fitted to my lifeboat. I won't be captured, Miss Courtney. I refuse to give Herr Hitler the satisfaction of parading me in chains through the streets of Berlin. And it is my conviction that there is no better way to die than fighting the enemy to the last.'

'Perhaps you might care to go inside, Miss Courtney?' Harriman suggested. 'For your own safety.' He was clearly worried that the images conjured up by Churchill's words might have unsettled her.

'No, thank you, sir. I was once on a ship that was sunk by Stukas, and it's an awful lot easier to jump into the water if you're on deck to begin with.'

'You were on deck in the middle of an air raid?'

'Yes, I was manning some anti-aircraft guns.'

'Were there no men to do that?'

'They were all injured or dead.'

'The girl stood on the burning deck, my dear Harriman, whence all but she had fled,' Churchill remarked. 'Now, this is a distinctly inadequate vantage point for any naval engagement. Might I suggest that we relocate to the sports deck, where we will be in the open air with a greater elevation and able to see to both port and starboard? Colville, would you be good enough to ask the captain if he could spare that young officer to keep us in the picture. As a former First Sea Lord, I flatter myself that I have a reasonable grasp of the rudiments of anti-submarine warfare. But it may be less familiar to my guests.'

'Of course, sir,' Colville said, and hurried away.

Churchill turned to Saffron. 'I hope I have not been too presumptuous in assuming that you would wish to join us?'

A few minutes later, Saffron was standing just aft of the first of the *Queen Mary*'s funnels. The young officer Churchill had requested – a lieutenant commander, whose name was Quicke – had joined them. Suddenly, from deep in the bowels of the ship there came a roaring, thunderous noise; seventy feet above her, the plume of smoke from the engines thickened and the deck beneath her feet trembled.

'Full speed ahead – that's the spirit!' Churchill exclaimed, and Saffron saw in his eyes the gleeful – almost manic – excitement of a much younger man, the Lieutenant Winston Churchill who had taken part in the last great cavalry charge in British military history at the Battle of Omdurman.

Another memory of her father suddenly came to her, and the excitement in his voice as he'd exclaimed, 'Good Lord! It says here that the *Queen Mary* will have a top speed of almost thirty-three knots. That's equivalent to . . . let me see, thirty-eight miles an hour. Why, she'll be the biggest speedboat in the world!'

'How fast can a U-boat go?' Saffron asked Quicke.

'About ten knots on the surface, four when submerged.'

'So there's not the slightest chance of a U-boat keeping up with us, then?'

'No, none whatsoever. That's why our escorts are sailing slightly ahead of us. No enemy could catch us from behind.'

'You mean they have to be ahead of us already, and hope to ambush us as we go by?'

'Exactly. Imagine a fairground shooting range, with ducks passing across the stand, and some chap trying to shoot them as they go by. The U-boat is the chap with the air rifle. We are currently aboard a very large, very grey duck.'

Churchill laughed. 'A capital description! I shall forever think of the *Queen Mary* as a large grey duck.'

'But actually, sir, it's much harder than a shooting range, from the U-boat commander's point of view. After all, the position of those fairground ducks is clear for all to see. But he does not know where exactly we are, or what course we are taking.'

'Or so we must fervently hope,' Churchill murmured.

'How fast does a torpedo travel, compared to the speed of this ship?' Saffron asked Quicke. 'You know, in case we need to get out of the way.'

He shrugged. 'Well, roughly, if we are going at full pelt, a torpedo is pretty much twice as fast. That's not exact, but it's a reasonable rule of thumb.'

Before Saffron could respond, Quicke said, 'Hang on.'

Something had caught his eye. He was looking across the deck, squinting. 'Excuse me, sir,' he said, then strode across to the starboard rail, which faced almost due north. No sooner had he got there than he raised his binoculars and looked out to sea. He turned and waved back towards the prime minister and his companions. 'I say, sir, come and take a look at this!'

Saffron followed Churchill and Harriman across the deck. 'Look, sir,' Quicke said, handing his binoculars to Churchill. '*Ottoman*'s caught the Jerries' scent.'

Sure enough, the slender little destroyer was turning from its westerly course on to a north-westerly bearing, and haring away across the water.

'Goodness, she's nippy!' Saffron exclaimed.

'Absolutely,' Quicke agreed. 'The O-class ships have a top speed of almost thirty-seven knots, so they can more than keep up with the *Queen Mary*.'

'So how did the *Ottoman*, as you put it, catch the scent?' Harriman asked.

'ASDIC, sir – or "sonar", as your American navy calls it. You tow a unit behind the ship that emits sound waves. When the waves hit something, they bounce back. A trained operator can tell if that something is a U-boat.'

'There goes *Ondine*, too!' Churchill cried.

Saffron could see the other destroyer cutting across the *Queen Mary*'s bows and racing to join the *Ottoman*. 'Always best to use two ships on a sub hunt,' Quicke said. 'If you've got two ASDIC readings, that helps to pinpoint the enemy's position. And it means one ship can attack while the other keeps track of the sub's movements.'

'Would you like a view of the ships through these, my dear?' Churchill asked, handing Saffron the binoculars.

'Thank you, sir.' Holding up the glasses, Saffron saw the two destroyers make another slight change in their respective courses. They were now converging, heading for the same position, about a mile up ahead, and roughly the same distance to starboard, away from the line of the *Queen Mary*'s course.

The *Ottoman* changed course once again, but the *Ondine* kept steaming on. Saffron understood what was happening: the *Ottoman* was getting out of the *Ondine*'s way, keeping her ASDIC homed in on the U-boat, while the other destroyer went in for the kill.

'*Ondine*'s launching her depth charges!' Quicke called out.

'You should watch this, sir,' Saffron said, handing the binoculars back to the prime minister.

A dozen or more black specks flew from the stern of the destroyer, arced high into the air, and then fell like a shower of meteorites into the water. A few seconds went by. Nothing happened. Then suddenly the water behind the *Ondine* was punched from below in a series of foaming, frothing white eruptions.

Surely nothing could have survived the cumulative power of so many explosions, but as he scanned the surface, Quicke grimaced and muttered, 'Damn! Missed!'

Now it was the *Ottoman*'s turn. She wheeled around and dashed towards the same patch of water that the *Ondine* had assaulted.

'Why isn't the U-boat moving?' Saffron asked.

Quicke shrugged. 'You tell me . . .'

'Oh, God . . .' Saffron whispered. The answer to her own question had just struck her, but before she could say anything there was another burst of depth charges, arcing through the air before plunging into the sea.

They waited. The seconds dragged on. The distance between the *Queen Mary* and the battle between the destroyers and the U-boat had closed.

Then the explosions came, in quick succession: a smattering that looked the same as the ones before, and then a vast geyser, streaked with grey and black. The noise of the explosion echoed across the water.

'Got him!' Quicke shouted. From the far end of the ship, Saffron could hear the Americans crowded onto the aft of the sports deck cheering the U-boat's destruction.

Churchill and Harriman were shaking Quicke's hand, all talking at once as they exulted in the victory.

But Saffron had fallen silent. She felt no joy at the U-boat's demise. Her eyes were fixed on the water between the *Queen Mary* and the site of the explosion.

'May I have the binoculars please, sir?' she asked Churchill.

'By all means,' he replied, handing them over.

Saffron looked back at the open water. She saw what she'd known was bound to emerge. Two parallel lines a fraction paler than the blue-black Atlantic water. The submarine had remained motionless because the captain was waiting for the perfect moment to strike. He was willing to sacrifice his own vessel, his own life and those of his crew for the chance to sink the *Queen Mary*.

'Torpedoes!' Saffron shouted from the top of her lungs, her voice clear above the joyful cacophony. She gestured frantically towards the two lines.

The celebrations fell silent in an instant. Quicke turned towards the rail, followed the line of Saffron's finger and gasped. 'Oh, bloody hell . . .' He ripped the binoculars from Saffron's hands with a cursory, 'Sorry,' took a closer look at the torpedo trail, then dashed to the foot of the ladder that led up to the bridge.

Quicke cupped two hands to his mouth and yelled, 'Torpedo! Starboard bow!'

There was no reply. The captain had already got the message. The noise from below increased and more smoke jetted from the funnel. Saffron could imagine the men in the engine room, watching the arrows on the dials that indicated the boiler pressure going further and further into the red.

The calculation was simple. The torpedoes had to cover about a mile to travel to the point where they would meet the *Queen Mary*. The ship needed half a mile to get past the torpedoes. The torpedoes were going twice as fast as the ship. You didn't need to be Einstein to work out that they were both heading for the same place at the same time.

A story from a play she'd once seen suddenly sprang into her mind: a man sees Death in the marketplace and, terrified, rides away as far away as he can, only to find the town where he finally halts is the very place Death has planned to meet him. This was what the ship seemed to be doing: heading for the exact place where the torpedoes would find her.

'Can the captain alter course?' Saffron asked Quicke.

'Yes, but an ocean liner isn't a destroyer,' he replied. '*Ondine* and *Ottoman* are both about three hundred and fifty feet long and weigh a little over two thousand tons fully loaded. So they're like a pair of whippets – skinny and nimble, and can turn on a sixpence, relatively speaking.'

His voice was quite calm, as though nothing dramatic was happening. Saffron knew he was using this little lecture as a distraction from a situation he could do nothing whatsoever to affect. But all the while, the torpedoes were getting closer to their target. She needed distracting, too. 'And the *Queen Mary*?' she asked.

'Ah, well, she's like a huge, lumbering, eighty-thousand-ton elephant. It's a lot harder for her to change course. And she would take many miles to slow down, let alone come to a halt, so we can't just stop and let the torpedoes go by. The only asset she's got is speed.'

'Not to mention, her hull is a thousand feet long,' Saffron said, trying to sound as casually stiff-upper-lipped as Quicke. 'So that's another three hundred yards to cover before the stern gets clear of the torpedoes' line of attack.'

'Yes, it is,' said Quicke grimly.

Saffron heard a commotion and turned to look. The Americans at the starboard rail were all pointing and shouting. Some were frantically looking around, as if trying to find a place to hide. Others – more resigned, perhaps – were staying still, watching, and making the calculations.

There was nothing to be done now except wait and hope that the numbers didn't add up the way Saffron thought they did. Maybe the submarine was further away than she'd estimated. Maybe the torpedoes were more sluggish than Quicke had thought. One way or another, she wouldn't have to wait long to find out.

Saffron wasn't afraid for herself. She was with the one man whose life would be guarded above all others. She noticed now that a dozen or so Royal Marines had gathered a few yards away, ready to clear a path to Churchill's lifeboat. She gave a half-smile as she thought, *the one with the machine-gun mounted on it.*

If she tagged along, her proximity to power, as well as her gender, would guarantee her a safe passage onto the lifeboat. 'Women and children first,' and all that. What worried her more, creating a sickly chill in the pit of her stomach, was the fate of the Americans. The number of men far exceeded the quantity of lifeboats. And what about the German prisoners, under lock and key on the very lowest decks? What about the wounded in their hospital beds? What about Stackpole? He'd said he had to get back to work. He was probably below decks, too.

'Get out, Clay,' Saffron muttered. 'Just get out.'

She looked back at the torpedo line. It was clearly visible now, far closer, heading for the very centre of the ship's hull.

The breeze had freshened, whipping up the water. The *Queen Mary* was bucking up and down as she ploughed through the ocean swell.

The two destroyers had turned back on themselves and were heading towards the *Queen Mary*. If the torpedoes hit, they would soon be there to pick up survivors.

The torpedoes were less than four hundred yards away. They were on course to hit the stern of the ship.

Two hundred yards away – less than ten seconds to impact. Saffron was alone by the rails. Quicke had discreetly herded Churchill and Harriman to the far side of the deck, as far away as possible from any explosion.

One hundred yards. The torpedoes were so close. The *Queen Mary* was travelling at top speed, but to Saffron it felt as if she was hardly moving at all.

She couldn't escape. The torpedoes were going to hit them.

Saffron closed her eyes and turned away to shield her face from the blast.

And then she heard a cheer, a huge roar that dwarfed the one that had greeted the sinking of the submarine. She looked back towards the stern and saw air force men jumping up and down, punching the air and hugging one another.

The torpedoes had missed, passing within a whisker of the stern. The next thing she knew, Quicke was at her shoulder, saying, 'The PM is heading below for a spot of brandy. He wonders if you would care to join him. He rather thinks you might need it.'

• • •

Lewandowski met Foxglove at eleven in the morning at a diner on M Street in Washington, close to Georgetown University, called Ma Franklin's. It was half-empty, most of the occupied booths filled with earnest academics debating the finer points of their subjects with one another or conducting affairs with their students. Four skinny young men, three of them bespectacled, two bearded, were having a heated discussion about a famous mathematical problem. *Either they're too feeble for military duty, or too brilliant to be wasted on a battlefield*, Lewandowski thought. *Or both.*

He had come straight from a building site in his dark blue denim overalls, grimy grey work shirt and heavy boots. Foxglove was, as always, smartly dressed. They were sitting in a corner booth, on brown leatherette benches. The booth next to theirs was empty. A set of building plans was rolled up on the table between them to explain the meeting: a builder meeting with his client, or maybe even an architect.

A waitress came to take their order.

'Just a coffee for me,' Foxglove said. 'Cream, no sugar.'

'And you, sir?' the waitress asked Lewandowski. It was the kind of bohemian, hipster joint where the staff wore their own clothes, and this one was in ballet flats, jeans rolled up to show her ankles, and a black sweater. Her blonde hair hung down over her forehead. Another student working her way through college.

'I'm hungry,' Lewandowski said. 'Gimme a coupla fried eggs, over easy, on hash browns, bacon . . . You got any links?'

'Sure.'

'Okay then, links and a stack of pancakes with maple syrup and cream. And black coffee – plenty of black coffee.' Lewandowski smiled. 'What's your name, honey?'

'Marion,' the girl replied, smiling back.

'Well, Marion, be a doll and get us a whole pot of java. How about that?'

'You got it. Gotta feed the working man, right?'

Foxglove watched Marion head to the counter to pass their order to the cook, waiting till she was out of earshot before saying, 'You may be interested to hear that my friends are meeting for dinner next week at a delightful residence, close to where I work. I have the time and place. I was wondering whether you or your colleagues were interested in making an appearance.'

Lewandowski smiled and nodded. That had been nicely done. 'Yeah, I heard from head office. They're interested in passing on a nice, warm message to your friends. You know, let them know exactly how they feel. Now they've just got to get approval from the chairman.'

'You mean the big boss?' Foxglove asked.

'That's the one,' Lewandoski said, a hint of a smile playing on his lips.

'Well, I'm glad to hear that the idea is being taken so seriously. But it might be hard for any of you to get into the event. There'll be someone on the door.'

'That's what we figured. But you'll be there, right?'

'Yes . . . Not sitting at the same table, of course,' Foxglove clarified. 'But certainly in the building.'

'Then you'll have to deliver the message. Do you think you can do that?'

Foxglove gave the matter a moment's thought. 'Will it require any technical expertise, or . . . how can I put it . . . specialist training? I haven't had any of that.'

'No, you just have to deliver a package and make sure that no one sees it until the big moment.'

'I can do that.'

'Can you, though?' There was no one within earshot, but still, Lewandowski lowered his voice. 'If this operation succeeds, there will be a lot of casualties, aside from the principal ones. Many of these will be your colleagues, even your friends. Does that not concern you?'

'Why would it?' Foxglove asked, with a shrug. 'This is a war. Thousands are killed every day. Their lives are of no importance.'

Lewandowksi looked at the person sitting opposite him. It struck him that he might, by chance, have stumbled upon the perfect assassin. He sat back in his chair as the waitress reappeared with his order. 'Marion, there you are,' he said with a grin. 'I was beginning to think you'd forgotten me. I'm starving to death here.'

Marion smiled sweetly as she set down the loaded plate. 'Well, this ought to set you right.'

Lewandowski gave a big Joey L laugh. 'I hope so!'

Another customer, across the room, was holding up an empty glass coffee pot and tapping it with his finger. 'Gotta run!' Marion said, hurrying away.

'There's something else,' Lewandowski said, turning his attention back to Foxglove. 'Information we've received from sources in London. Just so you know, we don't see it as any threat to our plans, simply an additional element to be considered.'

'Maybe you should just tell me this information, and let me assess its significance,' Foxglove said, adopting the superior tone of voice Lewandowski found so grating.

Lewandowski looked at Foxglove, acutely aware that although the diner was far from crowded, he still couldn't raise his voice to say what he felt. It only made matters worse that the slight hint of a smirk told him that Foxglove knew it, too. The words had been a deliberate taunt, even a tease. But being an objectionable human being did not necessarily lower an asset's value. Lewandowski took a deep breath, calmed himself and said, 'This is what we know . . .'

'I agree with you,' Foxglove said when Lewandowski had finished, mollifying him somewhat. 'I do not see a direct threat yet . . . but a potential one, perhaps.'

'And your response to that is?'

'Very simple. I will keep an eye on the situation. If I detect any real danger, I will let you know. We will then deal with it, definitively, at once.'

'So long as head office agrees—'

'The hell with them.' Foxglove gave a dismissive sniff, then added, 'And now, since you gave me your surprise news, here is mine. I heard this morning that there will be an additional guest at the party.'

Lewandowski frowned, fearing an unwanted complication. 'Anyone significant?'

Foxglove smirked. 'Well, that depends—'

'On what?'

'On whether you think that a former king of England is a man of any significance.'

• • •

'Come in!' said *Sturmbannführer* Preminger, in response to the knock on his office door. 'Ah, Hertz. What can I do for you, old boy?'

'I've been thinking about our beautiful murder suspect, Saffron Courtney. Perhaps we can do a little more than just observe her movements. Let us suppose, for the sake of argument, that she really *is* the Hatpin Girl. Tell me, Preminger, have you ever killed a man? I mean, at close range. Close enough to see and hear and smell every detail of his death.'

Preminger nodded. 'Yes . . . more than once.'

'Shocking, isn't it? No matter how necessary the act of killing might be, no matter how deserving the victim, still it lives with one, no?'

'True. Unless one is some kind of psychopath, it is impossible not to be affected.'

'I agree . . . and we are men, born with a natural hunter's instinct, raised and trained to fight for our country. Think how much more it must affect a woman, with all her emotions – a woman whose natural purpose is to give life, not take it.'

'Ach, no natural woman could do what the Hatpin Girl did.'

'She might if she had been taught to fight and kill. The British are now giving their female agents the same training as their men.'

'My God, the English are barbarians!'

'I know . . . but they cannot give those agents the same minds as men, or prevent them reacting like women. So, what if Miss Courtney has not reacted well?'

A smile grew at the corner of Preminger's mouth. 'Then she really does need a holiday.'

'But still, this is a war. A valuable intelligence asset cannot just take a leisurely summer vacation. Her bosses therefore decide that she must be put to some use . . . even if she is in a fragile emotional state. Very well, then. In a few days' time, Miss Courtney will arrive in America thinking that she is in a safe place, surrounded by her country's allies. But what if she were made aware that she was being watched? She would wonder, "Am I imagining this?" And then, "Who can it be?" And, "How do they know I am here?" Might she not become disconcerted, on edge, perhaps even sufficiently stressed that she would start making mistakes? And then might she not reveal things that would otherwise have stayed hidden? Or get herself into situations that she would otherwise have avoided? If you apply enough stress, even a solid iron beam can break, let alone a fragile female mind.'

'Ha! You're a devious old bastard, Hertz, but I like the way you think. So yes, let us find out just how fragile Fräulein Courtney's mind really is.'

• • •

Every square inch of the *Queen Mary*'s decks was packed with men trying to get a glimpse of New York City as the ship slowly cruised into Upper Bay, three miles or so from the southernmost tip of Manhattan, the Statue of Liberty clearly visible on the port bow. The two destroyers were still steaming ahead of her. An American battleship, painted in a camouflage pattern of dove and charcoal grey, passed the British flotilla on its way out to sea. Saffron gasped at the size of her gun turrets, each bearing three giant cannons, and imagined the factories and shipyards across the United States, safe from enemy bombs, churning out fleets of ships like this, countless squadrons of new aircraft, great armies of tanks. How could Hitler or Hirohito possibly hope to defeat them?

From her viewpoint at the forward end of the sports deck, Saffron could see US Army Air Forces personnel jammed tight against the railings, and all the way up the ladders between one deck and another. Ignoring the rain that had started falling an hour or so earlier, men had climbed onto the davits from which the ship's lifeboats were hung. Some had even risked the wrath of the ship's crew by perching on the lifeboats themselves. Others were leaning out of portholes, so that the flanks of the ship's hull were studded with human heads almost to water level.

Saffron was hoping to catch a glimpse of Clay Stackpole, perhaps even find a way to speak to him. But the crowds of American servicemen were so thick that even his tall frame did not stand out. And that was assuming he was able to enjoy the view. There were wounded flyers who needed medical attention. They could hardly be abandoned because a doctor wanted to take in the sights.

Saffron observed the glint of gold on Liberty's flaming torch and the ferries scampering back and forth across the bay that led to the city itself, fringed with piers and docks, then rising in rank after rank of mighty towers that disappeared into the mist and rain. She was barely conscious of the smile across her face, or the gleam in her eyes at the thought of what awaited her in this brave new world. Shops full of treasures that could no longer be bought at home. Smoky clubs in Harlem, where they played jazz music unlike anything ever heard on earth before.

Lost to the spectacular view, Saffron was not aware of the approach of another person until she heard a familiar voice beside her.

'A magnificent sight, is it not, Miss Courtney?'

'It certainly is, sir. Absolutely wonderful.'

Churchill took a puff of his cigar. 'Hambro tells me you're meeting Stephenson.'

'Yes, he's very kindly agreed to help set up some meetings for me in Washington.'

'Remarkable man, Stephenson – one of the best.' Churchill paused, drew deeply on his cigar and blew out the smoke in a long, gentle exhalation.

Saffron felt her stomach tighten. Her country's leader, the symbol of British courage and fortitude the whole world over, was considering something, and while it was possible he might have come up here into the rain simply to find some peace and quiet, she had a feeling that whatever he was contemplating involved her.

'Miss Courtney,' Churchill said, with an emphasis that made it plain she was the reason for his presence, 'it is possible that when you meet Stephenson, and should he form a good impression of you, he may entrust you with a task that is of the greatest importance. One, indeed, upon which the successful prosecution of this war may depend.'

'Yes, sir,' seemed the safest response Saffron could think of.

'He is aware, as am I, that asking such a thing of a young woman of your tender years is, to put it mildly, unconventional. But your service record is exceptional, and I have already cabled Stephenson to tell him that I observed you while this vessel was under attack, and you behaved with admirable sangfroid.'

'Thank you, sir.'

'Now, I must tell you that there are those who think that Stephenson is currently embarked on a pointless chase for a wild goose which does not exist. So, just as I have recommended you to him, let me also recommend him to you.'

'I gather he is an extraordinary man, sir,' Saffron said carefully.

'You gather correctly.' Churchill took another puff of his cigar as he weighed up his next words. 'Miss Courtney, I confess that I take the old-fashioned view that mortal combat is, and should remain, essentially a business for men. Despite your remarkable war record, I therefore feel uneasy commanding you to embark on any undertaking that might expose you to personal danger. Nevertheless, I ask – indeed, implore – you to listen to what Stephenson has to say, consider it with the utmost seriousness, and then do your duty as you see fit.'

'You can count on me, sir,' Saffron replied with an air of confidence that not many men would have been able to show.

'Good . . . good.' Churchill nodded. 'Then it only remains to wish you a pleasant stay in America, and bid you farewell.'

Saffron watched Churchill turn on his walking stick and move towards the stairs to the lower decks. She turned back to lean on the railings and look at the Manhattan skyline. But her mind was no longer on the city's magnificent buildings and what they might hold in store.

Gubbins had sent her to the United States on a diplomatic mission that he believed was crucial to the survival of SOE, an organisation that Saffron not only served, but loved. Now her prime minister had given her another mission. And though he had not specified what it was, he had made it clear that it was of vital importance to the war effort. Saffron was not sure how she would manage to do two jobs at once. But she did not feel apprehensive, let alone frightened. What she felt was an excitement that was something close to ecstasy.

Ninety minutes later, the Grey Ghost had been led into a berth on the Brooklyn docks by a pair of tugs, and disembarkation was beginning. The prime minister was first to set foot on American soil, but Saffron was not far behind. She stood in line to have her passport and travel documents examined, and opened her cases for inspection by the customs men. Since she was in uniform and travelling with the VIPs, they nodded her through with barely a glance. No one noticed the diminutive Beretta 418 pistol and twenty rounds of 6.35mm ammunition hidden amongst her underwear.

The gun had been given to Saffron by her father when she secured her first wartime job as General 'Jumbo' Wilson's driver, and had been her close companion ever since.

She smiled at the thought of retrieving the little weapon from its incongruous surroundings of silk, satin and lace and dropping it into her shoulder bag. As she walked out onto an open, tarmacked space the size of a parade ground, she saw trucks lined up in ranks, waiting to take incoming airmen to the railway stations from which they would start their journeys to new stateside bases. A smaller squadron of ambulances were ready to meet the wounded, and yellow taxicabs were lined up for anyone carrying a leave pass who wanted a ride to the bright lights of midtown Manhattan.

Saffron was about to hail one of the cabs. Her plan was to go to the Rockefeller Center, make contact with Stephenson or his staff, and see if they could advise her on where she might stay. But then she heard an American voice calling her name. 'Miss Courtney?'

She turned, and there stood a middle-aged man wearing a black peaked cap. His black suit, white shirt and grey silk tie were immaculate and his black brogues gleamed. His moustache was as neatly trimmed as the grass on a bowling green.

'Yes . . .?' Saffron replied.

'My name is Dalton, Miss Courtney. Mr Stephenson sent me. He apologises that he is unable to meet you here himself. But I'm to take you to your hotel. He'll be meeting you there.'

'Oh . . . thank you,' Saffron said.

Dalton smiled. 'Here, let me help you with those bags.'

He led the way to a black limousine with whitewall tyres, and held the passenger door open. Saffron entered a space that felt more like an elegant drawing room than the passenger compartment of an automobile. The floor was covered in a thick beige carpet, while the seats were upholstered in soft leather the colour of creamy toffee.

There was a low, gentle rumble as Dalton started the engine. He slid down a glass partition and turned to her. 'Would you like me to turn on the air conditioning, Miss Courtney? If you would prefer fresh air, the windows can be opened by pressing the buttons on the door beside you.'

Intrigued, Saffron pressed a button and the window slid silently down. A touch on the other button sent it back up to the top again.

'Oh!' Saffron exclaimed. 'I've never seen anything like this!'

'Only a few people have, ma'am. This is a Packard one eighty limousine, the first automobile in the world to offer air conditioning and electric windows. Only in America!'

Saffron surveyed her luxurious surroundings. 'Dalton, may I ask you a favour?'

'Of course, ma'am, what can I do for you?'

'Might I be allowed to sit in the front, with you? That would make it much easier for us to talk.'

Dalton gave a friendly chuckle. 'Sure, I'd be glad of the company.' He turned off the engine, got out, and helped her into the front seat.

As the car pulled away, Saffron saw the first of the army air forces men spilling out of the customs hall. She scanned the faces, but there was no sign of Clay. She turned to Dalton. 'I used to be a chauffeur, too, you know.'

He grinned. 'You're kidding me.'

'No, it's true. I was a general's driver, in the Middle East. I took him out to the battlefront in the Western Desert, and all round Cairo, Athens and Jerusalem.' Saffron laughed at the memory. 'I'd have made a great taxi driver in Cairo. I knew every side street, alley and shortcut in the city.'

'Say, what kind of car does a British general ride in anyway?'

'A very dusty one, if he's in the desert. And one much less impressive than this.' She wanted to have Dalton on her side by the time they reached the bridge that would take them from Brooklyn to Manhattan. And that's when she planned to start asking him some pertinent questions about his boss.

The Packard cruised over the Brooklyn Bridge and headed north on the East River Drive. 'You are now riding over a little bit of Bristol, England,' Dalton said, soon after they'd turned onto the six-lane parkway.

Saffron had been trying to steer the conversation to William Stephenson, but Dalton had deflected all her questions. This was another distraction, but it seemed rude not to respond. 'How so?'

'Well, when we send ships full of food and weapons to you guys in England, some of 'em land at Bristol docks. And I guess Bristol must have been bombed plenty by the Krauts, because the ships load up with rubble from the bomb sites there to use as ballast. When they get back home to the States, that same rubble is unloaded and used on construction projects. And this section right here, on up to 34th Street, is built on Bristol rubble.'

Before Saffron could respond to this nugget, her attention was caught by the sight of a man on a black-and-white motorcycle riding alongside the car. Just as American cars seemed bigger and smarter than English ones, so this motorcycle seemed longer, lower, sleeker and more powerful than any she had ever seen. The rider looked in her direction. He was as dashing as his machine, in a black leather jacket with a matching helmet and goggles over his eyes. He gave her a wave and rode away up the road.

A minute or so later they turned onto a street lined with residential properties, some with shops or small neighbourhood restaurants on their ground floors. They crossed a number of intersections, then Dalton pulled up at a set of traffic lights. 'See those trees, right up ahead?' he said.

'Yes . . .'

'That's Central Park. You should take a walk there, if you get the chance.' The lights went green and Dalton turned left, saying, 'And this is Fifth Avenue.'

Moments later, he was pulling to a halt outside a tall, stone-fronted building with a black awning on which St. Regis was emblazoned in gold capital letters. No sooner had Saffron emerged than a uniformed doorman was warmly greeting her and taking her case from the car.

Suddenly, Saffron heard a piercing wolf whistle. She turned, and on the far side of the Packard, sitting on his fancy motorcycle, was the man who had passed them just a few minutes earlier. He grinned again and roared away up the avenue.

Saffron smiled, thinking to herself that the mysterious bike-rider was as cocky as Clay Stackpole. Were all American men like that? Then she thought for a second. Was it just coincidence that he had passed by her again . . . or was she being followed?

She shook her head and told herself not to be silly. This was America, not the Netherlands. There were no SS here out to get her.

Saffron said goodbye to Dalton and was ushered into a lobby where the floor was patterned with different coloured marbles, polished to a mirror shine. The reception desk was marble, too, and the ceiling above it was painted sky blue and filled with flying cherubs.

As she absorbed the splendour of her surroundings, Saffron did not notice a small man in a dark grey suit stand and start to make his way towards her. He moved with a grace and lightness of foot that suggested he might once have been a dancer. Yet there was nothing flamboyant about him – quite the reverse. He seemed to glide effortlessly across the room, barely moving his arms or hands. And then, just as Saffron reached the reception desk, he appeared as if from nowhere beside her. 'Good afternoon, Miss Courtney, my name is William Stephenson.'

She turned and looked at the man for whom Churchill had such a high regard. He was middle-aged, with neatly brushed dark hair, showing the first signs of grey. He had a prominent nose and chin, like a less exaggerated Mr Punch. But it was his eyes that struck her most. They were very dark brown, almost black, and they looked at her with a concentrated intensity which told her at once that Stephenson's diminutive stature was misleading. This was a substantial, powerful man.

He turned to the receptionist. 'We'll go up to Miss Courtney's suite now.'

'Certainly, Mr Stephenson.'

The bellboy who had picked up Saffron's bags appeared with them on a gold-coloured trolley. 'Follow me please, sir, ma'am. The elevators are this way.'

'Your father contacted me a few days ago,' Stephenson said, as the elevator doors closed and they started to ascend. 'We exchanged a number of telegrams and came to a mutually satisfactory decision about the funding of your stay here in the United States. You will be well provided for.'

'Thank you, that's kind,' Saffron said.

'Not at all. Your father feels that you have earned it, and I agree with him.' Stephenson reached inside his jacket pocket and removed a folded telegram. 'He asked me to pass this on to you.'

Before Saffron had time to read the message, the elevator stopped and the bellboy led them to the end of a short corridor, past the doors to two other rooms. At the end was a single door. The bellboy took out a room key, opened the door and led Saffron into a small hallway. 'Your private dining room is just here, ma'am,' he said, pointing in one direction. He turned the other way and, as he pushed the trolley before him, said, 'Here we have your bedroom, bathroom and lounge. As you can see, this is a corner suite, so you look out onto Fifth Avenue and Central Park. Please follow me.'

Saffron entered a beautifully furnished drawing room with floor-to-ceiling windows on two sides. Through one of them, she could see a balcony with a small table and two chairs and beyond that, past a line of skyscrapers, the green expanse of a park running up the middle of the city.

'Oh, but this is magnificent,' she said. 'You really are too generous, Mr Stephenson.'

'Read your telegram,' he said.

> My darling daughter. Have instructed Stephenson to give you nothing but best and send bill to me. Also to provide one thousand dollars cash. I order you to spend it. You have earned every penny. Your mother would be very proud of you as are Harriet and I. Your loving father Leon Courtney.

Saffron burst into tears, caught unawares and overwhelmed as much by the mention of her long-dead mother as by her father's generosity. 'I'm so sorry,' she said, scrabbling in her bag for a handkerchief.

'Don't be,' Stephenson said.

As she gathered herself, Saffron was dimly aware of Stephenson quietly giving orders to the bellboy. By the time she had dried her eyes, her cases were in her bedroom, the bellboy had departed and Stephenson had reappeared beside her.

'I'm sorry,' she said. 'I'm afraid I haven't got off to a very good start.'

'Nonsense. You received good news from someone you love, who also loves you very much. Perfectly natural. Now, I'm afraid my diary is full for the rest of the day and this evening. I suggest you unpack, freshen up, maybe take a stroll in the park, and then take dinner in your suite, or downstairs in the Astor Court. My wife and I lived here at the St. Regis for quite a while at the start of the war. The food is excellent. I will see you at my office in the International Building of the Rockefeller Center at 10.30 tomorrow morning.'

'Yes, sir,' Saffron said, conscious that she was being given an order rather than an invitation.

'You can't miss the building. Just look for the statue of Atlas.'

'Like our PM, with the weight of the world on his shoulders,' Saffron nearly said, but instead she followed Stephenson out of the living room towards the front door of the suite. Stephenson was about to step into the corridor when he paused, and gave a half-smile. 'I almost forgot . . .'

He reached into the same jacket pocket from which he had extracted the telegram and pulled out a bulging letter-sized envelope. 'Your money,' he said, handing it to Saffron. 'Nine hundred and ninety-eight dollars in notes and . . .' He pulled a small paper packet from a trouser pocket. 'Two bucks in change. If you're just out walking around, the change and a couple of five-dollar bills will be more than enough. There's a safe in the room for the rest.'

'Thank you very much, sir,' Saffron said.

'Don't thank me, thank your pa . . . So, 10.30. Don't be late.'

• • •

Adomas Petrauskas was a second-generation Lithuanian-American, a stevedore in the Brooklyn Docks. He had many grievances in his life, but the one that animated him the most was his hatred of the Russians who had invaded and annexed his country in 1940.

The Third Reich had invaded the Soviet Union in June 1941, and within a single week expelled the Russians from Lithuania.

Inspired by the Nazis' single-mindedness, Petrauskas had presented himself to the German consulate in New York in September 1941, when the United States was still a neutral country, and declared himself ready to help the Nazi cause.

Just as all nations place intelligence agents amongst their diplomatic and consular staff, so there was an *Ausland-SD* man at the consulate. He met Petrauskas and agreed to pay him fifty dollars a month to keep an eye on shipping movements in and out of the Brooklyn Docks. When America entered the war that December, the German consulate was closed, and all its staff were expelled from the United States, the SD man included. So now Petrauskas was controlled by a Nazi sympathiser in the Swiss consulate called Hartwig Meyer, who received his information and paid him in return. Petrauskas was more than happy to take the payments. He was married with a baby son, and he had recently bought an expensive motorbike that was his pride and joy. He needed every cent he could get.

It was Meyer who had come to Petrauskas with the offer of an extra twenty dollars for a task that, he said, 'I think you will find quite agreeable.'

Damn right it was agreeable. Petrauskas had got a buddy to cover for him at work for a couple of hours. Then he rode his

1937 Harley Davidson UL into Manhattan, following a hot broad to her hotel. Meyer had told him, 'Let her know that you are there,' so he'd given her a wave while they were on the road and a wolf whistle outside the hotel.

Now he was in a phone booth on Fifth. He called Meyer and told him where the broad was staying. 'Good work,' Meyer said. 'Now, there is a Jewish delicatessen, Goldwyn's, on the corner of Bowery and East Houston Street . . .'

'Yeah, I know the place.'

'Good. Meet me there in one hour. I have one last task for you today. If you accomplish it successfully, I will pay you thirty dollars, not twenty.'

'Thirty bucks? I'll be there, Mr M. You can count on it.'

'Excellent. Now, do you have a toolbox of some kind?'

'Sure, for working on my bike.'

'And a cap?'

Petrauskas's voice sounded puzzled as he answered, 'Yeah.'

'Bring them both when you come to see me.'

Hartwig Meyer was sure that an attractive young woman, newly arrived in the most exciting city on earth, would not sit alone in her hotel room for the rest of the day but would want to go out and explore the town. There would therefore be a period of time, possibly several hours, when Miss Courtney's room would be unoccupied. This would provide an opportunity to take further action against her.

He had a contact at the St. Regis: a fellow Swiss, Rolf Haecki, who worked as a concierge. Haecki had no allegiance whatever to Nazism, but he had an unfortunate fondness for betting on the horses at Aqueduct and Belmont Park, which left him almost permanently short of money. Ten dollars was all it cost to buy his unqualified assistance.

Haecki was standing at the concierge desk when Meyer called him. He held his left hand up to his mouth so that none of the guests or fellow staff could overhear him as he said, 'You promise me that no one will be harmed? I won't do anything that hurts the hotel or its guests.'

'You have my word, Rolf,' said Meyer. 'No one will be hurt in any way. No damage will be done. Nothing will be stolen or borrowed. There won't even be a crease in the bedlinen.'

'So, what are you doing?'

'Nothing you need worry about. Absolutely nothing.'

Meyer took a table at Goldwyn's, close to the customers' payphone. He ordered a cup of coffee – cream, two sugars – and a couple of *rugelach* pastries, which looked like croissants filled with chocolate, raspberry jam and chopped walnuts. He took a copy of the *Wall Street Journal* out of his briefcase and was pleased to see that the Dow Jones had reached its highest level since November 1940. Meyer smiled to himself. Whatever his political convictions, he couldn't help but admire America's astonishing capacity for economic regeneration. *They will even manage to make a profit out of this damn war!*

The phone rang. No one paid any attention when he picked it up. This was a neighbourhood joint. Plenty of regulars who didn't have telephones of their own used this one.

'Miss Courtney has just left the building,' said Haecki. 'She's going for a stroll in Central Park. She asked for a map, and I gave her advice about what she should see there. She also booked a table in our main restaurant for seven o'clock. I imagine that when she returns from her walk she will freshen up in our ladies' cloakroom, spend approximately one hour eating her meal, and then return to her room at around eight.'

'Might she not go out to see a film, or go to a nightclub?'

'No. I asked her if she wished me to book anywhere, and she replied that she had a very busy day tomorrow and so wanted to get an early night.'

'You have been admirably thorough, my dear Rolf. Now, there is just one more thing I need you to do . . .'

'For ten dollars, only?'

'All right . . . I'll add another five.'

Meyer gave detailed instructions, then added, 'Please, Rolf, just promise me that the next call you make will not be to a bookmaker.'

'I swear it won't be,' said Haecki.

Meyer smiled to himself. He knew the poor man was lying. He would keep betting and keep losing. And as long as he did, he would be easily and cheaply bought.

Meyer had drunk most of his coffee and polished off his first *rugelach* when Petruskas arrived. He bought the Lithuanian a coffee and offered him the other pastry. 'It's delicious, but one is quite enough.'

Petruskas demolished the *rugelach* with the glee of a fit, active young man who knows he can soon burn off any amount of calories. *Ah, you just wait till you get a little older and your belly starts expanding*, Meyer thought, watching the performance.

'So, what do you want me to do, Mr M?' Petruskas asked, once his plate was empty.

After Meyer had given him precise instructions, Petruskas frowned. 'Is that it? I mean, it seems like . . . I dunno . . .'

'Almost nothing?'

'Yeah, exactly – almost nothing.' Then he grinned and said, 'But, oh boy, that dame is gonna go crazy.'

• • •

Saffron Courtney had seen the world, from the highlands of Kenya to the slopes of St Moritz. She knew Cairo as well as she knew London, not to mention Cape Town, Paris, Athens and Jerusalem. She spoke Swahili as fluently as English, could communicate in Arabic and in her local Maasai dialect, and had passable French and German. But when she stepped out of the St. Regis and onto Fifth Avenue and looked down a seemingly endless canyon of concrete and glass, filled with hurrying New Yorkers, hot dog stands, horn-tooting cars, trucks, buses and bright yellow taxis, Saffron felt like a naive, inexperienced ingénue, overwhelmed by the wonder and excitement to which no visitor getting their first taste of Manhattan was immune.

A burly doorman was whistling up a cab for another guest, a middle-aged businessman, who was standing on the sidewalk in a three-piece pinstripe suit and black homburg hat, impatiently glancing at his watch. The doorman couldn't help but grin when he saw the happiness on Saffron's face, and he touched his peaked cap in salute as she went by. Even the businessman spared a second of his precious time to observe her.

To Saffron, New York felt like a city untouched by war. In London, it was impossible to escape the looming shadow of death and destruction. The sky was filled with barrage balloons. The Luftwaffe had destroyed houses, shops and offices, leaving gap-toothed streets. Other buildings were damaged beyond repair, with their facades torn away, exposing joists and rafters, pipes, wires – even carpets and torn, bedraggled curtains – for all to see. Even those that had so far survived intact had been blackened by the dust, the smoke and the scorching flames that erupted with every exploding bomb.

London's inhabitants had a grey, exhausted, underfed pallor. Their clothes were shabby, their shoes worn out. But here in New York, at 10.15 on a bright spring morning, every building gleamed with the light reflecting off the windows that rose towards the sun. Faces looked healthy and well fed. Women were dressed in the latest fashions, and men wore suits that looked newly pressed, with crisp, freshly laundered shirts.

There was, though, one thing that both sides of the Atlantic had in common – women had taken over the jobs left vacant by men who had been called up. As Saffron walked downtown, she noticed that a lot of the cabs had female drivers. She smiled as one of them, forced to a sudden stop by a car braking in front of her. The woman gave a series of furious blasts on her horn, then leaned out of the window, waved her fist at the offending driver and gave him a piece of her mind. *Anything a man can do, we can do better!*

The weather was what a New Yorker would consider pleasantly mild, but in England counted as scorching. Saffron was still at heart an African, born and raised in the tropics. As she headed uptown towards the park, she basked in the warmth of the sun on her face and the feel of the breeze fluttering the skirt of her silk summer dress. After five days at sea, much of it cooped up in her cabin, she was looking forward to a proper walk. A quick scan of the map that the concierge had given her suggested that a circuit taking in most of Central Park would cover about five miles and take around two hours, and so it proved.

Saffron stood on a stone bridge over a pond and looked back towards the hotels that ran along the southern edge of the park, and the skyscrapers that rose behind them. She was dazzled by the vivid pink cherry blossom beside the reservoir and on the aptly named Cherry Hill. She entered a passage beneath one of the streets that cut across the park and found herself in a fairytale grotto supported by colonnades of arches and decorated with beautifully patterned ceramic tiles. A solo violinist was playing 'Danny Boy', and as the beautiful, heartbreaking melody filled the air, she thought of Daniel Doherty, the US Navy officer she had met at the SOE training school on the west coast of Scotland, and smiled wistfully at the memory of being in his arms. Then she laughed as she asked herself why she was so mad about Americans. *Talk about 'One Yank and they're off'!* Except, as she reminded herself, her undies had not come off. As the song said, a kiss was just a kiss, and there had only ever been one man with whom she had actually made love.

All in all, I've really been remarkably well behaved!

A couple of times Saffron caught herself stopping and looking again as a man passed her by. At first glance, they bore some resemblance to the motorbike rider, and each time she told herself to stop being so silly. There really was no reason why anyone would want to have her followed. So far as she knew, the Germans had no idea that she had been Marlize Marais. She'd left Belgium without being identified. And anyway, she wasn't in the Low Countries now. She was in America, and if she'd walked around London every day without the slightest fear of being followed by enemy agents, why should she worry here?

Saffron was just reassuring herself that her logic was sound when a man's voice called out, 'Hey, doll-face!'

She looked around and saw a thickset man, shaded by a blue and yellow umbrella, standing behind a metal chest perched on four small wheels. 'Me?' she asked, pointing to herself.

'Yeah, you,' he said. 'You look toisty.'

Saffron frowned. '*Toisty*?'

'Yeah, like you could use a drink.'

'Oh, you mean thirsty.'

'What I said.'

'Well, now you mention it, I am rather. What do you have?'

'Hey, what don't I have?' the man said, as Saffron walked up to his cart. 'I got Coca-Cola, RC Cola, Orange Crush, cream soda, root beer, you name it.'

'Hmm . . . Coca-Cola's the only one I've heard of, so I'll have that, please.'

'You got it, sweetheart. That'll be a nickel.'

Saffron was beginning to realise that America was a much more foreign country than she had imagined. 'I'm sorry?'

'Five cents. So, where you from?'

'London . . . England.'

'This is your first time in the States, right?'

'Yes.' Saffron opened her handbag and extracted the little packet of change that Stephenson had given her. She hadn't even looked at the little coins until now. 'I'm afraid I don't know any of these,' she said, putting a selection on the cart.

'Here, let me help you,' the man said, sorting them out. 'So, you got your nickel, that's five cents, which you need for this Coke. The dime there, that's ten. And yeah, it's smaller than the nickel and no, I don't know why, any more'n you do. And that there's a quarter – twenty-five cents.'

'Because it's a quarter of a dollar . . .'

'There you go, you're gettin' the hang of it. We'll make a Noo Yawker outta you yet.'

'I consider that an honour,' Saffron said, smiling. And as she walked away, she thought of the skyscrapers and the energy on the streets, and the sheer number of different fizzy drinks she could get from a single vendor in a park. She compared that now, not to London, but to Occupied Europe, and the crushing oppression, grimness and misery of life under the Nazis and thought, *They can't beat us. Not now. Not with America on our side*.

• • •

It was seven o'clock when Adomas Petruskas walked through the service entrance of the St. Regis Hotel and told the doorman that he had an appointment to see Mr Haecki. The doorman looked sceptical: this man he'd never seen before, coming in off the street and asking to see one of the concierges.

'You don't believe me, just call him,' Petruskas said. 'Tell him Adam Peters has arrived. He's expecting me.'

The doorman shrugged, muttered, 'What the hell,' and made the call. A few minutes later, Heacki appeared, looking very impressive in his hotel uniform. 'I'll deal with this,' he told the doorman, and then said, with a suitably haughty air, 'This way, Mr Peters.'

They went down a series of short corridors and then into a room that resembled a walk-in wardrobe, filled with racks of St. Regis Hotel clothing for kitchen staff, waiters, bellboys, housemaids and, finally, maintenance staff. Haecki handed Petruskas a boiler suit with the hotel's name embroidered upon it. He hesitated for a moment, then said, 'You promise me no harm will come to Miss Courtney? I asked Mr Meyer, but I need to hear it from you, too.'

'Buddy, I swear to you, there won't be no rough stuff.' Petruskas held his arms wide apart and said, 'Search me . . . I got nothing to hide. And I ain't lifting anything, neither. I'm not a criminal. I'm just a guy doing a job, same as you. And Mr Meyer is a respectable gentleman – a diplomat, for Pete's sake.'

Haecki nodded. 'Okay then, take the service elevator to the fourteenth floor. Turn right along the hallway. Miss Courtney's suite is the last room.'

'Got it,' said Petruskas.

'And you'll need this . . .' Haecki reached into a trouser pocket. 'It's the pass key. And I need it back, okay?'

'Sure thing.'

'Okay, then. When Miss Courtney finishes her dinner and goes up to her room, I will be able to see her walk across the main lobby. At that point, I will call you to let you know she is coming. After that, you just have to listen for the bell when the elevator stops to let her out. Agreed?' Haecki asked anxiously.

'The ring of the bell is my cue to leave. Sounds fine by me.'

'Good . . . so then you do what you have to do. There is a staircase, which is also a fire escape, right by the service elevator. It does not matter which method you use to get down to the bottom, you will end up in almost the same place. I'll be waiting for you there. And trust me, if you try any tricks, or decide you want that key for yourself, I'll go straight to Meyer. And maybe he's a gentleman, but you can bet he's got friends who are not.'

'Relax, pal. My intentions are all good. Do the job, collect my pay, go home to the missus.'

That seemed to satisfy Haecki. He returned to his desk. Petruskas changed into the overalls and took the service elevator to the fourteenth floor.

Less than a minute later, he was walking into Saffron Courtney's suite.

• • •

Saffron had decided to continue the process of getting to know America by picking up a selection of reading matter at a news-stand on Fifth Avenue. She bought the latest edition of the *New York Times*, partly because of its lead story about fifty thousand German soldiers and four generals being captured as the Allied forces kicked the German and Italian forces out of North Africa. But she was even more intrigued by a headline lower down the page: 'Bears beaten 7–6 by Bisons in 10th.' It sounded as intriguingly mysterious as one of the coded messages attached to the end of BBC news bulletins for the benefit of the French Resistance. And Saffron giggled to herself as she pondered the question of which would win an actual contest between a bear and a bison, as opposed to what turned out to be a baseball match between a team from Newark, New Jersey and Buffalo, New York.

Having worked up quite an appetite on her walk, she was looking forward to dinner back at the hotel restaurant. As soon as she was shown to her table, she ordered prawns for a starter and a fillet steak for her main course. The plump, juicy prawns were eagerly consumed while she flicked through the *The New Yorker*, whose cartoon cover showed two workmen repainting a dull, military green piece of artillery in a fresh spring colour to match the leaves on the trees all around it. The steak looked to her like an entire family's weekly meat ration on a plate, but she wolfed it down with an unladylike enthusiasm, while perusing a special 'Beauty Edition' of *Vogue* whose cover encouraged her to 'Look your best. Feel your best. Be your best.'

I don't know how good I look, but I feel absolutely splendid, Saffron thought, as she sipped the glass of red wine she had allowed herself, to follow the white she had drunk with her seafood. One of the features inside was called 'The backbone of beauty', and was illustrated with a picture of a pretty girl in a spotty dress walking side by side with a handsome naval officer in his dashing dress uniform. *That could be me and Danny*, she thought. And then, feeling a little disloyal, *But Clay looks just as good in his army air force kit*.

According to the article, the current ideal of beauty was 'part spine, part soul, part lipstick'. And one could easily spot a woman who possessed these qualities: 'It's the way she holds her head high, squares her shoulders, walks with purpose.' Duly instructed, Saffron signed the bill for dinner, then walked across the restaurant towards the elevators in a suitably purposeful style. As the lift rose towards her suite, she felt as though her time in America had got off to a perfect start. Tomorrow she would meet William Stephenson and discover what task he had in store for her. And she felt confident that Clay Stackpole would be making contact as soon as he was able.

The lift reached her floor. The smartly uniformed operator opened the door and said, 'Good night, ma'am,' as she stepped out into the corridor. She looked towards her suite.

She smiled to herself, looking forward to the comfort and unadulterated luxury that awaited her.

As Saffron walked down the corridor towards her suite, she saw a man walking towards her, wearing tradesman's overalls and a flat cap. His head was down, so she could not see his face.

As they approached each other, the man nodded, raised a finger to his cap in salute and said, 'Ma'am.'

He was perfectly polite. Close up, Saffron could see that his overalls bore the hotel's name, so he must be one of their maintenance staff. She had not seen him come through her door. He could easily have been sorting out a problem in another room. There was nothing at all to suggest that he was anything but a working man going about his business.

But still, there was something about him that set her nerves on edge. And then, just as he passed by, he turned his head a fraction, just to glance at her, and there was something about his smile that . . .

No, don't be so stupid! He's not the same man. He can't be.

And yet, even as Saffron forced herself to stay calm and keep walking, she could not rid herself of the thought that the man in the overalls really had been the man on the motorbike.

She turned back and looked down the corridor. The man was by a pair of swing doors, with a FIRE ESCAPE sign above them. He must have been thirty or forty yards away, but even at that distance, there was no mistaking the air of calculated, provocative mockery as he doffed his cap and disappeared through the door.

It was the same man, all right.

Saffron raced down the corridor, barged through the doors, saw that there was another lift and instantly discounted it. No one making a speedy exit would stop and wait for a lift to arrive. Taking a few more steps, she skidded to a halt at the top of the stairs. She bent over the metal handrail and looked down the stairwell, but there was no trace of the man, not even the sound of slapping feet on concrete steps.

She gave a frustrated sigh and shook her head. A fit man, taking several steps at a time, could easily have gone down two floors in the time it had taken her to get there. She heard a noise behind her, coming from the lift. It was on its way down, and the arrow above it was halfway between the numbers nine and ten.

Saffron told herself to forget it. If he had got hold of a hotel uniform, then why not hotel keys as well? And if he had a key, he surely would have used it to get into her room. When she reached her door, that supposition became a certainty. Like all personnel of British intelligence agencies, Saffron had been taught the simple trick of leaving a hair between the door and its frame when leaving a room. If the hair was still there when you returned, then there was no need to worry. If it was not, then someone had been inside.

There was no hair in the jamb. The maintenance man had been there.

Once in the suite, Saffron went straight to the safe. Her money was still there, not a dollar missing. Likewise, her jewellery was untouched, and her clothes had not been disturbed, including the ones she had thrown on her bed when she was changing for her walk. Her Beretta and all its ammunition were in her canvas shoulder bag.

So, he's not a thief. Maybe I was wrong to think he was the man on the bike. Maybe he really was just doing his job.

She called the operator and was put through to the concierge desk. Mr Haecki answered. He asked how she had enjoyed her walk and her dinner. She replied that both had been very agreeable. And then, as casually as she could, she asked, 'Have any of your maintenance staff been in my room this evening?'

'Please excuse me for a moment, madam, while I check,' Haecki replied. A moment later he said, 'No, madam, but if there is anything wrong, I can certainly have someone sent to your suite at once.'

'No, thank you, that won't be necessary.'

So, he wasn't staff and he wasn't a thief; what did that leave? To anyone with Saffron's training, the obvious next answer was 'saboteur'. She had been trained to make, place and detonate explosive devices small enough to kill a single target or big enough to blow a train off its tracks. She had been away from her room for more than three hours. In that time, she could have made a bomb big enough to blast half the hotel's fourteenth floor to smithereens.

She started looking: under the bed; behind the curtains; in the cupboards, the fireplace, the lavatory cistern; behind the bath and in the cupboard below the bathroom sink. She went back to her luggage and took all the clothes out, just in case the man had left something underneath garments that had appeared to be undisturbed.

But there was nothing to be seen, except for a total mess strewn across what had been a lovely, tidy hotel suite.

Saffron sat on the edge of her bed and racked her brain for another idea. Then she remembered a conversation at Baker Street about an old country house called Trent Park, which stood in what was now a north London suburb. The place was being used as a POW camp for senior German officers. It was far more comfortable than any normal camp, with agreeable grounds in which the captured generals, admirals and air marshals could stroll, or take more vigorous exercise. The idea was to relax them so that they would talk more freely, unaware that Trent Park was the one place in Britain where the Allies really did have ears.

Small microphones linked to listening posts had been built into the fabric of the house, and were hidden around the grounds. So every word the Germans said was recorded and then sifted for useful intelligence. Plainly three hours was not enough to build microphones into the walls of Saffron's suite. But it might have been long enough to hide some. But where?

Well, since microphones had wires, the obvious place to put them was where there already were enough wires that an extra one might not be noticed. So, cursing the fact that she did not have a screwdriver with which to open lamps or tele-phones, or look behind the front plates of sockets, Saffron checked every single electrical fitting. But all she achieved was to create an even greater mess, make herself even more tired and anxious, and add to the feeling of violation which the knowledge that a man had been in her private room had given her.

And that, she now realised, as the hands on her bedside clock moved towards midnight and she began the process of restoring some order to her surroundings, was the whole point. Someone wanted her to feel this way. They wanted her to feel spied upon and vulnerable. But who were they? And why were they going to such trouble?

Before she finally went to bed, Saffron locked her door and jammed a dining chair under the handle. If the man in the overalls came back, he damn well wasn't getting into her room a second time. But as she lay in bed, lights out but eyes still wide open, she thought of how close she had been to him in the corridor. It was touching distance, point-blank. And it was this thought that kept a last question going round and round in her mind . . . *Why didn't he just go right ahead and kill me?*

• • •

Saffron had not slept well. She told herself to forget everything that had happened. Someone was trying to unsettle her. Who they were and why they were doing it, she could not be sure. All she did know was that the best way to beat them was simply to ignore them. And she certainly wasn't going to waste Stephenson's time with this nonsense.

But she was still jittery enough to check that no one was watching her as she left the St. Regis, or following her as she walked along Fifth Avenue, heading uptown to the Rockefeller Center.

She passed the Gothic facade of St Patrick's Cathedral and looked up at its twin spires. They had once been the tallest structures in the city. But now, the temples of Mammon were rising all around them, putting God in his place. Across the road was the greatest of all Manhattan's tributes to the material world: the Rockefeller Center. And right before her eyes was the giant bronze figure of an almost naked Atlas, with his Superman muscles, holding up the heavens, just as Stephenson had mentioned.

She crossed the avenue, passed the statue and walked towards the revolving doors of the International Building's entrance. Above them, narrow windows, three storeys high, worthy of the cathedral opposite, seemed to confirm her feeling that this was a temple of other gods. And once Saffron passed into the soaring lobby, walled in green marble, with a ceiling of fiery copper leaf and escalators gilded in bronze, the sense of being in a palace or a place of worship grew even stronger.

Somewhere in here William Stephenson was waiting for her, and Saffron could not help but wonder why. Hard-won experience had given her an instinct for impending danger. It also told her that a man did not go out of his way to make life nice for a woman, unless he expected something in return. Normally that meant sex, but Stephenson had not been flirtatious. No, he wanted favours of a different kind.

So, get a grip, girl, she told herself. *Stephenson needs a proper SOE agent, not some neurotic, unstable, unreliable Nervous Nellie! So, square shoulders, head up, and bloody well walk with purpose.*

'Mr Stephenson is expecting you, ma'am,' said the immaculately uniformed and made up woman behind the reception desk. 'His offices are in Suite 3606. Take the elevator to the thirty-sixth floor and there'll be someone waiting for you.' The receptionist smiled with what seemed like genuine enthusiasm. 'Enjoy your stay in New York!'

'Thank you,' said Saffron, taken aback by this display of unabashed familiarity. It would take a formal introduction and several social meetings to produce such cheer in England. 'I'm sure I will,' she added, deciding that she quite liked the American style.

As she rode the elevator, Saffron realised she had never been as high as a thirty-sixth floor before, and that was still only just over halfway to the top.

The soberly dressed woman who greeted Saffron as she emerged from the elevator was more formal. 'Good morning, I'm Grace Garner, Mr Stephenson's personal assistant,' she said. 'I'll take you right in.'

Grace led Saffron down a long corridor, lined with doors whose frosted-glass windows bore the gold-painted names of the businesses and organisations that worked behind them. The British Passport Control Office was at the end. Grace opened the door and stood aside to let Saffron go in ahead of her.

She was confronted by a hallway which also served as a waiting area, to judge by the four chairs arranged around a coffee table on which lay a small pile of *Picture Post*, the British answer to *Life* magazine. Two corridors branched off the hall at right angles, and looking down them, Saffron realised that this office was much larger than she had imagined. Grace led her down one of the corridors, with office doors opening off it, and across a large open space that was subdivided into a warren of small cubicles, occupied mostly by men, all in civilian dress.

Everything Saffron had heard about Stephenson's operation had led her to imagine something on a much smaller scale, little more than a one-man band. But this was clearly a full-sized intelligence agency. *Can he really be paying for all of this out of his own pocket?* Saffron wondered. *Gubbins was wrong. He's even richer than Croesus.*

Grace led Saffron through another door, into what appeared to be an outer office containing two desks, one of them unoccupied. Another woman, seated behind the other desk, got to her feet as Saffron came in. 'This is my assistant, Pamela,' Grace said. 'Can we get you a cup of tea or coffee, Miss Courtney?'

'Coffee, please. White, no sugar,' Saffron said.

'I'll see to it,' said Pamela.

There was a door beyond the two desks, which now opened to reveal William Stephenson. He focused on Saffron with his searching eyes. 'Good morning, Saffron. Come in and let's get started.'

'That's quite a view,' said Saffron as she entered Stephenson's office. At the far side stood a sleek, modernist desk, on which three telephones – black, white and red – and an intercom box were arranged in a neat line. Beyond it, two large windows looked across the plaza towards Fifth Avenue and the cathedral.

'It's not bad,' Stephenson agreed. 'But there are better. Now, let's make ourselves comfortable over here.'

To one side of the room, a large framed map hung on the wall, showing Canada, the United States and the westernmost waters of the North Atlantic. Below it, two low, chrome-framed leather-upholstered sofas faced each other across a glass-topped table on which a brown manila file had been placed. Stephenson sat down by the file and motioned to Saffron to take a seat opposite him.

Pamela slipped into the room and silently placed two cups of coffee on the table. Saffron gave her a smile of thanks. Then she took her place, crossed her legs, smoothed down her skirt and waited for Stephenson's opening move.

'So, about your mission to Washington . . .' he began. 'I had my staff get in touch with a number of political and military figures whom I know to be sympathetic to the work SOE is doing. I underlined the importance of getting Allied agents into Occupied Europe, and gave them a few details about you. There was an excellent response. You will not be short of invitations to business meetings and social events. Both, in my view, are equally important.'

'Thank you,' Saffron said simply.

Stephenson reached for the file. 'This is a dossier that we prepared for you.' He slid it across the glass tabletop. 'It lists all your contacts, times of meetings and events, locations and so forth. There are half a dozen social invitations in there, too. We RSVP'd on your behalf.'

Saffron picked up the file and then set it down, unopened, on the table in front of her. 'That's very kind,' she said. 'What I'd really like, though, is some advice on what to say, what questions to ask, what buttons to push to persuade these men to look favourably on SOE.'

'I thought you might. The dossier also contains a list of talking points, and outlines the things these men want to hear. The main question you must be able to answer is this – how can SOE help the invasion of Occupied Europe when it comes? The only thing that matters to anyone in Washington is getting from the French, Belgian or Dutch coast to Berlin, as fast as possible, with the minimum number of dead Americans. If SOE can help with that, then you'll be in business.'

'Well, I can answer that question right away,' Saffron said. 'And I can do so on the basis of having been in both Belgium and Holland within the past few months and seeing the situation at first hand.'

'Good. Always start that way. It'll get everyone's attention. Now, let me play the guy from the Pentagon . . . What did you learn over there about the people's resistance to Hitler?'

'As matters stand, there's not much of it,' Saffron responded. 'There are very few people in resistance movements, and their efforts are sporadic and mostly ineffective.'

'Why's that?'

'The majority of people in the occupied nations are too frightened to rise up against the Germans. They know that if they get caught, they'll be interrogated, tortured and then executed without the benefit of a trial. From the perspective of the average Dutch or Belgian, it seems the Germans are going to be there forever.'

'If that's the case, why should we help you?' Stephenson pressed. 'What good can you do?'

'Because the tide of the war is turning. Once the French and Belgians and Dutch can see that the Germans are losing and that the Allies are on their way, then they will be ready to take action. And that's where the SOE comes in. We can supply local people with weapons, ammunition, explosives, radios. We can train them to bomb railway lines, assassinate local army and SS commanders, and carry out attacks on German patrols and motorcycle messengers. That all adds up to effective, destructive action that will tie up a great many German troops and make it harder for them to defend their empire in Europe against the invading Allied armies. And that will achieve both of the ends you specified – faster progress, fewer casualties.'

Stephenson gave a grunt of approval, which, Saffron guessed, was as good as a round of applause from a more demonstrative man. 'Good. That will go down well in Washington. Now, tell me, do you know personally how to undertake all these bombings, assassinations, ambushes and so forth?'

'Of course. We were all trained to do that.'

'Then I advise you to go into a few details – the tougher and bloodier, the better. Coming from a woman, that will get their attention.'

'By all means, if you think it would help,' Saffron said.

'I do.'

'Then that's settled.' One aspect of Saffron's journey to Washington had been wrapped up. Now she wanted to change the subject. 'I owe you an awful lot for all the help you're giving me,' she said. 'I feel I should do something in return. Brigadier Gubbins said you had something in mind. "Sleuthing" was the word he used. What exactly does that entail?'

Stephenson almost smiled. 'I was wondering when you'd ask. And the simple answer is that I need you to find out why a man has stopped sending letters to his godson. Because the success or failure of the greatest seaborne invasion in human history may depend on the answer to that question.'

'Oh . . .' said Saffron, unable to come up with a better comment on a mission that was so overwhelmingly important and so utterly baffling.

'Let me explain,' Stephenson said.

He got to his feet and walked over to the map on the wall. 'There!' he said, jabbing at a small pink dot on the map. 'That is the island of Bermuda, six hundred and some miles east of Cape Hatteras, North Carolina, and a British colony since 1607.'

'I hear it's a lovely place for a holiday,' Saffron said.

'Indeed it is. I strongly recommend it. But that's not why I'm pointing it out. I want to tell you about the one thousand, two hundred of your countrymen and women who are spending this war in the Princess Hotel, otherwise known as the Pink Palace, which is one of the oldest, biggest and smartest establishments on the island.'

'They're not on holiday, I imagine.'

'No, they have to do a lot of tough, often boring and repetitive work.'

Stephenson left the map and sat back down on the sofa. 'Three years ago, while the United States was still neutral, I helped negotiate a deal between the US and British governments by which all mail leaving the United States bound for Europe was intercepted and taken by flying boat to Bermuda, to be read by staff of British Imperial Censorship . . .'

'I didn't know there was such a thing,' Saffron said.

'That's the point – people not knowing.'

'Can I ask how you got the Americans to agree to that deal while they were still neutral?'

'With some difficulty. I argued that we would be able to help the US as well as Britain by uncovering Nazi spies based in America. The FBI didn't like that. Mr Hoover reckoned he could catch Nazis all by himself, thank you. The project hung in the balance for a while. But then we caught a lucky break. One of our people in Bermuda noticed a letter addressed to a gentleman called Lothar Frederick. And that was interesting, because "Lothar" was a code name for Reinhard Heydrich, who was second only to Himmler in the SS.'

'Until SEO assassinated him.'

'Indeed you did . . . Anyway, to cut a long story short, there were regular letters from a man who signed himself "Joe K", and they contained messages in invisible ink, plus diagrams of, for example, the US defences at Pearl Harbor.'

'Goodness! That's serious stuff.'

'Very. Our discovery started a process that ended with the FBI uncovering an entire Nazi spy ring. And Joe K, alias Kurt Frederick Ludwig, is currently cooling his heels in Alcatraz and no one complains about Bermuda anymore.'

Saffron thought for a moment. 'Would I be right in thinking that your people in Bermuda have uncovered another spy, by any chance?'

'You would be exactly right,' Stephenson replied.

'But you're talking to me, not the FBI, because . . .'

Stephenson said nothing, letting her complete the thought.

Saffron pondered for a second. 'You don't want them to know what you think is happening. And why wouldn't you want that? Why do you want to keep this in house? Okay . . . You're worried that this spy is one of us, aren't you?'

'Yes. I believe there is a spy working for the Germans in the British embassy in Washington. And within the next three weeks, Mr Churchill and President Roosevelt, along with their key military strategists, will sit down together to determine, amongst other things, the course of the war in Europe over the next twelve to eighteen months—'

'Including the invasion.'

'More than one invasion, I would imagine. There's more than one way into Europe.'

'So, if the Germans were to know our plans, that would be a total disaster. And if the Americans found out that it was all because of a spy in our embassy—'

'Yep – that would make it an even bigger disaster.'

'Still, don't you have to tell the FBI about your suspicions, no matter how awkward it might be?'

'Uh-huh.' Stephenson nodded. 'Pretty soon I won't have much choice. But what if Hoover advises the president that it's not safe to be meeting with Mr Churchill? The thought of the prime minister being sent back to Britain, having accomplished nothing . . . Think what that would do for morale in Britain, and what a gift it would be for Nazi propaganda.'

'Do you know anything about this spy? You must do, or you couldn't have worked out he was there . . . whoever he is.'

'That's a good question. Let me get the person who is best able to answer it.' Stephenson got up and walked to his desk. He pressed a button on the intercom. 'Grace, could you please ask Miss Araminta Keswick to join us?'

Stephenson returned to the sofa, moving himself up to one end to make room for another person. 'The young lady you are about to meet has a high level of security clearance. You and she can discuss your work in the certain knowledge that none of what is said will go any further.'

The door opened and Saffron turned her head to see a plump, bespectacled woman, dressed in grey trousers, a plain white shirt and a rather baggy pale blue cardigan. Her mousy hair was pinned into a ragged bun, from which stray wisps had escaped in a number of different directions. She was holding a manila folder, identical to the one that Stephenson had given Saffron.

Miss Keswick's smile as she saw Saffron was tentative, shy and distracted, as though her mind was somewhere else. But as she came closer and their eyes met, Saffron sensed a high-powered mind. Miss Keswick took her place on the sofa and glanced across at Stephenson. 'Would you like me to explain about Gerald now, sir?'

'Go ahead.'

'Well, then . . .' Miss Keswick gathered her thoughts and began her story. 'One day in the middle of January last year, I opened a letter to a Master Oskar Nykvist, in Östersund, Sweden.'

'It's a town in the middle of the country, a little less than four hundred miles from Stockholm,' Stephenson explained.

'Yes,' said Miss Keswick, 'and as I opened the envelope, I said to myself, "I wonder what Gerald is sending you this month." You see, I'd seen two of these letters before, and, as it later turned out, a couple of other girls had opened ones like them before me. And as I said those words, it suddenly struck me – "Is there something fishy going on here?"'

'What made you think that?' Saffron asked.

'Well, the letters were always dated the eighteenth of the month. They were sent every month, regular as clockwork, and they were all just signed "From your loving Godfather, Gerald." They were nice, cheerful letters. They seemed harmless. But there was something about that regularity. It didn't seem like the way a godfather keeps in touch with a young child.'

'But it is the way an agent communicates with their handler,' Saffron observed. 'So that if the schedule is ever broken, the handler knows something's wrong.'

'But the thing that really niggled at me,' Miss Keswick continued, 'wasn't the schedule. It was that the letters were written entirely in English – not a word of Swedish. Of course, Gerald could just have been helping Oskar to learn English, but you'd have thought that he'd still have thrown in the odd word in the boy's own language, maybe at the beginning, or when he was sending his love at the end.'

'I agree,' said Saffron. 'If Gerald's close enough to the family to be a godfather, he'd know a bit of Swedish. Could you tell anything about him from the letters?'

'Oh, yes. For a start, it was definitely an Englishman writing, not an American. That was obvious from the language he used. He was quite charming, actually.'

'Could it have been someone pretending to be English?'

'No, I don't think so. The tone seemed genuine. I knew the type of chap he was, too – well educated, from an upper-class or upper-middle-class family . . .'

'Public school, in other words.'

'Absolutely. And I don't believe that a foreigner could get it quite right, without any giveaways. Well, not unless they'd lived or gone to school in England. And even then, there would be the odd word or phrase that gave them away.'

'Tell her about the pictures,' said Stephenson.

'Absolutely, sir,' said Miss Keswick. 'So, Gerald's letters always contained an image of some kind. The first few were black-and-white photographs taken in Washington DC, presumably by Gerald himself. But after a while he switched to colour postcards of something typically American that would appeal to a small boy. Mickey Mouse, for example, or a shiny Cadillac, or a painting of Chief Sitting Bull. And there would always be a couple of lines in the letter about the postcard, but the card itself was blank, because, as we gathered from the letters, little Oskar was supposed to stick them all in an album which Gerald had given him for his birthday.'

'That's neat,' said Saffron. 'Was there a hidden message written on the blank side of the card?'

Stephenson smiled. 'Nice try. But no.'

'You got there quicker than we did, though,' said Miss Keswick. 'Even after I'd flagged the Gerald letters as something that could be of interest, it took three more messages before anyone at the Pink Palace asked that question.'

'An error, but understandable,' said Stephenson. 'Our people in Bermuda are dealing with tens of thousands of letters a week. Those Gerald letters were akin to a few grains of sand on a mile-long beach.'

'Of course, as soon as we thought there might be something on the cards, we started taking the whole thing very seriously,' Miss Keswick continued. 'We've got some terribly brainy boffins. They tested them with every method of detecting invisible ink they knew, but they couldn't find a thing. Then I had a eureka moment. The answer had been staring us in the face all along. The message was on the picture, not the blank side.'

'You mean, like a microdot?' Saffron asked. 'We have a magic tricks department at SOE that dreams up all sorts of gadgets, and I know they're working on that for us, too. An agent writes a message, photographs it, reduces the image to a microscopic size, and then sticks it onto . . . well, almost anything. And of course!' Saffron suddenly exclaimed. 'The words Gerald wrote about the card in the letters told the person at the other end where to look for the microdot.'

'That's right,' said Miss Keswick. 'Let me show you.' She opened her file and started shuffling through the papers. 'Once we decided we needed to keep an eye on the Gerald letters, we started photographing them all. So . . . ah . . . yes . . . Here is the postcard of Sitting Bull I was talking about.'

Miss Keswick handed Saffron a Victorian era image of Sitting Bull looking at the camera. His face was stern and commanding; his hair rested on his chest in two long plaits, and a single, magnificent feather was stuck vertically into the hair at the back of his head.

'And here is the letter that came with it. I've underlined the key words – "Isn't that feather splendid, sticking up behind his head?" The boffins looked at the bottom of the feather, just where it poked up behind his head, going over the whole area under a microscope. It took a while for them to find the microdot, but they got there in the end.'

'So how is the agent creating his microdots?' Saffron asked. 'As I understand it, that's a sophisticated procedure and it needs a lot of gear. Whoever's sending these messages must be well equipped.'

'That's not all. When we finally got into the microdot, we found a message that no one has been able to decode.'

Before Saffron could follow up, Stephenson put an end to the conversation. 'Thank you, Araminta, that was an excellent presentation. But I can take it from here.'

'She seems very bright,' said Saffron, as the door closed behind Miss Keswick.

'Oh, yes. She was recruited from Girton College, Cambridge, where she was lecturing in linguistics while working on her PhD thesis – "The Mathematics of Language". She has a particular interest in finding linguistic patterns that have characteristics similar to mathematical patterns, like the Fibonacci sequence.'

'I should have thought that would make her the perfect cryptographer.'

'You're not the only one to hold that view. We're having a hell of a fight to keep her. I fear Miss Keswick will soon find herself on a flying boat to Britain.'

'How utterly grim, after Bermuda.'

'Yes, but if she ends up where I think she will, she'll find her mind being stretched in ways no other place on earth can match. And for a mind as brilliant as hers, that matters more than sunshine and beaches.'

'I can well believe that,' Saffron agreed.

She sat back, waiting for Stephenson to continue the conversation. Instead, he rose to his feet and said, 'There's something I want you to see. Follow me.'

He led her out of the office, back down the hall to the elevators, and when one arrived, they took it to the top floor. Stephenson pushed open a door and Saffron was almost blinded by a sudden blast of dazzling sunlight, closely followed by the buffeting of a cool, fresh breeze. She blinked and realised she was standing in the middle of a roof garden – a green oasis five hundred feet in the air. Saffron heard the distant sound of a car horn coming from the avenue below. She looked out beyond the garden and gasped at the sight that met her eyes.

To her right, the even taller RCA building rose sixty-five storeys from Rockefeller Plaza. To her left, she could look down at the tops of the twin cathedral spires. But in front of her, the whole of lower Manhattan was laid out, avenue by avenue, street by street, block by block, progressing down the island in geometric ranks towards the sea.

'The skyscrapers of the Rockefeller Center have the best views in the city,' Stephenson said. 'Even better than the

Empire State Building, because from here you can actually see the Empire State Building.'

Sure enough, there it was, twenty blocks downtown.

'And that's the Chrysler Building,' Stephenson said, pointing to a gleaming silver art deco spire, much closer. 'One good thing about the war – there are no tourists in town, and no one else up here to bother us. Let's take a stroll around the garden. We can talk as we go.'

Stephenson set off without saying anything more, and to break the silence Saffron asked, 'Can you tell me about the German code even Miss Keswick can't break?'

Stephenson grimaced. 'I'm afraid not. Jerry hardly ever says anything that gets past our best people these days. But on this one, they're completely stumped.'

Saffron was never one to take no for an answer. 'Surely, if you know where the messages are going, can't you intercept them, or the person who picks them up?'

'My thoughts exactly. But a lot of intelligence officers in London resent the fact that I have Mr Churchill's ear, and they don't like the influence that my outfit has here in the States, any more than they like the things that you SOE people get up to. It required a lot of persuading and a word from Number 10 to make the Secret Intelligence Service take these Gerald letters seriously. Finally, in March, they sent someone up to Östersund from Stockholm. Of course, we knew that there was a risk of tipping German intelligence off, but we couldn't just sit on our backsides doing nothing. We were damned if we did and damned if we didn't. But the head of SIS assured me personally that their man was highly competent and half-Swedish, so he spoke the language like a native. I gave them the go-ahead.'

'What happened?'

'The SIS agent went to the address on the letters. It was to a tobacconist's shop with two flats above it. One was where the shopkeeper and his family lived. The other was rented out to a couple. They had a child, but she was a little girl, aged three, called Magda. The agent spoke to both families. He explained that he was an official from the local school board, and had been informed that a boy called Oskar, living at that address, had been missing school. Now he was trying to find out what was going on. Naturally, he had all the appropriate paperwork. Both families said they knew nothing about any child called Oskar, so our man said that there must have been a mistake, thanked them for their time and departed.'

'Isn't the obvious explanation that the shopkeeper himself was Oskar Nykvist?'

'Yes . . . except that SIS checked out all the people in that building, and they were, without exception, genuine Swedish citizens, born and raised in Östersund, with proper jobs and no connection to any known Nazi sympathizers. Just decent, law-abiding people.'

'Except that they aren't,' Saffron said. 'At the very least, one of them is acting as a courier, passing the messages on to the next person in the chain.'

'Of course, but good luck finding them without some kind of freak stroke of luck. Take that Joe K case. The FBI had their best people on the job. But they didn't have a thing until out of the blue, a man who called himself Don Julio Lopez Lido was hit and killed by a New York cab. It was an accident – Lido was jaywalking. But when the police went to the hotel room where he was living, they found a hoard of suspicious documents containing information about the US military, all written in German. This “Señor Lido” was an Abwehr agent called Ulrich von der Osten. The FBI joined the dots between Von der Osten and Joe K, alias Ludwig, and they rolled up a whole network. But if Von der Osten hadn’t tried to beat the lights on Seventh Avenue, they’d still be in business today.’

‘But this time, you can’t even talk to the FBI,’ Saffron said, ‘so the chance of catching the spy is even smaller.’

‘Not entirely. At least we know we’re looking for an Englishman.’

‘But how do you know he works at the embassy?’

‘We don’t, not for sure. But the embassy’s by far the biggest employer of British citizens in Washington DC. And there’s another thing. We intercepted ten messages. Eight contained postcards, but the first two contained original photographs. One of the photographs was of the British embassy, and it showed the classical portico at the front of the ambassador’s residence. That portico is not visible from the street. You have to be in the embassy grounds to see it.’

‘Presumably the embassy has lots of receptions and things like that. I seem to remember seeing newsreels of a tea party there for the King and Queen when they visited Washington before the war. Any guest could take a picture of the residence.’

‘Sure,’ Stephenson agreed. ‘That’s what the letter said. “I went to a party here, aren’t I lucky?” or something like that. Except there was no sign of a party in the photograph. No guests in smart clothes. No bar or buffet. Just a couple of men in suits walking in front of the building. Whoever took it was there during working hours.’

‘But that would be crazy, wouldn’t it? I mean, giving such an obvious clue.’

'Yes and no. After all, look at it from Gerald's point of view. You're sending innocent messages, with no suspicious content, to a neutral country. If you're working at the embassy, you probably know that your letter is going to be one of many, many thousands that our people sift through every week. Why should they pay any attention to it? And even if they do, your real message is coded inside a microdot, hidden in an image. So, irrespective of what the image portrays, what are the odds of anyone finding the message? We wouldn't have done so if it hadn't been for pure luck – an entirely unpredictable association of ideas inside Miss Keswick's brilliant mind.'

'Hmm . . .' Saffron tried to put herself into the mind of the agent. 'You said it was one of the first two messages. What if Gerald was new to this game and made a beginner's mistake?'

'They call that a rookie error over here. But I don't think this is one. You see, I believe we're dealing with someone who thinks he's better than us. I'll bet he doesn't think we're smart enough to intercept his messages. But in case we are, he wants to have a laugh at our expense. He's taunting us, saying, "I can show you where I am, and you still won't find me."'

'That makes sense. And if he was like that, the risk of exposure would be exciting, like a private thrill. So, what do you want me to do?'

'Keep your ears open and your eyes peeled when you're in Washington. I've been in touch with the ambassador, Lord Halifax. He knows that you're with SOE, here to liaise with OSS and muster support on Capitol Hill. But there's no need to tell the other embassy staff. None of them will be present at your private briefings or be invited to the social events you attend. And in any case, they'll have their hands so full dealing with the conference, they won't have time to waste wondering about you.'

'Our usual procedure at Baker Street is to tell people that we work for an outfit that sounds so tedious that no one would ever want to talk about it,' Saffron said. 'The Joint Technical Board is one name we use. That sort of outfit might send someone to talk to their equally boring opposite number in Washington.'

'That sounds perfect . . . Anyway, I suggested it would be nice if someone could put you up, so you didn't have to be alone in a hotel, or sitting by yourself in a restaurant. There won't be any room at the residence itself this week, for obvious reasons. Lady Halifax is, apparently, asking for volunteers.'

'I suppose I'd better wish her luck! But, sir . . .' Saffron stopped. There was a question she'd been wanting to ask, but she was worried it might sound as if she was teaching Stephenson to suck eggs.

She felt those eyes bore into her. 'What is it?' he asked.

'I was wondering . . . why don't you block this month's letter? Don't let it get to Sweden. As Miss Keswick said, wartime mail is unreliable. So, it would take two or three weeks at least for the Germans to be sure that their communications have been intercepted. You'd be buying some time.'

'Too late,' said Stephenson bluntly. 'There was no message on April eighteenth. Not to Oskar Nykvist, anyway. I made the wrong call about sending a guy to Östersund. That just told the Germans we were on to them. Now their man here knows that, too.'

Stephenson sighed, and for the first time Saffron sensed the pressure he was under. 'Two of the most powerful men on earth are about to begin the talks that will determine British and American military strategy for the next two years,' he said. 'And there's a very real danger that the Germans will have the whole thing served up to them on a plate.'

‘What about SIS? Can’t they look at the embassy staff?’

‘They claim they already have. They insist their men in the embassy have checked everything out, and there’s nothing to worry about. And they’ve persuaded Winston’s people to tell the old man that, too, but I don’t believe it for a second.’

Saffron said nothing, caught up in the thoughts that Stephenson’s words – ‘checked everything out, and there’s nothing to worry about’ – had just triggered. *Maybe I should tell him . . .*

He looked at her with a concerned frown. ‘Are you all right?’

‘Yes, it’s just something that happened. I wasn’t going to tell you, but—’

‘Does it have anything to do with Gerald?’

‘I don’t know.’

‘Well, why don’t you tell me and I’ll be the judge?’

So Saffron described the man on the motorbike who’d followed Stephenson’s limousine on the drive from the dock to the St. Regis.

‘Yes, Dalton told me about him,’ said Stephenson. ‘What of it?’

‘I’m sure I saw him again – at the St. Regis, when I was going to my room. I’d been out all evening. He was coming the other way, dressed in overalls, like a maintenance man. The way he looked at me, he wanted me to recognise him. And he’d definitely been in my suite, but the concierge’s desk had no record of any of their chaps being there while I was out. So he was working for someone else, presumably someone hostile. But I absolutely tore my suite apart, and I couldn’t find anything remotely suspicious. I was up half the night thinking about it.’

‘And what do you conclude now, in the light of day?’ Stephenson asked.

'Well, I may just be going a bit mad. All the stress of being undercover in the Low Countries ruining my nerves.'

'Or . . .?'

'That maybe this whole Washington business is just like my room. That I'll go round the bend trying to find something that just isn't there.'

'Or . . .?'

'That someone knows I'm here . . . and they want me to know it.'

'Why would they want that?'

'To unsettle me, I suppose. Put me on edge. Get me doubting myself.'

'Which they seem to have done quite successfully,' Stephenson said. 'But do you know what I think? This seems to me like a sign that we're on to something. Otherwise, why would anyone bother going to all the trouble they've taken over you?'

'I thought about that last night. But in that case, why not just kill me?'

'History suggests that you're not an easy woman to kill. But still, that is a good question.'

'Well, there's only one way to get to the bottom of all this,' said Saffron. 'I'd better get to Washington right away.'

'No, don't. The embassy's expecting you tomorrow evening, off the Congressional Limited. Stick to that schedule. The last thing we want is the woman who's putting you up to complain to a friend that you've turned up unexpectedly.'

Saffron nodded. 'The friend tells another friend, Gerald hears about it. He starts asking around about me. The next thing I know, I'm a target, and I don't even know who's targeting me.'

'So, the schedule stays.'

Stephenson led Saffron back to the elevators. 'Oh, one other thing,' he added, as he pressed the button. 'An army air force doctor, Lieutenant Stackpole, pitched up at our offices first thing this morning, just as we were starting work for the day. He said you'd met on the *Queen Mary* and agreed to meet in New York. Is that true?'

'Yes.'

'Good, because I told him he could reach you at the St. Regis. Now, I am under strict orders to look after you, from both your CO and your father. I even had a message from young Jock Colville first thing this morning, telling me that you'd made quite an impression on the PM. So, the least I can do is to invite you to join my wife, Mary, and me for dinner at the Copacabana club tonight.'

Saffron forced herself to smile, knowing she could hardly say no. 'That would be lovely, sir.'

Stephenson nodded. 'I think you'll like the place. There's a young man singing there tonight who's the talk of the town right now. Tables are like gold dust. A pal of mine called me up and offered me a hundred bucks for my reservation. Said his two daughters would kill him if he didn't get them in to see the show.'

'So, if I change my mind you can still turn a nice profit.'

Saffron said it deadpan, and for a moment she was worried that Stephenson had taken her seriously. But then he laughed and said, 'Ha! I guess I can. But I hope you don't. And look, if you'd like to see that doctor fellow, I get it. So, don't worry, he's welcome to join us. And us old folk will leave nice and early, right after the show, so you kids will be free to go out on the town together, make a real night of it.'

Saffron beamed. 'Thank you, sir. That all sounds wonderful . . . and no blackout to worry about. What bliss!'

'You're welcome. Stackpole will be reporting to the St. Regis at seven this evening. You need to be at the Copa by eight.'

There was a ping as the lift arrived. The doors slid open. 'It's coming up to midday,' said Stephenson as they got in. 'Mary will be here any minute.'

Sure enough, when they got back to the office a diminutive but elegantly dressed middle-aged brunette was there to meet them with a sweet smile, inspecting Saffron with shrewd brown eyes. 'The store clerks in the ladieswear department are going to love dressing you, my dear,' she said. 'Such a perfect mannequin figure.'

'Thank you,' Saffron replied. 'But I feel rather guilty for even thinking about shopping, when there's so much for me to do.'

'Don't,' said Stephenson. 'This is meant to be a holiday.'

• • •

The hour hand on the clock beside Saffron's bed had just reached seven, and she was about to give herself a dab of Chanel No 5 when the telephone rang. She picked up the handset and the concierge informed her that Lieutenant Stackpole had arrived. 'Please tell him that I'll meet him in the King Cole Bar.'

Then she pulled the crystalline top off the bottle and basked for a second in the pure femininity of the scent, smiling as she thought back to the moment when she had first laid her hands on it.

'You can't get proper French scent in London anymore,' Saffron had told Mary Stephenson. 'Not unless you have contacts in the black market, and even then, it's almost certainly fake.'

But the manageress of the Saks perfume department had said that she might have one or two bottles left for special customers. And since Mrs Stephenson was just such a lady, she would see what she could find. When the bottle had been presented to her in its little box, Saffron had been overjoyed. It occurred to her now that she might even have squealed, which was something she tried not to do as a rule.

It had been an auspicious start to an afternoon that, with Mary Stephenson's encouragement, had turned into a pampering session on an epic scale, as a result of which Saffron now had perfect red nails, an elegant new hairdo and a brand-new suitcase filled with her purchases, all wrapped in tissue paper by the Saks staff. Amongst her hoard were four pairs of nylon stockings. They were unobtainable in London, and were even becoming hard to get – and correspondingly expensive – in America as the US military discovered that this new miracle fabric was good for a lot more than women's hosiery.

Saffron was wearing a pair now. The feel of them against her skin was not as luxurious as her favourite French silk stockings, but the way they clung to her legs amazed and excited her. She had set aside two more of her purchases for the night ahead: a pair of black evening shoes and a dark, midnight-green velvet dress, whose fabric criss-crossed over her bust, boosting her relatively modest curves, then fell in a close-fitting sheath to her knees, emphasising her lithe waist, hips and legs.

She dabbed on the No 5, then took one last look in the mirror. Her reflection, an image of feminine sophistication, seemed like a stranger to Saffron. How long had it been since she had dressed for a night out? *Not since Hardy Amies took me to dinner at the Dorchester, then dancing at the Embassy Club*, she thought. *My God, that must have been eighteen months ago, maybe more.*

Saffron smoothed her dress, blew herself a kiss and felt a shiver of anticipation as she thought of what the night might bring. She picked up her coat and her evening bag and headed for the door.

Stackpole was leaning against the bar as Saffron walked in. She could feel his eyes on her as she made her way between the tables, enjoying the electric charge of knowing that a handsome man in a smart uniform was captivated by her.

He stood up with a broad grin. 'If I ever saw a more beautiful sight, I sure as hell don't remember. I ordered you champagne. I hope Krug is all right.'

He led her to a stool at the bar, then sat down beside her.

She nodded, took a sip of champagne, then made a little show of looking him up and down and said, 'You look quite spiffy yourself. I mean, I've seen worse.'

They both burst out laughing

'Here's to you,' he said, gently bumping his chunky bourbon glass against her delicate champagne flute. Saffron told him about Stephenson's invitation.

'So, are you bringing me along?'

'If you don't mind it being a foursome.'

'There could be twenty people round that table, you'd still be the only one for me.'

Stackpole took a swig of Old Forester, savouring the warmth of it on his tongue, then looked at the wall behind the bar. It was covered by Maxfield Parrish's thirty-foot mural of the real estate magnate and hotelier John Jacob Astor IV, sitting on a throne in the role of Old King Cole, attended to his right by three fiddlers and to his left by two servants bringing his pipe and bowl, as in the nursery rhyme.

'Now that sure is some fancy wallpaper,' he said, playing the cowboy again.

Saffron looked wide-eyed. 'They don't have murals like that in bars in Texas?'

'Oh, sure we do,' Stackpole said, smiling. 'I just meant it was a little on the small side.'

'Hmm . . .' Saffron looked at him. 'Maybe you can impress some girls with all that "everything's bigger in Texas" talk. But I come from Africa. I grew up with elephants wandering around in the garden.'

Stackpole grinned. 'Are you kidding me?'

'No, I'm serious. We have herds of elephant on our land, along with lions, rhinos, giraffes, zebras . . . It's Africa. There's nowhere on earth to compare.'

'Maybe when all this nonsense is over, you could take me there, give me the tour,' Stackpole said.

Saffron weighed him up. Behind his Texan bluster, she sensed a well of genuine feeling. 'So, do you have a sweetheart waiting for you back in Texas?'

Stackpole looked at her for a moment. *He's deciding whether to be completely honest or not*, Saffron thought, and when he nodded, 'Uh-huh,' the sting of disappointment was softened by her relief in knowing that he was a man who told the truth, even when he didn't have to.

'You?' he asked.

'Yes, there's a man,' she said. 'A fighter pilot. He's overseas. I don't know if we'll ever see each other again. He could die, or I could . . . or both of us, come to that. It's something that my girlfriends and I talk about a lot. You know, what we should do . . .'

'And what do they say?'

'That rather depends on the girl. But what a lot of us think is that you take your love, and you wrap it up and put it in a special, safe place in your heart, where nothing can happen to it. Then you close the door on that safe place, and you go and make the best of every minute of every day, because you never know if you'll still be here tomorrow.'

Stackpole nodded. 'I guess it's different for you in London, what with the bombing raids, and all. No one's going to drop any bombs on Galveston any time soon.'

'Or New York . . . and yet here you are,' Saffron said.

Stackpole smiled, but it was a wry, almost guilty shadow of his usual grin. 'Yeah, here I am.'

'Are you sure that's a good thing?'

'Tonight, right now? Hell, yeah.' Just as the grin had gone from Stackpole's face, so the usual light-hearted tone of his voice had given way to a new intensity. 'Everything about you is special, Saffron Courtney. Once a guy meets you, it kind of makes other girls look boring . . . like plain beef stew when you just ate chilli con carne.'

'I've never eaten that, but I'm guessing it's spicy.'

'Very.'

'I'll take that as a compliment. But there's one thing you're not taking into account.'

'What's that.'

'I'm dangerous. People tend to get hurt around me.'

'Oh, I'm sure that's not true.'

Saffron almost didn't answer. She couldn't quite work out why the conversation had suddenly taken such a serious turn. But she wanted to keep talking – not so much to tell Stackpole anything, as to work things out for herself.

'I'm afraid it is true,' she said. 'You know that head doctor I was talking about, that afternoon on the games deck?'

'Uh-huh.'

'He told me there's a saying in his business – there's no such thing as an accident. If people are happy and their lives are going well, it's not a matter of luck. It's because they act in a way that makes good things happen. They make positive, healthy choices. And if there's endless trouble . . . Well, that's because, subconsciously, they seek out . . . I don't know . . . lovers who will hurt them, or situations where they will fail.'

'I don't know about that,' Stackpole said. 'Sometimes folks just get lucky, and sometimes things go wrong, no matter what you do.'

'That's true. But the positive person, faced with hard times, finds a way to make them better. And a negative person, given good luck, finds a way to waste it.'

'Well, one thing you ain't is a negative person.'

'No, I'm not. But I am a person who finds herself in a lot of trouble on a regular basis. And that's not a coincidence, or a run of bad luck. It's because, deep down, I seek trouble out. I put myself in harm's way. And when it comes, I don't do the sensible thing and get away as fast as possible. Instead, I dive right in.'

'Are you doing that now?'

'I'm under strict orders from my CO to stay out of trouble. Go to America, have a nice time, be charming to powerful men, and come home.'

'And that doesn't appeal?'

'For a bit, yes. Look, I'm a girl, and I like girl things. You should have seen me in Saks today with Mary Stephenson. I bought an entire suitcaseful of new clothes. But here I am now, a few hours later, and I can just feel the other side of my nature screaming for attention.' Saffron sighed. 'Things are already getting . . . complicated. I'm going to get into trouble, I know I am. And, what's more, I'll have asked for it.'

She was waiting for Stackpole's answer, but instead he quickly looked at his watch.

'Well, I can tell you one way you're going to find trouble, and fast,' he said. 'It's damn near eight o'clock. The Copa's on East 60th Street, five blocks from here. I'm guessing your Mr Stephenson is not a man who stands for tardiness?'

'Absolutely not.'

'Then we'd better move on out, right now.'

They made it in good time, but not before Saffron had slowed down a couple of times to check that they weren't being followed. 'Are you okay?' Stackpole asked. 'You seem kinda jumpy.'

'Oh, it's nothing really.' She forced a smile.

Stackpole gave her a look that was more that of doctor to patient than a regular guy to his date. 'Okay, I believe you,' he said. But his tone made Saffron think, *No, you really don't.*

The Copacabana was located in the basement of a hotel, and was elaborately decorated in a tropical, Latin American style. A waiter led Saffron and Stackpole between thick white columns, designed to resemble palm trees, with spotlights in place of coconuts and leaves that spread like umbrellas over the patrons beneath. The waiter pointed to a table at the edge of the dance floor. 'Mr Stephenson is right over there.' Then he grinned and added, 'And it looks like he's got company.'

Sure enough, Saffron could see Stephenson talking to a middle-aged man, whose head seemed to be constantly turning away to glance around the room. His sharp eyes briefly met Saffron's as she walked towards him, then he tapped Stephenson on the arm and nodded in her direction.

Stephenson smiled at his guests and said, 'Ah, Winchell, may I introduce Lieutenant and Doctor Clayton Stackpole, and . . .' Stephenson paused for barely a second, considering his options, then continued, 'Miss Jane Smith. You must excuse Miss Smith, Winchell, if your name means nothing to her. She comes from Africa.'

Walter Winchell looked up at Saffron – for, in her heels, she towered over both him and Stephenson – and then, in an urgent, almost hectoring, voice said, 'Jane from Africa, huh? How does Tarzan feel about your new boyfriend?'

Saffron laughed. 'Oh, I haven't told him yet.'

'Then maybe I should. Eight hundred and twenty newspapers across this country take my column, Miss Smith, and more than twenty million Americans listen to my radio show. Hmm . . . "Me Tarzan. No Jane." That's what I call a story.'

'Winchell was just about to tell me why he's left his regular table at the Stork Club to come here for the evening,' Stephenson said.

'Let's just say there's an unexpected attraction at the Copa tonight,' Winchell said. 'And I'm not the only guy who wants to check it out. See over there, those three Italian signors with dames who definitely ain't their signoras? One of them owns this joint, though you won't see his name on any piece of paper at City Hall. Think I'll go say hello, pay my respects. Be seeing you, Stephenson.' Winchell gave two more nods as he said, 'Lieutenant . . . Miss Smith,' then made a beeline for the other table.

'So, who are those guys?' Stackpole asked.

'Mobsters,' said Stephenson. 'The one in the middle, wearing the spectacles, is Frank Costello. He's the one who owns this place. Allegedly. Now, let's sit down.'

'Isn't Mary coming?' Saffron asked, noticing that only three places had been laid.

'I'm afraid she's got a migraine, but she asked me to convey her sincere apologies and to say how much she enjoyed meeting you and witnessing your blitzkrieg on Saks.'

There was already a bottle of champagne in an ice bucket beside the table. A waiter handed out dinner menus that were several pages long. 'The Copa boasts of having more than two hundred and fifty items on its menu,' Stephenson said. 'But the best thing by far here is the Chinese food. Why don't I order us a selection for the table and you can eat whatever takes your fancy?'

The dishes of prawns, pork and beef, in a variety of spicy and sweet-and-sour sauces, accompanied by rice, noodles and an array of exotic-looking vegetables, were as delicious as Stephenson had promised, and far better than any Chinese meal Saffron had eaten in London. When the waiter came to take their order for dessert, she opted for the hot fudge ice cream sundae.

'You don't want something Chinese?' asked Stephenson. 'Lychees, perhaps?'

'I'm sure they would be delicious,' Saffron said. 'But after two years of miserable rationing in England, and even worse overseas, there are absolutely no circumstances in which I'm turning down the chance of ice cream, whipped cream, chocolate, fudge and nuts, with a cherry on top.'

'Good for you.' Stephenson laughed.

The sundae, when it arrived, was a towering skyscraper of sweet, sticky, sickly self-indulgence.

'Five bucks says you can't finish it,' said Stackpole.

'Ha!' Saffron scoffed, polishing it off efficiently. Then, feeling full, happy, and only slightly bothered by the fear that she might at any moment burst out of her dress, she sat back to watch the Copa's floor show.

High-kicking showgirls in glittering costumes that revealed endless legs, taut stomachs and barely covered bosoms strutted onto the dance floor, so close to their table that Saffron could almost reach out and touch them. They were accompanied by male dancers dressed like characters from *The Arabian Nights*, with baggy pants, bare chests and turbans. Their routines were a cross between ballet and circus acrobatics, and Saffron found herself clapping and cheering along with the rest of the audience, entranced by the dazzle, energy and sheer glamour of the spectacle.

Then the dancers scampered away and a short, bespectacled, middle-aged man appeared. He picked up a microphone stand in front of the band and pulled it into the middle of the dance floor. He tapped the mic to make sure it was working and said, 'Ladies and gentlemen, we have a very special attraction tonight . . .'

It was all Saffron could do not to burst out laughing. The man had a broad northern English accent, the last thing she had expected to hear in this all-American setting. 'Who is that?' she whispered to Stephenson.

'Monte Proser, he manages the place.'

'Well, he sounds like George Formby.'

'There's a young man from Hoboken, New Jersey, who's been making quite a name for himself lately . . .' Proser continued.

There was a buzz around the room. Saffron looked around and saw the young women in the audience – and some of the younger men – had begun to chatter excitedly, smiles breaking out on their faces, while the much larger number of older patrons looked either as baffled as she felt, or distinctly unimpressed.

'He had an engagement at the Paramount Theatre a while back that caused quite a stir, and lately he's been entertaining America on the CBS Radio Show *Your Hit Parade*, presented by Lucky Strike.'

Somewhere behind Saffron, a woman gave a stifled scream.

'Well, he's about to play a series of concerts and he wanted to give his new routine a dress rehearsal, so I said he was welcome to do it right here. And so, without further ado, I'd like to introduce . . .' He paused to let the tension build. 'Mr Frank Sinatra!'

A young man wearing black tie and a dinner jacket that seemed too big for his skinny frame walked up to the microphone. He looked at the audience and gave a cheeky, boyish smile. Saffron was struck by the contrast between his dark, Italian hair and piercing blue eyes.

Stackpole leaned across and spoke in Saffron's ear. 'I heard all the high school girls are crazy for this guy. They scream the place down. People call 'em bobby-soxers. Not sure the Copa crowd's that impressed.'

'Good evening,' Sinatra said. 'It's great to be here . . . singing for an audience that's old enough to drive.'

The drummer hit a rim-shot; the audience laughed. Sinatra grinned again, knowing he'd broken the ice. He turned to the band. 'Okay, fellers, take it away.' The music began. And then something extraordinary happened. Sinatra looked like a skinny boy, but he sang in a rich, supremely masculine baritone that seemed as effortless and natural to him as breathing. He sang words of love and loss like a man who already knew everything about men, women, and the games they played with one another. And he didn't follow the music so much as toy with it, bouncing the words off the beat in a way Saffron had never heard before.

'Man, that cat's got jazz!' Stackpole exclaimed, sounding surprised and impressed, like everyone else in the audience. As the applause grew with every song, Sinatra's playful self-assurance blossomed, and by the end, Saffron was on her feet calling for an encore with the rest of the crowd. Sinatra obliged and, after giving his final bow, went over and took a chair at Costello's table. 'There's a young man with powerful friends,' Stephenson murmured darkly.

A moment later the band struck up a tune. It was one of the songs Sinatra had just sung: 'All Or Nothing At All'.

Stackpole looked at Saffron. 'May I have the pleasure?' He turned to Stephenson and added, 'If you don't mind, sir?'

'By all means.' Stephenson smiled.

Stackpole led Saffron onto the floor.

Saffron had not been sure what to expect from Clay Stackpole on the dance floor. Men of his height often found it hard to move their limbs with any elegance, let alone grace. She thought of all the young, gangly Englishmen with whom she'd danced before the war. They didn't lead her, so much as grab her and drag her after them.

Stackpole was different. He seemed at one with the rhythm of the band, just as Sinatra had been. He took charge of the dance, so that Saffron was relaxed in his arms, but he was always as conscious of her body and its movement as he was of his own, constantly adjusting his lead to her response. Saffron felt seen and appreciated, and that was as arousing as the smell of him and the strength she could feel in his arms. She felt sure that Stackpole would be equally good in bed, and the thought of what lay ahead, an hour or two from now, made her press her body even closer to his.

Out of the corner of her eye Saffron saw a man walking across the dance floor, pushing his way between the dancers, oblivious to their objections. He was massive – at least as tall as Stackpole – but more heavily built, thick-necked with gorilla shoulders, a belly that pushed at the buttons of his shirt, and suit trousers stretched tight by his tree-trunk thighs. The lights shining on the dance floor picked out the sheen of sweat on the man's fleshy jowls. A half-smoked cigar was clamped between his teeth, and as he bore down on them, Saffron could imagine the stench of him, all smoke, booze and stale sweat.

She had seen men like this before, strutting down Dutch and Belgian streets, their natural arrogance and bullying nature amplified by their uniforms and jackboots. She stiffened at the memory and Stackpole felt it. He looked at her with a concerned frown and spoke over the sound of the band. 'Are you all right?'

Saffron was about to warn Stackpole of the man's approach, when a meaty hand clamped itself around his arm. 'Beat it,' the man growled. 'This one's mine.'

Stackpole wrenched his arm free, letting go of Saffron as he did so. 'What the hell do you think you're—'

The punch came from nowhere – a right hook that sent Stackpole staggering backwards for a couple of paces until he stumbled into another couple and fell to the floor.

The man paid no attention. He put his arm around Saffron's waist and pulled her close against his bulk, so she could feel his arousal, then pinned her arms to her sides. His breath was even more noxious than she had expected as he mumbled obscenely in her ear: calling her a whore, a slut and a bitch, painting a graphic picture of what he intended to do to her. Then he opened his mouth wide and licked up the side of her face, from her jawline, across her cheek and over her ear.

For a second, Saffron felt as though she was back in The Hague. She was already on edge, imagining enemies lurking in every shadow on every street between the hotel and the club. Now she could feel her self-control slipping away as panic gripped her, but then suddenly her mind cleared, her focus returned, and her SOE training took over.

The next few movements were as choreographed as a chorus girl's routine.

Saffron stretched her trapped arms to grab the hem of her dress and yank the tight skirt a few inches up her thighs. The thug now seemed the embodiment of all the men who had ever tried to hurt her. He gave a grunt of satisfaction, thinking that she was playing along, and reached down to get his hand between her legs. The dress rode higher, exposing Saffron's legs further . . . and freeing them.

Saffron raised her right leg and then stamped down as hard as she could, focusing all the force of the impact through her high heel into the top of the man's left foot, feeling the bones break like dry twigs. Barely a second later, before the excruciating pain of the impact had even registered in her would-be rapist's brain, Saffron had driven her right knee up and slammed it into his testicles.

He doubled up. His head came down and Saffron met it with the heel of her right hand, hitting him hard on the underside of his chin, while the freshly filed and painted fingernails of her left clawed at his eyes.

She stepped back to avoid the man's wildly flailing arms. He was crouched over, groaning, hobbling on one foot, unable to see. Saffron dodged the punches, then stepped up close to him, pressed her fingers tight together and aimed a single hard chop with the edge of her hand at the man's exposed neck.

He dropped like a sack of wet cement and Saffron could feel the floor juddering beneath her feet. Stackpole was still down, but propped up on one elbow now, shaking his head to try and clear it. The band had stopped playing. But none of the other dancers had had time to react to the unexpected explosion of controlled but brutal violence.

From the moment when the man had licked Saffron's ear, to him hitting the deck, fewer than ten seconds had elapsed.

She stood over him for a second, catching her breath. Her training had taught her that a fight wasn't over until the assailant was definitively disabled – preferably dead. But this was a nightclub, not a battlefield. The man no longer posed an immediate threat to her.

Saffron looked at the men and women standing motionless around her. Now that the fight was over, no one seemed to know what to do. A sardonic flicker of a smile crossed Saffron's mouth as she imagined their predicament. When a slender young woman had beaten a man twice her size to a pulp, what was there to do or say? She walked over to Stackpole, who was getting groggily to his feet, thinking, *So much for tonight* and, *Memo to self – never wear a tight dress if there's the slightest chance of a fight.*

'How are you feeling?'

'Embarrassed,' he said. 'Got caught by a sucker punch.'

He ran a hand up the side of his face and moved his jaw from side to side.

'What's the diagnosis, doctor?' Saffron was looking into his eyes.

Stackpole gave a rueful smile. 'I'll live.'

Suddenly a camera flash went off. Saffron blinked to clear her vision and looked around. A man's voice said, 'Over here, siss!' Without thinking, she turned her head and the camera flashed again, catching her looking into the lens.

'Damn!' Saffron muttered. The last thing she wanted was her face all over the New York papers. A moment later she saw the photographer pulling the flashbulb from its mounting, with another to replace it already in the palm of his hand. She turned away, putting a hand up to deny him another view of her face, and saw Frank Costello gesturing towards another man who was standing at the bar. Costello jabbed a finger in the photographer's direction. The man nodded and began walking swiftly towards the photographer, who was now trying to make his getaway, darting between the tables towards the exit.

He looked like a slippery little ferret, used to scrapes like this, and Saffron was sure he'd manage to slip away before Costello's man could get to him. But just as he got to a pair of double doors leading out to the street, another of Costello's heavies appeared in front of him. He turned with what Saffron had to admit was impressive agility and started sprinting in the opposite direction, but he had barely taken ten paces when a forearm like a leg of mutton shot out in front of him, catching him neatly across the throat and sending him crashing to the floor. He lay there, gasping for breath, while one of Costello's men stomped on the camera he was still clutching in his hand. Someone in the audience yelled in appreciation and started clapping, and soon the whole audience was joining in, releasing the pent-up tension of the last sixty seconds in riotous applause.

Stackpole managed a battered smile. 'Just another quiet night at the Copa!'

As Stackpole dusted himself down, Saffron noticed that Stephenson was standing beside them.

'Sorry, sir,' she said. 'Shouldn't have caused such a fuss.'

'Don't worry. You had every right to defend yourself. Though perhaps you didn't need to be quite so thorough.'

'Of course, no, sir.'

Saffron glanced towards Costello's table and saw Sinatra's piercing eyes and that impish smile. She smiled back; it was impossible not to. And then she saw that Sinatra was pointing at her. *No, wait . . . he's pointing behind me.*

Saffron let go of Stackpole's hand and turned around.

The assailant she thought she had disabled was staggering towards her. He was limping, wincing in pain every time his left foot had to bear his weight, and still bleeding from the scratch marks her nails had left on his face. He was slightly stooped, too, one hand pressed to his aching groin. But there was no disguising the fury in his eyes or his implacable determination to get his revenge.

Stackpole tensed, ready to defend her.

Saffron held out an arm to stop him. 'I'll deal with this.'

She waited until the man was close enough to strike. *And this time I'll make sure he doesn't get up*, she thought to herself. But instead of trying to grab her, the man started to reach inside his jacket, and Saffron cursed herself for underestimating the threat he posed.

Her breath caught in her throat, but the man did not pull a gun from his jacket. Instead, he pulled out what looked like a black leather wallet. He held it out towards Saffron and flipped it open.

There was a badge inside, shaped like a sun with golden rays. She read the words CITY OF NEW YORK POLICE and beneath them, LIEUTENANT.

The man's voice was slurred with drink and the force of the blow that Saffron had landed on his chin, but the words were clear enough. 'Yer under arrest . . . assaultin' a police officer.'

He gestured with his other hand. 'Hands toward me, together.' And as he pulled his cuffs from his back pocket, he leaned into Saffron's face, and said, 'I'm gonna make you pay, bitch. You hear me? I am gonna make you pay.'

There was a moment of silence, followed by a burst of chatter mixed with boos and shouts of protest. Saffron heard a man call out, 'Leave the dame alone!' and the woman beside him added, 'You attacked her, you bully!'

She looked round and saw that Sinatra's seat at Costello's table was empty. *He must have slipped out while everyone was distracted*, Saffron thought. His presence at the club would be enough to make the fight a story. She was not surprised that he didn't wish to make the news for the wrong reasons if he could avoid it.

Then Saffron noticed that Sinatra was not the only character in the drama to have left the scene. Walter Winchell had made his exit, too. She winced. It was one thing making a spectacle of herself in front of the gossips at the Copa, but if Winchell's boasts were to be believed, he gossiped to the whole of America. *Gubbins told me not to get involved in rough stuff and not to cause trouble, and I've done both*, Saffron chided herself.

She thought for a second. *No, this doesn't have to be a problem. Winchell has no idea who I really am. Thanks to Stephenson, he's only got the name Jane Smith. And Costello made sure there were no photos. With any luck, it will blow over and no one need know it was me.*

Costello, meanwhile, was taking charge. 'Proser, get this show back on the road. Start up the band, hand out free drinks, whatever it takes. Now, let's go talk about this somewhere quieter.'

'The hell we will,' the cop growled. 'This woman's coming with me.'

'You gotta be kidding, O'Bannon,' Costello replied.

Oh, so he knows him, thought Saffron. Then: *a policeman, in his club – of course he knows him.*

'You walk her from here to the exit, you'll start a riot,' Costello said. 'Come with me, we'll get this sorted nice and peaceful.'

O'Bannon glared at Costello's two silk-suited heavies. 'Okay, but those goons ain't comin' with you. I don't want no funny business.'

'You think I'd try something? Seriously?' Costello asked, sounding genuinely amazed. 'What, I don't know you belong to Vinnie Mangano? I ain't looking to start a fight with him.'

O'Bannon shrugged and grunted. 'Okay . . . but I'm cuffing her first.'

Costello rolled his eyes. 'Suit yourself.'

O'Bannon held up the pair of handcuffs. Saffron put out her hands and he snapped the cuffs shut around her wrists.

Costello's two men led the way towards a pair of swing doors at the back of the club, keeping the Copa's clientele at bay, followed by Costello, O'Bannon and Saffron, with Proser, Stephenson and Stackpole following behind them. The mood of the crowd had quietened, anger giving way to curiosity.

'This way,' Costello said, as they went through the door into a kitchen that was almost as big as the club itself, filled with busy chefs.

Stackpole kept close to Saffron as O'Bannon prodded her forward.

'How is it?' she asked, seeing Stackpole prodding the side of his face and moving his jaw.

Stackpole grimaced. 'I don't think anything's broken.' He glanced at O'Bannon. 'Can't say the same for him.'

'At least one severely fractured metatarsal,' Saffron said. 'Possibly more. Assuming I did it properly.'

'Can it, you two,' O'Bannon growled, still trying to play the tough guy.

Costello led them into a private office and leaned against the front of the desk. Behind him, the walls were covered with autographed photos of celebrities.

Saffron found herself in the middle of the room opposite O'Bannon. The other men were in a rough circle around them. Stephenson lurked unobtrusively in the background.

'Hey, Proser, you keep any booze in here?' Costello asked.

'Sure, Frank, in the cabinet. I can fix you anything you want.'

'Make it Scotches all round.' Costello looked around. 'That okay with you gentlemen?'

There were murmurs of agreement. 'How about you, sweetheart?' Costello asked Saffron.

'I'll take it straight, no ice, no water,' she said. The adrenaline rush from the fight was giving way to an edgy, unstable sensation, like a skidding car on an icy road. Flashes of memory were flickering in her mind – O'Bannon grinding himself against her, his words in her ear, his tongue against her cheek; Schröder in The Hague; the motorbike rider in his hotel uniform, grinning at her from the far end of the corridor – a jumble of images, past and present, all at the same time.

'The hell you will, bitch,' O'Bannon said, taking a step towards her and then wincing as he put weight on his injured foot.

'For Chrissakes, O'Bannon, give us all a goddamn break,' Costello said.

'Shut your guinea mouth, Costello. I'm taking her in.' The words were muttered more than spoken, but Saffron could see from the look of pure hatred on O'Bannon's face that he wasn't going to be satisfied until he'd paid her back in full for humiliating him.

'Are you kidding me?' asked Costello, incredulously. 'How many times were you the heavyweight champ of the NYPD? Three, was it?'

'Four . . . undefeated.' O'Bannon was talking to Costello, but his eyes were fixed on Saffron, running up and down her body, mentally stripping her.

'And now you're going to go back to the precinct house, looking like you just got run over by a truck, and you're gonna tell the guys there that some dame did that to you?'

'Sure I'm going to take this frickin' slut back to the station. Then I'm going to stick her in a cell, by herself, no one else around. Then I'm going to wait a while, till it's all nice and quiet. Then me and my buddies are going to go in there with our nightsticks and—'

Before O'Bannon could finish his sentence, Saffron closed the distance between them and stamped on his wounded left foot for a second time. As he bent double, howling in pain, she batted aside Stephenson's arm as he reached out to try and restrain her, then looped the chain of her cuffs around O'Bannon's neck while kicking the back of his standing knee. As he started to fall, she took a sharp step backwards, pulling the chain tighter in a vicious chokehold. As she listened to

O'Bannon's frantic gurgling as he fought to breathe, she could hear raised male voices, but they seemed to be coming from far away and she could make no sense of what they were saying. She only had one thought in her mind: to kill the man who had threatened to rape her.

Suddenly there were hands on her, grabbing her around the waist, forcing her arms up and over O'Bannon's head, then pulling her away from him. The red mist slowly cleared from Saffron's head, and as O'Bannon floundered on the floor like a fish on a trawler's deck, she became aware once more of her surroundings and the other people in the room.

A muffled voice was saying, 'Saffron . . . Saffron . . . Look at me.' She realised it belonged to Clay Stackpole. He was looking into her eyes, with a shocked expression on his face.

'Can you hear me?' he asked.

Saffron nodded.

'Okay, that's good. You almost killed him just now, you know that?'

She nodded again.

'Not that any of us would have blamed you, but, still . . .'

Stephenson handed her a large glass of whisky. 'Drink it,' he said. 'That's an order.'

Saffron nodded, took the glass and drank, closing her eyes as she felt the warmth of the alcohol spreading through her, calming her. She brought her breathing under control, keeping it slow and steady. 'Thanks,' she said, handing the half-empty glass back to Stephenson.

O'Bannon was struggling to get back on his feet.

Costello looked at his two men. 'Hold him. Get his keys.'

One of the men hauled O'Bannon up while the other patted him down and extracted a bunch of keys from a trouser pocket. He unlocked the cuffs.

'Thanks,' Saffron said, rubbing her wrists.

'You goddamn wop greaseballs,' O'Bannon croaked, trying to summon some vestige of authority. 'You'll be sorry for this.'

'Trust me, O'Bannon,' said Costello, 'I ain't the one with the problem. You think Mangano's gonna be happy when he opens the newspaper tomorrow morning and reads Winchell's column, all about how his pet flatfoot, the famous boxer, got his ass handed to him by a dame in front of half of New York? And then some wise guy tells him, "Yeah, boss, then she whipped O'Bannon a second time, even after he'd cuffed her!"

'You know how it is, Lieutenant. If you look bad, Mangano looks bad. If you get laughed at, he gets laughed at. And let me tell you, Vincenzo Giovanni Mangano is not a man who likes being laughed at. Not one little bit.'

Costello paused and then casually added, 'They don't call him "the Executioner" for nothin'.'

There was real fear on O'Bannon's face now, as well as pain, but he tried not to show it. 'Kill a cop? Are you kidding me? He knows the rules, same as you do.'

Costello shrugged. 'You better hope so . . .' Then he nodded at the man holding O'Bannon. 'Let him go.'

O'Bannon stumbled forward, placed his weight on his left foot and fell to the floor again, crying in pain as he did so.

'Here, let me have a look,' Stackpole said. 'I'm a doctor, and broken bones are my specialty.'

'Get away from me,' O'Bannon growled.

Their evening together might have just ended in disaster, but something important about Stackpole suddenly became clear to Saffron. O'Bannon, who had hit Stackpole with a cowardly sucker punch, was feeling sorry for himself. Stackpole, who had taken the punch, was trying to help him. That was the difference between a bullying braggart and a real man.

'Listen, Lieutenant,' Stackpole said forcefully. 'You need to go to an emergency room right now, before your foot swells up so bad they'll have to cut your shoe off.'

'Okay . . . okay . . .' O'Bannon conceded, his spirit broken. A taxi was ordered, with instructions to go to the club's service entrance. A burly sous-chef was assigned to help O'Bannon make his way across the kitchen.

Back in the office, Saffron was rubbing her wrists where the cuffs had chafed them and thinking about the second attack on O'Bannon. She knew now that what triggered her rages was not dark water, sudden noises, or any other form of unconscious stimulus. The trigger was vile, bullying men trying to rape her. And what happened next was that the men got what was coming to them. *I can live with that*, she thought. *Case closed.*

'Time we were on our way,' Stephenson said, clearly including Saffron in the 'we'.

'Thank you, Mr Costello,' she said. 'You helped me out of a very tight spot.'

'My pleasure,' he said, then he gave a rueful smile and added, 'You know, we were never formally introduced.'

'Saffron Courtney,' she said, extending her hand.

Costello bent his head, lightly kissed the proffered hand, then said, 'It's been a pleasure to meet you, Miss Courtney. And before you go, let me do you another favour. See, I guess you figured by now that that bastard O'Bannon is a dirty cop. In fact, he's a treacherous, two-faced snake. So to see you give him what he had coming . . . Well, that made my day. And I'll get a kick outta breaking Vinnie Mangano's balls, too, next time I see him. Now, here's what I'm going to do . . .'

Costello reached into his jacket and extracted a slim, black leather notebook and a gold pen. He opened the book, wrote something, tore out the page and handed it to Saffron.

'That's a telephone number,' he said. 'It's like . . . Who's the kid with the genie and the magic lamp?'

'Aladdin,' said Proser.

'Right, Aladdin. So this number is like that magic lamp. If you ever get in trouble, any time of day or night, anywhere in the country, you dial it. You tell the guy on the other end, Uncle Frank said you should call. You say you're his niece, Saffron. Then you tell him all about your trouble. And, hey presto! That trouble will magically go away.'

'Goodness,' said Saffron. Out of the corner of her eye she could see Stephenson. He was paying close attention to what Costello was saying. But he made no attempt to interfere. *He's as curious about this as I am*, she thought. *I wonder if he wants a magic lamp, too.*

'Now listen up,' Costello continued. 'If you call that number, whatever you want, you get. That's my gift to you, like a thank you for making my day. But you should know that you will then be in my debt. And one day, I may call on you, and ask you to perform a service of some kind for me. You understand what I'm saying?'

'Perfectly,' Saffron replied.

'You still want the number?'

'Please.'

Costello looked at Saffron, assessing her, but in a way that made it clear that his interest was entirely professional. He gave an appreciative nod. 'You are one dangerous lady. Whoever you are.'

Saffron looked back at him with her sweetest smile, feeling much better now. 'Yes,' she replied, 'I know.'

'Do you need a ride?' Stephenson asked. He, Saffron and Stackpole had been escorted to the service exit and out onto East 60th Street, where the Packard limousine was waiting.

'No, thank you,' Saffron said. 'I can walk back to the St. Regis.'

'Don't worry, sir, I'll escort her,' Stackpole said.

'I think we both know that she'll be looking after you,' Stephenson said, with a dry smile. He looked at Saffron. 'The Congressional express to Washington leaves Pennsylvania Station at six thirty in the morning, arriving in DC shortly before midday. Dalton will pick you up from the hotel at six. He will have your ticket. And wear your uniform. If the embassy sends someone to meet you, it will help them spot you.'

'Yes, sir,' Saffron said.

'Goodbye, then . . . for now.'

'Thank you, sir, for everything. And please thank Mary for me, too.'

'Of course . . . Have a good time in Washington.' He smiled, and added, 'Let me know how you're getting on, and if there's anything I can do . . .'

'Thank you, sir.'

Saffron watched the long black car drive away. Stackpole took her arm and they began walking down Fifth Avenue towards the St.Regis. He hadn't uttered a word of complaint all evening, but looking up at him, Saffron saw the tension in his face, and could only imagine the effort he was making to keep the pain at bay. As they came to the end of the block, she saw the sign of an all-night drugstore on 59th Street.

'Let's get something to make you feel a bit better,' Saffron said, and the fact that Stackpole didn't protest told her how much he was hurting.

Stackpole bought a bottle of codeine tablets and dropped two of them into his palm. 'You got any water I can wash 'em down with?' he asked the man behind the counter.

'No. But give me a nickel and you can have a bottle of Coke.'

Stackpole bought the drink, swallowed the tablets, then handed the bottle back to the storekeeper. 'Here, have the rest on me.'

He took Saffron's arm and they walked out onto the street.

'This wasn't how I imagined the evening ending,' he said.

Saffron snuggled closer to him. 'It doesn't have to end like this.'

'Oh, I don't want it to end, believe me. But that damn punch . . .' He shook his head.

'But you're still in one piece from the neck down?'

'Uh-huh.'

Saffron discreetly ran her hand across the front of Stackpole's trousers and giggled. 'So you are.'

'Oh yeah, the flesh is willing . . . most of it, anyways.'

Saffron was suddenly aware that she didn't just want Stackpole; she needed him, just to remind her that sex didn't have to be an act of abuse. It could be her choice, her desire, her joy. It could be fun.

'Well, I can see the problem,' she said, adopting a more businesslike tone. 'I would imagine that if you were to engage in, ah . . . vigorous movements of the lower limbs and torso, that would send pain shooting through the affected area.'

'Exactly so, Miss Courtney,' Stackpole replied, with equally exaggerated formality. 'And I confess, I have yet to think of a satisfactory solution.'

They had reached the steps leading up to the entrance of the St. Regis. 'Well, Dr Stackpole, I think I may have the answer to all your difficulties, if you will allow me to demonstrate . . . upstairs.'

'Sure.' Stackpole was showing signs of returning to his normal self. 'Lead the way.'

As they reached the top of the steps, the background noise of the traffic on Fifth Avenue was pierced by the squeal of brakes, the revving of an engine and a voice shouting, 'Watch where ya goin', ya lousy bum!'

Saffron turned her head and saw a motorbike racing away down the avenue, but she was too wrapped up in Stackpole to give it much thought. 'Typical New York!' she laughed, and walked with him into the hotel.

Barely a minute later, Saffron was unlocking the door to her suite.

'Holy moly . . .' Stackpole gasped as she led him down the inner hall to the living room. 'This isn't a hotel room. It's a goddamn palace.'

'Is it bigger than the hotel rooms in Texas?' she teased.

'Bigger'n any I ever walked into, that's for sure.'

'This is only part of it. I have a private dining room and . . .' She opened another door. 'A nice bedroom, too.'

'Not too shabby . . .' Stackpole agreed. 'So, is this where you plan to give your demonstration?'

'It is indeed, but first . . .' Saffron stood on tiptoe and kissed the bruised side of Stackpole's face.

'That helps,' he murmured. His voice was thick, his breathing heavier.

'Then I'll increase the dose.' She kissed him again, just below the first one, and then twice along his jaw, getting closer to his mouth until the next kiss was on his lips.

Stackpole grabbed her. His arms were around her waist, and as he pulled her tight against him, her fit, strong body suddenly seemed so fluid and insubstantial that, for the first time in her life, she felt her knees go weak as she lost herself in his kiss.

'Shit!' Stackpole jerked back, one hand up to his jaw, gasping in pain.

'Oh, my God, did I hurt you?' she asked.

'No . . . I just moved my jaw and . . . God damn! I swear, if I ever see that bastard O'Bannon again, I'll finish the job you started.' Stackpole looked at Saffron with pained, unhappy eyes and said, 'I guess it wasn't such a great solution after all, huh?'

Saffron raised a hand to his face. 'I'm sorry . . . I just got greedy and couldn't wait.'

He smiled. 'Baby, don't apologise . . . I wanted to kiss you from the moment I set eyes on you.'

'Well, I still have my answer to our problem . . . if you can face another try.'

'I'm willing to give it a go,' he said.

'All right, then. Since you still have the use of your hands . . .' Saffron spun round so that her back was facing him and added, 'Can you help me out of my dress?'

'You mean, like this?' Stackpole asked, slowly undoing the zip.

'Exactly.' Saffron stepped out of the dress and turned to face Stackpole in her black heels, stockings and silk lingerie. Without taking her eyes off him, she removed them, too.

'Whoa . . .' he sighed, his breath quickening at the sight of her.

'Now why don't I do the same for you?' Saffron helped Stackpole out of his clothes, her movements quickly becoming faster and rougher, her pulse racing as the feel of him beneath her fingers increased her desire.

Stackpole was built the way Saffron liked: broad shoulders, narrow waist and hips. He was lean and well-muscled, but not pumped-up. He had strong thighs and forearms, but his fingers were surprisingly long and slim: the hands of a pianist. *Or a surgeon*, she thought, longing for their touch on her body.

'All right,' she said, taking Stackpole's hand. She had to fight to restrain the urge to throw herself at him as she led him to the king-size bed. She pulled back the bedclothes and, wanting any excuse to bring their two bodies together, pressed close enough to murmur in his ear, 'Now, lie on your back.'

He gave her a crooked smile. 'Isn't that your job?'

'Mmm . . . but you're an invalid, so do what you're told.'

'Yes, ma'am.'

Stackpole lay down and put his perfect figure on display. That he was a man in the prime of his life was unmissably evident, and yet there was something about his vulnerability that added a surprising tenderness to the raw desire coursing through every cell of Saffron's body.

She got up onto the bed and straddled Stackpole, allowing herself a couple of seconds to look at him before putting her hands on his shoulders to support herself as she leaned forward, slowly lowering her body onto his. Grinding her hips and moaning softly, she gasped at the sweet shock of the touch of her nipples on his chest. Then she kissed him and whispered, 'Just lie back and enjoy the ride. I can take it from here . . .'

• • •

On the corner of Fifth and 42nd, Petrauskas was dialling Meyer's home number. He'd figured that a great-looking woman, staying in a swanky hotel, would have a hot date who'd take her somewhere fancy. He'd put on his only smart suit – the one he wore at weddings and funerals. Then he'd taken a couple of fat, fifty-cent Cuban cigars from a box that he'd picked up at the docks when a crate that came in from Havana 'went missing' one day, and put them in the top pocket of his jacket.

When he walked up to the Copa, the gift of those two cigars got Petrauskas past the doorman and into the joint. He'd been watching from the bar when the fight broke out, and the dame he'd been tailing, who looked like she'd never had to lift a finger in her life, beat the bejesus out of a guy twice her size, who turned out to be a cop. So when his call was answered, he said, 'Listen up, Mr M, 'cause, man, have I got a story for you.'

• • •

Saffron woke at five in the morning after three hours' sleep. She kissed Stackpole's sleeping face, rubbed her eyes, stifled a yawn, then pulled on a hotel dressing gown and went into the drawing room. She used the telephone to order coffee and breakfast for two. It crossed her mind that the hotel might be scandalised by the thought of an unmarried woman sharing her room with a man, then she told herself not to be so silly. What was the point of grand hotels, if not to use them for wild romantic flings?

She closed her eyes for a moment, and her mind instantly went back to the first time they had made love. She gasped at a memory so intense that for a moment she could still feel him inside her. *What a wonderful way to start the day!* she thought, then went to the bedroom. She sat on the side of the bed and brushed a stray lock of hair from Stackpole's face. His poor, battered jaw looked much worse than it had done the night before. Saffron kissed the swollen skin, now a vivid palette of purples, blues and black. She gently shook his shoulder, and when Stackpole gave a grunt in response, said, 'Wake up, sleepyhead. It's time to get moving.'

Stackpole had taken some more codeine before they went to sleep, and the bottle was sitting on the bedside table beside a glass of water. Saffron tapped two more tablets onto her palm and handed them to him, followed by the water.

'Breakfast of champions,' Stackpole muttered.

'I've got a real breakfast on the way,' Saffron said, enjoying the feeling of looking after her man and thinking of everything he might need. 'Give me a few minutes to wash and do my face, then the bathroom's all yours.'

Saffron had grown up drinking Kenyan coffee from her father's estate, and had never found anything to match it anywhere else in the world. But the silver jug of java she shared with Stackpole, as they feasted on scrambled eggs and crisp bacon, was fragrant and delicious. *Or maybe it's the company that makes it taste so good.*

They went downstairs at 05.55. Saffron checked out, and as they left the hotel, there was the indefatigable Dalton standing by the Packard to greet them.

At Penn station, Dalton found a porter to take Saffron's luggage to the train. Spring sunshine poured through the great arches of the glass and cast-iron roof as she and Stackpole walked across the vast station concourse. It was quiet. The crowds of office workers who would come pouring into the city from the suburbs would still be at home having breakfast. But there were serious men in business suits, and servicemen in uniform looking purposeful as they, too, marched to the train that would take them to the nation's capital. And when Stackpole led Saffron through Gate 14 and down to the platforms that stretched beneath the city streets, there were other couples, like them, saying their farewells, though in every other case, it seemed to be the man who was getting aboard the train and the woman who was being left behind.

Saffron had been hoping that the train might have been delayed, that she might have a little more time with Stackpole, but there was the porter, lingering for a tip and saying, 'You'd better get aboard, miss, she'll be on the way real soon.'

'I suppose I'd better say goodbye,' she said, blinking away a tear and clinging to Stackpole, not wanting to let go. 'I'll never forget last night.'

'Me neither,' he said, running a hand over his livid face.

Saffron gave a laugh. 'No . . . I suppose not. I hope you feel better soon.'

'Oh, my ugly mug will mend. Not so sure about my heart.'

'Darling, don't . . .' she said, so softly that he could barely hear her. 'We can't think that way. We mustn't . . .'

He nodded. 'No . . . I guess not.' He managed a smile. 'Maybe the song is right, and we'll meet again. It's a big world . . . but it's a small war sometimes. You never know who you're going to bump into.'

'Oh, darling, I hope I bump into you again one day.' Saffron heard the guard's whistle blow and knew that she had no choice but to step aboard. As the train moved off, she made her way along the rattling carriages until she came to her reserved seat. She sat down, gave a polite smile to the plump, late-middle-aged woman sitting opposite her and dabbed the last tears from her eyes.

A few minutes later, the train emerged from the tunnel that had taken it under the Hudson and started across a flat, swampy wasteland, marked only by battered old advertising hoardings and piles of scrap metal. The contrast between this barren desolation and the energy, bustle and glamour of the city felt like a sharp jolt of reality after the romantic fantasy of the past few hours. *You've had your fun*, Saffron told herself. *Now get a couple of hours' rest, then go back to work.*

She closed her eyes and was on the point of falling asleep when a memory, emerging dream-like from her subconscious, jerked her wide awake.

That motorbike, racing away down Fifth just as she and Stackpole had walked into the St. Regis – she'd seen it before. It was the same bike, and presumably the same rider, that had overtaken the Packard on the East River Drive. He'd given her a wolf whistle outside the hotel. He'd wanted her to know he was around two days earlier; she was sure he'd been in her hotel room, and he'd done his best to make her turn around and spot him last night.

Saffron suddenly wondered if he was the only man who'd been following her.

She ran her mind over her brief stay in New York. There had been a balding, middle-aged man in a cheap raincoat who'd bumped into her at the perfume counter, the ladies' lingerie racks and the luggage department of Saks.

'You seem to have an admirer,' Mary Stephenson had said, after the man nervously blurted, 'Oh . . . we meet again!' before scurrying away between the steamer trunks and weekend bags.

'Maybe he's following me!' Saffron had laughed. Because the idea was absurd. The only people who knew she was in the city were on the same side as her. *Unless there is a spy in the embassy, and he's found out and tipped off . . . well . . . who?*

And if the young man on the bike and the older man in Saks had been following her, why had they made a point of advertising their presence . . . and then not done anything? That wasn't the Nazi style. In Saffron's experience, the SS didn't fool around. They came after their targets and neutralised them with brisk and brutal efficiency.

But that's when they're on home turf. Maybe they can't do that here, in America. Maybe they're simply letting me know they've got their eyes on me.

Saffron considered it further and then smiled to herself. *Or maybe I'm just tired, and my brain has been turned to mush by a very late night.*

The only things she could be sure of were that her primary mission to Washington – gathering support for SOE – was not reason enough for German intelligence to put a tail on her. And while her secondary mission – to discover the identity of the spy in the British embassy, if such a person existed – might attract enemy interest, she had received her instructions less than twenty-four hours earlier, and only she and Stephenson knew about it.

Saffron was aware that the Abwehr had acquired advance knowledge of all SOE's operations in the Low Countries. But they had done that by breaking British codes and decrypting SOE's radio traffic. The discussion between her and Stephenson had been face to face, in private. No one else knew what had been said. Therefore no one else could act upon it.

Saffron went through her reasoning once more and could find no fault with it. She checked the time. There were more than five hours of the journey to go. If she could sleep for three of them, then spend the rest of the time refining what she was going to say to influential Americans, she might be of use to SOE by the time she arrived in Washington.

• • •

'Have you read Meyer's report from New York? Remarkable, is it not?' Preminger said, as he and Hertz talked over coffee and cigarettes at a cafe on Unter den Linden. This stretch of Berlin's most famous thoroughfare was as yet untouched by Allied bombs. Not far away, three Luftwaffe officers had stopped to talk to a couple of young women who had caught their eye. An old lady walked by with a string shopping bag filled with brown paper parcels of food. A nanny was telling her young charges to behave themselves while they scampered around her. One might almost forget there was a war on.

'I know – extraordinary,' Hertz agreed. 'This Courtney woman is given a suite at one of the most expensive hotels in New York, at a time when the British are short of US dollars. She spends the morning in Stephenson's office, then dedicates the rest of her day to shopping and self-beautification, before meeting some unknown American army air force officer. He takes her to a sleazy nightclub, run by gangsters and Jews, where she gets into a drunken brawl before spending the night with this officer in her hotel room . . . and yet . . .'

'Yes?' said Preminger as Hertz took a sip of coffee.

'I am beginning to think that she really might be Schröder's killer.'

'No, surely not. How could someone capable of living for months undercover, without once giving herself away, now behave with such total lack of self-control?'

'Well, she might have been traumatised, just as we said. And our plan to destabilise her might be working. And my people might have uncovered some very interesting evidence.'

'Ah, you sly dog, keeping that under your hat. Come on, then, out with it.'

'Well, as you know, the investigation into Schröder's death was carried out by members of the Berlin Murder Squad, the finest homicide detectives in the world, under the leadership of Kommissar Wilhelm Lüdtke. They established that the woman who killed Schröder was using the alias Marlize Marais, and had entered Belgium barely two months earlier, using papers issued by the Reich consulate in Lisbon. She claimed to be a South African whose father had lost all his money at the hands of the Jews. But what the police did not know, since Saffron Courtney was not a suspect, is that the Courtney family have been prominent in South Africa, as well as the British colonies of Rhodesia and Kenya, for several decades. Saffron Courtney herself was born in Kenya, but was educated partly in South Africa. She has close family members who are involved with security matters in that country, who could have helped her infiltrate organisations there, that are sympathetic to our cause. And finally, when members of those organisations were asked about Miss Marais, they said that she had made herself known, out of the blue, little more than a month before she appeared in Lisbon. Now, I have not yet established that Saffron Courtney was in South Africa over the Christmas and New Year period, but that should be possible to determine. And if it is . . .'

'The case is closed,' said Preminger with alacrity. 'My sincere congratulations, Hertz . . . Huh! Isn't it remarkable how a case that seems insoluble can be cracked open by a tiny, random event? A man sends a message so innocuous that he sees no reason to encrypt it . . . and suddenly we have our breakthrough.'

'So now it only remains to make that final connection.'

'Yes, and in the meantime, we in Section D have a good man in Washington – one of our best. I suggest we put him on to the case, while we wait for our superiors to decide what to do about Fräulein Courtney.'

'Oh . . .' Hertz smiled. 'I think we both know what that decision will be.'

• • •

Stephenson had been right about the uniform. Saffron was halfway across the crowded concourse at Washington Union station, trailed by a porter pushing her cases on his trolley, when she heard a well-bred English voice say, 'Miss Courtney, is that you?'

The voice belonged to a small, thin woman. Her hair was neatly set, her clothes were well made, but she conveyed an air of disappointment – even bitterness. Saffron could see it in her face, which might once have been pretty, but was now rendered plain by her tightly pursed, slightly downturned lips, her drawn, sunken cheeks and the heavy bags beneath her eyes.

Saffron doubted that the woman was past thirty, but she already looked like an old maid. *Don't be cruel*, she told herself. *Make an effort to like her. She won't tell you anything if you don't.*

She smiled brightly and answered, 'That's right.' A little laugh, then, 'How on earth did you know?'

The woman managed a hint of a smile in return and said, 'I was told to look out for a tall Auxiliary Territorial Service girl with dark hair and lots of luggage. You fit the bill to a T.'

'I suppose I do,' Saffron said, with another ice-breaking laugh. She held out her hand and said, 'I'm Saffron.'

'Millicent James,' the woman said, as they shook hands. 'I'm Lady Halifax's personal assistant. She apologises for not being here to meet you herself, but there's a bit of a flap on at the embassy.'

'Yes, I was on the *Queen Mary* with Mr Churchill. His arrival must have caused quite a stir!'

'Yes, well, that's just the half of it,' Millicent said, and before Saffron could ask what the other half might be, she added a brisk, 'Now, let's get you to my car.'

Millicent set off towards the middle of the three huge arches that led arriving travellers into the nation's capital. As she walked beside her, Saffron looked up at the barrel-vaulted roof that soared above them, as high as the nave of a great cathedral, covered in an intricate pattern of recessed, octagonal stone panels. 'Isn't it a magnificent building?' she said.

'Yes, I suppose it is,' Millicent replied, briefly coming to a halt, not to admire the view but to upbraid the porter, who had been trying to navigate Saffron's baggage through crowds of travellers rushing to and fro, with an irritated, 'Do please try to keep up!'

As Millicent began walking again, Saffron gave the porter an apologetic shrug. He rolled his eyes, and they exchanged grins before heading off in pursuit of Millicent.

'I heard that Lady Halifax was asking for someone willing to put me up,' Saffron said, once she'd caught up. 'Did she find any takers?'

'Yes, she did, as a matter of fact,' Millicent replied. 'Charlie and Mavis Playfair. Quite surprising takers, really, because he's going to be working like a mad thing for the next couple of weeks, and she's constantly off doing good deeds for charity. But they're certainly one of the more interesting couples you could be billeted with.'

'How intriguing!' said Saffron as they walked between a line of classical columns, passed under an arch and emerged onto a large, open plaza. A couple of electric trolley cars had stopped outside the station, and new arrivals were leaving them as those about to depart waited to climb aboard. In the distance, Saffron could see the dome of the Capitol Building. Despite everything she had told herself on the train, she stopped and looked around, scanning her surroundings for anyone who might look out of place, or make a show of their presence, as they had in New York.

'Is something the matter?' Millicent asked.

'No . . . sorry,' Saffron said, trying to put the idea of someone following her out of her mind. But it kept gnawing at her – the thought that someone, somewhere, wanted to know where she was and what she was doing. Or – which was worse – that they knew exactly what she was doing, and were now working out how to stop her.

Saffron gave Millicent her best carefree smile. 'Do tell me more about the Playfairs.'

'Well, now . . .' Millicent began, marching towards the cars parked in a circle around a large, white marble fountain at the centre of the plaza. 'Charlie is the Honourable Charles

Algernon Faversham Playfair, second son of Gerald, the fifth Earl of Charlton, although he always insists that he hates all that kind of palaver. He's a great one for left-wing politics, is Charlie, although, as you will discover, he still acts like the lord of the manor.'

'What's Charlie's job at the embassy?' Saffron asked.

'He's the political counsellor, which is the third most senior post, after Lord Halifax and the deputy head of mission, and he's not yet forty.' Millicent paused for a moment, as if flicking through some mental filing cabinet, and added, 'Thirty-eight, if I recall correctly. Amongst Charlie's many blessings, he is one of that lucky generation of men who were too young to be called up for the first war, and too old for the second.'

'Perhaps he's of more use as a diplomat than a soldier,' Saffron suggested.

'Very possibly,' Millicent replied, making it sound like a criticism. 'Still, he's undeniably the cleverest of all our people here, and he knows it. He also has most of the embassy typing pool, with whom I am obliged to share an office, drooling over his dashing good looks.'

'Does he know that, too?'

'Oh, yes, and exploits it ruthlessly whenever he wants something done. Mind you, I'm not sure how long Charlie's looks will last, given his alcohol consumption. Too much whisky and too many cigarettes can ruin the handsomest face. Don't you agree?'

'I suppose so,' Saffron said, 'although I can see why a man like that would seem tremendously glamorous.' Millicent clearly had a sharp eye and an even sharper tongue. That made her a potential source of useful information. But it also meant that Saffron had to be on her guard. Those beady eyes and attentive ears would also be directed at her. 'I can only imagine what Mavis must be like.'

'I very much doubt that,' Millicent replied.

'Why ever not?'

'Well, are you imagining some brilliant society beauty, with the looks and brains to capture a filthy rich aristocrat who's odds-on to be an ambassador before he's fifty?'

'Something like that, I suppose.'

'Well, think again. Our Mavis comes from Nottinghamshire. She's the only child of a coalminer and a woman who doled out the dinners in the local junior school. She's pretty, in a mousy sort of way, but you'd never know it because she's far too busy doing good in the slums of Washington to worry about her appearance.'

They had reached the car. Much like Millicent, it had seen better days. 'You can put the cases on the back seat,' Millicent told the porter.

Saffron opened her shoulder bag, pulled out her purse and gave the porter a dollar. 'Thank you kindly, ma'am.' The man touched his cap and gave her a smile, before turning his trolley around and heading back to the station.

'Ten cents would have been quite sufficient,' said Millicent as they got into the car.

'Well, the cases were heavy and he brought them all the way out here.' Saffron smiled. 'So how did Charlie and Mavis meet?'

'In Spain, during the Civil War. Charlie was posted to Madrid, where he made quite a name for himself at the Foreign Office by haring off to various battlefronts and sending dispatches back to London that were better than anything any war reporter was coming up with. He also spent some time with George Orwell – you know, that lefty writer. As I understand it, they were both King's Scholars at Eton, only a year or two apart, so they knew each other quite well, and of course Orwell was out in Spain, too, fighting for the communists.'

'I thought *Homage to Catalonia* was a wonderful book,' said Saffron, fighting back the temptation to point out that Orwell's experiences in Spain had left him bitterly opposed to communism and its dictatorial tendencies. 'My politics tutor at university was a tremendous admirer of Orwell. When he heard I didn't grow up in England . . . Kenya, before you ask . . .'

This time, Millicent's smile was a little warmer. 'I was just about to!'

'Well, my tutor said that if I wanted to understand the condition of the British working class, I should read *The Road to Wigan Pier*, and if I wanted to understand the condition of the Left, I should read *Homage to Catalonia*.'

'I haven't read it myself,' Millicent said. 'So, do tell me, does an idealistic working-class grammar school girl called Mavis Perkins, who got herself into Cambridge before running off to Spain and working as a nursing orderly in Barcelona, feature in it anywhere?'

'Not that I recall.'

'Well, that's what Mavis did. And she must have known Orwell, because the story goes that he introduced her to Charlie and the two of them fell madly in love right there and then.'

'It must have been wildly romantic . . . you know, a magnificent city, on the shores of the Med, in the middle of a war. Not that I've ever been to Barcelona, but I spent the first two years of this show in Cairo, with occasional trips to Alexandria, and then I was in Athens and Jerusalem for a bit . . . so I can imagine.'

'And did you fall madly in love?' Millicent asked.

'I wish! Unfortunately, I was too busy driving a general about the place for that kind of thing. But tell me more about Mavis. She can't be that mousy, if she had the gumption to win a place at Cambridge, let alone make a man like Charles Playfair want to marry her. And going off into the slums of Washington must take a certain amount of bravery.'

'I dare say.' Millicent sniffed dismissively. Clearly what appalled her was not the suffering of the poor, but the way they lowered the tone. 'Well, they bring it upon themselves. I'm told the filth is indescribable . . . and within spitting distance of the Capitol Building, too.' She glanced towards Saffron and said, 'Perhaps that's why Mavis spends so much time in their midst. It's like missionary work, but without the necessity to live in some malaria-ridden backwater of the empire. She can put on her little boiler suit, set off to minister to the poor folk, and be back at her agreeable house, with all its modern conveniences, in plenty of time for a sumptuous supper.'

Saffron was very tempted to give Millicent's cynicism the denunciation it deserved. But she was on an information-gathering mission. And that required at least a facade of civility. 'Mavis sounds like quite a character. What's she like when she's not on her "missionary work"?'

'Well, Mavis is terribly quiet at embassy garden parties and cocktail dos, but when she wants something she sets her chin, grits her teeth and somehow ends up getting her way. You see her whispering in Charlie's ear, and the next thing you know, there she is, chatting away to a senator.'

From the station, they had been driving through the sort of crowded, urban setting Saffron would have expected. But suddenly they were surrounded by wooded parkland uninterrupted by any signs of urban life, as far as the eye could see.

'Almost there,' Millicent said. 'Now, there's one last thing I should tell you. If Lady Halifax seems distracted, or not quite paying attention to you, please don't judge her too harshly. She lost one of her sons, Francis, killed in action in Egypt last year. And a few months ago, another of her boys, Dickie, lost both his legs. That was in North Africa, too.'

'Oh, the poor woman . . .' said Saffron. 'How awful for her.'

'Yes, she and the ambassador are longing to go home again to be with what's left of their family. He's begged to be relieved of his duties, but the Foreign Secretary won't hear of it, says his presence here is essential for the war effort.'

As she was speaking, Millicent's grip on the steering wheel had been getting tighter. Now her knuckles were white with tension. Then suddenly she banged her hand against the wheel and exclaimed, 'This bloody war! It's taking everything from us – everything!'

'Have you lost someone, too?' Saffron asked gently.

Millicent nodded, and said with painful formality, 'Flight Lieutenant Johnny Hamilton, DFC and bar. The only man I ever loved. We were engaged to be married. He'd got some leave sorted. My pa had booked our village church. Mother spent ages adjusting her old wedding dress to fit me. Three days before the wedding, Johnny took a new pilot who'd just been sent to the squadron, still wet behind the ears, up for a training flight over Kent. They were jumped by a squadron of Messerschmitts.'

Saffron reached into her bag and handed Millicent a handkerchief.

'Thank you.' Millicent dabbed her eyes, then straightened in her seat, as if ordering herself to buck up. 'According to Johnny's squadron leader he never stood a chance,' she said. 'Some vile bloody German shot him down . . . might as well have shot me, too. God, I hate those people! I wish I were a man – I'd make it my life's mission to kill the lot of them.'

'I don't blame you,' Saffron said, and then fell silent, needing a moment to sort out her own thoughts.

She had been forming a clear impression of Millicent James: *bitter, resentful, looks down on 'lesser' people, hates the Left, is equally disapproving of over-privileged aristocrats and over-ambitious proles*. The combination added up to a woman who might before the war have started conversations with words like 'Say what you like about Herr Hitler, but . . .' And a woman like that might easily associate with the kind of man whose pro-Nazi views were strong enough to lead him to betray his country.

But then had come the revelation about her dead fiancé. Saffron had no doubt that Millicent had been telling the truth about her man, his death and its effect on her. It explained her pinched face and her simmering anger, and however much Saffron disapproved of Millicent's views, she felt compassion for her. The Luftwaffe pilot who had killed Johnny Hamilton had robbed Millicent James of her love, her hopes for the future and her happiness.

'But do you know what really makes me cross?' Millicent added.

'No . . . what?'

'We needn't have had this blasted war at all. Poor Lord Halifax told everyone, again and again, "We should sue for peace." And he was right. We'd have kept our country, our king and our empire. Our young men would have stayed safe at home. There'd never have been a Blitz. Johnny and I would be married, and the Halifaxes would have their boys safe and well, without a care in the world.'

The car was slowing down. Across the road, Saffron saw a fence of high, spiked, black iron railings, broken by a series of stone-pillared gates. Beyond stood a large U-shaped red-brick building, with two protruding wings running down towards the street, decorated by a classical pediment at its centre.

'We're here,' Millicent said. She turned into the furthest gate, drove along the side of one of the wings, then turned towards an entrance in the side of the building. Above the entrance there were three windows: a large rounded one, flanked by two smaller, narrow ones, with the Union Jack fluttering above them.

'That's Lord Halifax's office,' Millicent said, glancing up at the three windows. As they drove through the arch, Saffron saw a shallow flight of stone steps to her right, leading to a glazed door. Millicent parked the car in a small courtyard beyond the arch, and said, 'Right, enough moping – let's go and meet Lady Halifax.'

• • •

The British ambassador's residence was built as an English country house in the heart of America's capital. It was an elegant, gracious, but still forceful reminder that while Britannia might not be the force she once was, she wasn't entirely finished, either.

The entrance that Millicent had driven past a minute earlier led to a hall from which a double staircase in grey marble rose in sweeping, mirror-image semicircles, with twin red carpets running up the steps.

'The residence is built on sloping ground, so we're actually going uphill to a second ground floor,' Millicent said, as Saffron looked around. The walls were painted in a pale grey that set off the brilliant white of the ceiling and the ornate plasterwork of the Corinthian pilasters that were set against the walls.

At the top of the stairs, a bridge to Saffron's right led across the stairwell towards a corridor that, lit by tall windows, stretched the entire length of the building.

'That's the door to the ambassador's study,' whispered Millicent, nodding to the left, as if speaking more loudly might penetrate the study's thick oak door, set within a classical arch.

'Have you ever been in there?' Saffron whispered back, finding herself playing along.

'Oh, yes,' said Millicent, raising her voice a little and holding her head higher as she added, 'Lady Halifax often asks me to pass messages on to His Lordship, so I'm in and out all the time.'

'What's it like?'

'Well, the walls are all panelled in oak. It's a little too masculine for my taste, of course, but entirely suitable for an ambassador and—'

Before Millicent could finish her sentence, the door opened and Jock Colville scurried out, moving, as always, as if he should have been somewhere else by now, like the White Rabbit in *Alice's Adventures in Wonderland*.

'Good Lord!' he exclaimed, bringing himself up short. 'Hello, Saffron, what on earth are you doing here?'

'Lady Halifax very sweetly said I could put my feet up here, while I wait for the kind lady who's volunteered to put me up.'

'Well, you've picked a hell of a time to arrive.' He looked around and in a quiet, conspiratorial voice added, 'Between you and me, a very eminent, but somewhat, ah . . . controversial personage has decided to make his presence felt . . . *with his wife*.' The last words were said with a weight that suggested they were of considerable significance. 'Anyway, must dash!'

'Wait a sec,' Saffron said. 'Could you tell the PM that I saw his friend in New York, and will be acting on their advice?'

A puzzled frown crossed Colville's face. 'I'm not sure I follow you, old girl.'

'Don't worry, he will understand – and he will be *very* glad to hear it.'

Just as Colville had emphasised 'wife', so she underlined 'very'.

'Well, I'm off to see him now, so I'll be sure to pass it on,' Colville said, getting the hint, before he raced away across the bridge. He turned right and disappeared. By the sound of his footsteps, Saffron guessed that he was heading up another flight of stairs.

'What was all that about?' Millicent asked, not even trying to mask her inquisitiveness.

'Oh, just a friend of Mr Churchill's who he wanted me to look up when I was in New York. He thought she could give me some useful advice about dealing with Americans. Which she did . . . and she took me shopping at Saks Fifth Avenue, too, which was wildly extravagant, but great fun.'

Saffron hoped that Millicent would be sufficiently put off by her spoiled-little-rich-girl story that she wouldn't pursue it. To encourage a change of subject, she added, 'What did Colville mean by the personage and his wife?'

'I couldn't possibly say,' Millicent replied. 'But the word "personage" is usually quite specific in its meaning.'

Having despatched that question, she returned to the scent she had been chasing.

'You seem to have struck up quite a friendship with Mr Churchill.'

'I wouldn't go that far. I was introduced to him aboard the *Queen Mary*. I was the only female in our part of the ship, so I dare say he just wanted some light relief. And then, as we were saying hello, a German U-boat appeared and let off a couple of torpedoes. They only just missed. So I suppose that made the occasion a bit more memorable. And then we bumped into each other again, just as we were coming into harbour. You know, leaning on the railings and admiring the view.'

'You're very casual about being attacked by a submarine.'

'Well,' said Saffron, deciding to take a different approach, 'it's not nearly as bad as being on a ship that's being dive-bombed by Stukas. That didn't feel casual at all.' She smiled sweetly and added, 'Shall we go and find Lady Halifax?'

'She instructed me to take you to the portico,' Millicent replied, doing her best to put Saffron back in her place. 'Follow me.'

They set off across the bridge and along the corridor, heels clacking on the black and white patterned marble floor, past the staircase that Colville had just ascended and a series of closed doors, until they came to a point, about halfway along, where light flooded in from both sides. To her right, open to the corridor, save for a line of marble columns, with the same white Corinthian capitals, Saffron saw an oak-floored room with a grand piano at the far end. 'That's the ballroom,' Millicent said.

'It's magnificent.'

'Not that magnificent. The Treasury panicked at the amount of money this place was costing and ordered a drastic cutback. The columns aren't marble. They're painted plaster.'

'Well, they look pretty splendid,' Saffron said. Peering further down the corridor, she saw what she had assumed was a window but was actually a pair of French doors that opened onto a flagstone path ending in a set of steep steps.

'Where does that go to?' Saffron asked, pointing towards the door.

'The ambassador's swimming pool,' said Millicent. 'Very lovely, and entirely out of bounds to anyone except for the Halifaxes and their guests. Now, if you'd just come this way . . .'

Millicent turned left, where three more sets of glazed doors looked out onto the embassy garden. The middle pair were open, and she led Saffron onto a terrace that sat beneath a portico, supported by more columns. Saffron tapped one as she walked out and said, 'I hope this isn't plaster.'

'No, that's stone. Quite solid.'

A wicker table had been laid for two with a pristine white cloth, silver cutlery and gleaming crystal glasses. A vase of freshly cut flowers sat upon a smaller table to one side.

'I'll let Lady Halifax know you're here,' Millicent said, disappearing into the house.

Saffron gazed across the gardens at the skyline, thinking that the Capitol dome seemed to be at the centre of every view of Washington, just as St Paul's rose over London. She concentrated on what Millicent had said. *What kind of a person is called 'a personage'?* Had she grown up in England, instead of Kenya, and been familiar with the nuances of upper-class etiquette,

Saffron would have known in an instant. As it was, she had to rack her brain and . . .

'Oh,' Saffron said, as it came to her. 'Personage' – in the way Colville and Millicent had used it – must refer to someone of royal rank. This royal was controversial, and the presence of his wife only added to the difficulties it caused.

Even a Kenyan girl knew what that meant.

The Duke of Windsor, formerly King Edward VIII, must be in Washington, accompanied by Wallis Simpson, the woman for whom he had abdicated the throne. So he, Churchill and Roosevelt were all in the same place at the same time, and suddenly Saffron was struck by another question. What if this embassy mole wasn't intent on getting information about the Allied invasion plans? What if his purpose was something more straightforward, more brutal – a strike at the Allied leaders themselves?

But the Duke of Windsor was infamous for being a great admirer of Hitler's. Why on earth would the Nazis want to kill him? And if that was not their intention, what did they intend to do with him?

Saffron Courtney had spent enough time in the conspiratorial world of secret intelligence to doubt there was any such thing as coincidence. Whatever the duke was doing in Washington, she refused to believe that it was purely a matter of chance.

Lady Halifax must once have been a ravishing English rose. Her features were modelled with the delicacy of fine porcelain: her cheeks were high, her eyes were gentle, her mouth, with its wide, slightly overhanging top lip, conveyed vulnerability as well as beauty. In Saffron's experience, women blessed with such perfect – almost regal – bone structure retained their looks all their life. But grief and loss had left their mark on Lady Halifax, just as they had on her secretary. Her eyes were dull, her skin dry, her hair wiry, and she was rail-thin, her limbs looking as frail as a china doll's.

The embassy staff had prepared a picnic lunch of ladylike sandwiches – crust-less rounds of ham, with a touch of mustard; egg mayonnaise and cress; and finely sliced cucumber – accompanied by a green salad. To Saffron, whose few days in America had not yet stopped her thinking like someone on meagre British rations, this was a real feast, and it was all she could do not to wolf the spread down in an instant. Lady Halifax, however, barely managed a mouthful.

Putting a single leaf on her fork. She took a nibble out of one corner of a cucumber sandwich and a quick sip of the chilled white wine that had been served with the food. 'It's Californian, I'm afraid,' she said distractedly. 'We have to save the French for official occasions.' She attempted a smile. 'And of course, we've set aside the best champagne and cognac for Mr Churchill's visits.'

'I gather that's essential!' said Saffron, doing her best to be upbeat.

Lady Halifax barely seemed to hear her. 'Anyway, it's really not too bad for an American wine.'

The wine, Saffron discovered, was delicious. So, too, were the sandwiches, but they might as well have been tap water and cardboard for all the pleasure Lady Halifax took in them.

'My husband tells me you spent the first two years of the war in North Africa,' she said. 'I never had the chance to talk to . . . Well, one received letters, of course, but, well, one can't help but wonder what it was like. You know . . . for our boys.'

'Surprisingly cold at night,' Saffron said, beginning with the most trivial but surprising thing she could think of. 'You could always tell the old hands because they made sure they had thick jumpers, greatcoats and sheepskin jerkins to keep them warm.'

'Tell me about the desert,' Lady Halifax said.

Saffron told her how it could be as brutal and unforgiving an environment as any human could be forced to endure, yet beautiful, too. She talked about a land war that was often as fluid as any naval engagement, with the battle lines sweeping like tides across eight hundred miles of the Mediterranean coast, deep into the heart of Libya, then back all the way to Egypt, before turning once again.

'It was nothing at all like the trenches must have been. It was exciting . . . I know, because I saw it. In fact, I was mixed up in it a few times.'

Lady Halifax hung on Saffron's every word as she recounted her adventures, and was equally enthralled as she described life in wartime Cairo. 'There are the most wonderful riverboats there. You can steam up and down the Nile, eating dinner and dancing to the band. It's heavenly. And the Great Pyramids are only just outside town. Of course, the fighting could be terrible. But if you asked any of the chaps who'd been sent to the desert, they wouldn't have missed it for the world.'

Saffron was trying, with all her heart, to make Lady Halifax believe that her two sons, one dead, the other mutilated, had not been sacrificed in vain. And she felt she was beginning to succeed. Lady Halifax's eyes seemed a little brighter, her smiles wider, her conversation more animated. And then Millicent James stepped onto the patio.

'Excuse me, My Lady, but I have a message for Miss Courtney. A Major General Donovan called from the Coordinator of Information's office. He wishes you to know that if you want to meet him to discuss your schedule in Washington, this afternoon might be the only time he can spare, and the sooner you get there, the better. He is apparently . . .' Millicent pursed her lips in an expression of both scepticism and disapproval. '. . . a very busy man.'

'Thank you, Millicent,' said Lady Halifax. She turned back to Saffron. 'Well, my dear, it seems you must be off. I've greatly enjoyed our conversation, and I do hope we shall have the chance to continue it before you leave Washington. Millicent, could you call a taxi for Miss Courtney? And have her luggage ready to be taken over to the Playfairs' house when Mavis returns home.'

'Yes, My Lady. Mrs Playfair told me that she would be home by five.'

'Ah, Millicent, how wonderfully efficient you are.' Lady Halifax glanced at her watch. 'Oh, goodness, is that the time? I'm afraid, my dear, that I must in any case desert you. I have a rather important little reception, which requires more formal attire.'

'With a duke and duchess?' asked Saffron, innocently.

Lady Halifax laughed, and for a moment Saffron caught a glimpse of the woman she had once been. 'Exactly so,' she said. 'But do feel free to wait here until your taxi arrives. Oh . . . and my husband tells me you're here to bang the drum for your unit, though he won't go so far as to tell me what that unit is.' She smiled to let Saffron know that she was being self-deprecating, rather than put out. 'Perhaps you could give Millicent a list of the meetings and social events you are planning to attend. I may well know some of the people involved, or their wives. I'll try to put in a good word for you if I can.'

• • •

'Miss Courtney, let me be blunt,' said William Donovan. Just months shy of his sixtieth birthday, he was silver-haired with what Saffron thought of as a headmaster's face: one whose expression suggested genuine care for the people over whom he ruled, combined with an unflinching refusal to accept anything but the highest standards from them. He wore a single general's star on his epaulettes and, though there was a relatively short line of medal ribbons on his jacket, they comprised, as Gubbins had suggested, the most prestigious awards for valour that the United States could bestow.

'Yes, sir.' Saffron was sitting opposite Donovan, and suddenly felt like a naughty schoolgirl. His office was on the first floor of a white building fronted by the columns that seemed obligatory for grand Washington properties, close to the Old Naval Observatory. Behind him, she could see a globe at least four feet in diameter, mounted in a wood and metal cradle like a boiled egg in a cup, symbolising the global reach of the Office of Strategic Services. Beyond that, dark wooden shelves laden down with books suggested the breadth of his intellectual interests.

Their meeting had begun well, as Donovan had talked her through the names on Stephenson's list of Washington bigwigs, describing each man's character, suggesting things that she should or should not say, and subjects to be raised or avoided. Having made sure to thank Donovan for the trouble he had taken, Saffron had said, 'There's something else, sir – another reason I'm here.'

He looked at her quizzically. 'Tell me.'

Saffron had outlined Stephenson's fears about an enemy agent at work in the British embassy. She had also offered Donovan her theory that the agent's real purpose might be more aggressive than merely passing on classified information. And that was when Donovan had decided to put her in her place.

'I have heard nothing but good things about you,' he said, making his words sound nothing like a compliment. 'Gubbins tells me you're one of his best operatives. Stephenson says that you could teach my men a thing or two about unarmed combat, and he is not alone in praising your fighting skills.'

Saffron wondered who else might have spoken about her to Donovan. But before she could follow the thought any further, he continued. 'I can think of few men whose opinions I value more highly than those two gentlemen. I also consider them both, Bill Stephenson in particular, to be my personal friends. But I believe Stephenson has set you off on a wild goose chase.'

'But, sir—'

'I've not finished.'

'No, sir.'

'Now, I am in the business of placing US spies on foreign soil. I leave the business of catching foreign spies on US soil to the Federal Bureau of Investigation. But I do have access to both American and British intelligence, and both nations are broadly in agreement. Neither of Nazi Germany's principal intelligence operations, the Abwehr or the SD, have any significant presence on American soil.'

'But—'

'You may say, "But Stephenson thinks the Nazi spy is a British double agent inside the embassy."'

That was indeed the point she was about to make.

'And I say – so what? You must know from your own experience that any agent operating in enemy territory needs local support. Wouldn't you agree?'

Donovan had been the senior partner in a Wall Street law firm between the wars. Now Saffron felt like a witness under hostile cross-examination. 'Yes, sir,' she said. 'That was the case when I was in the Low Countries. I made contact with resistance elements. I wouldn't have made it home without them.'

'And did they help you communicate with London?'

'Yes, sir.'

'Well now, do you think there are Nazi agents in the United States, communicating with Berlin, armed and ready to risk their lives to overthrow President Roosevelt? No, you don't. No one does, because every time a German submarine deposits an agent onto the Atlantic coastline of the United States, that agent swiftly finds himself in the hands of the FBI. Now, don't get me wrong. I can just about believe, in theory, that there could be a Nazi sympathiser within the British embassy. Hell, the ambassador himself has been accused of that – very unfairly, in my view. And we all know about your former king, and his willingness to shake Herr Hitler's hand.'

'He's about to arrive in Washington, sir – the former king.'

'Did Stephenson tell you that?' asked Donovan, in a tone of surprise.

'No, sir. I worked it out for myself.'

'Huh . . .' Donovan nodded to himself, filing that piece of information away. 'Interesting. But even if there was a Nazi sympathiser in the embassy, I don't believe he could operate without support on the ground. And if he was intent on carrying out some kind of assassination, which I don't for one second believe, then he'd need even more support to provide him with weapons and help him get the hell out of Dodge. And, as I say, there is no such support.'

Donovan's words had been intended to shut down Saffron's line of questioning, but she persisted doggedly. 'What you say may be possible. But just because people believe that there are no spies here, it doesn't mean that they're right.'

To tell someone of far higher rank that they were wrong, to their face, came perilously close to insubordination, but Saffron ignored the furious look on Donovan's face and pressed on. 'When I was in Belgium, I was told by the leader of the local fascist party that there were no active SOE agents in the Low Countries. Every single person we'd sent over there had been caught. He had been told so by the military governor of Belgium, General von Frankenhausen himself.'

Saffron paused for a second, before she delivered her punchline. 'And the fascist was right. Every SOE agent had been caught . . . except for the one he was talking to.'

Donovan harrumphed. He was still displeased, and that was putting it mildly. But it was hard to argue with someone who could speak from direct personal experience. Before he could come up with a response, Saffron adopted a more humble tone and made sure to sprinkle in the maximum number of deferential 'Sir's. 'Just suppose, for the sake of argument, sir, that Stephenson is right. Imagine that there is a spy in the embassy. How do you think I could set about finding him? Because if he is going to give away our military plans for the next two years, sir, I really don't have much time.'

Donovan looked at her as if weighing up the odds. He sighed. 'All right . . . Because Bill Stephenson is my buddy,

I'll say this, though I doubt it's anything you can't figure out for yourself. Your guy – if he exists – is going to be the last person you would expect, either because he seems meek and inoffensive, or because he's passionately anti-Nazi, or whatever. But, as you have so *eloquently* pointed out, you know what it's like to be undercover. It's damn stressful, right?'

'Absolutely, sir.'

'So, look for someone behaving like they're stressed, which is difficult, because everyone's stressed, all the time, because there's a war on. But maybe one guy's obviously drinking too much, or he's like a bomb about to blow – really on edge. And there's one other thing you've got to bear in mind. Let's just suppose, for the sake of argument, that this guy exists and is betraying his country to the Krauts. Maybe you won't have to look for him. Maybe he'll come looking for you. And he won't have to look far.'

Saffron looked puzzled. 'Why not, sir?'

'Because you just blew your cover.'

Donovan pushed a piece of paper across the desk. It was a slightly blurred copy of a newspaper cutting from the *New York Daily Mirror*, headed WALTER WINCHELL ON BROADWAY.

'Stephenson wired me this about an hour ago,' Donovan said. 'Read the lead item.'

Saffron did as she was told, and became more appalled with every word.

I went to the Copacabana Club last night. A little birdie told me that Frank Sinatra, the Hoboken kid with the baby-blue eyes who's got the nation's bobby-soxers swooning, was going to play a secret show. Well, the birdie was right. Sinatra was there all right, but he was just the warm-up act. For once the crooner had given his final bow, all hell broke out on the dance floor.

Enter a burly figure, whom eagle-eyed admirers of the noble art recognised as Police Lieutenant William O'Bannon, otherwise known as Bashin' Billy, the former undefeated heavyweight champion of the NYPD. Billy approached a young couple on the dance floor – a handsome army air force medic from Texas, Lt. Clayton Stackpole and his beautiful brunette partner, Jane Smith, who sounded like a fine English lady but assured me she came from Africa. Yes, Jane, from Africa . . . remind you of anyone?

When Lt. Stackpole objected to O'Bannon's presence, he got a right hook to the jaw for his pains. O'Bannon then laid his paws on Miss Smith. He whispered not-so-sweet somethings in her ear. Big mistake. That dame might be Jane, but she punched like Tarzan. Talk about a KO. Within seconds, Jane was standing over that copper like Joe Louis over Max Schmeling. And even Sinatra was applauding.

So, who was this Mauling Miss? Well, she shared a table with her fly-boy beau and William Stephenson, the Canadian-born multi-millionaire husband of tobacco heiress Mary French Simmons and close personal friend of Winston Churchill. Word is, by the time you read this, she'll be on the first train out of town. And every fight promoter in Gotham will be hot on her tail.

Saffron looked up from the page and sighed. 'I've barely been in Washington for three hours . . .'

Donovan shrugged. 'The evening paper in DC, the *Star*, syndicates Winchell. So they'll have that story on the streets . . .' he looked at his watch, 'I guess right about now. Could take a while for people to join the dots. But if there is a spy at your embassy, he'll soon know you just arrived from New York—'

'Ahead of schedule, because I had to leave fast.'

'And if he's senior enough to get his hands on classified information, he knows what Bill Stephenson's doing up there.'

Saffron sighed, feeling utterly deflated. Donovan leaned forward, seeing her disappointment. His eyes softened and his voice took on a more sympathetic tone. 'Will you let an old man give you some advice?'

'Of course, sir.'

'Very well, then . . . You have already gone above and beyond the call of duty on numerous occasions. Your service has been exemplary, and I do not say that lightly. But if you are the only person standing between the Nazis and the Allied war plans, then a great many good men have fallen down on their jobs. So do me a favour – obey your commanding officer's orders. Go fly the flag for SOE. Have a great time. Stay out of trouble.'

'Yes, sir,' said Saffron.

'Is there anything else?' Donovan asked.

'No, sir.'

'Very well, then. I've got to go – meeting at the Pentagon. One last thing . . . As a favour to Stephenson, I've assigned an officer to give you any assistance you may need getting around town. His office is down the hall, third door on the right.'

'Thank you, sir.'

Saffron got up, saluted Donovan, left his office and made her way along the hall, wondering why Donovan would appoint one of his men as her chaperone. If OSS was anything like SOE, no one had time for anything but essential activities. She counted the doors, opened the third, and walked in.

'Didn't I tell you this was a small war?'

She turned her head. Leaning against a desk, a grin contending with the swelling and vivid bruising across one side of his face, was Lieutenant Clayton Stackpole.

Saffron stood rooted to the spot.

Stackpole pushed himself off the desk. 'Aren't you going to say anything? I kinda thought you might be pleased to see me.'

Saffron gave a heavy sigh and shook her head. 'Honestly, I don't know what I think. Half of me wants to run into your arms, the other half wants to wallop the other side of your face.'

Stackpole took a couple of steps towards her. 'What did I do wrong?'

'What did you do?' repeated Saffron, amazed that he couldn't work it out for himself. 'You told me you were an army air force doctor when really you're an OSS agent. You made me think we would never meet again, when all the time you knew I was coming to Washington and you'd be here, too . . .' She stopped and frowned. 'And how the hell did you get here, anyway? There wasn't another express for hours.'

'I flew out of Teterboro Airport in New Jersey, across the river from Manhattan. Hitched a ride with a two-star air force general who was on his way to a pow-wow at the Pentagon. Because I swear, I really am an army air force doctor, and I do put guys from bomber crews back together. I came back stateside because I got seconded to OSS, but I'm not here to be a secret agent . . . well, not most of the time, anyway. My main job is to make sure that everyone we take on is fit enough for the job, and fix any of them that get broken.'

'Why didn't you tell me?'

'The same reason you don't talk about who you really work for. It's classified. And I truly didn't know you were coming to meet Wild Bill.'

'Were you ever going to let me know you were here?'

'If I got the chance . . . My plan was, find out where you were, make it sound like I'd just got new orders and . . . ask you out on another date. You know . . . seeing as how the first one went so well.'

Now it was Saffron who took a step towards Stackpole and reached out to touch his arm. 'It did go well, though . . . didn't it?' There was genuine uncertainty in her voice – that fear that the other person might not have felt the same way in the cold light of day.

Stackpole put his arms around her waist and pulled her close. 'It was the best night of my life,' he said. 'You're the most beautiful, amazing, smart and, I gotta be honest, scary woman I've ever met in my life, and—'

Before he could say another word, Saffron was kissing him, her hands on either side of his face, gently and tenderly, holding back the raging hunger she felt for him for fear of causing him pain, because then he might stop kissing her back.

Far too soon, Saffron felt Stackpole gently pushing her away. 'If we carry on much longer, I won't be able to stop,' he said, his chest still heaving. 'And if someone comes in and finds us making whoopee on the desktop—'

'Let them,' Saffron said, her voice thick with desire.

'No, trust me, it wouldn't be good for you. Washington is a town that runs on gossip. There's nothing folks here love more'n ruining other folks' reputations. No one would ever take you seriously.'

Saffron's face fell. 'Maybe they won't anyway. Did you see that Walter Winchell story about us?'

'See it? I've had everyone in the entire damn office ribbing me for needing a gal to rescue me.'

Saffron cooed, 'Poor baby,' then used that as an excuse to give him another kiss. 'So what are they going to think if they find out I'm "Jane Smith"?'

'Oh, don't you worry about that. You won the fight, and this is America. Everyone loves a winner.'

Stackpole gave her another kiss, then took her hand and walked her back to the desk. 'Why don't you sit down there,' he said, patting one end of the desk, 'and I'll sit here.' He perched at the other end.

Stackpole looked Saffron in the eye, wanting her to know he was being straight with her. 'You're right, I owe you an explanation. So, if you've got any questions, fire away.'

'When we met at Gourock, was that a set-up? Was any of it real?'

'It was all real,' Stackpole replied. 'Like I said, I really had been sewing fly-boys back together. But Donovan had already contacted me, so I'd done a couple of things for him.'

'Which you can't tell me about?'

'Not the specifics, no. But it was mostly, ah . . . liaison work with various British agencies.'

'Donovan knew I was coming to Washington. Did he know I'd be on the *Queen Mary*?'

'Sure, and since I was going to be on the same voyage, he said I should keep an eye out for you.'

'To what end?'

'Oh, nothing major. It was more curiosity than anything. Gubbins had given you quite a sell. Big Bill wanted to get my impression of you. But when I saw you on the dock, I swear I didn't know who you were. That was just a guy acting natural when he sees an incredibly beautiful woman suddenly appear right in front of him.'

'Then you found out who I was . . .'

'And suddenly I became much more interested in my assignment.'

Saffron looked at Stackpole with shrewd, appraising eyes, then nodded to herself. 'All right, I believe you . . . Did you tell Donovan that I'd been to see Stephenson?'

'Sure . . . and he told me what he reckoned Stephenson wanted to talk to you about.'

So, he knows about the spy theory. 'And what do you think?' Saffron asked, praying that he would be on her side.

'Well . . .' Stackpole shrugged. There was a brief silence. Saffron felt herself tense. 'Between you and me, I don't agree with Donovan.' Saffron fought the urge to throw herself across the desk and hug him. 'If Stephenson says there's a Nazi spy and you agree with him, that's good enough for me. And you remember what you said to me in that King Cole Bar – that you're a girl who gets into trouble, and you could feel trouble coming your way?'

Saffron nodded.

'Well, I feel it, too. You know, my family home is in Dallas, but we've got some land way up on the High Plains, about fifty miles south of Amarillo. I'll be riding out some days and the sky'll be clear blue, not a cloud to be seen, but you can feel that there's a storm coming, and the horse can feel it, too – gets all nervous and skittery. You know what I'm saying?'

'Yes, it's like that in Kenya, too.'

'Well, right now, I feel like that horse. I can feel the storm coming. And what I'm trying to say is, when it breaks, if you need help, don't call that damn gangster. You don't ever want a favour from him. Call me, and I'll be there for you. I promise. Although . . .' Stackpole made another attempt at a grin. 'As you may have figured out by now, I'm not a great fighter. I'm better at putting people together than busting them up.'

'Don't worry, having you on my side means everything.' There were many more questions Saffron wanted to ask Stackpole, but the first one that came to mind was a practical one. 'So what use does Donovan have for an army air force surgeon from Texas?'

'My mom is Russian. I speak the language fluently. It's on my service record. Guess someone must have tipped him off.'

Saffron was taken by surprise. 'That's extraordinary. Why didn't you tell me that before?'

He shrugged. 'I don't know.' Then a smile. 'Maybe we had more interesting things to talk about.'

'Well, tell me now, then.'

'Okay. Well, it starts with my dad. You know his name, right?'

It took Saffron a moment, and then she laughed. 'I assume he's King Clayton the Second.'

'You got it. Anyway, my old man was supposed to go into the family business, selling drilling gear to oil prospectors. But he wanted to be an artist. So, a couple of years before the last war, he went to Paris, sailed over third class, lived in a garret, discovered maybe he wasn't quite as great an artist as he thought. Mom's maiden name was Anastasia Kuznetskova. Her folks were aristocrats. They had a big old, falling-down palace in Leningrad and an estate that didn't produce enough money to pay the bills. They hoped Mom would marry some rich prince and rescue the family, but she said "the hell with that" and escaped to Paris, figuring she could make a living as a dancer. Dad met her in a cafe in Montmartre. They were both broke, hungry, getting nowhere, and if you ever ask them, they'll tell you, it was love at first sight.'

'How romantic!' exclaimed Saffron. No wonder Stackpole had found it hard to get excited about the girl next door.

'Yep, it sure is,' he said. 'Anyway, they got married. Dad took Mom back to Texas and that saved her life, because the rest of her family died in the revolution. I grew up speaking Russian along with English. Turns out to be a useful skill these days.'

'You mean, communicating with our Russian allies?'

Stackpole grimaced. 'Yeah, I can talk to them, and every time I do I think of my Russian family, that I never met, and remember they were killed by Communist bastards, just like them. And believe me, that'll be the next war. As soon as we've kicked Hitler's ass to hell, we'll be taking on Stalin.'

'Oh, for God's sake,' Saffron chided, 'we haven't remotely finished this war yet. It's a bit soon to be thinking about another one.'

'Well, we'd better,' Stackpole said, 'because the Russians sure as hell are.' He looked at Saffron and gave a gentle, almost sad smile. 'Let's not talk about that now, though, huh?' He reached across and ran a finger down her face. 'Oh, God, I wish we could just be together . . . alone.'

'Oh, me too.'

'Are you free this evening?'

'I don't know. I'm going to meet the couple who are putting me up while I'm here. They'll probably want to have supper with me. I can't brush them off.'

'No . . . I guess that would be kinda rude. But tomorrow night, maybe?'

'I'd love that.'

'Okay, let's put that in the diary. Give me a call around six?' Stackpole ripped a piece of paper from a notepad on the desk and scribbled down a number. 'This is my office number. It's where I spend all my waking hours.'

'I know that feeling.' Saffron put her arms around him. 'I can't wait.'

'But now . . .' he checked his watch, 'I'm late for a hospital appointment. I figured I really should get an X-ray. Gave myself doctor's orders.'

'Off you go, then,' Saffron said. 'I really need you to be fit and healthy.'

The OSS headquarters stood in an area of Washington known as Navy Hill. It was close to the Potomac river, about a mile due west of the White House. 'You should see the sights,' Stackpole had said as he walked her out of the building. 'Make a right on 23rd Street and it'll take you all the way to the Lincoln Memorial. You can walk it in ten minutes.'

Saffron took his advice, and soon found herself gazing up at the giant statue of the seated president, looking like an American Zeus upon a marble throne. Around him, the inner walls of the memorial were inscribed with the texts of Lincoln's greatest speeches. As she read his description of 'a nation dedicated to the proposition that all men are created equal,' and of a 'government of the people, by the people, for the people,' Saffron found, to her surprise, that her throat was tightening.

If New York had shown her the might, the glamour and the excitement of America, the Lincoln Memorial embodied the soul of the nation, its idea of itself, the goal towards which it was eternally striving. She knew that the real America fell short of the ideal that this memorial embodied, but there was something magnificent about a nation that was at least attempting to be worthy of its founding principles, just as there was a nobility to Britain's dogged refusal to bow before the Nazi onslaught.

'Stop being so soppy, woman,' Saffron muttered to herself as she wiped a tear from her cheek. But in truth, she was glad that she'd been so deeply moved. She spent most of her working life focused on the nuts and bolts of the challenges that confronted her. It was good to be reminded that there was a reason she was doing it.

But there was also a practical side to her sightseeing. Having cast her eyes on the newly opened Jefferson Memorial and peered through the White House towards the president's mansion, Saffron bought a city map at a news-stand on Constitution Avenue. She headed to the Washington Monument and took an elevator ride five hundred feet to the top of the marble and granite obelisk.

Looking down from each of the small rectangular windows of the observation deck, with her map in hand, Saffron pieced together a mental image of the city, memorising it in minute detail, to be retrieved whenever she needed to get her bearings. The ability to know where she was – and how to get out quickly – was essential to Saffron's survival if things turned nasty. As she took the ride down to the ground, it gave her a comforting sense of security to know that Washington DC could be added to the list of cities that were stored in her internal atlas.

She emerged from the monument shortly after five o'clock, walked to Constitution Avenue and hailed a cab. 'I was told to let you know that it's just off Foxhall Road,' she said to the driver. 'Down at the far end of the street, all the way to the park.'

'Got it,' he said, and drove off.

• • •

Just about the time that Saffron was arriving at the British embassy, an explosives expert called Marx was leaving his workshop, carrying a brown paper package. He made his legitimate money providing the charges, fuses and detonators used in quarries and on demolition sites, and so he was familiar with pentaerythritol tetranitrate, otherwise known as PENT, penthrite, or even nitropenta, which was the most powerful explosive on the market. There was approximately three pounds of PENT in Marx's parcel, and, following the instructions that he had been given, he took it to Griffith Stadium, on the corner of W Street and Florida Avenue, where Washington's baseball team, the Senators, were playing that afternoon.

Marx was used to working for what he called his private customers. They paid him much more than his standard commercial rate, and in cash. He, in turn, made a point of never asking any more than the absolute minimum number of questions required to meet his clients' requirements. It was safer that way. He therefore had no idea what the contents of his package were going to be used for, let alone the real identities of the people who'd paid for it. He knew that when it went off, the blast would be roughly equivalent to a dozen hand grenades. That was a hell of a bang, and it would make one hell of a mess. But he'd been paid in full, up front, so what did he care?

The man who sat next to Marx in the bleachers at Griffith Stadium, about twenty rows back, did not know Marx's name any more than Marx knew his. But he recognised Marx from the description he had been given, and he had the correct code word, so Marx gave him the parcel. The second man had no idea what was in it and no desire to find out.

Then Marx said, 'I need to take a leak.' He got up and, without looking back, walked to the nearest exit, never to return to his seat.

The second man watched a couple of innings of baseball, then he, too, left the stadium. He took a series of trolley cars and buses, followed by a railroad train across the state line to Hyattsville, Maryland. He got on and off more times than the journey required to make sure he wasn't being followed. In a bar next to the station, he approached a burly guy in a crumpled suit and said, 'Are you Spanish Johnny?'

The guy didn't look Spanish – not one bit – but he said, 'Who's asking?' He didn't sound Spanish, either.

The second man just said, 'Got a package for you.'

Spanish Johnny took the package and said, 'Thanks, it's for my niece.'

'I hope she enjoys it,' said the second man.

The script was complete. Spanish Johnny looked at the package and said, 'Not very big, is it?'

That was an impromptu line. The second man wasn't sure how to reply. He shrugged and left.

Jozef Lewandowski watched him go. He held the package in his hand, considered what it was intended to do, then put it in his battered briefcase, whose once black leather was grey with dust and flecked with spots of paint.

Lewandowski looked at his watch and thought for a moment about how long it would take to get home from Hyattsville. He picked up the case and walked up to the bar. 'Gimme another beer,' he said to the barman.

As he drank, Lewandowksi wondered about the strange situation in which he'd found himself. Within the next seventy-two hours, the bomb sitting in his briefcase would either detonate as planned – in which case his targets would be dead and he would be a hero – or it would not, in which case his targets would be alive and well and he would be a dead man walking. He drained his glass, muttered, 'Welcome to the Third World War . . .' and headed outside to his truck.

• • •

Saffron's cab ride took a little over fifteen minutes. It ended on a tree-lined street that ran along the side of a hill, filled with widely separated houses, ranging from large French-style country homes to smaller New England clapboard cottages. Finally the driver pulled up, and leaned back. 'Here you go, ma'am. This is it.'

Saffron got out to find herself standing in front of one of the cottages. It was the last house on the street. Beyond it was a T-junction with a road running along one side of the park, which was a long, thin strip of wild, almost unkempt woodland, that – as Saffron's map-reading and observations told her – ran down the west side of the city in a straight strip, about three miles long, all the way south past Georgetown to the Potomac.

Like most of the houses they had passed, the Playfairs' was set back from the sidewalk, a little up the hill. It had the simplicity and the charm of a child's drawing, with five windows, each with a set of black-painted shutters, punctuating its white facade. There was a single-storey extension to the right of the building.

Satisfied that she had established the basic geography of the neighbourhood in her mind, Saffron paid off the cabbie, took her luggage and climbed the steps to the front door.

The short woman who opened the door was dressed in denim dungarees and a pale blue cotton shirt with rolled-up sleeves, and she was holding a baby against her hip. Her sandy hair was partially covered by a floral-patterned cotton headscarf. She had freckles across her face, a broad smile and green eyes that seemed to exude energy and life.

'Hello,' she said, holding out her spare hand. 'I'm Mavis. You must be Saffron.'

'Yes. It's so kind of you to have me.'

Mavis grinned. 'You may not be thanking me after you've been here a day or two. Come in.' She led the way down the hallway. 'This,' she nodded at the baby, 'is Arthur.' From up ahead came the pattering of paws, a couple of enthusiastic barks and a blur of chocolate brown fur that hurled itself at Saffron. 'And that,' said Mavis, 'is Franco. He's a chocolate Labrador, so he's totally bloody daft, but he's a good lad, really.'

'Well, I think he's splendid,' Saffron said, giving Franco a two-handed scratch behind his ears. He growled contentedly, his tail wagging furiously as he looked up at Saffron with an expression that suggested he had fallen instantly in love.

'We're in the kitchen,' Mavis said. 'I was about to make some tea. Would you like a cup?'

'Yes please.' Saffron followed Mavis into a sunny kitchen which had oak cabinets, a large gas oven, a breakfast nook with a table for four, and an enormous, glossy, cream-coloured refrigerator. A young Black woman was standing by the table. She wore a pale lilac uniform dress, and was holding a battered handbag in the crook of her right arm.

'Saffron, this is Loretta,' Mavis said. 'She does a wonderful job looking after Arthur. Loretta, this is Saffron. She's staying with us for a few days.'

Loretta nodded shyly. 'Think I'll be going now, Miss Mavis, if that's all right by you.'

'Of course.'

Loretta gently stroked Arthur's head and headed towards the front door with Franco trotting after her, clearly hoping she was going to take him for a walk.

'Franco seems an odd name for a dog,' said Saffron, as Mavis put the kettle on the stove.

'That was Charlie's bright idea,' Mavis said. 'He thought it would be amusing to boss a fascist dictator around. You know – "Heel, Franco!", "Beg, Franco!", "Bad boy, Franco!". He didn't allow for the fact that Labradors never do a thing they're told. But you fall in love with them anyway.' She sighed. 'Typical Charlie. For such a clever man, he can be thick as two short planks sometimes.'

'Loretta seems sweet,' Saffron said, as the kettle whistle blew.

'She's a diamond,' Mavis said, pouring boiling water into a teapot. 'Part of me feels terrible, having staff. It goes against the grain. But then I think, I'm putting shoes on that lass's feet and food on her family's table. You have no idea of the poverty here, Saffron. There are terrible, filthy, rat-infested tenement buildings within spitting distance of the Capitol. It's unbelievable. The leaders of the richest country on this planet are lording it in that building, and less than four hundred yards away there are people with no jobs, no homes, no food, nothing. I know some people think I'm mad to spend my days working at a soup kitchen, but how could anyone with a conscience live here, knowing what was going on, and not want to do something about it?'

Mavis paused, smiled and said, 'There I go, on my soapbox again. Come on, I'll show you your room, then let's take our tea outside. It's a lovely afternoon, seems a pity to waste it.'

Arthur Playfair, it turned out, was seven months old. 'Born in America, so he's legally entitled to become the president one day.' Mavis laughed as she fed him his bottle.

Mavis seemed to Saffron to be totally at ease in her environment. Another woman from her background, going up to Cambridge, marrying into a family as grand as the Playfairs, and then living amongst privately educated diplomats and their equally privileged wives, might have tried to get rid of her East Midlands accent, or desperately tried to fit in. But Mavis was clearly proud of her roots and saw no need to deny them. And it said a lot for her husband that he had not wanted to change her.

'People can't work us out,' Mavis said. 'They can't understand why Charlie chose me when he could have had some posh Henrietta or Charlotte. It never occurs to them that we might love each other, and be good mates, and sod what class we come from.'

'I've met those Henriettas and Charlottes,' Saffron said. 'I know why he'd rather have you.'

'Thanks, duck,' said Mavis, lifting her cup of tea in salute. The front door opened and then slammed loudly shut. 'His lordship's home,' Mavis remarked with a roll of her eyes.

An upper-class male voice cried out, 'For God's sake, woman, get me a glass of whisky!'

'Get it yerself, yer lazy bugger!' Mavis called back.

'That bloody man!' Charlie Playfair declaimed from the direction of the living room.

'He means our beloved prime minister,' Mavis told Saffron.

'He's become so used to being adored that he cannot spot loathing, even when it's right in front of his face . . . Oh, hell and damnation, where's the bloody ice?'

Mavis shouted again, 'In the bloody freezer compartment, where do you think?'

'Granted, Roosevelt doesn't loathe Winston personally, but he hates the British Empire with a deep and abiding passion . . .' The voice was getting closer. Saffron heard the opening and closing of a fridge door, the cracking of ice being dislodged from a tray and the chink as the cubes hit the glass.

'God knows how many memos I've written trying to get people to see sense . . .' A tall, slim man in a dark blue suit appeared on the patio, with his tie loose and the studs of his stiff white collar undone at the neck. He had a full tumbler of whisky in one hand and a lit cigarette in the other.

Playfair nodded at Mavis, paid no attention to Saffron and took up a position at the edge of the patio, looking out at the garden. Saffron, in contrast, was paying close attention to him. Playfair's face was tightly drawn, with hollows beneath his prominent cheekbones, and no trace of sagging at the jawline or chin. He had a long nose, a dark five o'clock shadow and grey-blue eyes. His black hair, shot through with the first streaks of silver at the temples, was brushed back, but a lock had fallen loose across his forehead. He looked brilliant, highly strung and a little dangerous. Saffron could see why impressionable young typists would swoon over him.

'Finally, today I managed to get five minutes with the old boy.' Playfair was speaking towards the garden, but occasionally looking to check that he still had his audience's attention. 'I told him in no uncertain terms, FDR wants to see the empire gone, preferably by the end of the war. That's the one thing he, Stalin and Hitler all agree upon.'

'And Winston didn't believe you? Amazing,' Mavis said, with heavy irony.

'Pah! What can you expect from a man who was considered too stupid even for Harrow?' Playfair discarded the stub of his cigarette and ground it into the stone beneath his feet. Then, apparently remembering his manners, he turned and said, 'Can I get you ladies anything?'

'I'll have a beer, please, love,' Mavis said.

'What a good idea,' Saffron added. 'Can I have one, too?'

'By all means. Coming up.'

'Is Charlie all right?' Saffron asked, once he was out of earshot. 'He seems quite worked up.'

Mavis gave a dismissive snort. 'He's always like that. My husband's problem is that the rest of the world refuses to believe he knows everything about everything and bow down to him accordingly. Mind you, to do him justice, he's right about most things.'

'He doesn't seem to be in the least bit interested in me,' Saffron said, more as an observation than a complaint.

'All right, let's do something about that, why don't we?'

Playfair emerged from the kitchen a few moments later, carrying a tray with a bottle of whisky and two glasses of pale yellow beer. He put the tray on the table, handed the two beers to Saffron and Mavis, and refilled his glass.

'This is Saffron Courtney,' Mavis said. 'She's staying with us for a week, remember?'

'Ah, right,' Playfair said, with a discernible lack of interest. Then he paused, thought for a moment, and suddenly his face came alive with a beaming smile. 'Of course! The celebrated Manhattan Mauler herself, Slugging Saffron Courtney. The PM's pet pipsqueak Colville was showing me the paper barely half an hour ago, boasting that he knew you. Well, what an honour, champ, to welcome you to our humble abode.'

Playfair sat on one of the chairs facing the two women.

'And you must be the not-quite-so-well-known Pinko Peer, the Honourable Charles Algernon Faversham Playfair,' Saffron said. 'Did I leave any names out?'

'No more than five or six,' Playfair said, amused by Saffron's attitude and at last fixing her with his full attention.

'Millicent gave Saffron a lift from the station to the embassy,' Mavis said, apparently unperturbed by her husband's newfound fascination with their beautiful house guest.

'Ah, yes, that explains it,' Playfair said, still looking only at Saffron. 'Millicent disapproves of me. She can't forgive me for not dying for my country.'

'Is that fair?' Saffron asked. 'The poor woman lost her fiancé.'

Playfair lit another cigarette. 'I know, and I feel for her,' he said, exhaling smoke with every word. 'I just can't bear the way she uses her loss as a stick with which to beat any man of more or less fighting age who happens not to be in uniform.'

'Charlie did try to join up, you know,' Mavis said, coming to his defence. 'Trouble was, no one would have him.'

Playfair nodded. 'Absolutely true. It was a matter of age. I was thirty-five when the war broke out, and the army's looking for fresh-faced eighteen-year-olds. My service to king and country must thus be conducted as a member of the diplomatic corps. So here I am . . . And here you are, Miss Courtney, with your remarkably well-cut uniform and your intriguing decorations. So, what outfit do you serve in?'

'The Joint Technical Board,' Saffron answered.

The fake name didn't fool Playfair for a second. 'Oh, you're one of Gubbins' Baker Street irregulars. Of course, should have guessed. And that explains your brief sojourn with Stephenson in New York. He's frightfully hugger-mugger with SOE. So what on earth are you doing here? Shouldn't you be parachuting into France *pour encourager* our French Resistance chums?'

'France isn't my territory. And my assignment in Washington is really a sort of rest cure.'

Playfair's eyes narrowed as he looked at Saffron. 'And what assignment is that, exactly?'

'Chatting up generals and senators to get them to look favourably on our efforts.'

'Ah, yes . . .' Playfair smiled. 'But what's the real reason you're here, eh? Why did Gubbins send you off to see Stephenson?' He exhaled slowly, and then his eyes brightened and his smile reappeared as he came up with the answer to his own question. 'Oh, wait . . . Of course, silly me. You've been lent to Stephenson, haven't you? He's got you chasing up that ludicrous spy fantasy of his.'

'I don't know what you're talking about,' Saffron deadpanned.

'Oh yes you do . . .' Playfair gave an exhausted sigh. 'I can't believe this is all being dug up yet again. Listen, Saffron . . . Washington is the most important embassy we have, and there's more than one person in it qualified to handle counter-intelligence operations. Please believe me, I implore you, that they are entirely satisfied that Stephenson is barking up the wrong tree with his belief that we have a spy in our midst.'

'You seem very well informed about intelligence matters,' Saffron said.

'People are always saying that Charlie's really a spy,' said Mavis casually. 'And they're not wrong.'

'Yes, they are, my dear, and you know it,' Playfair said, with an edge of indignation. 'Look, Miss Courtney . . .'

'Please . . . call me Saffron.'

'Well then, Saffron, the truth is, I have at times done the odd favour for the intelligence bods. Lots of diplomats have. When I was in Spain, my travels took me to places and I met people that were of interest to SIS. I snapped the odd photograph, borrowed a document or two. All pretty innocent stuff, part and parcel of my job as a diplomat.

'Likewise, here in the United States, my role as political counsellor inevitably means that I pick up the odd bit of useful information. You know . . . an Irish Catholic congressman from New York is raising money for the Irish Republican Army. Or a Midwestern state governor with large numbers of German-American voters is privately expressing a worrying *tendresse* towards dear Adolf. That sort of stuff. Naturally, I pass it on.'

'Does anyone ever pass things back to you?' Saffron asked.

'Well, one has the odd chat, and, after all, the whole point of conversation is that information passes in both directions.'

Before Saffron could respond, the telephone inside the house started ringing. 'Oh, bugger!' Playfair muttered, before striding off to answer it. He reappeared a few seconds later and looked at Saffron. 'It's for you. And they called collect, so I'm paying.'

'I'm so sorry,' Saffron said, getting to her feet.

'The phone's in the kitchen, of all ludicrous places.'

Saffron went in, closing the garden door behind her, and picked up the handset. 'Hello?'

'Miss Courtney, my name is Jarvis. I work at the embassy. That is why I reversed the charges. It meant Playfair spoke to an operator, rather than me. He'd . . . um, know my voice at once.'

'I see,' said Saffron, wondering why Jarvis was so keen not to be identified by Playfair. His manner seemed hesitant – oddly nervous.

'Not to beat about the bush, Miss Courtney, I know why you're here, and I, er . . . I have information that you should see, concerning the men at the embassy who might be of interest to you. Perhaps we could meet up for a leisurely chat with another colleague of mine. There's a place called the Dupont Bar and Grill, off Dupont Circle. Any taxi driver will know it. I'll meet you at seven, but no need to tell the Playfairs. Mum's the word, and all that.'

Before Saffron could reply, the line went dead.

'Hmm . . .' she murmured to herself.

'I've got a date,' Saffron said, as she re-emerged into the afternoon sunshine.

'Ooh,' cooed Mavis. 'Is he handsome?'

'Very,' Saffron replied. 'Most of the time. But he's not at his best at the moment. A little bit battered and bruised.'

'Poor chap.'

'Poor me.' Saffron laughed. 'I'm the one who has to look at him.' She reached into her bag, took out her purse and extracted a dime. 'Silly me! I almost forgot . . .' She handed Playfair the coin and added, 'This is for the call.'

'I'll try not to spend it all at once,' Playfair said cheerfully. But then, almost as if he had known what the call was really about, his smile vanished. 'You're a lovely girl, Saffron Courtney. But you pick fights in clubs and you let Stephenson use you as a human foxhound. Your determination to get into trouble verges on the perverse.'

'Possibly,' said Saffron, affecting indifference, while smarting from the fact that Playfair had hit upon precisely the thing she most feared about herself.

'Does it worry you that one of these days you might get yourself into trouble that you can't get out of?' he persevered. 'I mean, what if this person you're chasing really exists? Wouldn't he be willing to do absolutely anything to carry out his mission?' He paused. 'Including killing you.'

It suddenly struck Saffron that Playfair might be talking about himself. But because she was in his house, and Mavis was sitting a few feet away, she laughed and said with a bravado she didn't feel, 'I'm quite hard to kill, you know.'

Playfair looked at her with blank, poker player's eyes. 'Better if no one tried, don't you think?'

Saffron couldn't make out whether Playfair was expressing genuine concern for her, or issuing some kind of threat. Neither his facial expression nor his body language gave anything away. But he had at least told her one thing. Behind all the banter, the core of Charlie Playfair was as cold and hard as a steel blade. And possibly as deadly, too.

• • •

The Dupont Bar and Grill was a fifteen-minute cab ride from the Playfairs' house. Saffron had changed into a blue polka-dot cotton dress with short sleeves, puffed at the shoulder. It was a pleasure to be out of her uniform, and dressed as she was the men she was meeting would be more likely to underestimate her, and thus give away more than they intended.

The maître d' led Saffron across the room to a table tucked away in a corner: the perfect spot for clandestine lovers and conspiratorial diplomats. Two men rose to greet her. One was quite small – shorter than her, even without heels. His pale, blinking, watery eyes peered at her through round gold-rimmed glasses. He was dressed in a light grey, double-breasted suit. His blond hair was already receding from his forehead, though he could not have been older than mid-thirties.

This, Saffron knew, must be Jarvis. His appearance perfectly matched the hesitant voice she had heard on the phone. The man next to him was very different. He was a head taller than Jarvis, for a start, sturdier, suntanned, and boasted an impressively full, black handlebar moustache. Though he couldn't have been more than five or six years older than Saffron, he was wearing the uniform of a group captain in the RAF, a rank equivalent to an army colonel, with a medal collection that put hers to shame. 'Jonathan Goodhouse,' he said, taking her hand. 'But my friends call me Jonty.'

He smiled with the confidence of a man accustomed to getting women into bed, and Saffron immediately perceived he was sizing her up as another potential conquest. She was not interested in obliging him, but she smiled sweetly all the same. If that was the game he wanted to play, she was happy to join in.

'Well, Saffron,' Goodhouse began, 'I hope you've got a hearty appetite.'

'Oh,' she purred, 'I'm absolutely famished.'

'That's the spirit! Can't bear a girl who pushes a lettuce leaf around her plate all evening.' He raised his hand and clicked his fingers to summon a waiter. 'I'll order for us both.'

'By all means,' Saffron said, wondering why so many men seemed to think women were incapable of deciding what they wanted to eat.

'Two quarter-pound cheeseburgers, medium rare, with French fries, pickles and slaw on the side,' Goodhouse told the waiter. 'What will you be having, Jarvis?'

'I rather fancy the . . . ah, Caesar salad, perhaps with grilled chicken.' He looked at Goodhouse somewhat nervously. 'If you don't mind me pushing some lettuce around?'

'Not at all, old boy, push away! And cold beers all round, what?'

It struck Saffron that she might not be the only one playing a role. Jarvis was nominally a first secretary, which made him at least as senior as an army major. He might also be an SIS agent. In both cases, someone, somewhere, held him in much higher regard than his meek and mild manner might suggest. And there was a predatory shrewdness in Goodhouse's eyes that went beyond mere lust. To win those medals, he had either shot down a lot of German fighters or flown a great many bombing missions. That made him tough, competent and not afraid of a fight.

She smiled to herself as she realised that they would be making the same calculations about her.

'So,' Goodhouse said, 'I hear you spent a few days in New York. What did you make of the place?'

'Oh . . . I thought the shopping was simply divine.'

'And the nightlife . . . I imagine a pretty girl like you must have been out on the town every night.'

So he knows about that damn gossip column. Saffron smiled. 'Yes, I even saw that new singer, Mr Sinatra. He had the dreamiest blue eyes.'

Jarvis finally entered the conversation. 'That's quite enough chit-chat, I think. Let us get down to business. You, Miss Courtney, have been seconded from the Special Operations Executive to pursue a theory promulgated by Mr Stephenson, who is *nominally* in charge of all British intelligence in the United States and Canada . . .'

Saffron noted the emphasis on 'nominally'. That was Jarvis telling her that neither SIS nor the diplomatic corps accepted this Canadian businessman's dominion over them.

'To the effect,' Jarvis continued, 'that the British embassy in Washington is harbouring a traitor. Correct?'

'Yes,' said Saffron. There seemed little point in denying it.

'We are here to dissuade you from that task. You see, Mr Stephenson is wrong, a point we hope to prove to your satisfaction this evening. Both the diplomatic and military wings of the British mission in Washington have much more important things to think about right now. Talks are taking place over the next two weeks that will determine the outcome of the war—'

'I am aware of that.'

'Then you will appreciate that we cannot be distracted by someone poking their nose into our business, in pursuit of wild theories that are entirely without merit.'

'That is not what the prime minister believes,' Saffron responded.

To her delight, Jarvis was taken aback. 'I'm sorry . . . Are you seriously suggesting—'

'We discussed the subject on board the *Queen Mary*. Of course, I can't divulge the details of our conversation, but I'm sure you know that Mr Churchill places great faith in Mr Stephenson's abilities.'

The waiter had reappeared with their food. 'Mmm . . .' Saffron groaned, appreciatively, as she took the first bite of her cheeseburger. 'What a splendid choice, Group Captain, it's delicious. Shall we all dig in?'

Meanwhile, you two can wonder what Winnie actually said to me, Saffron thought. *Chew on that, why don't you, you idiots?*

The food was quickly finished, the drinks consumed. Jarvis reached down to his feet and pulled up a black leather briefcase with a small royal coat of arms stamped in gold below the lock. He opened it and withdrew a foolscap manila envelope.

'I am going to pay you and Mr Stephenson a compliment,' he said. 'When the allegations of treachery were first raised, interviews were conducted with the nine men whose positions and security clearance allowed them to see classified documents of the kind that a spy, if he existed, might find of interest.' He paused. 'Actually, there were ten men with that seniority. But I hope you will agree that Lord Halifax, who served with distinction on the Western Front in the first war and served his country as both Viceroy of India and Foreign Secretary, is above suspicion.'

'The poor man lost his son, too,' said Goodhouse, to underline the point.

'Of course,' said Saffron, calmly. 'I don't think for one moment that Lord Halifax could be a traitor.'

'Glad to hear it. Carry on, Jarvis.'

'In this envelope are the summaries of the detailed reports on all nine men,' Jarvis said. 'A few lines have been blacked out. You may take it from me that the information in them, while classified, contains no suggestion of guilt, or even suspicion. Four of the men are serving military officers. They include the military attaché, Rear Admiral Mostyn-Clarke, and the respective attachés of the three services, of whom Group Captain Goodhouse is one.'

'All three of us have seen active service within the first years of this war, and Ken Jewell—'

'Brigadier Kenneth Jewell, the army's senior officer here,' Jarvis interjected.

'. . . won an MC at Passchendaele in '17, when he was nineteen, and another at Tobruk in '41. You'd get bloody short shrift if you accused him of spying for Jerry, I can tell you.'

'He made his feelings very clear in his interview,' Jarvis said. 'You can take it from me, Miss Courtney, that all our interviewees were far from happy to have their loyalty and patriotism questioned.'

And yet, thought Saffron, *one of them is Gerald, the loving godfather.*

'The five diplomats who were investigated were Mr Todd, who is the deputy head of mission . . . Mr Barrington, who is the minister counsellor defence, and therefore acting as the Foreign Office representative at the current conference . . . His deputy, Mr Samwell . . . Mr Brinton, who handles trade – accurate information about arms manufacturing, convoy cargoes and so forth – would be invaluable to the enemy . . . And finally Mr Playfair, the minister counsellor political, whom you, of course, have met.'

Jarvis handed over the envelope. 'The summaries are quite short.' He gave the faintest hint of a wry smile. 'Our masters are busy men. They don't have time for any document that takes longer than three minutes to read. But there's no need for you to hurry. Take your time. As one's teachers used to say . . . read, mark and inwardly digest. We gentlemen shall retire to the bar for a quiet drink. Let us know when you've finished. Goodhouse, perhaps you could order Miss Courtney some coffee.'

Saffron read the summaries. They were, as Jarvis had suggested, exonerations of all nine men. None of them had ever expressed the slightest support for Nazi political ideology, nor acted in any way suspiciously. None had any personal habits or weaknesses, from gambling debts to homosexual tendencies, that made them susceptible to blackmail.

The interviews had also covered all the journeys that the men had made around America that might have given them material worth passing to Berlin about military bases, ports, factory complexes, political rallies and so forth. The fact that they were all frequently out of town dispirited Saffron most of all. Gerald always posted his messages from Washington, but she felt sure that if she had access to all the men's detailed travel records, none of them would have been in DC on every day on which Gerald's messages had been sent. Of course, someone could have posted something for them. But still, she could see why Jarvis, and his superiors, were so sure that Stephenson was wrong.

But the letters were sent, and they were in code and someone was responsible for that, Saffron reminded herself, not wanting to lose her faith in the mission.

She saved the two summaries that interested her most for last, simply because she knew the men involved. Jonty Goodhouse, she discovered, was a fighter pilot. He had flown in the Battle of Britain, making eleven enemy kills, before being transferred to the Western Desert and from there to Washington. It never hurt to have one's government represented by a dashing young war hero, and Goodhouse had an impressive record by any standards, as did all four of the military men.

Goodhouse was, the report noted, a man of considerable sexual appetites. But since he was a bachelor, resolutely heterosexual and not known to seduce other men's wives, there were no grounds for blackmail. He was judged to be potentially vulnerable to a Mata Hari-style seductress, but there was no evidence of one snaring him yet.

I'd get him singing like a canary, Saffron thought, smiling to herself. Then she turned to the Hon. Charles Playfair.

At first, Saffron was disappointed. There was little that Millicent had not already told her, or that she had not observed for herself. Playfair was brilliant, arrogant, sometimes charming, and yet at other times equally obnoxious. He was vehemently anti-fascist, and his undisguised support for the left-wing Republicans during the Spanish Civil War had led to him being vetted for Communist sympathies. The report did not detail the findings of that investigation, but they couldn't have been damaging, or Charlie would not still be in his plum job.

But she was struck by the fact that almost a quarter of Playfair's summary had been blacked out. That was a higher proportion than any of the others, five of which were untouched. So, there were plenty of things about him – and she only had Jarvis's word that they did not directly pertain to the spy inquiry – that SIS did not want anyone to know.

Still, there was some interesting material left unredacted: *Like many men of his class and education, who have been separated from their parents at an early age and forced to fend for themselves, Playfair's apparently flippant exterior hides a much tougher, colder core.*

Saffron stopped reading. So, they had seen it, too. But then, she could say the same about a lot of the upper-class Englishmen she'd met over the years: all public-school charm on the outside; as icy, selfish and ruthless as paid assassins underneath.

What followed next intrigued her even more: *No evidence has been found that Playfair is spying for the enemy, nor should he be held in any suspicion. But . . .*

The rest of the sentence was lost beneath black ink. 'Damn it!' Saffron muttered. She held the paper up to the light to see if the lost words might be discernible, but no luck. 'But what?'

She put the summaries back in the envelope and carried it to the bar. 'Thank you, Mr. Jarvis,' she said. 'That was very useful. Clearly no evidence was found against any of the men who were investigated.'

'So, you'll tell Stephenson that?' Jarvis asked.

'Do I need to? Has he not seen these summaries?'

Jarvis looked edgy. He cleared his throat. 'No, as a matter of fact he hasn't, although he was informed of the investigation's general findings.'

'Why not?'

'For the same reason that your CO in London doesn't go around handing out your personnel file to every Tom, Dick and Harry. That is why I said we were paying you and Mr Stephenson a compliment. The access you have been given is truly exceptional. It required approval at a senior level. It was intended to persuade you that there is nothing to be gained in searching for a man who clearly does not exist. So, I very much hope that you will now assure me that you will desist from any further inquiries.'

That made the third time in a few hours that Saffron had been told to back off and abandon her mission. She could not decide whether it was just sheer stubbornness on her part – that bloody-minded Courtney determination to prove the world wrong – or a genuine faith in the evidence that Stephenson and the brilliant Miss Keswick had assembled. But whatever it was, she now felt even more determined to press on with her mission.

'There's only one thing I can assure you of, Mr Jarvis. I will continue to carry out my instructions from the prime minister.' Saffron looked in turn at the two men who had been sent to warn her off. 'As I am sure that you both would do, too, if he ever gave any to you.'

With that, she turned and headed for the exit.

• • •

As soon as Saffron returned to the Playfairs' house, she heard Mavis calling out, 'How was your date?'

She followed the sound of the voice into the drawing room. The Playfairs were sitting in armchairs, reading. Mavis put her book down and said, 'Come on, tell all!'

'Not much to tell,' Saffron said, knowing that the best cover always has an element of the truth. 'The poor boy is definitely off games. A peck on the cheek was about all he could manage. But I'm hoping he'll be feeling better before my stay is out.' To change the subject, she asked, 'What are you reading?'

'The latest Agatha Christie.' Mavis held up a hardback copy of *The Moving Finger*.

'Such a highbrow, my wife,' said Playfair, in affectionate mockery. He had risen from his armchair when Saffron entered the room, and was holding a cigarette in one hand and a copy of James Joyce's *Finnegans Wake* in the other.

'Intellectual snob!' retorted Mavis, throwing a small cushion at her husband and narrowly missing the whisky glass that sat on the table beside his chair.

Mavis turned her attention back to Saffron. 'I know it's not serious literature, but I love a good murder story.' She smiled. 'That's my guilty secret.'

'Mine, too,' Saffron replied. 'I think I'll head up to bed, if that's all right with you. I hardly slept a wink last night, and I haven't unpacked, so I'll do that and turn in. Oh, Mavis, do you have any notepaper and an envelope, by any chance? I've got to write something for Lady Halifax.'

'Of course,' Mavis said, getting up from her chair and walking over to an antique bureau. 'What's Lady H got you doing for her?'

'Oh, just an appointments list . . . in case I'm seeing anyone that she knows and can bend their ear on my behalf. Very kind of her, really.'

'I wish she'd bend some ears for me,' Mavis said with a laugh as she found what Saffron needed. 'There you are.'

Saffron went upstairs and started sorting out the contents of her suitcase and putting them away. She enjoyed the process of finding a place for everything, arranging her clothes and shoes, and all the paraphernalia required to wash and beautify herself, in the neatest, most orderly way. Tidying up physical objects also helped her set her mind in perfect order.

Going over the meeting at the bar and grill, Saffron thought that Jarvis and Goodhouse had succeeded in one respect. Having read the summaries of the nine potential spies, she had to admit that the investigation into them had not been a whitewash. The job had been done properly, and if there had been good reason to suspect any of the men involved, it would have been flagged. But there was no such reason. All nine men had emerged with their reputations intact.

And yet she kept coming back to the fact that the Gerald letters were real, and that someone, somewhere, had responded to the SIS man's visit to that apartment in Östersund by ceasing the correspondence. But maybe she was approaching the problem from the wrong angle. Instead of trying to find Gerald, maybe she should make sure that Gerald found her.

Thanks to that newspaper story, her arrival in the United States had been about as unsubtle as a stampeding herd of elephants. But perhaps there was a way of turning that to her advantage. What if she made her mission as obvious as possible? If there was no spy, then nothing would happen, a few men would say 'I told you so', and she could get on with buttering up powerful Americans on Brigadier Gubbins' behalf. But if the Nazis did have a man inside the embassy, he and his allies in Washington would surely want to stop her from getting in their way. And to do that, they would have to come out into the open, where she could see them and – hopefully – best them.

Saffron realised that offering herself as a sacrificial lamb, tethered for every passing tiger to see, was a risky strategy.

But given the potential threat to the Allies' war secrets, not to mention the lives of a prime minister, a president and a former king of England, then her life was a small price to pay.

And in any case, she concluded, she had survived everything that the war had thrown at her so far. *So I can bloody well survive this, too.*

With her mind made up firmly, Saffron went to bed and turned out the light. As she lay there, she realised there was one last question she had not properly considered: was Charlie Playfair the spy? He certainly fitted the criteria Donovan had put to her. He had access to classified information. He was known for his left-wing, anti-fascist views, so would never be thought of as a possible Nazi. His highly strung, hard-drinking character suggested a man under stress. And then there was that coldness. It was something Saffron had seen, perhaps to a lesser degree, in other men like him. Products of the boarding school system, as the report had mentioned.

That, of course, didn't make them all spies. But it did give them a gift for deception. The Playfairs had invited her to stay with them. That might have been a spontaneous gesture by Mavis, or it might have been Charlie wanting to have Saffron where he could keep an eye on her. But that would mean she could observe *him*. Most men with something to hide would shy away from that. But not Charlie. He'd think he was so clever that no one could outsmart him.

As she was drifting off, she heard a scuffling of feet and paws, and the sound of the front door opening and closing as one of the Playfairs took Franco out for a late-night walk. Satisfied that it was nothing to worry about, Saffron made herself comfortable, and within no time was fast asleep.

• • •

Joe Lewandowski lived in Congress Heights, on the Virginia side of the Potomac, with his wife Magda and their two children, Jake, who was five, and Suzy, who was three: two freckle-faced, golden-haired, all-American kids. Their neighbourhood was white, lower middle class, full of folks like them working hard to give themselves and their children a better life. Most of them lived in low-rise, red-brick apartment blocks, all nearly identical, but the Lewandowskis were in the minority of those who owned their own semi-detached home, with a basement and a yard behind the house.

Joe had built an aviary in his yard. It was about ten feet high and ran across the Lewandowskis' back fence, with netting that was held up by a slew of metal poles and wires. Any time the other moms from the children's kindergarten brought their kids over for a play date, the first thing the children would do, whatever the weather, would be to dash through the house and out the back door to go and look at the birdies. As often as not, their parents would follow them, too.

Magda was warm, friendly, and got on well with the other mothers, just as her senior officers back home had told her to do, but it was the aviary that made her house such a popular destination. The women could sit and chat, enjoying a slice of Magda's delicious *szarlotka* apple pie with their coffee, knowing that their children would be happily occupied outside. Most of Jake's friends were busy learning to identify every make and model of automobile, but Jake was the only one who could name the brightly coloured lovebirds and budgerigars, the zebra finches with their black and white striped tails, and the speckled quails, scurrying about on the floor of the enclosure.

If the kids' dads came over, they'd take a look at the birds, but the biggest attraction for them was Joe's ham radio setup in the basement. Joe would grab some brews and lead them down.

On the wall at the bottom of the stairs was a wooden plaque with the metal badge that named Joseph M. Lewandowski as a life member of the American Radio Relay League, call sign K4MRQ. Right next to it was his framed amateur radio licence from the Federal Communications Commission. Immediately, the other guys knew that Joe was serious about this stuff. And that was no surprise, because anyone who knew him knew that Joe Lewandowski was a guy who believed in doing things well or not at all. As he liked to say: '"Good enough" is never good enough.'

Joe's equipment was on the workbench against the far wall. 'Okay, let's start with this,' he would say. 'We got a professional quality microphone and headphones, good as you'll get in any radio station. This here is my Morse code key and Allied Radio Corporation deluxe oscillator, turns the keystrokes into signals.'

The guys would be impressed. 'Man, you can write Morse code?'

'Sure thing, one-twenty words a minute. If you ever have any emergencies, just come round here and I'll send out the SOS!'

Lewandowski saved his best gear till last: a grey metal box with a black fascia, dotted with knobs and switches, with two big, round, silver tuning dials. 'That right there is a military specification Abbott Instrument TR-4 ultra short wave transmitter-receiver, just as good as our guys on the battlefield get.'

One of Joe's neighbours, Bobby Muller, was a radio ham, like Joe. 'How did you get hold of a thing like that?' he asked, the first time he saw the transceiver, a note of suspicion in his voice. 'I thought all radios were going to the war effort. Was this black market or something?'

Joe laughed. 'Hell, no!' There was a pile of back numbers of *QST*, the radio ham's bible, on the workbench. Joe rifled through it, found the one he wanted and handed it to Muller.

'Here you go,' he said. 'December '41 edition.'

'Well, I'll be damned.' Muller sighed, looking at a full-page ad for the Abbott TR-4.

'The magazine arrives mid-November, right? I see the ad. I think, "Damn, that's a beauty," and then I figure I'd better buy it right away before the missus starts taking all my dough to pay for Christmas, you know what I mean?'

'Oh, I hear you, brother!'

'So, I send away for it right away and coupla weeks later, Friday December fifth, it arrives. Two days later the Japs bomb Pearl Harbor. Guess I got in just in time, huh?'

'You sure did.' Muller sighed. 'Man, I wish I'd done the exact same thing.'

With guys who weren't already experts, Joe would explain how with a set-up like this, you could send signals right around the world, bouncing them off a layer of the upper atmosphere called the ionosphere. 'Night-time's the best. Don't ask me why, but the signals go way further.'

Another time, his buddy Frankie Trentino had said, 'Wait, you could send a message to Berlin? Like, "Screw you, Adolf!"'

Joe had laughed. 'Sure . . . "Surrender now, you dumb Nazi bastard!"'

The way he saw it, this was another way of hiding in plain sight. As he'd tell Magda, if everyone knew he was a radio ham, then no one would be surprised to see the basement light glowing in the middle of the night. The aviary, though, was more like the kind of distraction a magician uses, so the audience doesn't see what he's really up to. Everyone was so busy cooing at the cute little birdies, even the other hams didn't notice that all the horizontal wires and the vertical poles added up to the ten-by-thirty-foot curtain array antenna Joe needed to get his signals across the Atlantic.

What amazed both Joe and Magda, however, was the simple fact that the state was happy to let Joe have a radio transceiver at all. The Constitution itself ensured that he could say whatever he liked, to whomever he liked, whenever he liked – and hear back from them, likewise – and the government had no right to stop him. There was not the slightest fear that the secret police would come barging through his door . . . because there were no secret police. What weakness, what decadence! Truly, the Americans were crazy.

Right now, though, at one in the morning, it was not Joe the contractor, but Jozef Lewandowski, the secret intelligence agent, who was sitting in his basement in his underpants, T-shirt and dressing gown, encoding a message he was sending to his bosses back home. An hour earlier he'd been woken by the phone ringing. He'd kissed Magda on the forehead and told her to go back to sleep, then went down to the kitchen where the phone was located.

'I told you not to call here,' he hissed, when he heard who was on the line. 'Emergencies only.'

'This is an emergency,' Foxglove had replied, and Lewandowski had been jolted by hearing a trace of anxiety – even fear – in Foxglove's voice.

'Tell me what it is and make it snappy.'

Foxglove had talked, and kept it quick, but now Lewandowski was worried, too. So he was sending a long message, providing a detailed update and assessment of the situation. His report would kick the mechanism of an all-powerful intelligence agency into gear. Meetings would be held. Commands would be sent out to agents in Britain and America, demanding further information, fast. Then, shortly after sundown in Washington – the middle of the night in Europe – Joe would come home from the bar where he had his regular beer after work, keeping that routine normal. He would wait for the message from home, then receive the instructions that he had requested.

And what the whole process amounted to was the answer to a simple question: 'Do you want me to kill Saffron Courtney?'

• • •

Saffron woke feeling refreshed, and opened the bedroom curtains to find bright sunlight filling the room. She had work to do today: a morning appointment at the Pentagon with a colonel who worked for General George Marshall, the US Army's Chief of Staff, then an invitation to speak at a tea party organised by the Daughters of the American Revolution.

Her briefings with Stephenson and Donovan had told her what to expect. Marshall was in charge of planning the invasion of Europe, so his man would want to know what SOE could do to assist. The message that Saffron intended to hammer home was simple: 'Every German soldier who fights the resistance is one less soldier fighting American soldiers. Every supply train that's halted by smashed railway tracks means less fuel for

German tanks and ammunition for German guns. Every wire cut is another vital message that doesn't get through to German HQ, or another order that doesn't reach the front line.'

Saffron knew what she would be saying was true. She believed SOE could make a difference. She was confident she could be persuasive. Also, she would be dealing with a straightforward, practical-minded man.

The Daughters of the American Revolution were another matter. They were an organisation comprised of women who could trace their lineage back to ancestors who had fought in or supported the American War of Independence. Their motto was 'God, Home and Country'. When Stephenson had told Saffron about them, she had asked, 'Won't they dislike me for being British? After all, their ancestors fought a war to kick us out.'

'True, but remember, their ancestors were also the descendants of British immigrants,' he'd replied. 'They grew up as subjects of the Crown. So really, they're as British as Americans get. Just remind them that you're a colonial, too. Tell them lots of inspiring stories about fighting the wicked Nazis and fascists. Be a warrior princess. You'll have them eating out of your hand.'

Saffron was not so sure about that. She imagined the Daughters as hard-boiled middle-aged matrons. *Give me a randy old army officer any day. Far easier to twist round my little finger!*

As she washed and dressed, Saffron realised that it was a relief to be thinking about how best to promote SOE, instead of obsessing about Nazi spies.

There was a knock on her door.

'Come in!' Saffron called.

The door opened and Charlie Playfair stuck his head through it, showing no signs of wear and tear after the previous evening's whisky consumption. 'The chef wishes you to know that breakfast is served.' He grinned. Saffron walked down and found that Mavis had made eggs, bacon and all the trimmings. 'I thought I'd give you a proper English breakfast,' she said. 'Since you can't get one in England.'

With the garden bathed in sunshine, Franco curled up in his dog bed and Playfair reading the *Washington Post* while the two women chatted, it was a scene of perfect domestic bliss. Mavis was wearing the same dungarees as she had the day before, but her pale blue shirt had been replaced by a red and white checked one, and a red patterned headscarf to match. 'I'm all day at the shelter,' she said, 'but Loretta will be here soon. What time did you say your first meeting was?'

'Ten forty-five, at the Pentagon.'

'Hmm . . .' Mavis thought for a moment. 'You could catch a bus on Foxhall, take it to Georgetown University and then change to an Arlington bus. That should take you all the way to the Pentagon. But it's such a lovely day. Why don't you walk to Georgetown through the park? Loretta can come with you some of the way. She can bring Arthur in the pram, give him some fresh air.'

'That would be lovely. I can't decide whether to come back here afterwards and then change into civvies. I've been invited to tea by the Daughters of the American Revolution. Do you think I should put on a proper dress?'

'I don't honestly know,' Mavis said.

Playfair lowered his paper and said, 'It has to be the uniform. They'll take you more seriously. If you pitch up in a floral frock and start yakking on about killing Jerries and blowing up bridges, they won't believe a word you say.' He looked at his watch. 'Right, time to scarper.' He gave a theatrical sigh. 'Off for another gruelling day of trying to save our glorious leader from himself.'

Saffron waited while Mavis tilted her head to receive her husband's goodbye kiss. 'Before you go, could you do me a favour?' she said. 'I've written out that list of appointments for Lady Halifax. I don't suppose you could drop it off for her at the embassy?'

'Of course,' he replied. 'My pleasure.'

'I'll nip up and get it, then.' As Saffron ran upstairs, she thought, *If there is someone in the embassy who wants to come after me, that piece of paper is a tasty piece of bait – particularly if that person is Charlie Playfair.*

• • •

Lewandowski was used to getting by without much sleep. That was just as well, because he was up again by six, calling his men and organising a schedule that meant between them they could have eyes on Saffron Courtney twenty-four hours a day. The more they knew about her routine, the easier it would be to capture and kill her, should the order come.

He took the first shift, turning up at the house where she was staying shortly after seven in the morning. The location suited him, the house being close enough to the park that it was possible to watch it from the woods. There were trails through the park, but few people using them. He sat up against a tree with a book in his hands, and none of the passers-by gave him a second glance. When he'd been there a couple of hours, a man who'd passed him going one way saw him when he was coming back. He'd stopped, grinned and said, 'Must be a good book!'

'*Grapes of Wrath*,' Lewandowski said, holding it up.

The man nodded approvingly. 'Steinbeck's the best!' And then he moved on.

Charles Playfair left the house at 08.50, got into his car and drove away. Lewandowski knew that he was going to the British embassy, two miles away. He estimated the journey time at eight minutes.

Mavis Playfair emerged a short while later, turned right, and began walking up the street towards Foxhall Road. Her drab clothing made it obvious that she was going to carry out her charity work in the slums. Washington DC was, in many respects, a city that had more in common with the old rebel South than the unionist North, and many of Lewandowski's American friends held views about its Black population that were worthy of the Ku Klux Klan. Lewandowski strongly agreed. It was one of the few subjects on which he did not have to feign his views.

Around 09.30, two women came out of the house. One was the Playfairs' servant, a Negress, in a pale lilac housecoat, pushing a pram. The other was tall, slender, dark-haired, wearing military uniform. So that was Saffron Courtney; for a moment, Lewandowski looked at her as a man rather than an agent. 'But if the order comes . . .' he murmured to himself as the Courtney woman helped the servant manoeuvre the pram down the steps to the street. They walked to the corner and crossed the road towards the park.

Here we go, Lewandowski thought, and melted into the trees.

• • •

'So, how did you come to work for Mavis Playfair?' Saffron asked, as she and Loretta started off down the path that would take her to Georgetown.

'We met down at the soup kitchen,' Loretta said, and it was clear she had been in the line for free food, not helping to dole it out. Loretta's story, it turned out, was an all too common tale of poverty, family breakdown and deprivation. She was born in Mobile, Alabama. Her father had left home when she was ten, leaving her mother and her three siblings: two younger sisters, Mary and Dionne, and a brother, Wilson, who was the baby of the family. Their mother had tried her best to support them, taking any jobs she could get. But there was little work for anyone in the Depression, and still less for those who were Black.

They'd moved to Washington to live with her mother's aunt, who had a tiny apartment in the north-east of the city. But the aunt had died and the landlord had evicted the family when Loretta's mother couldn't pay the rent. Since then they'd lived hand-to-mouth. 'And then I met Miss Mavis, ma'am, and I guess she just about saved our lives. See, Miss Mavis, she don't see colour, just people. It's like the Bible says, we all have one father. The Lord is the maker of us all.'

Talking to Loretta, Saffron could see what had drawn Mavis to her, out of all the countless impoverished, beaten-down souls who passed through the soup kitchen. She was bright, full of life, obviously capable of much more than fate had so far allowed her, if she was only given a chance. She worked at the Playfairs' house five days a week, so that Mavis could help out at the soup kitchen whenever she was needed. The pay was two dollars fifty a day, plus bus fare, which Loretta regarded as more than generous.

'Miss Mavis don't know for sure when she be gon' down the kitchen. Could be five days, could be one. Like this week, she worked yesterday and today. Not workin' tomorrow, maybe the day after. Next week, could be different. That's why I come every day, just so's there's always someone for Arthur. Weekends . . .' Loretta's voice tailed off. She asked, 'You all right?'

Saffron had stopped dead. She thought she sensed someone moving through the woods, as if keeping track of them. She looked around, but couldn't see anybody. She shook her head. Evidently, she was still jumpier than she liked to admit after those incidents in New York. 'Sorry, it was nothing . . . You were about to tell me about your weekends.'

'Uh-huh . . . I work in a bar across town. It gets kinda rowdy sometimes, but I'm used to that, don't let it bother me none, 'cos I know it's payin' for my night school. I go three evenings a week. Gonna get my high school diploma in a year or two. I won't let nothing stop me from doin' that, no matter how many jobs I have to work.'

'I'm sure you won't.' Saffron felt humbled by the young woman's determination, and painfully aware of the privileges she enjoyed and the comforts she took for granted.

They came to a clearing in the woods. 'This here is Miss Mavis's thinkin' seat,' Loretta said with a grin, indicating a bench. 'When we go out together, she always says to me, "You take care of baby, Loretta. I'm just going to have a little think."'

Loretta's imitation of Mavis's accent was uncannily accurate. Saffron laughed and asked, 'Does Mavis ever tell you what she thinks about?'

Loretta shook her head. 'Nope. Sometimes I ask her what's on her mind, but she just says, "Oh, this an' that." All I know is this is a real peaceful spot, where a person could sit and put their mind at ease. And Miss Mavis, she needs to do that from time to time, the amount of work she does, helping folks.'

'I bet.' Saffron heard a gurgling coming from the pram. 'Someone's waking up.'

Loretta smiled. 'I'd best be getting back. Pretty soon this little feller's gon' be crying for his milk. Been a real pleasure talking to you, Miss Saffron.'

'We must do it again very soon,' Saffron replied.

Saffron watched Loretta pushing the pram back up the path, singing softly to the baby as she went, and was about to turn around and head into the city, when a thought struck her. Mavis Playfair always liked to sit on this bench, in private. That could simply mean it was a good spot to think in peace, away from her husband, her baby and her work. Or it could mean something else.

Saffron hoped with all her heart that she was wrong. She liked and admired Mavis, and wanted to believe she was the person she seemed. But her mission required her to suspect everybody. And her training had taught her that a park bench was an ideal place for a spy, or a trusted courier, to leave and pick up messages.

Torn between the desire to do her job, and the fear that this might mean exposing the Playfairs as traitors, Saffron walked slowly around the bench, then got down on her haunches to give it a closer examination.

Nothing. But that might only mean that there was no current message passing one way or the other. She said to herself, *I'll have to keep coming back.*

• • •

From his hiding place in the trees, Lewandowski frowned as he watched Saffron examining the bench, trying to work out what she was up to. And then the penny dropped, and a grin spread across his face. When the time came to capture Miss Courtney, he now knew exactly how he was going to do it.

• • •

In all of humanity there were two men, and two alone, the very mention of whose names made millions shudder in fear. They were both tyrants, warmongers and genocidal psychopaths, and one of them, at this moment, was sitting at his desk in his private office at the heart of a bunker protected by concrete walls several metres thick, deep in a forest in Eastern Europe. He was stroking his moustache, another feature that he shared with his counterpart, who was also his deadliest foe.

'Tell me again why I should agree to this,' he said.

The only other man in the room was bespectacled, not particularly tall or imposing, and seemingly innocuous. He had very short, neat hair, a high forehead and unremarkable features. It was the face of a teacher or a bank clerk: an instantly forgettable, provincial nobody.

He was, in fact, one of the greatest murderers in the history of the world. As the commander of his nation's security apparatus, the mechanism through which all its people and those of conquered nations were observed, disciplined and oppressed, he was responsible not only for the armies of spies and secret police, but also the torturers and firing squads and the vast network of camps to which millions were sent, but from which almost no one ever returned. His master saw liars, traitors and enemies wherever he looked, and this harmless-looking henchman duly hunted down and eliminated them.

Now, though, he had another role: that of the only man capable of standing in front of the great leader and telling him something that even approximated to the truth, instead of what he wanted to hear.

'Because this is a unique opportunity,' he said. 'The Americans and the British are meeting, as we speak, to discuss their invasion of Europe.'

'They're taking their time about it. Why are their ships not massing in the English Channel? Why not invade this year?'

'That is precisely the question the Americans have been asking the British. They wanted to be in France by now. But the British are cautious. They have been at war for a long time and learned many hard lessons. They do not want to move until the Luftwaffe has been knocked out, guaranteeing them total air superiority.'

'What does Göring have to say about that?'

'What he always says – that the Luftwaffe can, and will, defeat the British and American air forces.'

The leader grunted, though whether it was in agreement with Göring's view, or scepticism at such blithe confidence, even his most loyal lieutenant could not discern.

'The British also want to build up enough men and matériel to ensure they and the Americans gain a solid foothold on the first day of the invasion.'

'Do they really think they can break the Atlantic Wall? Concrete, steel and guns, all the way from the Arctic Circle in Norway to the Spanish border? It is surely impenetrable.'

'Not yet, no . . . but next year, maybe. Our men in London have been sending back the current industrial production figures, in Britain and America. To take one example, the production of aircraft in both nations this year will be roughly double compared to the year before. Next year, it will double again. Between them, they will produce somewhere between one hundred thousand and one hundred and fifty thousand aircraft between now and the end of next year, and they are anticipating that the final figure will be at the high end of that scale.'

'Those numbers are propaganda.'

'No, my leader, they are the official, secret estimates, intended for the eyes of Roosevelt, Churchill and their most senior politicians and military commanders. And they are compiled by men who pride themselves on finding out the truth, however unpalatable.'

Neither man needed to be told unspoken words: *which is not the case here.*

The leader looked at his underling. Everyone who had ever had personal dealings with him knew that look, and what it meant: a decision was being made. *Shall I let this man live, or order him killed?*

The man took off his glasses and rubbed them on his handkerchief, as a distraction while he waited for the verdict.

'And what about tanks and ships?' asked the leader, stretching out the moment almost to breaking point. 'Surely if aircraft production is at this level, then other manufacturing must suffer. There is only so much steel in the world, and only so many workers.'

The man shook his head, trying to conceal his relief that he had been given this opportunity to clinch his argument. 'No, there is no decline. Production of everything from motorbikes to battleships is increasing, in line with their aircraft. And, of course, American factories are entirely safe. No one can bomb them. While even the British are suffering far less damage to their factories and docks than before. And Britain can call upon the natural resources of Canada and Australia, the limitless manpower of India. Their nation may be smaller and weaker than America, but they still have their empire.'

The leader stroked his moustache thoughtfully and the bespectacled man decided this was the moment to press his argument home.

'This opportunity that we have been given to strike is one we simply cannot afford to let slip. We may never again have an asset who is in a position to remove both men with one blow. And even if another chance does present itself, it may be too late. We are very close to the point when sheer industrial power will make the victory of the Western allies inevitable, both in Western Europe and the Pacific. Once they set foot in France, they will not stop until they get to Berlin.'

The man paused. This was the truth that everyone who had the slightest capacity for objective judgement understood – everyone except for the leader. To insist on its veracity was a huge risk – perhaps even a fatal one – but he had come too far now to turn back.

'Go on . . .' The leader's hooded eyes gave nothing away. Was he on the point of being persuaded, or simply handing out more rope for an underling to hang himself with?

The man took a deep breath. 'If we strike now, then everything changes. Roosevelt and Churchill are more than just leaders. They are symbols of their nations.'

'A cripple and a drunk,' said the leader. 'What kind of symbols are those?'

'The British people are all drunks themselves. They do not think worse of Churchill for his champagne, his brandy and his cigars. And they love him for his stubbornness, his refusal to surrender. As for Roosevelt . . . Well, he brought an end to the Depression—'

'No, the war did that.'

'It certainly helped, yes. But when Roosevelt spoke to America after the humiliation of Pearl Harbor, he turned a nation of isolationists into one that would fight in every theatre of war from the English Channel to the Pacific.'

'You sound as if you are in love with these men yourself.'

The man bowed his head. 'I am merely pointing out the symbolic hold these men have over their people, and the collapse of morale that will inevitably follow if they are killed. This moment of instability, on both sides of the Atlantic, will give us a unique opportunity that we must seize. If we strike with all our force, then we can win the next war before it has even begun. By the time the Americans and the British wake up to what is happening, it will be too late. We will have seized everything.' He dared to venture a semblance of a smile. 'Who knows, we may not just be in Rome and Paris, but in London, too.'

Silence fell. The underling told himself to be patient. He had said all he could say. Perhaps more than he should. Now all he could do was wait.

The silence stretched on into minutes while the leader considered. The other man could feel beads of sweat beginning to prick his forehead. Finally he spoke.

'Our enemies will not simply accept their fate. They will try to take revenge. Why should I risk that?'

'Let them try!' the man said. 'You have millions of men willing to sacrifice their lives for the cause, and the reward . . .'

The man paused, as a gymnast might do before launching into their most daring somersault.

'The reward is the world itself.'

His leader waited a beat, then finally smiled. 'Very well. Tell our people in Washington to proceed with the operation, and make it clear that failure is not acceptable. Do I make myself clear?'

'Oh, yes, my leader. Our agents will know exactly what that means.'

• • •

In the end, Saffron's meeting with the colonel from General Marshall's staff was a distinct success. At first he'd balked at her suggestion that the efforts of resistance fighters behind German lines could be worth an extra army division to the invading Allies. But she did get him to accept the basic principle that SOE's role as an enabler, co-ordinator and supplier of paramilitary forces in Occupied Europe provided tremendous value for the money and manpower invested in it.

'Can you get that written into the formal invasion plans?' she asked.

The colonel laughed. 'Well, I can't guarantee that, I'm afraid, but I will promise you that I'll write a very positive report of our meeting and make sure that General Marshall personally sees it. Does that sound like a deal?'

'It certainly does,' Saffron replied, wondering how long it would take the colonel to say what he wanted in return. Not long, was the answer.

'And since I'm doing you a favour, maybe you could do one for me. How about dinner?'

'Well, now . . .' Saffron smiled teasingly. She had been trained to use any and every means at her disposal to fulfil her missions.

And she was happy to string the colonel along if it gave SOE a formal role in the invasion. 'That sounds like a charming invitation, but if I just say "yes", then what's to stop you taking advantage of me, and never keeping your side of the deal?'

'I'm a very honourable man.'

'I'm sure you are, Colonel, but I'm a cautious woman. You show me General Marshall's signature on your report, and then ask me to dinner again.'

The colonel grinned. 'You drive a hard bargain.'

Saffron gave the colonel the full benefit of her sapphire eyes. 'Do I look to you like the kind of woman who'd be easy?'

• • •

The death warrant of a single enemy spy could be signed off by any senior officer. More important decisions, however, required authorisation at a far, far higher level. Jozef Lewandowski was not faithful to his wife Magda. There was no reason to be, since theirs was the ultimate arranged marriage: two agents assigned to each other by their superior officers. Agency doctrine made it mandatory for such couples to have intercourse with each other. Regular copulation was good for both mental and physical health. It also helped agents maintain the fiction that they were in a conventional relationship. Furthermore, by producing children they reinforced an image of normality, making it easier for them to assimilate with their American co-workers, neighbours and friends.

None of that, however, altered the fact that both male and female agents were also often required to use sex as a means of recruiting intelligence assets, either by blackmail or seduction. Some people would hand over information out of fear that their dirty secrets might be revealed. Others did it in the deluded belief that the agent targeting them was genuinely besotted with them. All that mattered was the result.

Lewandowski had a regular assignation with a female asset at the Imperial Hotel, a grand name for a down-at-heel establishment about half a mile north of the US Capitol, not far from Union Station. And now the woman he bedded there was walking through the dingy lobby, trying to ignore the peeling wallpaper, the sticky, unwashed linoleum and the permanent fug of smoke and sweat hanging in the air.

She signed herself in as Mrs Mary Jones, just below Lewandowski's signature in the name of Bill Schmidt. It was a German surname, but this was America, where those were even more common than Italian or Irish. The desk clerk had never bothered to ask for any proof of identity, since this was the kind of establishment where the guests would be expected to use aliases. She stepped into a rickety elevator, which pulled itself upwards, like an old man rising from an armchair, to the third floor, where her assignations took place. By the time the elevator door opened again, she was herself already beginning to breathe a little more heavily, just thinking about what was to come.

Lewandowski had not expected to derive any personal pleasure from having sex with this asset. In fact, he had been a little concerned that he would not be able to manage it at all. She was one of those women who dressed to hide their figures rather than accentuate them, and whose outward persona of high-minded respectability conveyed no hint of sensuality or lust. But when Mrs Jones had first undressed in front of him, he realised he need not have worried. She instantly seemed to strip herself of all her inhibitions, becoming as wanton in private as she was respectable in public.

Her shapeless – even frumpy – clothes had given no hint of the fullness of her breasts, or the slenderness of her waist. Mrs Jones also liked to be, as she put it, 'manhandled'. She enjoyed rough treatment and liked to dish it out in return. Lewandowski would take off his undershirt on an evening after one of his assignations to reveal a back criss-crossed by livid scratches. Magda had once admitted to him that such vivid evidence of passion upset her. 'You must find me very dull, when I do not do that,' she'd said. 'Or maybe it is your fault that I do not want to do it.'

'Don't be ridiculous,' he'd replied. 'You know it means nothing to me. It's just work.' But both had known that the scratches said otherwise. And the misery that Mrs Jones had brought to their lives made them feel more like a real married couple than anything else.

So now, Lewandowski was lying on the bed in Room 346 of the Imperial Hotel, rubbing his shoulder, while Mrs Jones lay on her side, her head propped on one hand, looking up at him.

'Does it hurt?' she asked, without a trace of sympathy.

Lewandowski looked at the bite marks. 'Yes,' he replied.

'Look on the bright side. I left your back alone. I thought I'd do things a little differently this time . . .' She smiled. 'Since it is a special occasion.'

Lewandowski grunted non-committally.

'So, did you bring it?' she asked, as another woman might inquire of a lover about a promised gift, like a box of chocolates or a diamond ring.

'Yes.'

'Can I see it?'

Lewandowski drew on his cigarette. He thought for a second, and then shrugged before stubbing out his cigarette in the ashtray on the bedside cabinet, then walked across the room, passing through a thin beam of afternoon sunlight coming through a crack in the curtains. Outside a tram rattled by, briefly drowning the noise of people on the bustling street. A car tooted its horn.

Lewandowski had arrived carrying a tin lunch pail, the kind many working men took to work. He opened it and extracted a brown paper parcel.

'Is that enough?' asked Mrs Jones, looking at it quizzically.

'Yeah, plenty.' He put the parcel on the bed. 'Now, pay attention. . .' All thoughts of sex were gone as he gave Mrs Jones a detailed series of instructions.

When the demonstration was over, Mrs Jones wrapped the parcel back up and put it in her handbag. 'I'd better get going,' she said.

They barely spoke as they got dressed, and remained silent in the elevator down to the lobby.

Out on the street, Mrs Jones was about to resume the role of a woman who had just had an assignation with her lover, and lean into the kiss that would have to last her until the next time they met, when she caught sight of a man walking towards them. He was the last person she expected to see in such a rough, impoverished district, where brown and black faces far outnumbered the white. 'Oh, hell!' she muttered.

'What is it?' Lewandowski asked.

'Trouble.'

• • •

The Secret Intelligence Service had long employed talent-spotters: academics at top universities who kept their eyes open for students with gifts that the service could use. Brian Jarvis had been exceptionally bright, with a particular gift as a linguist. He spoke passable German and was fluent in French and Italian. His real passion, however, was Spanish, particularly in its various Latin American forms. It was the surprising ability of this blond Anglo-Saxon to converse like a native with a Mexican, Argentinian or Peruvian – adapting to each nation's particular pronunciation and slang without difficulty – that had brought him to America.

He was thus able to converse in Spanish with one of the Secret Intelligence Service's most prized assets in Washington DC: Consuela Balcázar, the wife of the cultural attaché at the Mexican embassy. Her husband, Rodrigo, was as tall, dark and attractive as a more masculine, moustachioed Rudolph Valentino. Consuela had the sort of leggy, curvaceous body that bomber crews painted on the noses of their planes, with tumbling raven hair, pouting lips and come-hither eyes to match. And every item of clothing she wore, every lick of makeup on her face, every twitch of her body as she walked across a room, was designed to emphasise her charms.

In a town that usually valued power more than beauty, the Balcázars stood out as a glamorous couple, and were greatly prized by hostesses seeking to spice up their social events. But theirs was a marriage of convenience. Rodrigo ignored the fact that Consuela had countless affairs with the men of the Washington diplomatic corps, while she ignored the fact that he liked diplomats, too. Each understood that the other made them respectable, and they got on well as friends, so theirs, in fact, was one of the capital's happier marriages.

Consuela, however, had another, more secretive string to her bow: she was a dedicated anti-fascist. SIS had discovered this by chance in early 1940, when a British diplomat had joined the long list of Consuela's conquests and had been surprised to discover that her political passions were as highly developed as her sexual ones. He had tipped off one of his intelligence contacts that she might be worth cultivating as an asset in the fight against fascism.

Knowing that men will say almost anything to impress a woman, no matter how secret the information, Consuela had jumped at the chance to combine her two greatest interests. In the two years before Pearl Harbor, when Germany still had an embassy in Washington, her affair with one of the Reich's military attachés had yielded a remarkable amount of high-grade intelligence material. Even now, her dalliances with diplomats from Spain and various South American countries whose governments were sympathetic to the Nazis continued to produce golden nuggets of information.

Consuela liked to meet Jarvis at a restaurant called La Granja Roja, tucked away in the maze of rough, working-class backstreets behind Union Station. Not only did it serve the best Mexican food in town, it was also located in a neighbourhood where no self-respecting diplomat would be seen dead.

Jarvis sympathised with their qualms. As he walked along the street, he felt small, white and feeble, but the thrill of a couple of hours in the company of a woman as wildly attractive as Consuela trumped his fears.

She took a feline pleasure in toying with this mouse of a man. 'You know I can never make love to you as long as we are working together,' she once told him. 'Everything would become too complicated. But when this war is over . . . When

Hitler and his gang of bandits have been destroyed . . . Then, if you are good, I will show you how I make men tell me their secrets.'

As she spoke, Consuela had looked at Jarvis in a way no woman had ever done, with eyes so wanton he found himself overwhelmed with an intoxicating cocktail of terror and desire. And though he knew she was teasing – and even taunting – him, Jarvis had never felt as infuriated or humiliated by Consuela as he had been by Saffron Courtney.

After he had gone to such great lengths to provide her with the proof that there were no traitors within the British embassy, she had dismissed it all, to his face, with icy condescension and disdain. Damn it, she had even had the sheer gall to drop the prime minister's name as she was doing it. And the way she had suggested that he and Goodhouse would obey Churchill's orders, too, 'if he ever gave you any', clearly suggested that she thought the very idea was absurd.

Consuela, by contrast, even if she wasn't attracted to him, at least respected him, understanding the important job he did at the embassy.

On this particular day, Jarvis had left his lunch with Consuela Balcázar feeling in an exceptionally good mood. She had produced some interesting titbits about Nazi plans for post-war hideaways in Argentina and Uruguay, should the Reich not last the predicted thousand years. His belly was full of the spicy Mexican food that was a delicious contrast to the dull, stodgy fare usually served up in England, and he felt pleasantly drowsy from beer and tequila. Even the street life around him seemed less intimidating than usual.

Jarvis was so relaxed that, at first, he did not notice the white couple emerging from a seedy hotel about thirty yards ahead of him, and was almost on top of them by the time his foggy brain had realised that he knew one of them, and he found himself saying: 'Good Lord, what on earth are you doing here?'

There was no reply. Or if there was, Jarvis didn't register it above the sudden, sobering shock of realisation: William Stephenson and Saffron Courtney had been right all along . . . but also terribly wrong. There *was* a spy, and there *was* a dreadful threat, but neither was what they thought.

Jarvis had to get back to the embassy, fast. He needed time to get his thoughts in order before he sent a signal back to London. 'Oh, well, lovely seeing you,' he said, hurrying away while trying not to break out into an actual run. Above all, he mustn't give himself away. But as he squirmed his way between the people crowding the narrow sidewalk, Jarvis had a terrible feeling it was too late. He had seen recognition in the man's eyes, too. Not who he was, but what he represented. A threat that needed to be neutralised at all costs.

• • •

'His name is Jarvis,' Mrs Jones said. 'He knows me.'

Lewandowski nodded. 'Go,' he said. 'I'll deal with this.'

She turned and strode briskly away in the opposite direction, without looking back. Lewandowski drew a bead on Jarvis and set off in pursuit.

Lewandowski was perfectly capable of tailing someone without giving his presence away. But this was different. He wanted his prey to know he was coming after him. In fact, he wanted him to be scared to fucking death. It was plain just looking at Jarvis's feeble figure, and how flustered he had been, that he would not be the kind of man to remain calm under pressure. He would panic, and make a mistake, and then Lewandowski would strike.

As he elbowed his way down the street, Lewandowski was whispering under his breath, 'Come on . . . Come on . . . Look around.' And then Jarvis did turn his head and their eyes met for a second, and that was when the Englishman did start running – or tried to run. There were too many people on the sidewalk, and he lacked the physical force to barge them aside. Lewandowski, on the other hand, with his bull-like physique and snarling expression, was much more intimidating, and people hurried to get out of his way, like the Red Sea parting for Moses.

Brian Jarvis had been bullied at school, so he was accustomed to feeling afraid. But this was like no fear he had ever experienced. For the first time, he was actually running for his life.

If only he could get off this blasted street! As he wormed his way past the bars, barber's shops and bodegas, Jarvis's eyes darted frantically from one side to the other, looking for a means of escape.

Then suddenly he saw the entrance to an alley ahead. Jarvis was already out of breath, his heart hammering with exertion and mortal terror, but somehow he summoned a burst of fresh energy and barged his way forward. He reached the alley and peered in.

It was a dead end.

No, wait . . . There was a narrow gap between the side of the alley and the wall at its end. Surely he could squeeze through. He glanced back the way he had come. He couldn't see his pursuer. *So he can't see me!* he thought, hope suddenly springing up.

He raced down the alley.

Lewandowski had held back, merging into the crowd until he could see where his target was heading. He saw him turn into the alley, and smiled.

Before he had arranged his assignations at the Imperial Hotel, he had made a thorough reconnoitre of the area, scoping out potential escape routes if he was compromised. And that alley was definitely not one of them.

Jarvis reached the far end and stopped. What he'd thought was a back way out of the alley was a mirage: just a recess in the wall, leading nowhere.

He looked round frantically. There was a door on either side of the alley – what must be the back entrances of stores on the main street. He yanked the handles, but neither of them budged. There were fire escapes above the doors, too. But Jarvis couldn't jump high enough to grab the ladders.

He was trapped.

Jarvis looked back the way he had come. The man who had been following him was standing at the other end of the alley, looking straight at him.

Jarvis hammered on one of the doors. 'Help! Help! For God's sake, someone help!'

Nothing happened. The man was buttoning up his jacket. He reached into his trouser pocket, and there was a click and the glint of steel. A flick knife.

The man started walking towards Jarvis. 'Please . . . Please . . . Don't hurt me,' he begged. 'I won't tell anyone, I swear, not a soul.'

The man did not reply. He kept walking at the same steady pace.

Jarvis knew he was a dead man. Unless . . .

When he was a boy, he had been made to play rugby. He hated it. So far as he was concerned, it was not so much a sport as an opportunity for bullies to beat him in broad daylight and be applauded by the games teacher for doing so. But as a result, Jarvis had learned to weave and dodge, to avoid the bigger boys.

He took a deep breath, then ran as fast as he could straight at the big bully with the knife in his hand who was going to take his life.

The other man watched him come with a bemused smile on his face. At the very last moment, Jarvis feinted to his left, then, as the man shifted his weight in response, darted the other way. He heard the man grunt in surprise, and felt the wind on his cheek as he slipped past. He'd done it! He fixed his eyes on the entrance to the alley and pumped his arms for all he was worth.

Suddenly his feet slipped from under him as a hand grabbed his collar and pulled. The next moment, he'd been shoved up against the wall, his forehead scraping the rough bricks. He tried to scream, but a meaty hand covered his mouth. Sensing what was about to come, his mind filled with the image of Consuela Balcázar, and the thought that now he would never know what it was like to make love to her.

The last thing he felt was the blade of the knife being forced deep into his guts.

Lewandowski withdrew the knife and stepped back as Jarvis's body slumped to the ground and a pool of blood began to spread around him.

Glancing around to make sure that no one had seen him, Lewandowski wiped the blade of the knife clean with a handkerchief, snapped it shut and put it back in his pocket. He reached into Jarvis's suit jacket and removed his wallet, then checked the other pockets for ID of any kind. There was none. He took a thin wad of cash and Jarvis's driving licence from the wallet and put it in his pocket, then wiped the wallet with the same handkerchief and tossed it on the ground beside the body. The story told by this gruesome tableau was obvious. A well-dressed white male had unwittingly strayed into a part of the city where human predators would see him as easy prey.

It would take a day, at least, for the body to be identified. The police, under pressure to find a perpetrator, would fall back on their usual solution: they would look for a Black man to blame, as surely as the Berlin criminal police would look for a Jew. Lewandowski saw no likelihood of his being linked to the killing. Still, he needed to take precautions.

The front of his jacket was spattered with blood, as was the right sleeve. Lewandowski took it off. He checked his shirt. There was blood on his right cuff, but otherwise it was clean.

He rolled up his shirtsleeves, folded his jacket and slung it over his shoulder, then he strolled back up the alley to the street, where he quickly blended into the crowd.

Lewandowski's truck was parked eight blocks away. As he walked, he decided he would have to tell his masters back home what had happened. He trusted they would understand the necessity of acting on his own initiative. A problem had been dealt with. The mission was still on track. Jozef Lewandowski drove away with the satisfaction of a man who knows he has done his job well.

• • •

The Daughters of the American Revolution seemed divided in their opinions after Saffron had recounted her personal experiences of being trained as an agent and going undercover in the Low Countries. Some – she hoped, the majority – agreed that teaching young women to fight, kill, sabotage and steal, before sending them into enemy territory, was proof that the so-called weaker sex could be as brave and tough as any male. Other, more traditional matrons were aghast that the feminine values of gentleness, delicacy and empathy could be cast aside in favour of the sort of brutish behaviour that had hitherto been the exclusive province of men.

Saffron wondered what they would have thought if she had given them the full, unexpurgated account of what she'd been through, instead of the censored version. But she did her best to reassure them that, for all her apparently mannish ways, she was enough of a girl to have loved shopping in Saks and listening to Frank Sinatra. 'And,' she asked, 'is it really such a bad thing if women have the ability to defend themselves against men?'

Having said her piece and answered various SOE-related questions, Saffron chatted amiably with her hostesses over tea and cakes, moving from one table to another like a human pass the parcel. Several of the Daughters had read the Winchell column and, having discovered that she was 'Jane Smith', were agog to know all the details.

Saffron was happy to amuse and entertain them. She was not trying to persuade her audience with military logic. Her job was to charm them enough that they would speak warmly about her to their influential menfolk. And, she thought to herself, as she gave her umpteenth blow-by-blow account of her retaliation against O'Bannon, surely they were more likely to do that if they knew she responded to unwanted advances with a swift knee to the offending groin rather than a swoon into her would-be suitor's arms. She did, however, stop short of saying that O'Bannon had ended up in hospital. It was one thing being known as a gutsy gal who could defend her virtue; a crazed, vengeful hellcat was quite another.

As the event drew to an end, Saffron found her mind turning to the evening ahead. She wondered where Stackpole would take her for dinner, what she should wear, and what else he had planned. He'd not mentioned where he was living in Washington, let alone whether the two of them could safely and discreetly spend the night there. And should she even be thinking about Stackpole, if there was a traitor somewhere in the city, plotting who knew what?

'Miss Courtney?'

Saffron realised a slim, well-dressed woman in her fifties was standing beside her.

'Oh, I'm so sorry,' Saffron apologised. 'I was miles away.'

The woman gave a shrewd but kind smile. 'Thinking about handsome army air force officers?'

'How did you guess?'

'Well, I don't blame you in the slightest. More fun than a bunch of old women like us.' She held out her hand. 'I'm Cynthia Hackenstedt.'

'How nice to meet you, Mrs Hackenstedt,' Saffron replied, glancing at the rings on her other hand. 'I hope I wasn't too boring.'

'On the contrary, my dear. Lady Halifax told me that I would be entertained by you, and I am pleased to say that you lived up to your billing.'

'Thank you,' said Saffron. 'How kind of Lady Halifax to have called you, and to have been so flattering.'

'Well, she's a fine lady, and a smart one, too. And she thinks I can be of use to you.'

'How intriguing. Do tell me more.'

'It's very simple. My darling husband Morty is otherwise known as Mortimer J Hackenstedt, the senior Democrat senator for Connecticut and the chairman of the Senate Committee on Foreign Relations.'

'That sounds incredibly grand.'

'Oh, well, you know how men love their fancy job titles. Say, why don't you join us for dinner? You can tell him everything you told us ladies about your splendid organisation.'

Saffron's heart fell. She couldn't possibly turn down a chance to meet an influential American politician in his own home. That was precisely the kind of thing Gubbins had sent her to do. Her date with Stackpole would have to be postponed, along with all thoughts of spies.

She fixed the most grateful smile she could manage on her face. 'Thank you so much, I'd be delighted to accept. This will be good practice for me. I've got to speak to a couple of members of the Senate Armed Forces Committee tomorrow.'

'Then tell me their names,' Mrs Hackenstedt said, 'and I'll make sure Morty fully briefs you about them.' She winked. 'I mean, tells you all the good stuff you're not supposed to know.'

'That does sound intriguing!'

'Good – then that's settled. Now, we live in Chevy Chase, which is right on the edge of town, but you won't have any trouble getting a cab to take you there. Here, let me give you my card.'

Cynthia's address was on 27th Street NW. A minute's more conversation revealed that everyone called her Cindy, and Saffron should arrive at 19.30. 'Morty insists on dinner at eight . . . and not a second later,' Cindy said.

'I'll be there on the dot of seven-thirty, then,' Saffron assured her. She said her goodbyes to the DAR ladies, but as she stepped out onto the street, looking for the nearest telephone to call Stackpole, her mind suddenly switched to Charlie and Mavis. Maybe there was something she could do this afternoon. It probably wouldn't provide an answer, or at least not right away, but the more she thought about it, the surer Saffron became: *The bench . . . Everything depends on the bench.*

• • •

While Saffron was speaking to the Daughters of the American Revolution, Clayton Stackpole was in his office, combing the service records of men who were being considered for active service in the OSS to see if there were any obvious medical issues that might disqualify them. He had just read through the nineteenth of more than two hundred files, knowing that he was expected to file a full report in three days' time, when there was a knock on the door.

Bill Donovan's secretary popped her head around the door. 'The boss wants to see you, Clay.'

'Did he say why?'

'No, just that it's extremely urgent.'

Stackpole got up and hurried to Donovan's office, wondering if Saffron needed help. She was a girl with a nose for trouble all right, and it was possible that in the twenty-four hours since he had last seen her, she had succeeded in finding it.

'How's the jaw today?' Donovan asked as Stackpole entered his office.

Stackpole rubbed the side of his face. 'Bruised, but not broken. I'm okay.'

'So you're fit enough to operate . . . as a surgeon, I mean?'

'Sure.'

'Good, because I need you in a car to National Airport, fast. There's a DC-3 waiting for you.'

'Who's the patient?'

'One of our best trainees – guy called Wermuth.' Donovan pronounced the name like the drink Vermouth. 'He just smashed the hell out of his right leg on a training exercise in the Blue Ridge Mountains. He's been taken to some place called Banner Elk, North Carolina.'

'Do they have a hospital there?'

'The population is less than a thousand, so no. But they've got a doctor, and he's filled our guy up with morphine and put his leg in a splint. They're sticking him on a stretcher, putting it in the back of a truck and taking him to Johnson City, Tennessee, about forty miles away. That's the nearest hospital. There's an airport about fifteen miles from there called McKellar Field. The DC-3'll get you there in around two hours. You'll go straight to Johnson City, and put Wermuth back together.'

'Don't they have surgeons in Johnson City?'

'Maybe, but I don't know them, and I'll bet they don't have your experience of emergency surgery.'

'Thank you, sir. But this guy, Wermuth . . . He must be something special to get this kind of treatment.'

Donovan nodded. 'Yeah . . .' He looked at Stackpole, deciding how much to tell him. The Texan wasn't just an agent sworn to secrecy; he was a doctor sworn to respect his patients' confidentiality. And he didn't strike Donovan as a man who would betray either of those oaths.

'There's an outfit in France called the FTPF,' Donovan said. 'Stands for *Francs-tireurs et partisans français*. They're the biggest and most effective resistance force fighting the Nazis. When the day comes to invade Europe, we're really going to need them on our side.'

'If they're killing Nazis, can't we take that for granted?'

'You'd think . . . but they're also communists. So they don't exactly trust us, or the Limeys. But they trust Wermuth, because he was one of their top guys. Got arrested by the Gestapo, never gave them a thing. Then the FTPF busted him out of jail and smuggled him out of France, over the Pyrenees. One of these days we're going to put him back in, get him back to the FTPF, get them working for us. Could be crucial to the success of the whole invasion.'

'I'll put him back together, sir,' Stackpole said. 'You can count on that.'

'Good man. So, fix him up, make sure he's recovering okay, then get back here, fast as you can. I'll give you twenty-four hours more to finish that report. But not a minute over.'

'Yes, sir. You can count on me.'

'Good man. There's a driver waiting for you outside.'

Less than twenty minutes later, Stackpole was in the air, rising into the skies above northern Virginia. And then it struck him: *Damn! I didn't call Saffron!*

He cursed his stupidity for not leaving her a message, apologising for blowing their date and letting her know when he'd be back. Then he told himself not to be ridiculous. She, of all women, would understand that things happened unexpectedly. They were fighting a war, after all. And if there was one thing Stackpole had learned in New York, it was that if there ever was any trouble, then he was much more likely to need Saffron's help than she was to need his.

• • •

Lewandowski had asked his bosses a question. When he got home from work, he received their reply. His orders were to remove Saffron Courtney from the equation. She was to be captured and interrogated, to ascertain how much she and her superiors knew about the Foxglove operation. Once she had given up as much as she was ever going to, Lewandowski would kill her. Her body was to be disposed of, without a trace, so that the people she worked for could not be sure that she was, in fact, dead.

The business of the Courtney woman, however, was a minor matter compared to the second order he was given. The assassination had been approved at the highest level. Complete success was demanded. Failure would not be tolerated.

Lewandowski was considering the quickest and safest way to get the news to Foxglove when his phone rang. 'I was just about to call you,' he said, when he heard who was on the line.

'We just got the okay from the boss . . . and I mean the big boss.'

'All right,' Foxglove said, 'but there's just one problem. They've changed the date and time. It's happening tomorrow evening, not the day after.'

'Why?' Lewandowski asked, always alert to any sign of exposure or betrayal.

'I think it's just that the principals' schedules changed.'

'Hmm . . .' Lewandowski considered how this news might affect his plans. 'This makes no essential difference to us. You have what you need. We can bring our side of the operation forward. Now tell me, how much do you think the Courtney woman knows?'

There was a pause. 'I think she's closer than she realises. Did you play hide-and-seek as a child?'

'Of course, every child does.'

'Well, imagine we're all playing hide-and-seek. You and I are hiding in a closet. Saffron Courtney is in the same room. She's looking under the bed. She hasn't yet opened the closet door. But when she does . . .'

'I understand,' said Lewandowski. 'Then we shall both proceed as planned . . . and I will deal with Courtney before she opens that closet door.'

• • •

Saffron called Stackpole's office and was told that he was away, dealing with a medical matter, expected back the following afternoon. She took a tram to the Georgetown end of the park and then walked, stopping on the way at the bench and finding nothing there.

She arrived at the Playfairs' house shortly after six and talked to Mavis for a few minutes about their respective days at the opposite ends of the social spectrum. 'Next time you see those Daughters of the Revolution,' Mavis said, 'tell them they should come down and take a look at our soup kitchen. You mark my words, there'll be another bloody revolution if the rich in America don't do something about the suffering of the poor.'

'I'm having dinner with one of them tonight,' Saffron replied, 'and her husband, who's a senator, so I'll see if I can persuade them. That reminds me, I must get to 27th Street in Chevy Chase by seven-thirty. When do I need to get a cab?'

'Oh, quarter past should be fine,' Mavis said. 'I'll call you one.'

'Thanks so much. Righto, I'd better go and make myself presentable.'

Saffron showered, then changed into an evening dress she had bought at Saks, which was rather more demure than the one she'd worn for her infamous evening at the Copa.

The Hackenstedts were a pleasant, impeccably mannered couple, and the young man whom Cynthia had drummed up to be Saffron's dinner partner was a clean-living fellow from the senator's office, whose spindly physique and thick-lensed spectacles explained why the armed forces had no need of him. The food was good, the conversation was untaxing, though a little earnest, the senator paid close attention to what Saffron said about SOE, and gave her pen portraits of the men she would meet the next day that were useful, but scandal-free. It was hardly the most exciting night out, but as a working dinner it had served its purpose, and Saffron's thanks were sincere as she said her goodbyes.

Her cab pulled up outside the Playfairs' just as Charlie was bringing Franco back from his late-night walk. 'It was blissfully brief this evening,' he said, as they entered the house. 'Some nights I walk halfway round Washington before this blasted hound decides to do his business. Tonight, though, we were five yards into the trees when he sniffed some fascinating message left by another dog, posted his reply and trotted happily home.'

Playfair's description of canine messages left in the woods was casual, light-hearted stuff, the sort of thing any dog owner might say. But it was all too close to the thoughts that had been swirling round Saffron's mind all day. And as he had done the previous evening, he left her wondering: *was that an innocent remark? Or was he taunting me, letting me know that he's the spy and daring me to take him on?*

The following morning Saffron woke at six, pulled on a pair of trousers and a jumper, grabbed her bag, and was out of the house and into the park while the Playfairs and their dog were still asleep. It was a beautiful morning. The air was cool and fresh, and the sun was peeking through the trees as Saffron made her way along the path.

Twice she thought she saw a movement out of the corner of her eye. The second time, when the path made a U-turn around a copse of trees, she took advantage of the opportunity and circled back through the woods, returning to the path, where anyone tailing her would have lost visual contact. Now she would be behind whoever was watching her, following his trail.

There was no one on the path. But the instinctive feeling that there were eyes on her remained. Saffron found it strangely encouraging. If someone was following her, then she must be on to something. But was she in any immediate, physical danger? *No*, she decided. *If they wanted me dead, they'd have done it by now*.

Saffron reached the bench, then crouched down beside it. She looked at the front left leg. There was nothing suspicious to be seen. She ran her eyes along the crosspiece that supported the front of the seat. Again, nothing. Then she looked at the front right leg.

And there it was, at the top of the leg: a yellow chalk mark so faint that no one who was not deliberately looking would ever spot it, still less give it a second thought.

Saffron sighed. She had so hoped not to find this; so badly wanted the Playfairs to be the delightful people they seemed to be. But this was right out of the manual – standard procedure for SOE, and now it seemed for the Abwehr, too. In any male–female couple, the man is the senior agent and the woman is the courier. Why? Because no one suspects a woman, particularly a woman with a pram. And the baby is a bonus, because if you want to hide a message, who wants to go poking around a dirty nappy?

Saffron felt along the back of the seat-leg and found what she was looking for: a small, flat canister, no bigger than a quarter and no thicker than three stacked together, stuck to the bench with a bit of chewing gum. She pulled it off and opened it. Inside was a rolled-up message. The print was tiny, but just legible to Saffron's sharp eyes: twenty-five characters, in five groups of five.

Saffron took out her notebook and copied the characters. It was obviously some sort of code, but hopefully Araminta Keswick or another one of Stephenson's tame cryptologists would be able to crack it. True, they'd not yet been able to decipher the lengthy messages left in the microdots, but short messages between an agent and their handler, intended to be read and swiftly acted upon, would use a much simpler code. 'We'd better bloody well hope so, anyway,' Saffron muttered.

She put the paper back in the little canister and carefully stuck it back exactly where she had found it. Then she stood up and looked at the bench. In a few hours Mavis and Loretta would walk past, pushing Arthur in his pram. Mavis would tell Loretta to walk on while she had her little think. She'd pick up the message, ready for Charlie when he got home from work.

Saffron shook her head. *That poor baby . . . What will become of him?* The Playfairs' callous disregard for Arthur angered her almost as much as their betrayal.

Feeling utterly miserable, she made her way down the path, out of the park, then up the street to Foxhall Road. It was the busiest thoroughfare in this part of north-west Washington. There was bound to be a phone booth somewhere, and Saffron was confident there'd be someone on duty at Stephenson's office at any time of the day or night.

Both assumptions proved to be correct. When she called New York, collect, the call was accepted and a calm, efficient woman took down the message as Saffron dictated it to her, still in the five-character groups, along with the request to decode it as quickly as possible.

'Could you please tell Mr Stephenson that I believe this is a very important lead, and it is almost certainly time-sensitive,' Saffron said. 'I will call back when I have finished my morning appointment, soon after midday.'

'Mr Stephenson is always at his desk by seven,' came the reply. 'I'll make sure he's alerted the moment he arrives.'

Saffron returned to the Playfairs' house, getting a friendly 'Good morning!' from the newspaper delivery boy as he cycled past, going the other way. With every step she took, the knowledge of their betrayal weighed more heavily on her mind. Entering the kitchen, where breakfast was now in full swing, she did her best to smile brightly as she explained that she hadn't slept very well, so she'd gone out for a walk in the hope that fresh air would liven her up a bit. As she did her best to eat a piece of toast and drink a mug of tea, Saffron watched Mavis feeding Arthur, and Charlie playfully swatting Franco with his rolled-up copy of that morning's *Washington Post*, fresh from the delivery boy's satchel. She prayed that maybe, even now, they might prove to be who they claimed.

Back in her room, Saffron washed and then changed into an elegantly tailored pair of black trousers, a white silk blouse and a short, fitted, grey-blue jacket in lightweight tweed, with flat black shoes. The look was a trifle mannish, perhaps, but it was sufficiently smart to pass muster at her Senate meetings, while enabling her to run – and, if necessary, fight – a lot more easily than a skirt and heels would allow. She looked again in the mirror, then put a brooch on her jacket and added a short pearl necklace, worn inside the collar of her blouse.

Having established her femininity for the benefit of the men she was about to meet, Saffron went into the guest bathroom, locked the door, sat down on the floor and stripped down her Beretta pistol.

She heard a voice from downstairs – Charlie exclaiming, 'Bloody hell!'

As she reassembled the gun, she heard heavy male footsteps and the front door opening and slamming shut. Seconds later, the Playfairs' car started up and drove away at speed. Had something spooked Charlie? Or had he just remembered that he had an early meeting that morning?

Saffron concentrated on checking that her weapon was ready for action: a bullet in the chamber, a full magazine in the grip and a second clip in her shoulder bag. Satisfied that everything was in order, she went downstairs to say goodbye.

Loretta had just arrived. She gave Saffron a warm smile. 'Morning, Miss Saffron. How you doin'?'

'I'm fine, thank you, Loretta. How about you?' Saffron tried to sound cheerful, as a wave of pent-up anger, betrayal and hurt surged through her. Here was a sweet, bright, incredibly hard-working girl, and soon her job and the security it brought to a desperately poor family would be ripped away. How could the Playfairs do that to her?

Saffron had intended to ask Mavis why Charlie had dashed off, but now she just wanted to get out of the house as fast as he had done, and it was all she could do to keep her voice friendly as she said 'See you later!' to Mavis and gave her a peck on the cheek.

'Wait a second,' Mavis called out as Saffron headed towards the front door. 'There's something in the paper that you really—'

'Sorry, no time!' Saffron replied, opening the door and stepping out.

As she smoothed herself down, took a calming breath and set off for the Senate Office, Saffron wondered whether she should have listened to the men who told her not to worry her head with spies and plots and concentrate on enjoying her stay. *Just this once, could you have turned away from trouble?* But she had chosen to ignore them. She'd set a stone rolling, and now it was a matter of where it would stop, and who it would crush along the way.

• • •

While Saffron walked up to Foxhall to catch the bus into the city, the man who had been following her since she had first set foot outside the Playfairs' front door two hours earlier emerged from the woods. He strolled along the road running along the edge of the park until he came to a black Chrysler CO sedan. He got in, opened the glove compartment, took out the microphone handset that was wired to a battery-operated short wave radio in the boot and checked in with Lewandowski.

'You called it right, boss,' he said. 'She fell for it hook, line and sinker.' He paused and then added, 'She's good, though. She's observant. Had to work real hard not to get spotted.'

The conversation was in English. In the unlikely event that anyone was listening, it was better to sound like a bunch of hoods than foreign agents. The man described in detail what Saffron had done by the bench, and how she had immediately gone to find a pay phone. 'I don't know where she called, but I figure it was long-distance 'cause she called collect, didn't put no coins into the box.'

'I know exactly who she was calling,' Lewandowski replied. 'I know what she was asking him, too.'

'You got this under control, then, huh?'

Lewandowski didn't feel the need to reply.

• • •

Hidden in the trees, less than twenty metres away, the cultural attaché at the Portuguese embassy, Caetano Macedo, watched the scene with mounting irritation. It had taken him two days of patient investigation, and gentle teasing of information out of his opposite number at the British embassy, before he had tracked down Saffron Courtney to the house where she was staying. And then, when he had dragged himself out of bed at the crack of dawn, he had got there to find that some other bastards had beaten him to it.

Typical Germans! He admired them as a nation and believed passionately in the principles of National Socialism, but their excessive thoroughness could be an irritation sometimes. It might have made sense to someone in Prinz-Albrecht-Straße to have two sets of spies working the same case, but he had now wasted a great deal of time for nothing, and that was unacceptable.

What made it worse was that he was himself an agent in PIDE, the Portuguese state security agency. That was why the SD used him. They knew he could do more than just observe. They should have had more respect for his status as a fellow officer.

Macedo made his way back to the Portuguese embassy, drafted a furious message to Berlin, encoded it and transmitted it. Only then did he have second thoughts. Maybe he had gone too far this time. No, that was ridiculous. The SD were thousands of miles away. What harm could they do him here?

• • •

Millicent James had never seen her mistress so angry. 'Honestly, it's too much!' Lady Halifax had exploded, within minutes of Millicent arriving for work that morning. 'Yesterday morning I was told, out of the blue, that we would be having three of the most important men in the world to a private luncheon in two days' time. Now, as if that were not trying enough, my darling husband has seen fit to inform me that because of "scheduling complexities" . . .' Lady Halifax managed to imbue those two words with a lifetime of suppressed frustration, '. . . the event is now a dinner, to be held this evening. I told Edward, "I am the lady of the house. Social occasions are my responsibility. But I cannot execute that responsibility if I am kept in the dark."'

Lady Halifax paused, and when she spoke again, the anger in her voice had been overlaid by something else: the anxiety of a woman who dreads the possibility that she might fail in her duty, and thereby let other people down. 'No one seems to understand that a dinner party is an entirely different occasion from a luncheon. I now have just over nine hours to agree a new menu with the chef, for which he then must buy ingredients . . . and make sure we have wine in the cellar to match the food . . . and have the entire interior of the residence cleaned and tidied . . . and arrange the table decorations and seating plan. And now it transpires that every detail must be approved by the bloody Americans!'

Half an hour later, Millicent was standing beside the long dining table at the British ambassador's residence, around which thirty people could sit in comfort, clutching the notebook in which she had been writing down every detail of the dinner party plans as they were being formulated. Lady Halifax, meanwhile, was feeling no happier, even if her language had become more restrained.

'I'm sorry, but I really am finding this rather trying,' she said, looking as though she might at any moment spontaneously combust with the quivering heat of her rage.

Millicent suppressed a smile at the puzzled frown on the face of Mrs Dufoy, the White House official charged with ensuring that the president's personal needs were met. Clearly, she was having a hard time making sense of the contrast between the polite understatement of Lady Halifax's words and her volcanic body language.

The rugged, crew-cut US Secret Service officer leading the team responsible for the president's safety had conspicuously not volunteered his name to anyone. He was currently busy making sure that there was no line of sight for a gunman outside the building to anyone sitting at the table. The social niceties of the meal were none of his concern.

Jock Colville, however, spent his life reading the moods of his master, Mr Churchill, and the various politicians, military leaders and wealthy hangers-on who surrounded him, and he, like Millicent, grasped the gravity of the situation.

'I am awfully sorry, My Lady,' he said. 'But I'm sure we can find a solution, if we put our heads together.'

'I would hope so, Mr Colville. It should not be too difficult to arrange four men around a table.'

'Indeed . . . but these are four exceptional men.'

'The president will be the only head of state attending the meal,' said Mrs Dufoy, firmly. 'Therefore, he should sit at the head of the table.'

'That is usually the place occupied by the host,' Lady Halifax pointed out. 'Which would mean my husband, the ambassador.'

'On the other hand,' said Colville, 'since we are in a British embassy, this counts as British soil, and Winston Churchill is the prime minister of the United Kingdom of Great Britain and Northern Ireland. One would think – and he will certainly think – that he should take precedence.'

'Thank God the duke gave up his throne,' Lady Halifax sighed. 'At least he has no claim to the top seat.'

Charlie Playfair had been walking through the residence with a purposeful stride and a file under one arm, looking like a busy man. But he'd stopped by the colonnade on the side of the dining room, leaning on one of the pillars with an amused half-smile on his face as he listened to the argument over the seating plan.

'Oh, hello, Playfair,' Colville said, spotting him. 'You're a clever chap. Do you have any bright ideas?'

'Maybe they could take it in turns . . . you know, everyone moves round one place after each course. Soup . . . starter . . . main course . . . pudding. That's four, so they'd each get their turn. Though one would have to make sure that the drinks moved with them, of course. Champers for Sir Winston, Martinis for President Roosevelt . . . isn't that the standard order at the bar?'

There was a brief silence as the group around the table tried to work out whether Playfair had been making a serious suggestion, or simply mocking them. Before they could decide, Playfair said, 'Might I ask you a favour, Dorothy?'

'By all means,' Lady Halifax replied, as Millicent did her best to mask her resentment. *Damn Playfair!* The casual familiarity of calling Her Ladyship by her first name, that automatic presumption that he was her equal, and her unthinking assent, were infuriating.

'Just want to borrow Colville for a second. No more than one quick question, really.'

'Of course.'

As Colville strolled over to the pillar where Playfair was waiting, Lady Halifax and Mrs Dufoy had a brief discussion about Playfair's suggestion. Now it was Mrs Dufoy's turn to be upset. 'Was that gentleman not aware the president is confined to a wheelchair, and cannot just swap seats at a moment's notice?'

Millicent, meanwhile, was busy making adjustments to an arrangement of roses in a glass vase that had been placed on one of the console tables positioned at intervals along the dining room's walls. This took her closer to Colville and Playfair and enabled her to overhear their conversation, even though both men were keeping their voices down.

'Have you seen any of the local papers this morning?' Playfair asked.

'God, no,' Colville replied. 'No time for that sort of thing. Not with the conference to worry about.'

'Well then, you won't have seen the headlines about an unidentified man who was stabbed to death in an alley yesterday.'

Colville frowned. 'Which is important because . . .?'

'He was one of our chaps. No one knows that yet – not officially – but there was a hell of a flap here when we all saw the artist's impression of the man and recognised him at once. Next thing we knew, a police captain arrived at the embassy, saying that the murdered man had been wearing clothes made in Britain, so naturally they were coming to us for assistance in identifying him. I was given the job of making the captain feel at home, buttering him up and extracting the maximum amount of information from him, while giving as little as possible in return.'

'Though you promised to give him the fullest possible co-operation—'

'Naturally.'

'So what did he tell you? Are there any security implications the PM needs to be told about?'

'The police don't think so. They think this was just another robbery in a nasty part of town. Crimes like that can easily turn violent. It seems the killer used a flick knife, which the captain told me was suggestive of a, quote, "small-time hoodlum". A professional "hit man", as they call paid assassins here, would have used a gun. Also, the killer emptied the victim's wallet and took his driving licence – that's the reason they couldn't identify him – which suggests that money was the motive. Apparently licences have a certain value in the criminal world, since they can provide a false identity . . . like passports, I suppose.'

'My God, how awful – murdered for a few dollars and a scrap of card.'

'I know, but I'm afraid that sort of thing happens a lot here. If you start walking north from the Capitol or take a wrong turn out of Union Station, you can go from classical grandeur to festering, violent slumland in the space of a block or two. The poor chap just stepped on the wrong side of that line.'

'So there's no reason for the PM to change this evening's schedule?'

Playfair gave a thoughtful shake of the head. 'No . . . As far as the embassy is concerned, we're following the advice of the police. This is a personal tragedy, but it has no political bearing.'

'So he doesn't really need to know at all . . .'

Playfair shook his head. 'There are much more important things for one of the two great leaders of the free world to worry about.'

'Thank heavens for that. We're very keen, to put it mildly, to have at least one meeting with the president on our sovereign territory. You know, just to remind him we see this as a meeting of equals. Anyway, must get back to planning dinner. Thanks for filling me in.'

The two men had done their best to be discreet. But Millicent had still caught enough of their conversation to note the care with which Playfair had avoided saying the name Jarvis.

Charlie Playfair didn't say anything about the Secret Intelligence Service, either, she thought, *though everyone always said Jarvis was head of station. He's keeping that nice and quiet. Doesn't want anyone thinking too hard about what really happened.*

Millicent gave a little shake of the head, as she followed her train of thought. *No one does – not the embassy, not Churchill's staff – and no one's ever going to know for sure what happened to Jarvis. If he really was an agent, then SIS won't let anyone tell the local police that. There's no one in the embassy who's capable of investigating the case. And SIS won't send anyone all the way here to do it. What's the point? By the time anyone from London gets here, the trail will be stone cold. And anyway, there's a war on. They've got more than enough to worry about at home.*

Then she caught a glimpse of the Secret Service agent out of the corner of her eye, and had to suppress a bitter smile as she thought: *We haven't told the Americans that he's one of ours. No one wants to risk Roosevelt having second thoughts about dinner. Poor little Jarvis, no one gives a damn about you . . . Everyone's got bigger fish to fry.*

As Playfair departed and Colville turned towards the dining table, Millicent stepped away from the vase of flowers. 'Much better,' she said. She then approached Lady Halifax again. 'Perhaps I might make a suggestion, My Lady?'

'Please do,' Lady Halifax said. 'It can't possibly cause more trouble than anything the rest of us have come up with.'

'Well, it strikes me that, however they were arranged, the four gentlemen might feel a little lost around a long table in a large dining room. Perhaps if the meal were held in the morning room . . .? It might feel more . . . intimate. And, of course, the table in there is round, so it has no head, so everyone is on equal terms. In addition to which, there is only the one door to the room. I imagine the gentlemen looking after Mr Roosevelt would find it much easier to guard.'

The Secret Service man turned and glared at Millicent. 'Did you say "one door"?'

'Yes, that's right. And there are three windows – two that look out over the garden, and another internal window onto the stairwell.'

'Well now, that sounds just grand, because this place . . .' He waved a hand at the colonnade which ran along one side of the dining room, leaving it, like all the residence's grand reception rooms, open to the main corridor. 'This is not good for our purposes. Not good at all.'

Lady Halifax turned her eyes to Mrs Dufoy. 'Does the president have any objection to round tables?'

'I don't believe so,' she conceded.

'Mr Colville?'

'I can't see Winston having a problem with circularity, no.'

'Then let us go and inspect the morning room.'

They set off without a word of acknowledgement to Millicent. But as she was following the others out, the Secret Service man sidled up to her and murmured, 'Nice work.'

'Thank you,' said Millicent, glad that someone had noticed that she had easily solved a problem that had stumped the embassy's brightest intellects. She looked at her watch. 'It's almost eleven. Would you like me to organise some coffee for you and your men?'

'No, we always work right through without a break.'

'Are you sure?' Millicent looked up at the tall, broad-shouldered agent and put on her most winning smile. 'After all, this is British soil. And we always stop for elevenses.'

'Well, that's very quaint, ma'am, but we're Americans.'

'Fair enough, you win. Look, I must dash now, can't miss any of the dinner plans. But I'm Lady H's right-hand woman, as it were. I know everything about this place – what's what and who's who. So if you need any information, please don't hesitate to ask.'

The Secret Service man smiled, revealing gleaming white teeth unlike any that Millicent had seen in the mouth of an Englishman. 'Thank you kindly, ma'am. I might just do that.'

'Might I ask your name?' Millicent inquired.

The agent gave a wry smile as he shook his head. 'Sorry, ma'am, but there's a reason they call us the Secret Service.'

'Oh . . .'

'But if it makes it easier, you can call me . . . I don't know . . . How about Bob?'

Millicent smiled. 'Agent Bob.'

'At your service, ma'am.'

Millicent smiled and hurried off towards the morning room with a spring in her step. She remembered a line from a movie she'd recently seen – something like, 'This could be the start of a beautiful friendship.'

• • •

Saffron walked out of the Senate Building and checked her watch: 12.20. Stephenson would be expecting her call by now. She looked around for the nearest phone booth.

There was only one she could see, about a hundred yards away on the far side of a busy road. Saffron started walking towards it, then had to stand by the roadside, humming with frustration and impatience before the pedestrian light turned green. The booth was empty as she crossed the road.

A burly man in oil-stained mechanic's overalls appeared out of nowhere and beat her to the phone. He dialled a number and, while he was waiting for an answer, turned, looked at her and gave a shrug that was somewhere between an apology and 'Screw you, lady, I got here first.'

Someone must have answered, because he put a coin into the box and started talking.

The name of the man who had claimed the phone booth was Novak. In the office of his building company, Lewandowski listened as Novak talked. 'Whatever she was doing at the Senate Office, she's out. And she wants to make a call. She's giving me the evil eye right now, matter of fact.'

'Then let her make her call. Do you think she suspects you?'

'I'm pretty sure she just thinks I'm an asshole.'

'Okay. Now hang up, disappear . . . but don't lose her.'

As the call was being made, Saffron thought over the events of the past couple of hours. The day before, her work for SOE had been a distraction from thoughts of spies and conspiracies. This morning it had been its opposite. Even as she was talking to the junior senator from Delaware and then, after him, the chief of staff for the senior senator from Ohio, she had not been able to rid her mind of the little canister and what the message inside it might mean. But despite being distracted, the Senate meeting had not been a total disaster.

She had been able to say her piece, give plausible answers to the questions she was asked, and describe life in Occupied Europe from the inside. If there was one thing that had become clear over the past forty-eight hours, it was that first-hand descriptions of dinners with SS officers never failed to impress. But Saffron played her trump card when she passed on Cindy and Mortimer Hackenstedt's personal best wishes to the men she was meeting. Forget the war. Forget Europe. In Washington, nothing was more impressive than the fact that she had dined with such an eminent political couple, in their own home. If the Hackenstedts had taken her seriously, lesser mortals felt obliged to do the same.

A few yards away, the man got off the phone and left the booth. 'All yours, lady!' he called out with a grin.

Saffron dashed into the booth before anyone else could claim it and called New York. She was put straight through to Stephenson.

'I've got good news,' he said. 'Miss Keswick has been working on that message with a chap from our Bermuda operation who's in town this week – one of the best. The code is not the one that was used on the Gerald letters, so they're confident of cracking it.'

Saffron's spirits fell at those last few words. 'But they haven't yet?'

'It's only a matter of time. I spoke to Miss Keswick half an hour ago and she reckoned it would be no more than a couple of hours. Do you think there's an imminent danger of something crucial happening in the next two hours?'

'Maybe . . . I don't know . . .' Saffron sighed. Stephenson was a precise man. He did not like dealing in vague maybes. 'I don't have any knowledge of an imminent danger, no,' she admitted.

'Then it's not worth worrying about. Meanwhile, what is your news? How did you get hold of this text?'

Saffron ran through a quick summary of the previous forty-eight hours, starting with Donovan's scepticism, and taking Stephenson through her interactions with the Playfairs, culminating in the discovery of the message hidden on the park bench.

‘Are you suggesting that he’s the agent and she’s the go-between?’ Stephenson asked.

‘It’s common practice in SOE. But what really worries me, sir, is this . . . What if this isn’t just about information? What if someone’s planning something like an assassination or an act of sabotage?’

‘Do you really think Charles Playfair has the guts or the skill to kill people?’

‘I think he’s tougher than he makes out. He wasn’t afraid to get involved in the Spanish Civil War.’

‘But why would he do it? It feels absurd even to ask this, but did either of the Playfairs give the slightest indication of any sympathy for Nazi Germany?’

‘No, sir, none at all.’ Saffron thought for a moment. ‘Of course, if they did think that way, they’re both far too clever to show it. But I don’t think the Playfairs are pretending to have left-wing principles. They’re completely sincere about that.’

‘And yet there was a message left, presumably for her, though we don’t know for sure, at a bench where she regularly sits.’

‘It could be a coincidence,’ Saffron said. ‘I almost hope it is.’

‘Huh,’ Stephenson grunted. ‘I guess we’ll soon find out one way or the other. In the meantime, go get some lunch. Call me again at two. We should have a decoded message by then.’

• • •

SS-Brigadeführer Konrad von Meerbach was blessed with an impressive combination of power and privilege. His rank, equivalent to an army major general, was bolstered by a close friendship with *Reichsführer* Heinrich Himmler, the head of the SS, who could consider himself the second most powerful man in the Third Reich, behind only the Führer himself. This relationship, in turn, was founded on Von Meerbach's immense wealth as the current head of an industrial dynasty fit to rival the Krupps and Thyssens, thanks to which he was the owner of the Schloss Meerbach, a castle that loomed over the northern shoreline of the Bodensee, looking towards the Swiss Alps on the far side of the lake.

Von Meerbach was a generous host to the many Nazi officials who were his guests. His mistress was a dear friend of Eva Braun and Magda Goebbels. To cap it all, Von Meerbach was a hereditary count. And though the German National Socialist Workers' Party, as the Nazis were properly known, was supposedly a revolutionary movement opposed to the class system, even its most senior, ardent members had a streak of crashing snobbery.

For all these reasons, Von Meerbach was accustomed to getting what he wanted. And on this lovely spring morning, with the sun shining through the leaves of the lime trees on Unter den Linden, it appeared that he was, once again, about to have one of his wishes granted. For although he was not, strictly speaking, an officer in the SD, when he took a strong personal interest in one of that agency's investigations, no one was going to stop him from getting involved.

'So,' he said, looking at the two SD officers in their freshly pressed uniforms and gleaming boots, standing to attention on the far side of his huge mahogany desk, 'I gather that we have successfully identified the murderer of *Hauptsturmführer* Karsten Schröder. Is that correct?'

'Yes, sir,' said one of the officers.

'And you are?'

'*Sturmbannführer* Karl-Heinrich Hertz, *Herr Brigadeführer.*'

'You were the one who first made the identification?'

'Yes, sir.'

'And it was the Englishwoman, Saffron Courtney?'

There was a peculiar intensity to the way Von Meerbach said the name – a combination of repressed excitement and revulsion.

'Yes, sir.'

'How can you be certain?'

'Well, sir, the woman known as Marlize Marais was the last person seen with Schröder before his death, close to the site where the body was found. The police are satisfied that she killed him. Marais was a British agent. She entered the Reich, having sailed from South Africa, via our consulate in Lisbon, and made her way from there to the Low Countries. In Belgium, she joined the staff of the VNV, the local National Socialist Party, through which she had access to German personnel in both Belgium and Holland. She later escaped from Belgium on an RAF Lysander aircraft, which is a model used by the so-called Special Operations Executive, or SOE, to take agents in and out of Reich territories, particularly in northern Europe.'

Hertz paused, to allow Von Meerbach to ask any questions. Instead, the *Brigadeführer* waved a hand and said, 'Carry on . . .'

'Yes, sir . . . So, we know from captured SOE personnel that Saffron Courtney is an SOE agent, and that she works in the Belgian section of that organisation. We now also know that she arrived in Cape Town in January, aboard a British troopship. We have local men, loyal to National Socialist principles, who observe enemy shipping in and out of the harbour there. Miss Courtney was the only woman to disembark from the ship, and she is said to be very striking—'

Von Meerbach gave a little grunt at that, then waved his hand again.

'Very soon after that,' Hertz continued, 'this so-called Marlize Marais made her first contact with members of the Ossewabrandwag organisation, an Afrikaner nationalist organisation that has been steadfast in its support of the Führer and the Third Reich. Courtney, alias Marais, used her charms to persuade these men to write letters of recommendation, which she then used in Portugal and the Low Countries as proof that she, too, was on our side.

'The description of Marais given by these men exactly matches the description of Saffron Courtney given by our man at the Cape Town docks. Likewise, the description of Marais given by the members of the VNV exactly matches that given by former SOE agents, captured and turned by the Abwehr. There can be no doubt at all that Marais and Courtney are one and the same person.

'So, to use the policeman's formula, Miss Courtney had the means to kill Schröder, because her SOE training includes unarmed combat. She had the opportunity, because they were alone in a park in the dead of night. And she had the motive, because she is an enemy of the Reich.'

'Very good, *Sturmbannführer* Hertz . . . very good. You have done an excellent job, and I feel sure that the Reich will express its gratitude to you in due course.'

'Thank you, *Herr Brigadeführer*.'

Von Meerbach nodded, then turned to look at the other officer. 'If your comrade is Hertz, then you must be Preminger . . .'

'Yes, sir.'

'And you are in Section D, which covers the American sphere, which, I gather, is where Fräulein Courtney now finds herself.'

'Yes, sir.'

‘And do you know her precise location?’

‘She is in Washington DC, sir. I have already arranged for her to be placed under surveillance.’

‘Excellent.’ Von Meerbach smiled. ‘So, when I issue the order to have Miss Courtney executed, as befits a murderess, you are the man who will organise that execution.’

‘In theory, sir, yes.’

Von Meerbach frowned. His jaw clenched, and the good humour in his voice had been replaced by a tightness – a man trying to keep his temper in check. ‘What do you mean, “in theory”?’

‘Well, sir, we don’t actually have anyone in the United States who is qualified to carry out that kind of operation.’

‘I’m sorry . . .’ Von Meerbach was a very large man, and he was beginning to run to fat. His pale complexion reddened rapidly at his rising fury. ‘Are you telling me that the Overseas Security Service of the Reich has not got a single man who can do to Saffron Courtney what she did to Karsten Schröder?’

‘I’m afraid so, sir . . . and nor does the Abwehr. None of the Reich intelligence agencies have been able to get trained operatives capable of assassination and sabotage into the United States, any more than the British have been able to get any agents into the Low Countries—’

‘Except for Saffron Courtney.’

‘Yes, sir, except for her . . .’ In increasing desperation, Preminger went on. ‘I should say, however, that we do have sympathisers of various kinds, both Americans and also foreign diplomats. They provide us with information and can carry out low-grade work. Two such men carried out a successful operation of harassment and mental destabilisation against Courtney in New York.’

'But I don't want "harassment" and "mental destabilisation",' Von Meerbach sneered. 'I want a bullet in the back of that English whore's head! And I don't care if you have to swim across the Atlantic, I want you to make sure it happens. And don't you look so smug . . .' Von Meerbach turned his blazing blue eyes on to Hertz. 'You can damn well go with him. And between you, you had better put that sack of perfumed shit in the ground, or I will make sure that you are both doing guard duty in a concentration camp for the rest of your lives. No, forget that . . . I'll make you prisoners in that camp!'

Hertz and Preminger both shouted, 'Yes, *Herr Brigadeführer*,' snapped their heels and gave a Nazi salute. It was only when they had not only left von Meerbach's office, but were outside the building, on the street, lighting cigarettes with shaking fingers, that Preminger said, 'What the hell was that all about? I mean, I know Von Meerbach has a temper. He's famous for it. But that . . . That was personal. He really hates that woman.'

'Yes, it was as if he knew her . . . but goodness knows how. Is it really true? Do we not have a single damn agent in the whole United States?'

'No – not one.'

'My God. Then we'd better hope that someone else kills her fast, or we are in serious trouble.'

• • •

Charlie Playfair was in his office at the embassy, writing a report on the views of US senators about the invasion of Europe, when his secretary buzzed him to say there was a foreign-sounding lady on the line. 'Put her through,' he said, knowing who it must be. He'd been expecting her call all day.

Consuela Balcázar did not beat about the bush. 'You swore to me that there would be no danger!' she exclaimed, speaking to Playfair in Spanish, just as she had done with Jarvis. 'Now a man is dead. What if I am next?'

Playfair tried to reassure her. 'Don't worry, my darling, you won't be.'

'How do you know?'

'Because I'm certain that Jarvis was unlucky. He was in a rough part of town and doubtless some local criminal saw him as easy meat.'

'I'm still frightened,' Consuela purred, unable to restrain her seductive instincts even at times of crisis. 'Come to me tonight. I need you to comfort me and make me feel safe.'

'I don't think I can – not at such short notice. Anyway, don't you have a date with Jorge or Carlos?'

The two names belonged to the deputy Spanish ambassador and the consul general of Uruguay. 'Don't be mean,' Consuela said in a pouting tone.

'I'm not being mean, dear heart, just factual.'

'Well, all right, then. Maybe I am seeing Carlos. But I can cancel him at a moment's notice. He will be upset, of course, but then I will promise to see him in two or three days' time and his sadness will disappear.'

'Yes, but I have a wife who is expecting me home for supper.'

'But this is a time of crisis, no? One of your people is dead. Of course you must work late tonight.'

'Well, maybe . . .'

'Come – please – because I am in danger.'

'No, you aren't, I assure you – but I will do my best.'

Playfair hung up, inwardly cursing the day his path and Consuela's had crossed. He should have ended his affair with her long ago. Not only did it pose a terrible threat to his marriage, but he had sworn blind to SIS that he would end his relationship with her once she became a British intelligence asset. The trouble was, Consuela was addictive. Sex with her was on an entirely different level from any other woman he had ever bedded. He could not give that up. And yet, Playfair had no doubt that he truly loved Mavis, thought of her as his best friend, felt certain that she would never betray him, and he had no desire to leave her. *How can all these things simultaneously be true?* he wondered, with a philosophical sigh at the complexities of life, sex and love.

A moment later there was a knock on his door and in strode Millicent James. The sight of her, purse-lipped and disapproving, would normally have driven any thought of sex from Playfair's mind. But today Millicent seemed to be in an unusually good mood. There was a bloom on her cheeks and a sparkle in her eyes. *Good Lord,* Playfair thought, *she looks almost attractive.*

For once, he thought a cheery greeting might be in order. 'Hello, Millicent. You look very bonny today, if I may say so.'

'Oh . . .' she said, taken aback by his unusually friendly greeting. 'Thank you . . . Yes . . . Well . . . I have a message for you, Mr Playfair.' She handed him a neatly folded piece of British embassy notepaper. 'I wrote it down verbatim.'

'Thank you.' Playfair scanned the note, doing his best to contain his excitement as the blood started pounding through him again. 'Thank you very much indeed.'

Millicent gave a puzzled frown at his gleeful tone, then turned and left the room. Playfair waited a minute or so, to make sure Millicent had truly gone. He would not have put it past her to be pressing her ear to his office door. He picked up his telephone again and dialled a number he knew by heart.

'Good news,' he said when Consuela picked up. 'I may be able to make it after all.'

• • •

Saffron knew she needed to eat. All her instincts were telling her that the Stephenson assignment, which had been simmering for the past forty-eight hours, was about to come to the boil. She might soon be calling upon all the strength and energy she possessed. But her nerves were jangling, and she barely tasted the bowl of tagliatelle carbonara she ordered at an Italian restaurant a couple of hundred yards from the Senate Office Building.

Much of the tension was frustration at not yet knowing the contents of the coded message. But there was something else that was nagging at her, like a word on the tip of her tongue.

Saffron was distractedly lifting a forkful of pasta to her mouth when the realisation suddenly struck her.

The man who had beaten her to the phone call – there was something about the way he'd spoken. Saffron thought hard, tried to hear again in her head those three words: 'All yours, lady.' There had been a heaviness to the voice that was more Germanic than, say, Italian or French. Or was it more Eastern European?

Maybe that didn't mean anything. Lots of Americans spoke with the accent of the country they or their parents came from. But then Saffron thought of the way he had looked at her as he was placing the call. Men always looked at her. That was a fact of life. But somehow he'd looked at her as if he knew who she was.

But if he'd been following her, why make his presence so obvious by beating her to the phone?

Saffron sighed. The answer was obvious. She had deliberately put temptation in Charlie Playfair's way by giving him her appointments schedule to pass to Lady Halifax. Now a man with a Germanic accent was tailing her and passing on her movements to his boss.

Or I'm making this all up, and he was just a man who beat me to the phone and wanted to talk to his wife . . . or his mistress . . . or his bookie . . .

Saffron thought about her short walk from the phone booth to the restaurant. She couldn't recall seeing anyone following her, but if she were honest with herself, she'd been too absorbed by her conversation with Stephenson to be paying proper attention. She checked the time: 13.15. Forty-five minutes until she could make that call to New York. And this time she'd make sure she found a phone booth without anyone tailing her.

Having a plan took the edge off Saffron's tension. She ordered a bowl of chocolate ice cream – another indulgence long forgotten in London – and a strong, bitter espresso. She powdered her nose, paid her bill and left the restaurant at precisely 13.40.

There was a huge department store across the street from the restaurant, covering most of a block. That meant it had multiple exits. Saffron went into the store, browsed some cosmetics stands and flicked through a couple of racks of dresses, scanning her surroundings as she did so. She didn't see anyone suspicious.

The store was busy. Saffron made her way through the other shoppers as quickly as she could without breaking into a run, took a zigzag path across the ground floor, and left by a different door from the one by which she'd entered.

The map of the city that she'd memorised when looking down from the Washington Monument told her that Union Station was fewer than ten blocks away. Stations had telephones and lots of entrances and exits. That was where she would go. Saffron crossed the street, heading north.

Behind her, a black Chrysler sedan came to a sudden stop. A man quickly got out and the sedan moved off. The man crossed the street as Saffron had done and set off after her.

Saffron walked on, slipping into doorways every now and then to check behind her and see if anyone stopped at the same time. She saw no one.

She arrived at the station at 13.58, saw a long line of wooden telephone booths and quickly occupied one. This time, no one tried to beat her to it. She took her pen and notebook out of her bag, called Stephenson's number and was put straight through. He didn't beat about the bush. 'My people decoded the message. Can you write it down?'

'Yes . . . go ahead.'

'The message is in English. It reads, "Urgent meet Shadow 3127MNW 19."'

Saffron gave a sharp intake of breath. 'So Gerald does exist.'

'I never doubted it.'

'And he is Charlie Playfair.'

'That's a reasonable assumption. The rest of the message is presumably an address and time for a rendezvous. If I recall, M Street is in Georgetown. There are lots of restaurants, bars, coffee shops. I imagine the rendezvous is at one of them.'

'And the one-nine means they're meeting at seven p.m. I had better be there.'

'Yes, but now I am going to give you two orders, on my and Gubbins' behalf. First, your job is just to observe the rendezvous, and confirm Gerald's identity. You are not – repeat, *not* – to engage in any way with either Gerald or "Shadow", who must be his controller. This is a matter of covert surveillance. Do I make myself clear?'

'Yes, sir. But what if no one believes me? I've already had two chaps from the embassy telling me that there's no spy and they don't want me snooping around, looking for one. And General Donovan made it very clear that he took the same view. If I start claiming that I've identified an agent they've all told me doesn't exist—'

'They won't want you telling them that they were wrong. Yes, I can see the problem . . .'

'Particularly me being a woman.'

'Well, then, you'd better get a man who can tell them that he saw Shadow, too. An American would be good. Might make it easier to persuade Donovan . . .' A tone of wry amusement entered Stephenson's voice. 'Why don't you ask Lieutenant Stackpole to accompany you?'

'He's in the OSS, sir,' said Saffron. 'I wondered whether you knew that.'

'Yes, Donovan told me . . . but only after you'd arrived in Washington. He added that Stackpole's role was almost entirely medical. He's useful to have around, as a Russian speaker, but he's not a field agent, like you, which would explain why he was easy meat for that cop at the Copa. You'd do well to bear that in mind.'

'Yes, sir . . . And of course I'd be delighted to have Lieutenant Stackpole with me. But I'd be disobeying an order from General Donovan.'

'You are not under Donovan's command. As much as I like and admire him, it is not for him to say what you should or should not do.'

'No, sir . . . But General Donovan is Lieutenant Stackpole's CO, and I wouldn't want to get Stackpole into trouble by involving him in all this.'

'Hmm . . .' There was a moment's silence while Stephenson pondered. 'If you do as I have asked, and simply observe the situation, then there is no reason why Stackpole should be in any trouble at all. You arrange with him to meet for dinner. You don't say anything that suggests that this is any more than a social encounter. If you see nothing suspicious, then no harm has been done. But if, on the other hand, you do get evidence that Playfair is up to something, then you pass that information immediately to me and it will be followed up, without you or Stackpole being involved. And I entirely agree with Donovan that you can't be getting into any rough stuff.'

'But what do I do if I see something that might put other people in danger?'

'Call me. I'll deal with it. In the meantime, find a place to eat that overlooks the rendezvous point. Keep an eye out for Mr Playfair . . . or anyone else from the British embassy, for that matter.'

'The only one I'd recognise for sure is a man called Jarvis, who's with SIS.'

'Not anymore,' said Stephenson. 'Jarvis is dead.'

Saffron was taken completely by surprise. 'But I only saw him a couple of days ago . . . What happened?'

'He was stabbed in an alley in a rough part of town.'

'That explains it . . . Playfair left his house this morning earlier than usual. I heard him shouting "Bloody hell!" and he was out of the door and into his car like a scalded cat.'

'I'm told there was a hell of a flap at the embassy when people saw the morning papers. The police didn't have the victim's ID, but everyone knew who he was. Then the question became – what, if anything, to tell the police, or the White House? Perhaps I should have told you about all this earlier. I assumed you already knew. But this doesn't change anything from our point of view. And let me say this again – do not engage with Gerald or Shadow. Do not allow yourself to be spotted. Understood?'

'Yes, sir,' Saffron said, doing her very best to mean it. She knew she would be tempted to pull out her gun and charge into the place where Playfair and his contact were meeting. But she swore to herself that this time she would stay out of trouble and be a good girl. Well, maybe not entirely good. After she carried out the surveillance and dutifully reported what she and Stackpole had seen, she would consider her working day over. And then she planned to be a very naughty girl indeed.

• • •

In Berlin, SD *Sturmbannführer* Preminger was shouting into the telephone. 'Our man saw your man engaged in surveillance. I can give you the address of the damn property!'

Preminger held the handset away from his ear as a furious denial came back at him from Abwehr headquarters. 'This is ridiculous,' he muttered to himself. 'You have not heard the end of this.' He slammed the handset down.

A few minutes later he was in Hertz's office. 'You know,' he admitted, after he had given his colleague an account of the conversation, 'I almost believe him. I mean, suppose it were the other way around and the Abwehr had been calling me, after they had stumbled on to one of our operations, I would not deny that the operation was happening.'

'I suppose not,' said Hertz. 'After all, you would want them to go away, and why would they do that, if you had not given them a reason to do so?'

'Exactly. I would be firm, but calm. I would say that it was none of their damn business, but if they did anything that harmed our operations, I would take this matter to the highest reaches of the SS – so high, in fact, that Himmler himself would hear of it. And then the Abwehr would soon find themselves buried under an avalanche of shit.'

Hertz laughed. 'Maybe you should do that anyway!'

'Maybe . . .' Preminger nodded. 'But in the meantime, Hertz, we are faced with another question. If the Abwehr is not carrying out surveillance on Saffron Courtney, who the hell is?'

'Our Japanese allies?' suggested Hertz, though he sounded far from convinced.

'No. What interest would they have in Courtney? She works for SOE. They do not conduct operations in the Far East. Besides, Macedo assumed that the men he had spotted were German, so they must have looked European.'

'Italians, maybe? That will be where the Allies go next, now that Tunisia has fallen.'

Preminger sighed. 'Ach . . . I don't know. But let us pray that whoever they are, they can take care of Saffron Courtney, permanently. Because if they don't terminate her, Von Meerbach will surely terminate us.'

• • •

In Johnson City, Tennessee, Clayton Stackpole, wearing a white doctor's coat over his army air force uniform, was standing beside the bed in which Gilbert Wermuth lay with his plaster-encased left leg suspended in traction. The private room was spartan, but spotlessly clean. A china vase filled with flowers stood beside the glass of water on the bedside table.

There was nothing to suggest the six-and-a-half hours of messy, bloody work it had taken Stackpole and the local doctors and nurses to clean the wound caused by a compound fracture of Wermuth's left tibia: to remove stray scraps of bone, and bits of dirt and even grass that had entered the wound; to cut away pieces of muscle that may have been contaminated by dirt and bacteria; to reassemble and pin the broken bone; and then to close and stitch the incision that ran the full length of Wermuth's leg.

Stackpole yawned. He had not gone to bed until past two in the morning, and though he had slept through till eight he was still dog-tired. The DC-3 had been fitted out with passenger seats, rather than the bare metal benches used for troop transportation, but the flight back to Washington would be loud, bumpy and uncomfortable. Stackpole didn't care. He was planning on being asleep all the way.

He looked at his patient. 'How are you feeling?'

Wermuth did his best to smile. 'Better than this time yesterday. How long before I'm fit for duty?'

'You had a compound fracture. That's a serious break. It'll be four to six months before you're walking unaided.'

'I've got to be able to do more than walk.'

'You can expect to recover well enough to lead a normal life. But you'll never be as fast or strong as you were before your accident.'

Stackpole watched Wermuth slump back onto his pillows. 'Don't worry,' he said. 'Maybe you won't be able to run the hundred-yard dash, but you'll still be a valuable asset to OSS.'

'Thanks, doc. I guess I should count myself lucky, right?'

'Right. Now take it easy, okay?' Stackpole left the room and walked down the hospital corridor towards the exit. A driver was waiting outside to take him to the airport. He could still get back to Washington by six. Maybe Saffron would be free for dinner. And then they'd make up for missing last night.

• • •

Lewandowski was too experienced to take anything for granted. He had seen apparently flawless operations go to hell at the last minute, had seen too many officers pay the ultimate price for their failures. But the hook had been set, and unless everything his sources had told him about Saffron Courtney was wrong, she would not be able to resist taking the bait.

Her behaviour had certainly been that of a professional preparing for action. The thoroughness of her counter-surveillance routine on the route between the Italian restaurant where she had lunched and Union Station, where she made another call – presumably to Stephenson in New York – testified to that. It was only a stroke of luck that two of his men – having lost her in the department store – happened to be driving past the exit at the precise moment she emerged onto the street.

The tail had been restored, but she had disappeared into one of the station's telephone booths, and Lewandowski called his man off. He knew where she would be heading shortly before seven in the evening. They would pick her up on M Street easily enough.

What mattered now was making sure that her capture and removal were carried out with the minimum fuss, so that no one passing by would even know a kidnapping had taken place, still less who was responsible. Lewandowski had calculated the sequence of events to the last second. Now he needed his men around him so that they could be given their assignments and drilled in their execution.

In an old, abandoned tram shed in Arlington, not far from Lewandowski's home, where a trolley car company had once serviced their vehicles, he had used whitewash to mark out a full-scale outline of Ma Franklin's Diner and the surrounding streets.

When Lewandowski's men arrived at the tram shed, he began to tell them what they had to do.

• • •

In Saffron's experience, the hardest part of war was the waiting. Once the action began she was focused on the task in hand, and felt no fear or anxiety. It was sitting around with too much time to think that gave her the jitters. She had almost five hours to kill before Playfair – alias 'Gerald' – met his handler Shadow, but luckily she had several tasks to complete by then, so her mind would be fully occupied. Time to get to work.

The most important was a thorough reconnoitre of the building where the rendezvous would take place, and the area around it. She needed to find somewhere she could observe anyone who entered or exited the building, without being seen herself. And she needed to get hold of Stackpole.

The route from Union Station to M Street passed within a short distance of Navy Hill. Two trolley cars and a short walk brought her to the front entrance of the OSS building. She showed her ID at the front desk and asked for Lieutenant Stackpole. A call was made to his office, and a minute later a plain-looking woman in her thirties appeared. 'Miss Courtney?'

'Yes, that's me.'

'My name is Lucille Shaw. I work in General Donovan's office. I'm afraid Lieutenant Stackpole is still away.'

'On his medical mission?'

'Exactly so. He performed an emergency operation and it went very well.' She looked at Saffron and pointedly added, 'Lieutenant Stackpole is a remarkable man.'

As if I'm not good enough for him . . . Saffron controlled a sudden jab of irritation. 'When are you expecting him back?'

'He should be here in Washington by eighteen hundred hours, and I'm sure he'll come in to report to General Donovan. Can I take a message for him?'

Saffron thought for a moment. 'Not yet. But if I called your office within the next hour or so, once I've sorted out some plans for the evening, might I leave a message then, please?'

'Of course,' the PA said, smiling pleasantly, while her eyes gave Saffron a thorough examination, assessing whether she was worthy of the lieutenant's company.

Saffron was sure that the chilly Miss Shaw had read the Winchell story, added two and two together, and was now preparing to report back to the other secretaries. There might, she decided, be some resentment that she had landed the remarkable Lieutenant Stackpole and one of them had not. More reason to give Miss Shaw no cause to say anything bad about her.

'Thank you so much, that's awfully kind,' Saffron said sweetly, with an ingratiating smile.

'Oh, that's no trouble at all,' replied Miss Shaw, with equal insincerity.

Saffron took another trolley car on a short journey to M Street, and got off at a stop a block short of her destination. She walked to the junction with 31st Street and started counting off the numbers until she came to 3127. She looked at the name, painted in olde worlde Gothic script across the plate-glass windows: Ma Franklin's Diner. Then she looked across at the other side of the street. Directly opposite was McGinty's Irish Bar. It, too, had windows facing the street, albeit smaller, tinted and partially obscured by curtains. Saffron shrugged. It would be trickier to observe the street from the bar than from the diner, but also more difficult for anyone outside to spot her.

She would check out the bar in due course. First she wanted to recce the layout of Ma Franklin's Diner and see if there was a service exit. It would also be useful to find out who lived on the first and second storeys of the building. Saffron pushed open the door.

She had not been in a traditional American diner before. She took a seat at the counter. A man in cook's whites was standing by a gas hob, waiting for the next order of hot food, indicating that there was no separate kitchen. The dining area was mostly occupied by tables and chairs, with brown leather banquettes forming separate cubicles along one wall.

Saffron wondered where an agent would choose to sit if meeting his handler. The banquettes would provide more privacy, but they offered only a limited view of the rest of the room and would make a quick exit difficult. If she were in enemy territory, she would want to be able to see trouble coming and escape it fast. But then again, Gerald wouldn't think of Washington as a potentially dangerous environment. Nor would his handler. This wasn't like Occupied Europe. There were no SS men strutting around, checking people's papers; no secret policemen from the Gestapo lurking in the shadows. The two of them would probably care more about not being seen or overheard. So when Gerald arrived at seven o'clock, she reasoned, he'd head for a banquette.

Saffron turned her attention to the other customers. A couple of women surrounded by their bulging shopping bags were chatting over cups of coffee and slices of cake. Two middle-aged men hunched over a chessboard on the table between them. A quartet of young men and women, presumably students, paused their heated debate about the morality of the bombing campaign against Germany to joke with the young waitress who'd brought over their colas and milkshakes. An intense young man sitting at the next stool to Saffron, his curly brown hair already prematurely receding, frowned in concentration as he digested the wisdom of Bertrand Russell's *Principia Mathematica*.

Saffron ordered a cup of tea. When she had finished and paid for it, she asked her waitress for directions to the ladies' room. It was at the back of the diner, through a door that opened into a short a corridor. Doors to male and female lavatories stood on one side, facing another door into what Saffron imagined was the diner's storeroom.

There was also a door at the end of the corridor. It was unlocked. Outside was a broad alley running the full length of the block, opening onto 31st Street at one end and Wisconsin Avenue at the other. A couple of vans, a small flatbed truck and some cars were parked at the back of the premises, where their owners presumably worked. To her left was another, narrower alley, barely wide enough for a car to drive down, that led back along the side of Ma Franklin's to M Street.

I could walk down the alley and come in through the back door, she thought. *That could come in handy.* And if the door happened to be locked later on, that wouldn't be a problem. Lock-picking was one of the many skills taught to SOE agents. *And if all else fails, I can just shoot the bloody thing open.*

She walked up the alley, back onto M Street and crossed the road to McGinty's Irish Pub. She didn't need to go in. It was enough to check that there were tables by the windows, so it would be possible to observe anyone going in to or coming out of the diner. And she'd be able to see the alley, too, just in case Gerald had the same idea about coming in through the back door.

But what if he approached the door via the access road at the back? He could get to that from 31st Street or Wisconsin Avenue. He wouldn't have to come down M Street. That meant a second pair of eyes was vital.

Saffron found the nearest phone booth, called OSS and asked for Lucille Shaw. She dictated a brief message with the time and place of their date, and then added, 'Be sure to tell him he mustn't be late!'

'Mad about the boy, huh?' said Miss Shaw, softening just a little.

'Rather, yes.'

'Well, I can't promise I'll see him. But I'll be sure to put your message on his desk where he can't miss it. And, sweetie . . .'

'Yes?'

'Try to appear a little less desperate when you see him. Guys don't respect girls who don't make them work for it.'

'Thank you, that's such good advice.'

Saffron hung up the phone, livid. *I don't believe it! Getting lessons about men from a dried-up old spinster!* But it was a job well done. No one at OSS could be in any doubt that she had asked Stackpole out on a date; there was nothing remotely professional about it.

So now it was back to waiting again. It was just before four o'clock: three hours to go. Looking around, Saffron saw a movie theatre on the block beyond Wisconsin Avenue, whose sign proclaimed in big red letters that it was showing *Sherlock Holmes in Washington*, starring Basil Rathbone as the great detective. That would have to do. When she got to the theatre, the gum-chewing lady in the ticket booth told her that the B-movie had already started. 'But trust me, honey, you ain't missed much.'

'Can I ask, what does Sherlock actually do in Washington?'

'Tracks down a Nazi spy – something like that.'

Saffron laughed. 'Perfect. Maybe he can give me some advice.'

The woman looked at her with a puzzled expression, then shrugged. 'Whatever you say . . . That'll be thirty cents. I got candy, too, if you want it.'

• • •

Fifteen minutes into Stackpole's flight back to Washington, the DC-3 hit serious turbulence and was soon being thrown around the sky like a rodeo rider on an angry steer. Stackpole was enough of an air force man not to be too concerned. The DC-3 was a sturdy aircraft. It could take worse punishment than this. Still, he desperately wanted to get back to Washington, and the bad weather looked as though it might delay them. He got up from his seat, and holding on to whatever support he could find, made his way towards the cockpit.

'How you doin'?' Stackpole shouted as the pilot turned and acknowledged his presence. 'Is it gonna be like this all the way to DC?'

'Why . . . you got a hot date?' the pilot shouted back.

'That's the plan.'

The pilot looked across at his navigator. 'What do you reckon, Jack? Is the doc here gonna get back in time to see his gal?'

'Weather report said that a storm front was moving south from the Great Lakes, over Ohio toward the Appalachians,' came the reply. 'Guess it just arrived. But I reckon we should be through it soon.'

The pilot turned back to Stackpole 'So . . . this date. Is she—'

His words were suddenly drowned by an explosive clap of thunder.

'Damn, this is fun!' the pilot exclaimed, wrestling the controls to keep the plane stable. 'So, come on, then, doc, describe this gal for us. We need the full picture.'

Stackpole decided to play along, if only to take his mind off the very real possibility that he was going to be violently sick if the turbulence continued for much longer. 'She's tall . . . long, long legs.'

'Sweet ass?'

'Very. Dark hair, almost black, but amazing blue eyes, lips you just wanna kiss all day and night—'

'Oh, yeah!' the navigator shouted. 'Say, can I take a turn after you?'

'I'd advise against that, son, on medical grounds. See these bruises on my face?

'Uh-huh.'

'The man who put 'em there was a heavyweight boxing champ. Right after he did that to me, he tried to put his filthy hands all over the gal I'm talking about. She gave him such a whippin', he ended up in hospital.'

The co-pilot's eyes widened. 'For real?'

'Damn straight. She beat the crap out of him.'

There was another bolt of lightning, another deafening blast of thunder, and then, as suddenly as they had flown into the storm, they were out the other side of it. The pilot wiped the back of his hand across his brow. 'Well . . . that was really something, wasn't it?' The other two men nodded.

'Okay, then, let's get you to your date, lickety-spit.' The pilot looked across the cockpit at the man sitting beside him. 'Just one thing I need to know from you, Jack. Where the hell are we now, anyway?'

• • •

Millicent James had become firm friends with Agent Bob. He had positioned himself like a guardsman in the main corridor outside the morning room, to keep an eye on anyone going in or out of the salon where the president would dine. As a result, he had seen a lot of Lady Halifax's personal assistant.

She had been darting in and out with her handbag hanging from the crook of her elbow, running a never-ending set of errands for Lady Halifax. 'Here, let me check that,' Agent Bob had said, when Millicent made her first sortie. He looked into the handbag and, seeing Millicent's notebook, a hairbrush, a purse, a hankie and sundry other bits of feminine clutter, nodded. 'Nothing personal, just gotta check.'

'Of course, Bob,' Millicent said, smiling demurely. 'I quite understand.'

'Can I ask what your purpose is?'

'By all means . . . Lady Halifax wishes me to ensure there are no pink flowers in the centrepiece on the table or the arrangements on the side tables. She feels they would be inappropriate for a gentlemen's dinner.'

'Do you think any of the men would even notice?'

'That's not for me to say.'

'Then I guess you'd better go in.'

He opened the door, closed it behind her once she was inside, and returned to his station in the main corridor. Millicent emerged a few minutes later, clutching a white peony with the faintest tinge of pink. 'Can't be too careful,' she said.

The second time, she told him that she had to check that the four places were set at exactly equal distances apart. 'Now you know why I always have to carry my bag,' she said, extracting a tape measure from its depths, and opening it for his inspection.

On the third occasion, she came in clutching a white napkin, which she unfolded to reveal four fish knives. 'Can you believe it – the butler laid the wrong fish knives?' she said, rolling her eyes.

'Ma'am, I don't even know what a fish knife is,' said Agent Bob, waving her through without bothering to inspect her bag.

A couple of hours went by. It was 18.21 when Millicent arrived with a dustpan and brush. 'We can't have a single speck of dust – not one,' she said, as he opened the door for her.

A minute later, out of curiosity, Bob opened the door, and there was Millicent, on her hands and knees, brushing the carpet underneath the table. As he closed the door again and turned back to the corridor, he shook his head in amazement. *And I thought we were dedicated.*

• • •

Sherlock Holmes, it turned out, found catching a German spy in Washington a lot easier than Saffron did. She left the movie theatre at 18.40 and walked back up M Street towards McGinty's. On the way, she passed a news-stand where copies of the final edition of the *Washington Star* had just been delivered. A banner headline on the front page screamed: WAS ALLEY BODY A BRIT?. Below it, in smaller bold type ran the strapline: BRITISH EMBASSY WORKING TO IDENTIFY VICTIM OF SLAYING.

Saffron handed over a nickel and bought a copy. In the pub, she was disappointed to find that Stackpole wasn't there yet. She went to the bar and bought a tonic water with ice, lemon and a dash of bitters.

'Sure you don't want some gin in that, too?' the barman asked.

Saffron smiled. 'No, thank you. It doesn't really look good, a woman drinking alcohol alone.'

'Believe me, lady, we get plenty of those.'

She paid for the drink and looked towards the window. There were three tables with a view of M Street. Two were occupied. She took the third.

Saffron laid the newspaper down in front of her. She glanced briefly at the opening paragraph, which simply repeated, with only slightly more detail, what the headlines had announced. There was a quote from a homicide detective in the Metropolitan Police Department, saying that his officers were concentrating their efforts on members of the criminal gangs known to operate in the area where the killing took place.

Saffron felt a stab of guilt for the way she had treated Jarvis when they had met two nights earlier. He had not deserved to be at the wrong end of her bad mood. But she could not dwell on that now.

She looked through the window, across M Street, focusing her attention on the entrance to the diner. She glanced at her watch: 18.52. Where was Stackpole? Saffron couldn't believe that he would deliberately stand her up, so something must have happened. But what?

She thought about calling OSS. There was bound to be a phone in the pub somewhere. But she couldn't risk Playfair arriving the moment her back was turned. The surveillance was in danger of falling apart before it had started. Too many people were sceptical about her mission. They wouldn't be convinced by anything she told them unless there was someone else – *A man*, Saffron thought, bitterly – to back her up. *Where the hell are you, darling?*

Saffron watched a couple walk up to the diner, his arm across her shoulder, hers around his waist. They paused a moment by the front window and he said something that made her smile as they walked in. Saffron envied them, wondering whether she and Stackpole would ever be able to spend time together like a normal couple. Then she drove the thought from her mind. She was supposed to be on the lookout for two male spies, not daydreaming about a pair of young lovers.

She drummed her fingers impatiently on the tabletop. She checked her watch again: 18.58. Still no Stackpole, and still no Gerald. Across the road, she saw a woman walking towards the diner. She looked familiar, somehow, but her high-collared coat hid her features, and she was wearing a hat with a brim that threw a shadow over her face.

'I guess your date didn't turn up, huh, sweetheart?'

The man who'd spoken was middle-aged, paunchy. He was wearing a business suit, but with his tie loosened and a cigarette hanging from the side of his mouth. His face was damp with perspiration and his breath stank of booze.

'He's on his way, actually,' she said, then turned her face back to the window. The woman was approaching the door of the diner. The last thing Saffron needed at this moment was some boorish oaf distracting her.

The man shook his head. 'No he ain't, and we both know it.'

'Please, go away,' Saffron said, without turning around.

She kept her eyes on the window. The woman was at the door, and the light from inside the diner was illuminating her face.

The man put a sweaty hand on Saffron's shoulder.

'I said, go away,' Saffron hissed. 'Beat it. Scram!'

The hand stayed where it was. Saffron looked for a second longer at the woman's face, imprinting it on her mind. Then she brought her right hand over the hand on her shoulder. Grabbing it tightly by the wrist, she got up from her chair, joined her left hand with her right, and twisted the man's wrist while bringing his hand up hard behind his back.

'Let me go, you bitch!' the man shouted as he tried to reach around with his other hand and grab her. Saffron had time to glance through the window as the woman stepped inside.

The woman was Mavis Playfair.

Saffron gave the lecherous drunk's arm another painful yank, then pushed him away. 'Now . . . get lost.' As he stumbled towards the exit, rubbing his arm, followed by a jeer or two from the drinkers at the bar, Saffron's attention had already returned to the diner.

She could see Mavis in the diner, clearly looking around for someone, before a waitress showed her to a table. Saffron could see the waitress talking to her and Mavis shaking her head. *My God, how ironic! She doesn't want to order until her man arrives either.*

Saffron should have felt elated. She had finally proved Stephenson right. Gerald really existed. *Except that she's Geraldine*. And now that she thought about it, Mavis perfectly fitted Donovan's description of the spy as the last person anyone would suspect. There she was every day, going to work amongst the poor, serving food to Black people, giving work to a young Black woman. It was the perfect cover for someone whose whole life was a lie.

Saffron wished it had been anyone other than Mavis, but the facts were undeniable. The message on the park bench – her favourite bench – had been for her. She had answered the summons. Now all that remained was for her handler, Shadow, to make his appearance. Or maybe Shadow was a woman, too? And where was Stackpole? Saffron didn't just need his help; she longed to have him next to her. But the time went by and Stackpole didn't appear. Mavis sat at her table. After a few minutes, she ordered something, and soon afterwards a cup and a teapot were brought to her table. But like Saffron, she remained at the table alone.

Saffron began to wonder if she had been blown. If so, Shadow would not risk being seen with Mavis. It struck her that she had not been looking out for anyone tailing her between the cinema and the pub. Her mind had been on what lay ahead of her.

It was 19.15 when Mavis appeared to accept that she had been stood up. She placed some coins by her teacup and got up to leave. Saffron thought about Stephenson's orders. He had told her to stay put, no matter what. But that order assumed that Shadow was going to turn up. In his absence – and with Stackpole not being there either – it was up to Saffron to confront Mavis and force her to reveal Shadow's identity.

Saffron got up and walked out of McGinty's. The street outside had become more crowded as the evening had drawn on: couples walking arm in arm; small groups of students and soldiers; people spilling in and out of the bars and restaurants; a line forming outside the movie theatre for the 19.30 showing. She saw Mavis exit the diner and look around. *Maybe she's still hoping Shadow will come*, Saffron thought, as she spotted a gap in the traffic and started to cross the street.

As if she sensed her presence, Mavis suddenly turned her head in Saffron's direction. For a second their eyes met, and Mavis looked at her uncertainly, as if she wasn't sure it was really her.

Saffron was about to wave and call out. But then she felt a hand grip her left arm above the elbow. There was a hard prod in the small of her back, which she recognised at once as the barrel of a gun, and a man's voice in her ear, giving calm, precise instructions.

'Walk towards the alley. Do not look around. Do not make a sound. Everything nice and easy.'

Saffron did as she was told. From his voice she knew it was not the man who'd beaten her to the phone, but the accent was similar: not German, but Eastern European. Suddenly the realisation hit her. *They knew I'd be here. They left the message for me to find!*

So be it. Saffron had wanted the enemy to show themselves, and now they had. She felt her adrenaline levels rising, the body's instinctive response to threat, preparing her to fight or flee. But she was not afraid. She had been trained to deal with attacks from behind, and that included a gun in the back. So now, as the man behind her prodded her towards the alley, away from all the passers-by, Saffron's eyes were darting from side to side, assessing her surroundings, calculating possible courses of action and likely outcomes.

They walked past the diner. Out of the corner of her eye Saffron caught a glimpse of Mavis, watching her go by, a puzzled look on her face, as if she couldn't understand what Saffron was doing there. It certainly wasn't the self-satisfied look of an agent whose clever trap had just been sprung.

Saffron wanted to go over that in her mind, but there was no time. They were in the alley, where the light was gloomier. Another man was coming towards them from the far end, blocking off Saffron's exit.

'Stop,' the man behind her said. 'Do not move.'

He lifted her shoulder bag away from her body and threw it against the wall of the diner, well out of reach.

He wasn't holding her arms now, so Saffron could put her hands up, in the universal gesture of surrender. 'Please,' she whimpered, wanting them to think she was beaten. 'Don't shoot.'

The man coming towards them came to a halt, maybe twenty feet away. He reached inside his jacket and pulled out a long-barrelled revolver.

'Don't move,' the first man told her.

The man behind Saffron switched the gun to his left hand and started patting her down with his right. There was nothing to find. He looked towards the man opposite them and said something in a foreign language that Saffron could not understand. Then she saw the man kneel down by her bag and open it.

Saffron closed her eyes for a second, picturing a sequence of precisely choreographed movements, just as she had been trained to do. And then, at the instant when she was about to move, she heard a familiar voice call out her name. The man opposite her shouted something. His words were not in English. But a warning sounded the same in any language.

Saffron felt the man behind her push her to one side. She saw the other man raise his long-barrelled gun from where he knelt. And as he fired, she heard herself scream, 'No!'

• • •

It was seven o'clock by the time Stackpole got back to the OSS headquarters on Navy Hill. The place was half-empty, and Donovan must have sent the secretarial staff home because their desks were cleared and their coats, hats and bags were gone. The boss would still be at work, though – Stackpole was sure of that – and he would want a first-hand report of Wermuth's condition.

Stackpole knocked on Donovan's door and received the summons to enter. He spent five minutes describing Wermuth's injuries, the surgical procedure he had conducted and the results as he had observed them before leaving Johnson City.

'Is he going to be any use to us?' Donovan asked.

'Not for a while. He'll be on his feet in a matter of weeks, but he'll need crutches for some time after that, and it could be six months before he can walk unaided. Don't count on getting him back before the New Year.'

'We'd better hope they delay the invasion to summer of '44,' Donovan said. 'What's the best we can hope for?'

'He'll be capable of intelligence gathering, liaising with resistance groups, maybe supervising their training. Don't expect anything physical, though. I doubt he'll ever be passed fit for combat.'

Donovan nodded. Stackpole took his leave and went to his own office, planning to call the Playfairs' place and see if Saffron was around. He'd picked up the handset and was about to dial the number when he saw the note on his desk, written in a female hand.

Saffron Courtney called at 16.23, asking for you. I told her you were expected back at 18.00. She said to meet her at McGinty's Irish Bar at 3124 M Street NW, at 18.45. And please don't be late. She was very insistent about that!

Stackpole checked his watch. It was already 19.10. 'Dammit!' he muttered. 'Should've come straight here, instead of seeing the boss.'

Stackpole thought for a moment about telling Donovan where he was going. But that would take time, and he was already almost half an hour late. Saffron had asked for his help, and he had left her by herself. There wasn't a second to waste.

He ran from his office, through the building and down the stairs to the ground floor. Bursting through the front door, he dashed down the tarmac driveway that led to 23rd Street.

Then he stopped and looked around. There wasn't a cab to be seen.

Stackpole turned left and began running again. A couple of blocks up the street, 23rd Street hit Washington Circle, where a bunch of streets and avenues converged. He was still a hundred yards away from the circle when he got lucky and flagged down a passing cab with its yellow light shining. Stackpole dived into the back and shouted, 'Get me to McGinty's Irish Bar at 3124 M Street, fast as you can.'

The driver grinned. 'That thirsty, huh?'

Stackpole handed him a ten-dollar bill.

'Just get me there!'

'You got it, buddy.'

The driver floored the accelerator and the taxi raced up the street. It was 19.13.

The early evening traffic was light and the cab cut through it, horn blaring, lights flashing. They overtook sedans, trucks and trolley cars, and sent unwary pedestrians crossing the street dashing for the sidewalk. Less than four minutes had elapsed before they were pulling up outside McGinty's.

Stackpole got out. He was about to walk into the bar when something caught his eye: a movement on the far side of the street; a familiar outline. He stopped. As the cab pulled away, Stackpole dashed into the road, oblivious to the traffic, shouting. 'Saffron! Saffron!'

• • •

The man facing Saffron fired three times in quick succession. The man with the gun to her back turned his head to see if the shots had hit their target. Saffron desperately wanted to do the same thing. But first she had to get free.

She spun to her left.

The man had been distracted by the shots, but now he turned with her, keeping his gun trained on her – but still a beat behind as she chopped the edge of her raised right hand onto his left wrist. His hand sprung open and the pistol dropped to the ground. It was a long-barrelled revolver, the same as the other man's.

Saffron kept turning until she and the man were face to face. She jerked her knee up towards his groin, but he was too fast, twisting to take the impact on his thigh. Frustrated, she slammed the heel of her hand into his chin, but without enough force. He grunted but didn't go down.

In desperation, Saffron dived for the gun, grabbed it with both hands and rolled forward, hearing the boom of the other man's gun as it fired again. Finishing up on one knee, facing the far end of the alley, she brought the revolver up and fired two quick shots. The man staggered back, then dropped to the ground. Saffron turned towards her first assailant. He was running down the alley, towards the street. She raised the gun again, but did not fire. There were people gathering at the end of the alley, trying to see what was happening. She didn't want to hit an innocent bystander.

Jumping to her feet, Saffron started running, chasing after the fleeing man, passing Stackpole lying motionless on the ground. He was on his back, with his arms spread out. As she reached the end of the alley, a pickup truck pulled up. The fleeing man opened the passenger door and dived in. As the truck roared away, Saffron noted the name on the side: AOK CONTRACTORS.

People began clustering around her, asking her what had happened, and whether she was all right. Then they saw she was carrying a gun and backed off. She called out, 'Please, someone – call the police! And an ambulance!'

Before anyone could ask any more questions, Saffron ran to Stackpole. He was still alive, his face contorted in pain, his torso slick with blood, more black than red in the gloom of the alley, sluggishly spreading with each feeble beat of his failing heart.

Saffron kneeled beside him. She put her assailant's revolver down and clasped Stackpole's right hand. He tried to smile, and her heart almost broke at the desperate effort he was making.

'Sorry I'm late,' he whispered.

'That's all right. I knew you'd come,' Saffron said, forcing back the tears, knowing she had to stay strong. 'Just hold on, stay with me, there's an ambulance on its way.'

'No point . . .' Saffron saw Stackpole summoning up the last of his energy. She could see the fierce concentration in his face. He looked at her with imploring eyes, needing her to understand what he was about to say, then uttered one word: 'Russians.'

Then he was gone.

Saffron was vaguely aware of more people spilling into the alley from the street. She felt a tap on her shoulder, and then a calm, authoritative male voice said, 'Excuse me, ma'am . . . I'm a doctor.'

'Too late for that,' she said.

The doctor ignored her, crouching down over Stackpole's body, searching for any faint sign of life.

Saffron picked up one of the revolvers and got to her feet. She saw her bag, lying by the wall where it had been thrown. She walked over to pick it up with her back to the doctor and crammed the gun into the bag. It was a .44 Magnum, which was a tight fit, but she didn't want it lying around with her prints on it, and the way the night was going, for all she knew it might come in handy. But these calculations were unconscious, all those months of training kicking in, short-circuiting the grief that threatened to overpower her.

As she walked back towards the street, the onlookers moved out of Saffron's way, seeing the distress etched upon her face. She barely heard the English voice calling, 'Saffron! Saffron!' until Mavis took her by the arm and said, 'Come with me.'

Mavis led Saffron to the end of the block and around the corner, away from M Street to a less crowded stretch of sidewalk. 'Are you all right?' she asked.

Saffron nodded. The shock of Stackpole's death was slowly clearing from her mind. She was regaining her faculties, her mind returning to her mission. But before she could say anything, Mavis said, 'I don't understand. If you were here, why didn't you come into the diner? I was waiting for you, like you asked.'

Saffron grabbed Mavis's arm.

'Hey, that hurts!' complained Mavis, but Saffron ignored her.

'What do you mean, "Like you asked"?' she demanded.

'I didn't ask you to be here – Shadow did.'

Mavis looked at her in bafflement. 'Who the hell is Shadow? *You* asked me to meet you at the diner.'

Saffron let go of her arm. She took a deep breath. 'I'm sorry I hurt you. But this is important . . . Who told you that I wanted to meet you?'

'Charlie – he called me up this afternoon. He said that Millicent James had asked him to tell me that you wanted to meet at the diner.'

Saffron had a sense of pieces falling into place, though the puzzle was still not quite complete enough to see the full picture. 'I haven't spoken to Millicent since the day I arrived here,' she said.

'So why did she think you wanted to meet me?'

'I don't know,' Saffron lied, as the truth became clear to her. Millicent was the spy. She had helped her handler lure Saffron to M Street by getting Mavis to act as the bait. *They wanted me neutralised, out of the way. But why now?*

'So, where's Charlie?' Saffron asked Mavis.

'He's at the embassy. All the senior staff are there this evening.'

'Why?'

'There's a do on. It's supposed to be totally hush-hush, but you know Charlie, he couldn't resist dropping hints about who was coming.'

'Who?' Saffron demanded.

Mavis smiled. 'Well, you won't believe this, but I reckon the ambassador's having Winston, President Roosevelt and the Duke of bloody Windsor round for dinner.'

'Oh, no . . .' Saffron could hardly believe that her worst fears – ones she hardly credited herself – were coming true. There was going to be an assassination attempt. She was sure of it. The opportunity to kill a president, a prime minister and an abdicated king was too good to pass up. And if there was an enemy agent on the inside, and the one person who might work out what was going on was removed from the equation . . .

Saffron did her best to keep the near-panic out of her voice. 'Do you know what time the guests are arriving?'

Mavis shook her head. 'But Charlie said that he had to be in the receiving line by ten to seven.'

'So, assume a seven o'clock arrival time, dinner at half past . . .' Saffron checked her watch. It was almost 19.35. They'd have sat down by now. That was the time to do the job: when all the targets were in one place, around a table. 'Did you drive here?' she asked.

'No,' said Mavis. 'I came on the trolley car. Charlie's the driver in the family.'

'Right, then, this is what we've got to do. You get to the nearest phone. Call Charlie at the embassy. Tell him that the ambassador and his guests are in serious danger. No . . . make that mortal danger. I think someone's trying to kill them.'

Mavis's eyes widened. 'Oh, God, there really is a spy, isn't there?'

'Yes . . . and there's an assassination plot. I can't prove it yet, but tell Charlie he's got to believe me – and then find a way to convince everyone else there, too.'

Even as Saffron said the words, she knew what an impossible task she was giving Charlie Playfair. 'And he's got to tell the guards on the gate to let me in. I'm going up to the embassy now. I just hope to God I won't be too late.'

'Is Charlie going to be all right?' Mavis asked, looking at Saffron with terrified eyes.

'I don't know . . . I really don't. Oh . . . and one more thing . . .'

'Yes?'

'Tell Charlie that if Millicent James is at the embassy, and I'll bet my bottom dollar she is, then grab her, lock her up, and for God's sake don't let her out of the building.'

'Millicent . . .' Mavis never finished the sentence. Saffron had spotted a taxi and was running into the road, arm aloft, to flag it down.

• • •

Lewandowski was sitting at the wheel of his truck, parked in one of the quiet residential streets of Georgetown, half a dozen blocks north of M Street, cursing his misfortune. Taking out the Courtney woman was supposed to be the easy part: lure her away from the embassy, force her into the alley-way, and problem solved. Two of his men would dispose of her; the rest would stand ready to extract Foxglove when her job was done. But then the American had arrived, charging into the alley. He was plainly a hopeless amateur, but he had been the random element that disrupted Lewandowski's careful calculations.

Courtney had escaped. And now she would know that her suspicions had been well placed. But would she realise the magnitude of what was about to happen? Lewandowski found that hard to believe, yet he had to proceed on the assumption that now she knew everything.

And then Lewandowski caught a lucky break: a message coming over the radio in his truck. He had kept three men in reserve: Novak and two others. They'd been sitting in a parked car about a block away from the diner. Now they came into play.

'She's getting into a taxi on 31st Street, heading north,' Novak said. 'What do you want us to do?'

'Follow her.'

'Got it!'

As his men got moving, Lewandowski kept talking. 'She'll be making for the embassy. Wait till you're north of Rock Creek. The road is clearer there, less traffic. That's where you stop her.'

'By any means necessary?'

'Whatever it takes. She must not get to the embassy.'

'You got it, boss.'

Lewandowski checked the time and smiled. *Even if she does reach the embassy, she's going to be too late.*

• • •

Millicent James almost felt sorry for Agent Bob. He was still on duty, standing like a loyal dog outside the morning room, while his invalid master dined inside.

What a stroke of luck that ludicrous argument about who should sit where had been! Bob had been right – the dining room was completely exposed. That would have made it harder for Millicent to hide the bomb Shadow had given her. But then the argument had happened, and she had had that sudden moment of inspiration and suggested an alternative that made it all so much easier.

Millicent had almost been caught out when Bob had suddenly decided to check on what she was doing. Ten seconds earlier, and he would have seen her pressing the lump of PENT – an explosive which, Lewandowski had assured her, was two-thirds more destructive than TNT – against the underside of the Georgian mahogany dining table, right by the single leg that supported it. There was a magnet stuck into the top of the explosive. On the top of the table, underneath the silver bowl containing the centrepiece that Millicent had been fussing over, was the steel disc that she had placed there, to which the magnet was attracted.

Now she was standing on the terrace, where it had been decided, since this was a pleasant spring evening, Lady Halifax would enjoy a light supper with the Duchess of Windsor.

The weather might have been balmy, but the atmosphere at the table was anything but. Neither woman had eaten more than a morsel of her food. Their conversation, meanwhile, had been icy, stilted, painfully commonplace, the politeness forced, the mutual dislike palpable.

To an upper-class Englishwoman like Dorothy Wood, Lady Halifax, the duchess would always be Wallis Simpson, the calculating, disreputable American divorcee who had seduced the Prince of Wales and then, once he became King Edward VIII, lured him into a marriage so unsuitable that it forced his abdication from the throne. And she had, as every member of London high society knew – or, at least, believed – been making love to the German ambassador, Ribbentrop, even as she played at being a royal consort. To the duchess, on the other hand, a woman like Lady Halifax was the living embodiment of everything she hated about the British upper class and their ironclad snobbery.

Millicent despised them both equally. It was as well that she had placed herself in the shadows, ostensibly so that her presence would not be intrusive, but more importantly, so that they could not see the smile on her face as she contemplated what was about to happen, by her calculation, in a little more than five minutes.

Suddenly the chilly peace of the terrace was disturbed by the sound of raised voices coming from inside the building. 'Millicent, go and see who's making that terrible racket,' Lady Halifax commanded.

'Yes, My Lady,' Millicent said. She walked through the double doors into the main corridor. The source of the noise was immediately apparent. Charlie Playfair was standing by the entrance to the morning room, having a furious argument with Agent Bob. Millicent made her way as stealthily as she could along the corridor. She was used to going unnoticed by her social superiors.

'I'm telling you, we have to get them all out of there!' Playfair insisted.

'And I'm telling you, they ain't budging,' Bob retorted.

'But they're not safe!'

'The hell they ain't!'

The door of the morning room opened and Lord Halifax poked his head out. 'What in hell's name is going on here!'

'This man wants to remove you and your guests from the morning room, Your Excellency,' Bob said.

'Is this true, Playfair?' Halifax asked.

'Yes, Your Excellency. I have reason to believe you're in great danger.'

'And what reason would that be?'

'I've received a message from Miss Courtney—'

'You mean, that little girl who works for Stephenson?'

'Yes, sir.'

Halifax snorted. 'Don't be so absurd. Go back to your office, Playfair. And we shall have words in the morning.'

Millicent considered her options. She should leave the embassy right now and make her escape. But her orders were to make sure that the device had exploded and confirm the casualties before she contacted Shadow. But Millicent had her own reasons for staying at the embassy. She wanted to hear the bomb go off, to see the horror on everyone's faces, to bask in the knowledge that she – Lady Halifax's despised, disregarded dogsbody – had fooled them all.

I'm going to kill you, Mr Churchill – yes, me, boring little Millicent, who all the snobby diplomats look down on and laugh at – and there's nothing that you, or Mr Roosevelt or any of his Secret Service agents can do to stop me.

But as much as Millicent wanted to be in the vicinity of the bomb when it exploded, she had no intention of being one of its victims. So instead of going back to the terrace, which was adjacent to the morning room and would certainly catch some of the blast, she went up the private circular staircase that led to the residence's bedrooms. She would find an empty room, as far from the morning room as possible, wait for the blast, and then re-emerge to survey the results.

She checked the time again. It was 19.46 by her watch. The bomb was fitted with a ninety-minute fuse. She had activated it at a little before 18.25. Less than ten minutes to go.

• • •

While Lewandowski had been talking to his men, and Millicent was waiting on her mistress, Saffron had been sitting in a taxi, urging the driver to throw caution to the wind and put his foot down. Why now, of all times, did she have a cabbie who was calm, patient and polite? He seemed willing to let other drivers cut in ahead of him, never raced to get through the lights before they turned red, was always slow to accelerate when they turned green.

Saffron was close to despair. Forget an assassination – Churchill and the others would have died of old age by the time the taxi got there. 'For God's sake, drive faster!' she screamed.

The driver was having none of it. 'Don't you speak to me like that, lady, or I'll kick you out of my cab.'

'Right then,' Saffron replied. She reached into her handbag, extracted the .44 Magnum revolver and held it to the back of the driver's head. 'Drive as fast as this useless jalopy will go, or I'll blow your brains out all over the windscreen, dump your body on the street and drive the bloody thing myself.'

'Okay! Okay! Just put the gun down!'

Now the taxi started moving. 'Good. Don't slow down. Not for anything.'

Saffron slumped back into the passenger seat, with the Magnum in her right hand, tapping the barrel against the palm of her left while she thought her way through the idea that Millicent James was a spy. It seemed absurd, but what better cover could there be than that of an apparently insignificant woman, who held a job whose title – personal assistant – made it respectable for a middle-class woman, yet which was, in essence, no different from being a servant?

Saffron remembered standing outside the ambassador's office and Millicent saying, 'I'm in and out all the time.' Of course she was, and since everyone knew that no one would be surprised to see her enter that private sanctum – even if Lord Halifax himself were not present. Millicent only had to say that her ladyship had asked her to fetch something and no one would think anything of it . . . because no one thinks anything of her.

But why had Millicent done it? Why had she even considered betraying her country to begin with? Intellectuals like Charlie and Mavis Playfair might be driven by ideology, but Millicent was nothing like them. She was motivated by her emotions more than her intellect. So, although the assassination would have massive political consequences, Saffron was willing to bet that they would be of no consequence to Millicent. She was doing this for reasons that were deeply personal.

Somehow Millicent had found the enemy agents who could help her. Had she sought them out, or had they approached her? To an intelligence agency, the private secretaries of powerful men and women were always desirable assets. And a honeytrap wasn't always just a beautiful young woman seducing gullible men. A man could easily win over a lonely woman by making her feel desired, loved, special. Millicent must have dreaded the thought of living the rest of her life alone. Unloved, emotionally barren, happiness a fading prospect, she would have presented an easy target for a man who was trained to exploit her vulnerabilities.

But who had that man been working for? Donovan had been insistent that the Nazis did not have a significant secret intelligence presence in the United States.

And then it finally hit Saffron.

Russians.

The last word Clayton Stackpole had uttered before he died. He'd said that the next war would be with Russia. And it looked as if it had already begun.

Saffron put her head in her hands and moaned as she thought of Clay, his face creasing in agony, his life force ebbing away, all the joy and passion she had known with him turning into mournful silence.

The taxi driver leaned over. 'You all right, lady?'

'Fine,' Saffron said, fighting to contain her grief.

Dusk was falling over the city as they left the built-up heart of Washington and crossed into the semi-rural, suburban stretch of Massachusetts Avenue on which the British embassy stood. The road was made even darker by the tall trees on either side, and most of the cars they passed had their lights switched on.

This was the way that Millicent had driven Saffron, the day she'd arrived in Washington. And then it struck her: something that Millicent had said when they were sitting side by side in her car. Something Saffron had completely misinterpreted. And then, finally, she understood it all, and in the same instant, realised that understanding didn't make a bit of difference.

They're all going to die!

The cabbie was driving at full pelt now, quickly overtaking cars whose drivers were taking it easy, relaxing behind the wheel as they made their way home. But someone else was also driving fast, and quickly catching up with them.

Saffron turned to look out of the rear window and her eyes were instantly dazzled by a pair of oncoming headlights.

'Step on it!' she shouted to the driver.

He tensed his shoulders but it was too late. Suddenly his body was jolted forward onto the steering wheel as the car rammed into the back of the cab.

That was enough to really make the cabbie put his foot down. He sped up the avenue, jinking past a slow delivery van. The car behind followed.

The avenue was two lanes wide in both directions. The taxi was in the right-hand lane, doing more than fifty miles an hour. The pursuing car came up the inside lane, going even faster. As it pulled almost level with the taxi, Saffron could make out flared front wheel arches flowing down past the long snout of the bonnet towards the passenger compartment. It looked like something from a gangster film, with running boards for Hollywood hoodlums to stand on, firing their Tommy guns.

But this was no movie.

And the men in the car weren't actors.

The Russian driver nosed his car in towards their yellow cab to force them off the road. Saffron saw a passenger window at the back of the car roll down and a gun barrel emerge. She ducked down just as it was fired, the bullet smashing the rear window of the cab.

'Shit, lady, what in Christ is going on?' the cabbie shouted.

Saffron lifted her gun to her shoulder. She had already fired two bullets, so there were four rounds left.

The taxi was rocketing along at almost seventy, its engine howling. A small gap opened up between the two cars as the cabbie pushed the taxi's engine to the limit. Very soon, that gap would close. Saffron had to act now.

Two more shots from the car behind smashed into the taxi's bodywork. Saffron steeled herself, took a deep breath, then turned, kneeling on the back seat to fire three quick shots through the shattered rear window, into the driver's side of the oncoming car's windscreen.

For a second or two, nothing happened. A sickening feeling gripped Saffron's stomach. She had used up all but one of the Magnum's rounds. She still had her little Beretta, but at this distance its bullets would have little impact.

Then suddenly, the long bonnet slewed violently and the lights swung past as the car cut across the road behind the cab. It hurtled into a telegraph pole that crashed down like a sawn tree, crushing the passenger compartment. Saffron saw a lick of flame around the bonnet. Any second now the car would be burning, and if the impact hadn't killed the men inside, the fire certainly would.

The taxi driver slowed, then braked sharply and pulled to the side of the road. He slumped over the wheel. 'I can't go no further,' he said. He was trembling all over.

Saffron saw the embassy up ahead. She got out her purse, extracted a handful of twenty-dollar bills and handed them over. 'That should cover the damage. With a tip for being a careful driver,' she added.

She darted across the road and ran towards the main gates of the embassy, her bag flapping against her body. When she reached the guard box, a man stepped out onto the pavement in front of her. It was Charlie Playfair.

'It's no good,' he said. 'They won't believe me.'

'Take this,' Saffron said, throwing her bag towards him. She didn't want it slowing her down. She sprinted towards the entrance to the residence with Playfair trailing behind her. 'They're in the morning room!' he shouted and stopped, bent over, his hands on his knees, the bag dangling down between them.

It was 19.51.

Saffron retraced the steps she had taken on her first visit to the residence, running through the arch beneath the ambassador's study, up the steps to the entrance, through the lobby and up the stairs. It was only when she turned right, along the landing leading to the main corridor, that she realised she didn't know where the morning room was. She saw the ramrod-straight figure of a man in a plain black suit standing outside a door up ahead to the left. He must be a guard. And inside that door would be the people he was guarding.

Saffron slowed to a brisk walk, gathering her breath as she approached the man. 'Is this the morning room?' she asked.

'Yes, ma'am,' he answered, in an American accent, 'but you'd better move right—'

Before the guard could finish his sentence, Saffron looked to her left, pointed down the corridor and let out a high-pitched squeal of alarm. As the guard turned to see what had provoked her reaction, she pushed him with all her strength and sent him staggering away from the door.

Saffron opened it and walked in. She considered screaming 'Get out!' but decided that her best option was to appear as calm and competent as possible. Four pairs of male eyes turned towards her, while she scanned the room. *Where would I put the bomb?* The answer was obvious: *In the bullseye.*

'Why, Miss Courtney, what an unexpected pleasure,' said Churchill. 'Mr President, gentlemen, may I—'

'I'm sorry, sir,' said Saffron, dropping to her knees between the prime minister's chair and the duke's. 'Do excuse me.'

'I say. . .' drawled the duke, with an amused expression on his face.

She crawled under the table, all too aware of the absurd impression she was creating. And maybe the joke was on her. There was no bomb to be seen.

It was 19.53.

'Where is she?' growled an American voice from the door – the guard.

Lord Halifax shouted, 'Get out of there, woman!'

Saffron did not respond. She knew she was right. She had to be right.

She reached out and felt around the far side of the central column that supported the table . . . and touched a small, oblong package, wrapped in paper. She kept moving until she could see the bomb. Then she wrapped her hands around it and pulled. It did not budge.

'There's a bomb under the table,' Saffron replied, trying to keep her voice steady. 'It's at least two pounds of plastic explosive with a basic timer fuse stuck in it. Can't tell if it's booby-trapped. It's attached to the underside of the table by a magnet. There must be something metal on top, holding it in place.'

Now the message got through. Chairs were already scraping back as the voice said, 'Mr President, gentlemen, I must ask you to clear the room as soon as possible . . . Ma'am, you'd better let me handle this.'

'Just find the damn metal. It's probably under the flowers in the middle of the table.'

Saffron heard something heavy being moved and a moment later the bomb dropped into her hands. She crawled back out, got to her feet, held out the bomb, and said, 'See?'

'Holy shit!' gasped the guard. 'Get rid of the damned thing!'

Saffron was already running out of the door and down the corridor, with the American at her heels. 'Open the doors!' she shouted as they passed the startled figures of Lady Halifax and the Duchess of Windsor coming in from the terrace to see what all the fuss was about.

The guard overtook Saffron and aimed himself at the French doors at the end of the corridor. He barged into them with his shoulder and they burst open. Saffron ran on, heading into the garden along the flagstone path and leaping up the three sets of steps. She passed under the pergola that opened onto the ambassador's swimming pool and hurled the bomb with all her strength.

The bomb arced through the air, splashed into the swimming pool, disappeared for a moment, then exploded in a wild, booming geyser of water that rained down on Saffron and the guard. They both hit the ground and covered their heads as the earth shook and the air was torn by shock waves.

After a few seconds, the guard picked himself up and shook his head. 'Damn, that was close!' He held out his hand to help Saffron to her feet. 'People round here call me Bob. Helluva thing you just did.'

Saffron smiled. 'Hi, Bob, I'm Saffron. I'm sorry I shoved you.'

He shrugged. 'Good thing you did.'

They started walking back towards the residence, water dripping from them onto the grass. 'That was pretty impressive, the way you smashed through those doors.'

'Well, I was a linebacker in college.'

'What's a linebacker?'

'It's a football position, on the defence. Your job is to stop the guy on the other side.'

'Well, that explains it . . . You just never learned to stop a girl.'

Bob laughed. 'I guess not.'

They walked into the building through the broken doors, to be met by the Halifaxes and their guests. Churchill had a cigar in one hand and a tumbler of whisky in the other. 'As I was saying before we were so rudely . . . ah, interrupted . . . Mr President, Your Graces, my Lords, ladies and gentlemen . . . may I introduce Miss Saffron Courtney?'

Half an hour later, Saffron was standing in Charlie Playfair's office, flicking through the Washington phone directory, looking for the address of AOK Contractors.

Millicent had been found where she had been hiding upstairs, and was awaiting interrogation by the senior SIS man at the embassy and a team of FBI agents who were on their way. Dinner had been resumed. Everyone in the embassy had been instructed in the clearest possible terms that none of what had happened would ever be discussed at any time, anywhere, with anyone.

Saffron had been the heroine of the hour. She should have been basking in their adulation and quaffing champagne. Instead, she felt only emptiness. While she was occupied with getting to the embassy and thwarting the assassination plot, the loss of Stackpole had been set to one side. But now there was nothing to hold back the crashing waves of grief that pounded against her heart.

She tried to tell herself not to be sentimental. It was a flame that had briefly burst into life and then had been just as quickly extinguished. If he were still alive, how much more time could they have had together? Her work in Washington was as good as done. There would have been a few more meetings with American top brass to whip up support for SOE. But she had completed her task.

So, they could never have had more than a short, blissfully intense affair before they both returned to their everyday lives on opposite sides of the Atlantic. But she knew in her heart none of that mattered. What mattered was the terrible, absolute, irreversible loss of a man she had loved, however briefly. And the knowledge that he had died trying to rescue her. It was her fault that he was dead.

'Are you okay?' Playfair asked.

'Sorry,' she said. 'Miles away.'

'I was going to say that I'll be here for an hour or so. I've been given the task of writing this evening's events up for the official dispatch to the Foreign Office. But if you don't mind waiting, I can give you a lift back to our place . . . Now you know that it's not a nest of spies!'

'Thanks,' Saffron replied, 'but I need to tidy up some loose ends.'

As Playfair was talking, she had found AOK's address, and it had tripped a switch in her mind. Her mood had changed. She didn't want to wallow in her pain.

'Ah . . .' Playfair looked at her for a moment, wondering whether she would tell him what those loose ends were, but concluded that it was probably better for him not to know. 'Well, we'll see you in the morning, then.'

Saffron turned to go, and then stopped and looked back at Playfair.

'Yes . . .?' he said, when she hadn't spoken for a couple of seconds.

'I won't be back in the morning. Something important I have to do. Could you have my luggage sent on to the St. Regis Hotel in New York, please?'

'Of course.'

'Please send Mavis my love and tell her how grateful I am to her, and you, too, Charlie, for putting me up.'

'My pleasure. I'm only sorry we didn't have more time to talk. I like to be challenged. Keeps me on my toes.'

'I'll remember that if we ever meet again. And one other thing . . . Tell whoever's going to question Millicent James that she was recruited by the Russians. The Third Reich had nothing to do with it.'

As Saffron turned to leave, Playfair called out, 'Wait! How do you know?'

'That's a long story. But if she goes on about how much she hates the Nazis, believe me, she's telling the truth.'

'Oh, Christ!' Playfair muttered. 'That's going to complicate matters.'

'Yes, I suppose it is.'

'But if she was in bed with our Red friends, why she would want to kill the two men who were leading the fight against fascism?'

'I think she was only interested in one of them – Churchill.'

'Because . . .?'

'The love of Millicent's life was an RAF pilot. They were engaged to be married. She is obsessed by the idea that if we had sued for peace after Dunkirk, as Halifax wanted, her fiancé would have lived and she would now be a happily married woman.'

'But Churchill kept us in the war.'

'Exactly. So, you know . . . a life for a life.'

Playfair gave a rueful shake of the head. 'She must have felt so clever, so important, fooling everyone all this time.'

'You fool people, too, Charlie.'

He gave one of his charming, impish smiles. 'Shhh . . . don't tell a soul.'

Saffron left the office and walked through the embassy, back out onto Massachusetts Avenue. There were two police cars parked by the wreckage of the Russians' car, but otherwise the street was quiet as she turned right and started walking downhill towards the centre of Washington. The police paid her no attention. She was just a woman taking a walk on a beautiful evening.

Saffron was clear about what she was going to do next. She wasn't motivated by her sense of duty; her mission was over. What she had to do next was personal. She wanted revenge. And this wouldn't be over for her until she'd taken it.

A lone cab went by with its yellow light shining. Saffron flagged it down and told the driver where to take her. 'You sure, lady?' the man asked. 'This time of night? Alone?'

'Just drive, please,' she said.

As they proceeded down the avenue, Saffron thought about the consequences of what she was about to do. She couldn't leave a trail. If the police came after her she would get no protection. The British embassy, Donovan, Stephenson, Gubbins . . . none of them could be seen to give her public support. Maybe they would hush it up. But more likely they'd leave her out in the cold.

Saffron turned to the driver. 'It sounds like you know the place we're going.'

'Sure. It's an old shed where they used to service trolley cars. It was pretty much abandoned for a while, but I heard some guy bought it out – construction or something.'

'How long will it take to get there?'

'This time of night? Five minutes.'

'All right, can we stop at the next public telephone? I need to make a call.'

'Whatever you say, lady.'

The cabbie pulled over a few hundred yards up the road. Saffron made her call. As she got back in, she looked at her watch. *Ten minutes . . . that should be enough.*

• • •

At the back of the tram shed stood a prefabricated hut, a couple of rooms with large windows that looked out over the shop floor, so that the management could keep an eye on the workers and make sure no one was slacking or stealing.

Lewandowski used one of the rooms as an office for himself and Magda, who came in three mornings a week to handle any correspondence, keep track of supplies and do the bookkeeping. He was there now, with a packet of cigarettes, a half-empty bottle of vodka, a loaded Remington .44 Magnum revolver and a small cardboard carton of ammunition on the desk in front of him.

On one side of the desk was a telephone. Foxglove had orders to call and deliver a single word – 'Glory' – if her plan had succeeded. The phone had been silent all night. There was a radio on the desk, too – the regular domestic kind, tuned to a local station. Lewandowski had listened to it for a couple of hours, hoping that the programmes would be interrupted by a sudden bulletin, read by a stunned announcer, barely able to get the words out, saying that the president was dead.

He was sure now that there would never be any such bulletin. The plan had failed.

Lewandowski had sent his one remaining man home. 'Pack your bags, take your family and leave the city. Drive as far as you can. Keep your head down and hope that nobody finds you.'

He had been tempted to do the same, but knew that any attempt at flight was pointless. He was already doomed. The only question was, how many other people would have to die, too?

At this very moment, in the Soviet embassy on 16th Street, the senior officer of the People's Commissariat for State Security would be debating with Ambassador Gromyko how best to deliver the news to Moscow. They could eliminate Foxglove and Lewandowski immediately and demonstrate their eagerness to clean up the mess, but that would mean they had acted without orders. In the paranoid atmosphere of the Kremlin, the question would be asked: why had they killed the failed assassins? Were they simply covering up another plot?

Or they could ask Moscow for permission to carry out the clean-up killings, which might provoke fury for not having dealt with the matter immediately themselves. In circumstances like this, when something had gone wrong, and bad news had been delivered to Stalin, there was no such thing as a right answer.

Lewandowski was a dead man. The only question was the precise time and place of his death. *But that is true for everyone, from the moment we are born, so why should I worry now? Nothing has changed except the timing.*

He longed to hold his children one last time. He even wished that he could bid Magda a proper farewell. But that would only bring danger to them, too. Magda had been kept insulated from the assassination plan for her own protection. She knew nothing. As long as that remained the case, no one had any need to hurt her.

Ha! Who am I kidding? Lewandowski reached for the vodka. *They will kill Magda, and the children. Everyone will be under suspicion. No one will be spared.*

Lewandowski thought about his parents. They had been true believers in the Communist cause who had travelled to Leningrad before the first war, believing that Russia would be the birthplace of global socialism. They had been proved right. Lewandowski's father had known Lenin and Trotsky. He had followed one, rejected the other, and risen in the party. He had been proud of his son's service to the Motherland. *What would he think of me now?*

Lewandowski was lifting the vodka bottle to his mouth when he heard a car engine. He put the alcohol down. The tram shed was in an industrial area, surrounded by small factories and workshops. There was virtually no traffic at night. The sound of the engine changed. It was idling. Lewandowski heard a car door slamming.

He picked up his revolver. He had not expected this moment for another two or three hours. Gromyko must have ordered prompt action: one shred of good news for Moscow. *So be it, then.* Lewandowski steeled himself. He would go down fighting. After all, even dead men had their pride.

• • •

Saffron paid the driver and got out of the cab. She could see now why the cabbie had been reluctant to drop a woman passenger off here alone. It was a dark, foreboding industrial wasteland – whose factory sheds, warehouses and chimneys rose from empty streets, barely lit by a smattering of street lamps and the occasional glow of spotlights over company signs.

She checked her watch. The driver had been as good as his word: a shade under five minutes. So now she had five more to work with, and that was enough. 'The gunfight at the OK Corral lasted thirty seconds,' her SOE combat-shooting instructor had once said, with expletives before the words 'gunfire', 'corral' and 'seconds'. He'd then added, 'And the moral of that story is, either the other bastard's dead in double quick time. Or you bleedin' well are.'

It had better be him, then . . .

On the far side of the road Saffron saw a high chain-link fence, topped with barbed wire. A painted sign attached to the fence read AOK CONTRACTORS KEEP OUT, but the gate beside it was open. Someone was expecting company.

Saffron walked through the gate onto a tarmac forecourt where three sets of disused tram tracks led into an unlit building that was perhaps a hundred feet wide and at least forty high. It was open to the elements at the front, like an aircraft hangar. Its outer walls were brick, but the space between them was covered by three glass vaults, each rising over a set of tracks, supported by two lines of slender cast-iron pillars, linked by iron arches that ran down the building from front to back, like the pillars of stone along the nave of a Gothic cathedral, disappearing into the darkness.

The truck that Saffron had last seen escaping down M Street was parked a few yards into the building. She could dimly make out piles of timber, cement bags and other building supplies. Between them, the floor was bare, save for white marks roughly painted in a pattern of lines and squares.

So, this was where her hunt for the embassy spy would end. Saffron opened her bag, took out her Beretta and the spare magazine, then put the bag on the ground. She stuck her spare magazine in the back of her trouser waistband. With her gun in her hand, and the safety catch off, she started walking.

Saffron could now see a low structure, built within the bigger one. There was a dim glow in one of its windows, cast by a single light suspended from the ceiling. She saw the outline of a man moving beneath the light.

Her quarry was there. And he was waiting for her.

Suddenly the light in the office went out. A couple of seconds later, Saffron heard breaking glass, and almost immediately the lights inside the main expanse of the tram shed burst into glaring life.

Saffron had started running the moment she heard the glass smash. She knew what it meant. By the time the lights came on, she was dashing towards the truck.

An explosive boom echoed off the iron and glass as the first shot was fired, followed by the high-pitched metallic screech of a bullet ricocheting off a pillar a couple of feet ahead of her. Saffron dropped to a crouch, barely able to shelter her body behind the metal column. She was still only halfway to the truck.

At this range, the Beretta was useless. She somehow had to get closer to him.

A mad dash across ten yards of open ground would be suicide.

But there was another way. *I could just drive the bloody truck.*

Saffron moved a fraction to get another glimpse of the broken, unlit window. A bullet seared the air within inches of her head, followed an instant later by the boom of the high-calibre pistol.

She took a deep breath and leaned the other way, extending her arms outside the pillar and firing three quick shots in the direction of the window. She wouldn't do any damage, but just the sound of gunfire at close range was enough to keep a man's head down.

The echo of the final shot had barely died away before she had sprung to her feet and was running in a low crouch, three quick paces, then a jink to one side, then to the other, enough to break her rhythm and force the shooter to adjust his aim.

The gun boomed again. Saffron took one more step and hurled herself full length, diving for the shelter of the truck as another bullet smashed into the bodywork, just above her.

The truck was parked at a slight diagonal. She could get around the side of the vehicle and into the cabin without exposing herself to fire. The moment she sat down in the driver's seat, she'd be a sitting duck, but that was a problem for later. First, she had to start the engine.

Saffron knew how to hot-wire a car, but that required tools and time, and she had neither. As she made her way from the back of the truck to the driver's door, she reasoned that this was a working vehicle that would be driven by more than one person. It was parked in a secure compound, so the keys might be kept in the truck.

She peeked around the front of the pickup to make sure the Russian hadn't ventured out from his refuge. She couldn't see him, but she fired two more shots at the window anyway. She opened the driver's door, crawled onto the seat and was suddenly showered with glass as the windscreen exploded. Five shots.

How many has he got left? If he's using a Remington, like the others, it's only one. But it could be a different gun, with a bigger magazine. No . . . why would he have a different gun? All right, it's one round – just one. Then he'll have to reload.

Saffron reached across the cabin and rummaged through the glove box for the keys: nothing. She ran her hand across the top of the dashboard and only encountered chunks of laminated safety glass. Then she glanced up at the sunshade folded against the cabin roof. She reached up and yanked the shade down.

The sixth shot was a bullseye. It punched a hole through the dead centre of the shade as Saffron snatched her hand away, and the keys clattered into the footwell. She grabbed them and stuck them in the ignition. Now for the riskiest part of her plan. She slid into the driver's seat, her feet on the pedals and her body down as low as it would go while still being able to drive.

Saffron turned the key.

The engine fired.

She disengaged the handbrake, slammed the car into gear and floored the accelerator. Her mind flashed back to the *Queen Mary*, just as the torpedoes were racing towards it. *Momentum is mass times velocity . . . and this is a heavy truck.*

As it began to move, Saffron turned the wheel to the right, then straightened back up. She risked a glance to make sure she was going in the right direction and changed up into second as the truck picked up speed.

Still in the driver's seat, Saffron opened the door beside her . . . watched the hand on the speedometer inching around the clock . . . heard the sound of the gun firing . . . then slammed the truck into neutral and threw herself out of the cab.

Lewandowski had been trained to fight, shoot and drive when drunk. All Russian agents were. But that was a long time ago, and now he found he was badly out of practice. The vodka had slowed his reactions. He had wasted too many seconds wondering what a woman was doing here, rather than the men from the embassy, and that had prevented him from taking the initiative. His aim had been affected. He had only missed by fractions, but those fractions were the difference between him killing the woman, and her killing him. He'd been clumsy. When he opened the carton to get another six rounds to reload his .44 Magnum, his fingers had struggled to loosen the tightly packed ammunition and load the chamber.

The last shots he fired as the truck barrelled towards him were too late to stop it. As it smashed into the office in an explosion of glass and wood, he was too slow to get out of the way. He was in mid-air, diving to his left as the nose of the truck hit him below the waist, shattering both his thigh bones and pulverising his legs. The impact drove him against the wall and crushed his shoulder and right arm. Lewandowski was still alive when he hit the floor. But death was close . . . he could feel its dark chill seeping into him.

Saffron picked herself up from the floor, wincing at the stabbing pains in her elbows and knees. She would be a mass of bruises in the morning, but there were no broken bones or sprained joints. Like all SOE agents, she had been taught how to parachute jump, and leaping from a moving truck required similar skills on landing.

The front of the office had been obliterated and the gun had fallen silent. Saffron hesitated, wondering whether the truck might explode, but there were no flames or smoke, so she headed into the wreckage.

When she found the man, he was lying in a widening pool of blood against the far wall, to one side of the truck. He still had his gun in his right hand, but the arm above it was badly fractured.

'Hello, Shadow,' Saffron said.

He managed a faint ghost of a smile. His voice was a croaky whisper, forced from a face grey-white with pain. 'You have Foxglove?'

'Yes.'

'And the bomb?'

'It went off . . .' Saffron saw what she thought was a flicker of hope in his eyes, and added, 'In the ambassador's swimming pool.'

'Ah . . .'

'The gate was open. You were waiting for someone.'

'My own people.'

'No loose ends.'

'No . . .' He looked at her and spoke so quietly she could barely hear him, until she realised he was pleading. 'Kill me. I'm dead anyway. But the pain . . .'

'Good, I'm glad it hurts. You killed my friend.'

'Please . . .'

Saffron thought a man like this would not break under interrogation. But maybe now, when he had nothing to lose, he might answer one question. 'Tell me this . . . You're Russian?'

He managed to nod.

'So . . . why?'

Another flicker of the corners of his mouth. 'Because we are at war.'

'Then my friend was right.' She raised the Beretta and put two rounds into his chest.

Saffron reached down and took the wallet out of the inside pocket of the man's jacket. There was a driving licence in the name of Jozef Lewandowski, complete with his home address, along with a few small denomination banknotes and two photographs: a pretty, smiling blonde woman, and two golden-haired children.

Lewandowski had obviously been living undercover for a while. Maybe he'd married an innocent American girl who had no idea of his true identity and purpose. But more likely, his wife was also an agent, like him. They'd known what they were doing. They'd known the risks, and yet they'd brought these children into their world.

Saffron remembered how angry she had been with Charlie and Mavis when she thought that they had betrayed Arthur and Loretta, as well as their country. As she put the wallet back in Lewandowski's pocket, she thought, *No, it was his fault. And he killed Clay. There's no need to feel guilty. I won't be having nightmares about this.*

• • •

Saffron had cut it fine. Barely three minutes after Lewandowski had died, she heard the cars driving through the gates and across the forecourt to the shed. She'd taken cover behind a pile of timber, in case the Russians turned up earlier than expected.

Two vehicles came to a halt under the glass roof: a drab grey sedan and a much smarter, bigger black limousine with white-wall tyres. The doors opened and half a dozen men appeared. Five of them were armed, two with handguns, three with Thompson sub-machine guns. The armed men were dressed casually, their hair slicked back.

The sixth man, however, was different. He was tall, slim, dressed in an immaculate midnight-blue suit, with a black hat, and he appeared to be at ease in his surroundings.

'You reckon the damn broad's even here, boss?' one of the hoodlums asked.

'Yeah,' another one chimed in, 'I don't see her nowhere.'

These men were not Russian agents.

'The damn broad is right here,' Saffron said, stepping out from her cover. 'She just wanted to make sure you were the men she was expecting.'

The man in the blue suit looked at her. 'Are you expecting anyone else?'

'Russian agents, maybe, coming to kill a man who failed them.'

'I got the impression from New York that he was already dead.'

'He is now. Not when I placed the call. Your men will find him over there . . .' She pointed towards the wrecked office. 'Right beside the truck.'

The boss turned to his men. 'You heard what she said – get on with it.'

The hoodlums returned to the cars and started unloading their gear. Saffron saw a rolled-up tarpaulin and a couple of petrol cans. Their boss turned back to her and smiled, revealing perfect white teeth. 'So, you called in the clean-up crew in advance, before you'd done it?'

'I wanted to save time.'

'I like your style . . . Miss Courtney, isn't it?'

'Yes, Saffron Courtney. And I'm pleased to meet you, Mr . . .'

'Meyer . . . my name is Henzel Meyer. I'm an attorney. My clients have a lot of friends in Congress. It's my job to maintain good relations with them.'

'And Frank Costello is one of your clients?'

He didn't answer.

'I understand,' Saffron said. 'So . . . let's get down to business. There is only one body to deal with. But a lot of shots were fired. I wouldn't want the police to find any of my rounds. I was, ah . . . working freelance, as you might say. No official authority.'

'These men are good at their jobs. And they are . . . discreet.' Meyer looked towards the truck, then back at Saffron. 'He was over there, and you drove the truck straight at him?'

'Yes. It was the only way.'

'Impressive.' Meyer glanced towards his men, busy amid the wreckage. 'We can leave them to get on with their work. Can I give you a ride, Miss Courtney?'

'Thank you.' It was her turn to smile. 'Would you be going anywhere near the St. Regis Hotel in New York, by any chance?'

Meyer laughed. 'Ay-yay-yay! Such *chutzpah*!' He paused. 'Sure, why not? My driver is in the car. He can get us there, and you and I will talk. I think maybe I'll learn some things. And who knows? Maybe you will too . . .'

• • •

'I gather you got a ride up from DC from one of our Italian friends,' said Stephenson, shortly after nine the next morning.

'Strictly speaking, I got a lift from a charming Jewish gentleman,' Saffron said. 'But, yes, he has Italian friends. How did you know?'

Saffron lifted a delicate bone-china cup to her lips and sipped freshly brewed coffee. They were breakfasting at the St. Regis. She had arrived at two in the morning, having called from a gas station north of Philadelphia to say that she was on her way. The night manager had been entirely unruffled and admirably efficient. Her original suite had another occupant, but he promised her a large room overlooking Fifth Avenue at a significantly reduced rate. Saffron had grabbed a few hours' sleep before being woken by a call from the receptionist to say that Stephenson was downstairs. Ten minutes later she'd joined him, having showered, but still wearing the previous day's grimy clothes.

All around her, wealthy New Yorkers and visitors to the city were eating and chatting, and the only hint that there might be a war on was the presence of a few scattered men in the immaculately pressed uniforms of senior officers.

'Frank Costello was good enough to call me this morning to say that you were in town.' Stephenson smiled. 'We do a fair amount of business.'

'How so?'

'The Mafia controls the unions, and the unions control the docks. Men like Mr Costello ensure that the dockers don't come out on strike, thereby ensuring that the convoys that keep Britain alive can run without interruption. It is a contribution to the war effort. And, of course, the Italian–American community is keen to do all it can to help free Italy from the Nazis.'

'Very bad for business, I should imagine, the Nazis.'

'Quite so . . .' Stephenson paused. 'You realise that you are now in Costello's debt?'

'Yes . . . but I needed the kind of help that only he could give me. And to tell the truth, I'm curious to find out what he asks me in return.' Saffron reached for an almond croissant and added, 'Why didn't you tell me about the dinner at the embassy?'

'Because no one told me.'

'I thought you were in charge of all British security in the Americas.'

'I am – and I should have been informed from the moment the idea was first mooted.'

'So why weren't you?'

'Why do you think?'

It wasn't a rhetorical question. He was testing her powers of analysis. Saffron pondered for a moment as she savoured her pastry, then smiled and said, 'Everyone at the embassy knew you'd want to cancel the dinner because of the spy who didn't exist. But the dinner was too important politically and diplomatically, so they kept you out of the loop.'

'Exactly . . . but they were right about one thing. There wasn't a Nazi spy.' Stephenson grimaced and shook his head. 'I shouldn't have been so fixated on the goddamn Germans.'

'Well, that's understandable,' said Saffron. 'We all were. They're the enemy.'

'Yes, but not the only enemy.' Stephenson sighed. 'British Intelligence has been worried about the Communist threat since 1917, but Hitler came along and we took our eyes off the ball. Sure, the Americans have started talking about the "Red Menace", as they call it. But everyone thought it would be a post-war issue, you know, once Adolf was out of the way. We had no idea it would become this real, this fast.'

'So . . . what's going to happen now . . . with the Russians?' Saffron asked.

'Nothing – not in public. Privately, the ambassador will be summoned to the White House and be informed, in very strong language, that both Britain and the United States know that Soviet agents attempted to assassinate the leaders of their two countries.'

'Presumably, he'll simply deny everything?'

'Of course . . . as he would have done if they'd succeeded. We'll pretend to accept that denial, and that, along with the fact that the president and prime minister are still alive, will be all that keeps the Allies together.'

'What I don't understand, though, is why Stalin would be willing to make enemies of us now. Isn't he desperate for us to open a second front in Europe to ease the pressure on Russia?'

'Yes, he is . . . or was. But ever since Stalingrad, the tide in the East has changed dramatically. Hitler will make one last push this summer. But if the Red Army can repel it, which we have good reason to believe they will, they can break the back of the Wehrmacht and begin the march on Berlin. Now . . .'

Stephenson took a sip of coffee before continuing. 'The assumption on all sides has always been that we will, at some point, invade France and then drive into Germany from the west, as the Russians do from the east. But suppose Stalin is thinking that he can do the whole job by himself . . . Then why stop at Berlin? Why not roll up the entire Nazi empire, all the way to the Channel?'

'Would he really do that?'

'Why not? Like the song says, "Wider still and wider, shall thy bounds be set." If that was good enough for the British Empire, why not a Soviet empire?'

'I suppose so . . .' Saffron conceded. 'And if Roosevelt and Churchill were both gone, that would rob us of our leaders, and God knows what might happen then.'

'Well, disunity in the British and American political classes, for a start, as all the major players and their followers fought like cats in a sack to fill the vacancies in the White House and Number 10.'

'Wouldn't the American vice president take over automatically?' asked Saffron.

'Name the vice president,' came the blunt reply.

'I'm ashamed to say I can't.'

'I don't blame you . . . His name is Henry A. Wallace. He was a pretty good Agriculture Secretary, but he's no war leader, and there's an election coming next year. So Washington would be all caught up in that when it should be thinking about beating Hitler.'

'I'm not sure I can see another great leader emerging in Westminster, either.'

'Exactly – so the leaders of both governments would be weaker, and as the saying goes, the fish rots from the head.

Next thing you know, there'd be divisions between our two nations, each blaming the other for the disaster, and suddenly all the will and energy that is driving us to victory would just flicker and fade like a dying light bulb. Meanwhile, the Russians could do whatever they liked.'

'But that didn't happen. They lost.'

'Did they? Russians are chess players. They think several moves ahead. Last night they made one that might have given them checkmate. All they risked was a couple of pawns. So now they develop a new line of attack. My guess is that Stalin will use Roosevelt's hatred of the British Empire to drive a wedge between him and Churchill.'

'You sound like Charlie Playfair.'

'That's because I read his position paper. You know, in his own way, Playfair is a real patriot. It kills him to think that his prime minister is being taken for a fool. And he's not consoled by his certainty that America's president is being fooled, too.'

Saffron said nothing.

'What is it?' Stephenson asked.

'I was just thinking how right Clay was,' Saffron said sadly. 'He said that we should already be preparing for the next war – the one between the West and Russia.'

'He was right.'

Saffron looked despondent. 'Oh God, why can't it just end? Why do we have to keep on fighting?'

'Because that's what people have always done.'

'Well, I wish we didn't.'

'So, let's talk about something else. What are you planning to do next?'

Saffron smiled. 'I was hoping you might find me a nice comfy berth on a ship home.'

'How about a seat on an aeroplane?'

'That would do nicely, too. But first, I'm going to buy some clean clothes to keep me going until my luggage arrives. Then I'm going to spend the day being a tourist – the Empire State Building, the Metropolitan Museum . . . you name it. This evening, I'm heading up to Harlem, looking for men with names like Bird, and Dizzy, and Thelonious.'

'Never heard of them.'

'Neither had I until Clay told me about them. They're jazz musicians. He said they play in a style called bebop, like no other music on earth. It's so new and so wild that it's never been recorded. You have to go to tiny clubs after hours to hear it. I plan to find it, and listen to it . . . and I'll think of Clay Stackpole – the conversations we had, how we laughed, and how it felt when he held me in his arms. And you know what?'

Saffron looked at William Stephenson with a softness and sadness in her eyes that he hadn't seen before.

'What . . .?' he asked.

'It's entirely possible that I'll cry.'

DON'T MISS WILBUR SMITH'S OTHER ACTION-PACKED COURTNEY ADVENTURES . . .

LEGACY OF WAR

The war is over, Hitler is dead – and yet his evil legacy lives on. Former Special Operations Execute, Saffron Courtney, and her beloved husband, Gerhard, only just survived the brutal conflict, but Gerhard's Nazi brother, Konrad, is still free and determined to regain power. As a dangerous game of cat-and-mouse develops, a plot against the couple begins to stir. One that will have ramifications throughout Europe. . .

Further afield in Kenya, the last outcrop of the colonial empire is feeling the stirrings of rebellion. As the situation becomes violent, and the Courtney family home is under threat, Saffron's father, Leon Courtney, finds himself caught between two powerful sides - and a battle for the freedom of a country.

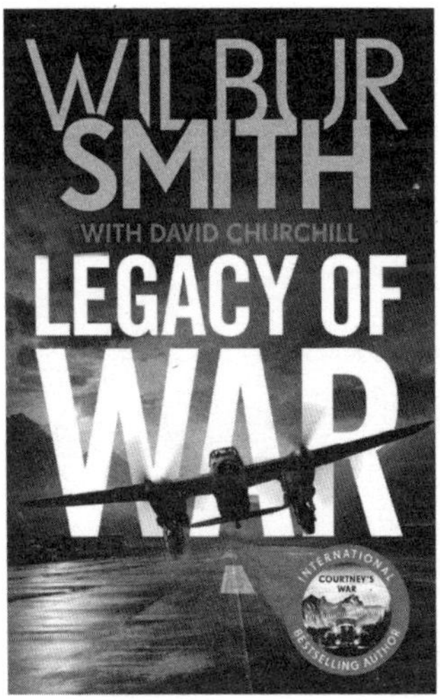

Legacy of War is a nail-biting story of courage, rebellion and war.

AVAILABLE NOW

DISCOVER THE BIRDS OF PREY SEQUENCE IN WILBUR SMITH'S EPIC COURTNEY SERIES

The earliest sequence in the Courtney family adventures starts in 1667, amidst the conflict surrounding the Dutch East India Company. In these action-packed books we follow three generations of Courtney's throughout the decades and across the seas to the stunning cliffs of Nativity Bay in South Africa.

AVAILABLE NOW

DON'T MISS WILBUR SMITH'S EPIC NEW KINGDOM SERIES

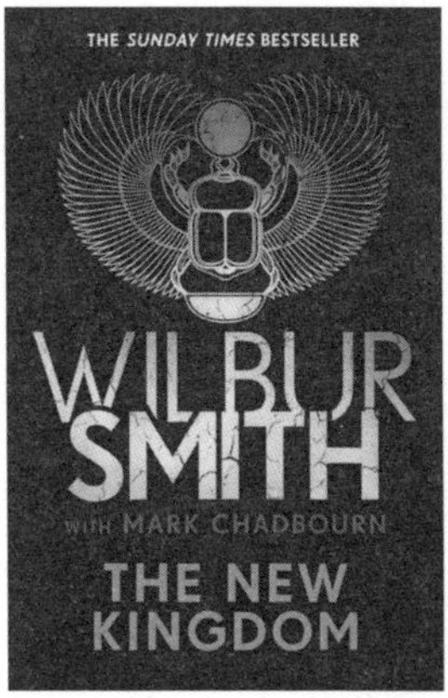

AVAILABLE NOW

AND LOOK OUT FOR . . .

COMING AUGUST 2025

WILBUR SMITH
THE POWER OF ADVENTURE
Visit the brand-new Wilbur Smith website to find out more about all of Wilbur's books, read the latest news, and dive into Wilbur's adventure notebooks on everything from the Boer War to the Skeleton Coast.
And if you want to be the first to know about all the latest releases and announcements, make sure to subscribe to the Readers' Club mailing list. Sign up today and get a preview of the next epic Wilbur Smith adventure!
Join the adventure at
WWW.WILBURSMITHBOOKS.COM